Arthur C. Clarke is without question the world's best-known and bestselling science fiction writer; his seventieth birthday in December 1987 was marked by the unveiling of a plaque at his birthplace in Somerset. He has won innumerable international awards for his fiction, for his scientific writing, and for his inspirational role as one of the chief prophets of the space age. His collaboration with Stanley Kubrick on *2001: A Space Odyssey* set new standards for SF films. As the presenter of the TV series *Arthur C. Clarke's Mysterious World* and its successors, Clarke has become a household name. He lives in Sri Lanka.

Gentry Lee combines two remarkable careers: on the one hand he is a screenwriter, whose credits include Carl Sagan's *Cosmos* series; on the other he is a distinguished space scientist, being chief scientist on NASA's deep space exploration programme. His collaboration with Arthur C. Clarke was born when he was assigned by Warner Bros. to script the film of *Cradle* from Clarke's extensive treatment.

Also by Arthur C. Clarke and Gentry Lee in Orbit

CRADLE

ARTHUR C. CLARKE and GENTRY LEE

Rama II

ORBIT

An Orbit Book

First published in Great Britain in 1989 by Victor Gollancz Ltd
This edition published in 1990 by Orbit Books a Division of
Macdonald & Co (Publishers) Ltd
London & Sydney

ISBN 0 7088 4833 8

Reproduced, printed and bound in Great Britain by
BPCC Hazell Books
Aylesbury, Bucks, England
Member of BPCC Ltd.

Orbit Books
A Division of
Macdonald & Co (Publishers) Ltd
Orbit House
1 New Fetter Lane
London EC4A 1AR
A member of Maxwell Macmillan Pergamon Publishing Corporation

Contents

1
Rama Returns

The great radar pulse generator Excalibur, powered by nuclear explosions, had been out of service for almost half a century. It had been designed and developed in a frantic effort during the months following the transit of Rama through the Solar System. When it was first declared operational in 2132, its announced purpose was to give Earth ample warning of any future alien visitors: one as gigantic as Rama could be detected at interstellar distances – years, it was hoped, before it could have any effect on human affairs.

The decision to build Excalibur had been made even before Rama had passed perihelion. As the first extraterrestrial visitor rounded the sun and headed out toward the stars, armies of scientists studied the data from the only mission that had been able to rendezvous with the intruder.

Rama, they announced, was an intelligent robot with absolutely no interest in our Solar System or its inhabitants. The official report offered no explanations for the many mysteries encountered by the investigators; however, the experts did convince themselves that they understood one basic principle of Raman engineering. Since most of the major systems and subsystems encountered inside Rama by the human explorers had two functional back-ups, it appeared that the aliens engineered everything 'in threes'. Therefore, since the entire giant vehicle was assumed to be a machine, it was considered highly likely that two more Rama spacecraft would be following the first visitor.

But no new spaceships entered the solar neighbourhood from the empty reaches of interstellar space. As the years passed the people on Earth confronted more pressing problems. Concern about the Ramans, or whoever it was that had created that drab cylinder fifty kilometres long, abated as the lone alien incursion passed into history. The visit of Rama continued to intrigue many scholars, but most members of the human species were forced to pay attention to other issues. By the early 2140s the world was in the grip of a severe economic crisis. There was no money left to maintain Excalibur. Its few scientific discoveries could not justify the enormous expense of assuring the safety of its operation. The great nuclear pulse generator was abandoned.

Forty-five years later it took thirty-three months to return Excalibur to operational status. The primary justification for the refurbishment of Excalibur was scientific. During the intervening years radar science had flourished and produced new methods of data interpretation that had greatly enhanced the value of the Excalibur observations. As the generator again took images of the distant heavens, almost nobody on Earth was expecting the arrival of another Rama spacecraft.

The operations manager at Excalibur Station did not even inform his supervisor the first time the strange blip appeared on his data processing display. He thought it was an artifact, a bogey created by an anomalous processing algorithm. When the signature repeated several times, however, he paid closer attention. The manager called in the chief Excalibur scientist, who analysed the data and decided the new object was a long period comet. It was another two months before a graduate student proved that the signature belonged to a smooth body at least forty kilometres in its longest dimension.

By 2197 the world knew that the object hurtling through the solar system toward the inner planets was a second extraterrestrial spacecraft. The International Space Agency (ISA) concentrated its resources to prepare an organised mission that would intercept the intruder just inside the orbit of Venus in late February 2200. Again humanity looked outward, toward the stars, and the deep philosophical questions raised by the first Rama were again debated by the populace on Earth. As the new visitor drew nearer and its physical characteristics were more carefully resolved by the host of sensors aimed in its direction, it was confirmed that this alien spacecraft, at least from the outside, was identical to its predecessor. Rama had returned. Mankind had a second appointment with destiny.

2

Test and Training

The bizarre metallic creature inched along the wall, crawling up toward the overhang. It resembled a skinny armadillo, its jointed snail body covered by a thin shell that curled over and around a compact grouping of electronic gadgetry astride the middle of its three sections. A helicopter hovered about two metres away from the wall. A long flexible arm with a pincer on the end extended from the nose of the helicopter and just missed closing its jaws around the odd creature.

'Damnit,' muttered Janos Tabori, 'this is almost impossible with the copter bouncing around. Even in perfect conditions it's hard to do precision work with these claws at full extension.' He glanced over at the pilot. 'And why can't this fantastic flying machine keep its altitude and attitude constant?'

'Move the helicopter closer to the wall,' ordered Dr David Brown.

Hiro Yamanaka looked at Brown without expression and entered a command into the control console. The screen in front of him flashed red and printed out the message, COMMAND UNACCEPTABLE. INSUFFICIENT TOLERANCES. Yamanaka said nothing. The helicopter continued to hover in the same spot.

'We have fifty centimetres, maybe seventy-five, between the blades and the wall,' Brown thought out loud. 'In another two or three minutes the biot will be safe under the overhang. Let's go to manual and grab it. Now. No mistakes this time, Tabori.'

For an instant a dubious Hiro Yamanaka stared at the balding, bespectacled scientist sitting in the seat behind him. Then the pilot turned, entered another command into the console, and switched the large black lever to the left position. The monitor flashed, IN MANUAL MODE. NO AUTOMATIC PROTECTION. Yamanaka gingerly eased the helicopter closer to the wall.

Engineer Tabori was ready. He inserted his hands in the instrumented gloves and practised opening and closing the jaws at the end of the flexible arm. Again the arm extended and the two mechanical mandibles deftly closed around the jointed snail and its shell. The feedback loops from the sensors on the claws told Tabori, through his gloves, that he had successfully captured his prey. 'I've got it,' he shouted exultantly. He began the slow process of bringing the quarry back into the helicopter.

A sudden draught of wind rolled the helicopter to the left and the arm with the biot banged against the wall. Tabori felt his grip loosening. 'Straighten it up,' he cried, continuing to retract the arm. While Yamanaka was struggling to nullify the rolling motion of the helicopter, he inadvertently tipped the nose down just slightly. The three crew members heard the sickening sound of the metal rotor blades crashing against the wall.

The Japanese pilot immediately pushed the emergency button and the craft returned to automatic control. In less than a second, a whining alarm sounded and the cockpit monitor flashed red. EXCESSIVE DAMAGE. HIGH PROBABILITY OF FAILURE. EJECT CREW. Yamanaka did not hesitate. Within moments he blasted out of the cockpit and had his parachute deployed. Tabori and Brown followed. As soon as the Hungarian engineer removed his hands from the special gloves, the claws at the end of the mechanical arm relaxed and the armadillo creature fell the hundred metres to the flat plain below, smashing into thousands of tiny pieces.

The pilotless helicopter descended erratically toward the plain. Even with its onboard automatic landing algorithm active and in complete control, the damaged flying machine bounced hard on its struts when it hit the ground and tipped over on its side. Not far from the helicopter's landing site a portly man, wearing a brown military suit covered with ribbons, jumped down from an open elevator. He had just descended from the mission control centre and was clearly agitated as he walked briskly to a waiting rover. He was followed by a scrambling lithe blonde woman in an ISA flight suit with camera equipment hanging over both her shoulders. The military man was General Valeriy Borzov, commander in chief of Project Newton. 'Anyone hurt?' he asked the occupant of the rover, electrical engineer Richard Wakefield.

'Janos apparently banged his shoulder pretty hard during the ejection. But Nicole just radioed that he had no broken bones or separations, only a lot of bruises.'

General Borzov climbed into the front seat of the rover beside Wakefield, who was sitting behind the vehicle control panel. The blonde woman, video journalist Francesca Sabatini, stopped recording the scene and started to open the back door of the rover. Borzov abruptly waved her away. 'Go check on des Jardins and Tabori,' he said, pointing across the level plain. 'Wilson's probably there already.'

Borzov and Wakefield headed in the opposite direction in the rover. They travelled about four hundred metres before they pulled alongside David Brown, a slight man, about fifty, in a new flight suit. He was busy folding up his parachute and replacing it in a stuff bag. General Borzov stepped down from the rover and approached the American scientist.

'Are you all right, Doctor Brown?' the general asked, obviously impatient to dispense with the preliminaries.

Brown nodded but did not reply. 'In that case,' General Borzov continued in a measured tone, 'perhaps you could tell me what you were thinking about when you ordered Yamanaka to go to manual? It might be better if we discussed it here, away from the rest of the crew.'

Dr David Brown remained silent. 'Didn't you see the

warning lights?' continued Borzov after a short pause. 'Did you consider, even for a moment, that the safety of the other cosmonauts might be jeopardised by the manoeuvre?'

Brown eventually looked over at Borzov with a sullen, baleful stare. When he finally spoke, his speech was clipped and strained, belying the emotion he was suppressing. 'It seemed reasonable to move the helicopter just a little closer to the target. We had some clearance left and it was the only way that we could have captured the biot. Our mission, after all, is to bring home –'

'You don't need to tell me what our mission is,' Borzov interrupted with passion. 'Remember, I helped write the policies myself. And I will remind you again that the number one priority, *at all times,* is the safety of the crew. Especially during these simulations ... I must tell you that I am absolutely astonished by this crazy stunt of yours. The helicopter is damaged, Tabori is injured, you're lucky that nobody was killed.'

David Brown was no longer paying attention to General Borzov. He had turned around to finish stuffing his parachute into its transparent package. From the set of his shoulders and the energy he was expending on this routine task, it was obvious that he was very angry.

Borzov returned to the rover. After waiting for several seconds he offered Dr Brown a ride back to the base. The American shook his head without saying anything, hoisted his pack on to his back, and walked off in the direction of the helicopter and the elevator.

3

Crew Conference

Outside the meeting room in the training facility, Janos
Tabori was sitting on an auditorium chair underneath an
array of small but powerful portable lights. 'The distance
to the simulated biot was at the limit of the reach of the
mechanical arm,' he explained to the tiny camera that
Francesca Sabatini was holding. 'Twice I tried to grab it
and failed. Dr Brown then decided to put the helicopter
on manual and take it a little closer to the wall. We
caught some wind....'

The door from the conference room opened and a
smiling, ruddy face appeared. 'We're all here waiting for
you,' said General O'Toole pleasantly. 'I think Borzov's
becoming a little impatient.'

Francesca switched off the lights and put her video
camera back in the pocket of her flight suit. 'All right,
my Hungarian hero,' she laughed, 'we'd better stop for
now. You know how our leader dislikes waiting.' She
walked over and put her arms gently around the small
man. She patted him on his bandaged shoulder. 'But
we're really glad you're all right.'

A handsome black man in his early forties had been
sitting just out of the camera frame during the interview,
taking notes on a flat, rectangular keyboard about a foot
square. He followed Francesca and Janos into the
conference room. 'I want to do a feature this week on the
new design concepts in the teleoperation of the arm and
the glove,' Reggie Wilson whispered to Tabori as they sat
down. 'There are a bunch of my readers out there who

find all this technical crap absolutely fascinating.'

'I'm glad that the three of you could join us,' Borzov's sarcastic voice boomed across the conference room. 'I was starting to think that perhaps a crew meeting was an imposition on all of you, an activity that interrupted the far more important tasks of reporting our misadventures or writing erudite scientific and engineering papers.' He pointed at Reggie Wilson, whose ubiquitous flat keyboard was on the table in front of him. 'Wilson, believe it or not, you're supposed to be a member of this crew first and a journalist second. Just one time do you think you can put that damn thing away and listen? I have a few things to say and I want them to be off the record.'

Wilson removed the keyboard and put it in his briefcase. Borzov stood up and walked around the room as he talked. The table in the crew conference room was a long oval about two metres across at its widest point. There were twelve places around the table, each one equipped with a computer keyboard and monitor slightly inset into the surface and covered, when not being used, by a polished grain top that matched the quality simulated wood on the rest of the table. As always, the other two military men on the expedition, European admiral Otto Heilmann (the hero of the Council of Governments intercession in the Caracas crisis) and American air force general Michael Ryan O'Toole, flanked Borzov at the end of the oval. The other nine Newton crew members did not always sit in the same seats, a fact that particularly frustrated the compulsively orderly Admiral Heilmann and, to a lesser extent, his commanding officer Borzov.

Sometimes the 'non-professionals' in the crew would cluster together around the other end of the table, leaving the 'space cadets', as the cosmonaut graduates of the Space Academy were known, to create a buffer zone in the middle. After almost a year of constant media attention, the public had relegated each member of the Newton dozen to one of three subgroups – the non-pros, consisting of the two scientists and two journalists; the

military troika; and the five cosmonauts who did most of
the skilled work during the mission.

On this particular day, however, the two non-military
groups were thoroughly mixed. The Japanese interdisci-
plinary scientist Shigeru Takagishi, widely regarded as
the world's foremost expert on the first Raman
expedition seventy years earlier (and also the author of
the *Atlas of Rama*, required reading for all of the crew),
was sitting in the middle of the oval between Soviet pilot
Irina Turgenyev and British cosmonaut/electrical engineer Richard Wakefield. Opposite them were life science
officer Nicole des Jardins, a statuesque copper-brown
woman with a complex French and African lineage, the
quiet, almost mechanical Japanese pilot Yamanaka, and
the stunning Signora Sabatini. The final three positions
at the 'south' end of the oval, facing the large maps and
diagrams of Rama on the opposite wall, were occupied by
American journalist Wilson, the garrulous Tabori (a
Soviet cosmonaut from Budapest), and Dr David Brown.
Brown looked very businesslike and serious; he had a set
of papers spread out in front of him as the meeting
began.

'It is inconceivable to me,' Borzov was saying while he
strode purposefully around the room, 'that any of you
could ever forget, even for a moment, that you have been
selected to go on what could be the most important
human mission of all time. But on the basis of this last set
of simulations, I must admit that I am beginning to have
my doubts about some of you.

'There are those who believe that this Rama craft will
be a copy of its predecessor,' Borzov continued, 'and that
it will be equally uninterested and uninvolved with
whatever trifling creatures come to survey it. I admit it
certainly appears to be the same size and same
configuration, based on the radar data that we have been
processing for the past three years. But even if it does
turn out to be another dead ship built by aliens that
vanished thousands of years ago, this mission is still the
most important one of our lifetime. And I would think
that it demands the very best effort from each of you.'

The Soviet general paused to collect his thoughts. Janos Tabori started to ask a question but Borzov interrupted him and launched again into his monologue. 'Our performance as a crew on this last set of training excercises has been absolutely abominable. Some of you have been outstanding – you know who you are – but just as many of you have acted as if you had no idea what this mission was about. I am convinced that two or three of you do not even read the relevant procedures or the protocol listings before the exercises begin. I grant you that they are sometimes tedious, but all of you *agreed*, when you accepted your appointments ten months ago, to learn the procedures and to follow the protocols and project policies. Even those of you with no prior flight experience.'

Borzov had stopped in front of one of the large maps on the wall, this one an inset view of one corner of the city of 'New York' inside the first Raman spaceship. The area of tall thin buildings resembling Manhattan skyscrapers, all huddled together on an island in the middle of the Cylindrical Sea, had been partially mapped during the previous human encounter. 'In six weeks we will rendezvous with an unknown space vehicle, perhaps one containing a city like this, and all of mankind will depend on us to represent them. We have no way of knowing what we will find. Whatever preparation we will have completed before then may well be not enough. Our knowledge of our preplanned procedures must be perfect and automatic, so that our brains are free to deal with any new conditions we may encounter.'

The commander sat down at the head of the table. 'Today's exercise was nearly a complete disaster. We could easily have lost three valuable members of our team as well as one of the most expensive helicopters ever built. I want to remind you all, one more time, of the priorities of this mission as agreed to by the International Space Agency and the Council of Governments. The top priority is the safety of the crew. Second priority is the analysis and/or determination of any threat, if it exists, to the human population of the planet Earth.' Borzov was now looking directly down the table at Brown, who returned the commander's challenging look with a stony stare of his own. 'Only after those two priorities are satisfied and the Raman craft is adjudged harmless does the capture of one or more of the biots have any significance.'

'I would like to remind General Borzov,' David Brown said almost immediately in his sonorous voice, 'that some of us do not believe the priorities should be blindly applied in a serial fashion. The importance of the biots to the scientific community cannot be overstated. As I have said repeatedly, both in cosmonaut meetings and on my many television news appearances, if this second Rama craft is just like the first – which means that it will ignore our existence completely – and we proceed so slowly that we fail even to capture a single biot before we must abandon the alien ship and return to Earth, then an absolutely unique opportunity for science will have been sacrificed to assuage the collective anxiety of the world's politicians.'

Borzov started to reply but Dr Brown stood up and gestured emphatically with his hands. 'No, no, hear me out. You have essentially accused me of incompetence in my conduct of today's exercise and I have a right to respond.' He held up some computer printout and waved it at Borzov. 'Here are the initial conditions for today's stimulation, as posted and defined by *your* engineers. Let me refresh your memory with a few of the more salient points, in case you've forgotten. Background Condition #1: It is near the end of the mission and it has already been established that Rama II is totally passive and represents no threat to the planet Earth. Background Condition #2: During the expedition biots have only been seen sporadically, and never in groups.'

David Brown could tell from the body language of the rest of the crew that his presentation had had a successful beginning. He drew a breath and continued. 'I assumed, after reading those background conditions, that this particular exercise might represent the last chance to capture a biot. During the test I kept thinking what it would mean if we could bring one or several of them back to the Earth – in all the history of humanity, the only absolutely certain contact with an extraterrestrial culture took place in 2130 when our cosmonauts boarded that first Rama spaceship.

'Yet the longterm scientific benefit from that encounter was less than it might have been. Granted, we have reams of remote sensing data from that first investigation, including the information from the detailed dissection of the spider biot done by Dr Laura Ernst. But the cosmonauts brought home only one artifact, a tiny piece of some kind of biomechanical flower whose physical characteristics had already irreversibly changed before any of its mysteries could be understood. We have nothing else in the way of souvenirs from that first excursion. No ashtrays, no drinking glasses, not even a transistor from a piece of equipment that would teach us something about Raman engineering. Now we have a second chance.'

Dr Brown looked up at the circular ceiling above him. His voice was full of power. 'If we could somehow find and return two or three different biots to the Earth, and if we could then analyse these creatures to unlock their secrets, then this mission would without doubt be the most significant historical event of all time. For in understanding in depth the engineering minds of the Ramans, we would, in a real sense, achieve a first contact.'

Even Borzov was impressed. As he often did, David Brown had used his eloquence to turn a defeat into a partial victory. The Soviet general decided to alter his tactics. 'Still,' Borzov said in a subdued tone during the pause in Brown's rhetoric, 'we must never forget that human lives are at stake on this mission and that we must do nothing to jeopardise their safety.' He looked around the table at the rest of the crew. 'I want to bring back biots and other samples from Rama as much as any of you,' he continued, 'but I must confess that this blithe assumption that the second craft will be exactly like the first disturbs me a great deal. What evidence do we have from the first encounter that the Ramans, or whoever they are, are benevolent? None at all. It could be dangerous to seize a biot too soon.'

'But there's no way of ever being certain, Commander, one way or the other.' Richard Wakefield spoke from the side of the table between Borzov and Brown. 'Even if we verify that this spaceship is exactly like the first one, we still have no information about what will happen once we make a concerted effort to capture a biot. I mean, suppose for a moment that Dr Brown is right, that the two ships are just supersophisticated robots engineered millions of years ago by a now vanished race from the opposite side of the galaxy. How can we predict what kinds of subroutines might be programmed into those biots to deal with hostile acts? What if the biots are integral parts, in some way that we have not been able to discern, of the fundamental operation of the ship? Then it would be natural, even though they are machines, that they would be programmed to defend themselves. And it is conceivable that what might look like an initial hostile act on our part could be the trigger that changes the way the entire ship functions. I remember reading about the robot lander that crashed into the ethane sea on Titan in 2012 – it had stored entirely different sequences depending on what it –'

'Halt.' Janos Tabori interrupted with a friendly smile. 'The arcana of the early robotic exploration of the solar system are not on the agenda for today's post mortem.' He looked down the table at Borzov. 'Skipper, my shoulder is hurting, my stomach is empty, and the excitement of today's exercise has left me exhausted. All this talk is wonderful, but if there's no more specific business would it be out of line to suggest an early end to this meeting so that we will have adequate time, for once, to pack our bags?'

Admiral Heilmann leaned forward on the table. 'Cosmonaut Tabori, General Borzov is in charge of the crew meetings. It is up to him to determine –'

The Soviet commander waved his arm at Heilmann. 'Enough, Otto. I think that Janos is right. It has been a long day at the end of an extremely busy seventeen days of activity. This conversation will be better when we are all fresh.'

Borzov stood up. 'All right, we will break for now. The shuttles will leave for the airport right after dinner.' The crew started preparing to leave. 'During your short rest period,' Borzov said as an afterthought, 'I want all of you to think about where we are in the schedule. We have only two more weeks left of simulations here at the training centre before the break for the end of the year holiday. Immediately thereafter we begin the intensive prelaunch activities. This next set of exercises is our last chance to get it right. I expect each of you to return fully prepared for the remaining work – and recommitted to the importance of this mission.'

4

The Great Chaos

The intrusion of the first Raman spacecraft into the inner solar system in early 2130 had a powerful impact on human history. Although there were no immediate changes in everyday life after the crew headed by Commander Norton returned from encountering Rama I, the clear and unambiguous proof that a vastly superior intelligence existed (or, as a minimum, *had* existed) somewhere else in the universe forced a rethinking of the place of Homo sapiens in the overall scheme of the cosmos. It was now apparent that other chemicals, doubtless also fabricated in the great stellar catacylsms of the heavens, had risen to consciousness in some other place, at some other time. Who were these Ramans? Why had they built a giant sophisticated spacecraft and sent it on an excursion into our neighbourhood? Both in public and private conversation, the Ramans were the number one topic of interest for many months.

For well over a year mankind waited more or less patiently for another sign of the Ramans' presence in the universe. Intense telescopic investigations were conducted at all wavelengths to see if any additional information associated with the retreating alien spaceship could be identified. Nothing was found. The heavens were quiet. The Ramans were departing as swiftly and inexplicably as they had arrived.

Once Excalibur was operational and its initial search of the heavens turned up nothing new, there was a noticeable change in the collective human attitude toward the first contact with Rama. Overnight the encounter became a historical event, something that *had* happened and was now completed. The tenor of newspaper and magazine articles which had earlier begun with phrases like 'when the Ramans return ...' changed to 'if there is ever another encounter with the creatures who built the huge spaceship discovered in 2130....' What had been a perceived threat, a lien in a sense on future human behaviour, was quickly reduced to a historical curiosity. There was no longer an urgency to deal with such fundamental issues as the return of the Ramans or the destiny of the human race in a universe peopled by intelligent creatures. Mankind relaxed, at least for a moment. Then it exploded in a paroxysm of narcissistic behaviour that made all previous historical periods of individual selfishness pale by comparison.

The surge of unabashed self-indulgence on a global scale was easy to understand. Something fundamental in the human psyche had changed as a result of the encounter with Rama I. Prior to that contact, humanity stood alone as the only known example of advanced intelligence in the universe. The idea that humans could, as a group, control their destiny far into the future had been a significant lynchpin in almost every working philosophy of life. That the Ramans existed (or had existed; whatever the tense, the philosophic logic came to the same conclusion) changed everything. Mankind was not unique, maybe not even special. It was just a question of time before the prevailing homocentric notion of the universe was to be irrevocably shattered by clearer awareness of the Others. Thus it was easy to comprehend why the life patterns of most human beings suddenly veered toward self-gratification, reminding literary scholars of a similar time almost exactly five centuries earlier, when Robert Herrick had exhorted the virgins to make the most of their fleeting time in a poem that began, 'Gather Ye Rosebuds While Ye May; Old Time is Still A-Flying....'

An unrestrained burst of conspicuous consumption and global greed lasted for just under two years. Frantic

acquisition of everything the human mind could create
was superimposed on a weak economic infrastructure
that had been already poised for a downturn in early
2130, when the first Raman spaceship flew through the
inner solar system. The looming recession had been
postponed throughout 2130 and 2131 by the combined
manipulative efforts of governments and financial
institutions, even though the fundamental economic
weaknesses were never addressed. With the renewed
burst of buying in early 2132, the world jumped directly
into another period of rapid growth. Production
capacities were expanded, stock markets exploded, and
both consumer confidence and total employment hit all
time highs. There was unprecedented prosperity and the
net result was a short-term but significant improvement
in the standard of living for almost all humans.

By the end of 2133, it had become obvious to some of
the more experienced observers of human history that
the 'Raman Boom' was leading mankind toward disaster.
Dire warnings of impending economic doom started
being heard above the euphoric shouts of the millions
who had recently vaulted into the middle and upper
classes. Suggestions to balance budgets and limit credit at
all levels of the economy were ignored. Instead, creative
effort was expended to come up with one way after
another of putting more spending power in the hands of a
populace that had forgotten how to say 'wait', much less
'no', to itself.

The global stock market began to sputter in January
2134 and there were predictions of a coming crash. But to
most humans spread around the Earth and throughout
the scattered colonies in the solar system, the concept of
such a crash was beyond comprehension. After all, the
world economy had been expanding for over nine years,
the last two years at a rate unparalleled in the previous
two centuries. World leaders insisted that they had
finally found the mechanisms that could truly inhibit the
downturns of the capitalistic cycles. And the people
believed them – until early May 2134.

During the first three months of the year the global

stock markets went inexorably down, slowly at first, then in significant drops. Many people, reflecting the superstitious attitude toward cometary visitors that had been prevalent for two thousand years, somehow associated the stock market's difficulties with the return of Halley's Comet. Its appearance, starting in March, turned out to be far brighter than anyone expected. For weeks scientists all over the world were competing with each other to explain why it was so much more brilliant than originally predicted. After it swooped past perihelion in late March and began to appear in the evening sky in mid-April, its enormous tail dominated the heavens.

In contrast, terrestial affairs were dominated by the emerging world economic crisis. On May 1, 2134, three of the largest international banks announced that they were insolvent because of bad loans. Within two days a panic had spread around the world. More than one billion home terminals with access to the global financial markets were used to dump individual portfolios of stocks and bonds. The communications load on the Global Network System was immense. GNS data transfer machines were stretched far beyond their capabilities and design specifications. Data gridlock delayed transactions for minutes, then hours, contributing additional momentum to the panic.

By the end of a week two things were apparent – that over half of the world's stock value had been obliterated and that many individuals, large and small investors alike who had used their credit options to the maximum, were now virtually penniless. The supporting data bases that kept track of personal bank accounts and automatically transferred money to cover margin calls were flashing disaster messages in almost twenty percent of the houses in the world.

In truth, however, the situation was much much worse. Only a small percentage of the transactions were actually clearing through all the supporting computers because the data rates in all directions were far beyond anything that had ever been anticipated. In computer language, the entire global financial system went into the 'cycle slip' mode. Billions and billions of information transfers at lower priorities were 'postponed' by the network of computers while the higher priority tasks were being serviced first.

The net result of these data delays was that in most cases individual electronic bank accounts were not properly debited for hours, or even days, to cover the mounting stock market losses. Once the individual investors realised what was occurring, they rushed to spend whatever was still showing in their balances before the computers completed all the transactions. By the time governments and financial institutions understood fully what was going on and acted to stop all this frenetic activity, it was too late. The confused system had crashed completely. To reconstruct what had happened required carefully dumping and interleaving the backup checkpoint files stored at a hundred or so remote centres around the world.

For over three weeks the electronic financial management system that governed all money transactions was inaccessible to everybody. Nobody knew how much money they had. Since cash had long ago become obsolete, only eccentrics and collectors had enough banknotes to buy even a week's groceries. People began to barter for necessities. Pledges based on friendship and personal acquaintance enabled many people to survive temporarily. But the pain had only begun. Every time the international management organisation that oversaw the global financial system announced that they were going to try to come back 'on-line', and pleaded with people to stay off their terminals 'except for emergencies', their pleas would be ignored, processing requests would flood the system, and the computers would crash again.

It was only two more weeks before the scientists of the world agreed on an explanation for the additional brightness in the apparition of Halley's comet. But it was over four months before people could count again on reliable data base information from the GNS. The cost to human society of the enduring chaos was incalculable. By the time normal electronic economic activity had been restored, the world was in a violent financial downspin that would not bottom out until twelve years later. It would be well over fifty years before the Gross World Product would return to the heights reached before the Crash of 2134.

5

After the Crash

There is unanimous agreement that the Great Chaos
profoundly altered human civilisation in every way. No
segment of society was immune. The catalyst for the
relatively rapid collapse of the existing institutional
infrastructure was the market crash and subsequent
breakdown of the global financial system; however, these
events would not have been sufficient, by themselves, to
project the world into a period of unprecedented
depression. What followed the initial crash would only
have been a comedy of errors if so many lives had not
been lost as a result of the poor planning. Inept world
political leaders first denied or ignored the existing
economic problems, then overreacted with a suite of
individual measures that were baffling and/or inconsistent, and finally threw up their arms in despair as the
global crisis deepened and spread. Attempts to
coordinate international solutions were doomed to failure
by the increasing need of each of the sovereign nations to
respond to its own constituency.

With hindsight, it was obvious that the internationali-
sation of the world which had taken place during the
twenty-first century had been flawed in at least one
significant way. Although many activities – communications, trade, transportation (including space), cur-
rency regulation, peacekeeping, information exchange,
and environmental protection, to name the most
important – had indeed become international (even
interplanetary, considering the space colonies), most of

the agreements that established these international institutions contained codicils which allowed the individual nations to withdraw, upon relatively short notice, if the policies promulgated under the accords 'no longer served the interests' of the country in question. In short, each of the nations participating in the creation of an international body had the right to abrogate its national involvement, unilaterally, when it was no longer satisfied with the actions of the group.

The years preceding the rendezvous with the first Raman spaceship in early 2130 had been an extraordinarily stable and prosperous time. After the world recovered from the devastating cometary impact near Padua, Italy, in 2077, there was an entire half century of moderate growth. Except for a few relatively short, and not too severe, economic recessions, living conditions improved in a wide range of countries throughout the time period. Isolated wars and civil disturbances did erupt from time to time, primarily in the undeveloped nations, but the concerted efforts of the global peacekeeping forces always contained these problems before they became too serious. There were no major crises that tested the stability of the new international mechanisms.

Immediately following the encounter with Rama I, however, there were rapid changes in the basic governing apparatus. First, emergency appropriations to handle Excalibur and other large Rama-related projects drained revenues from established programmes. Then, starting in 2132, a loud clamour for tax cuts, to put more money into the hands of the individuals, reduced even further the allocations for necessary services. By late 2133, most of the newer international institutions had become understaffed and inefficient. Thus the global market crash took place in an environment where there was already growing doubt in the minds of the populace about the efficacy of the entire network of international organisations. As the financial chaos continued, it was an easy step for individual nations to stop contributing funds to the very global funds and organisations that might have been able to turn the tide of disaster if they had been used properly, that were vitiated first by the near-sighted political leaders.

The horrors of the Great Chaos have been chronicled in thousands of history texts. In the first two years the major problems were skyrocketing unemployment and bankruptcies, both personal and corporate, but these financial difficulties seemed unimportant as the ranks of the homeless and starving continued to swell. Tent and box communities appeared in the public parks of all the big cities by the winter of 2136-37 and the municipal governments responded by striving valiantly to find ways of providing services to them. These services were intended to limit the difficulties created by the supposedly temporary presence of these hordes of unemployed and underfed individuals. But when the economy did not recover, the squalid tent cities did not disappear. Instead they became permanent fixtures of urban life, growing cancers that were worlds unto themselves with an entire set of activities and interests fundamentally different from those of the host cities that were supporting them. As more time passed and the ten communities turned into hopeless, restless cauldrons of despair, these new enclaves in the middle of the metropolitan areas threatened to boil over and destroy the very entities that were allowing them to exist. Despite the anxiety caused by this constant Damoclean sword of urban anarchy, the world squeaked through the brutally cold winter of 2137-38 with the basic fabric of modern civilisation still more or less intact.

In early 2138 a remarkable series of events occurred in Italy. These events, focused around a single individual named Michael Balatresi, a young Franciscan novitiate who would later become known everywhere as St Michael of Siena, occupied much of the attention of the world and temporarily forestalled the disintegration of society. Michael was a brilliant combination of genius and spirituality and political skills, a charismatic polyglot speaker with an unerring sense of purpose and timing. He appeared suddenly on the world stage in Tuscany, coming seemingly out of nowhere, with a passionate religious message which appealed to the hearts and minds of many of the world's frightened and/or disenfranchised citizens. His following grew rapidly and spontaneously and paid no heed to international boundaries. He became a potential threat to almost all the identified leadership coteries of the world, with his unwavering call for a collective response to the problems besetting the species. When he was martyred under appalling circumstances in June 2138, mankind's last spark of optimism seemed to perish. The civilised world, which had been held together for many months by a flicker of hope and a slim threat of tradition, abruptly crumbled into pieces.

The four years from 2138 to 2142 were not good years to be alive. The litany of human woes was almost endless. Famine, disease, and lawlessness were everywhere. Small wars and revolutions were too numerous to count. There was an almost total breakdown in the standard institutions of modern civilisation, creating a phantasmagoric life for everyone in the world except the privileged few in their protected retreats. It was a world gone wrong, the ultimate in entropy. Attempts to solve the problems by well-meaning groups of citizens could not work, because the solutions they conceived could only be local in scope and the problems were global.

The Great Chaos also extended to the human colonies in space and brought a sudden end to a glorious chapter in the history of exploration. As economic disaster spread on the home planet, the scattered colonies around the solar system, which could not exist without regular infusions of money, supplies, and personnel, quickly became the forgotten stepchildren of Earth. As a result almost half the residents of the colonies had left to return home by 2140, the living conditions in their adopted homes having deteriorated to the point where even the twin difficulties of readjustment to Earth's gravity and the terrible poverty throughout the world were preferred over continuing to stay, most likely to die, in the colonies. The emigration process accelerated in 2141 and 2142, years characterised by mechanical breakdowns in

the artificial ecosystems at the colonies and the beginning
of a disastrous shortage of spare parts for the entire fleet
of robot vehicles used to sustain the new settlements.

By 2143 only a very few hard-core colonists remained
on the Moon and Mars. Communications between Earth
and the colonies had become intermittent and erratic.
Monies to maintain even the radio links with the outlying
settlements were no longer available. The United Planets
had ceased to exist two years previously. There was no
all-human forum addressing the problems of the species;
the Council of Governments would not be formed for five
more years. The two remaining colonies struggled vainly
to avoid death.

In the following year, 2144, the last significant manned
space mission of the time period took place. The mission
was a rescue sortie piloted by a Mexican woman named
Benita Garcia. Using a jerryrigged spacecraft thrown
together from old parts, Ms Garcia and her three-man
crew somehow managed to reach the geosynchronous
orbit of the lame cruiser *James Martin*, the last
interplanetary transport vehicle in service, and saved
twenty-four people from the complement of a hundred
women and children being repatriated from Mars. In
every space historian's mind, the rescue of the passengers
on the *James Martin* marked the end of an era. Within six
more months the last remaining space stations were
abandoned and no human lifted off Earth, bound for
orbit, until almost forty years later.

By 2145 the struggling world had managed to see the
importance of some of the international organisations
neglected and maligned at the beginning of the Great
Chaos. The most talented members of mankind, after
having eschewed personal political involvement during
the benign early decades of the century, began to
understand that it would only be through their collective
skills that any semblance of civilised life could ever be
restored. At first the monumental cooperative efforts that
resulted were only modestly successful; but they
rekindled the fundamental optimism of the human spirit
and started the renewal process. Slowly, ever so slowly,

the elements of human civilisation were put back into place.

It was still another two years before the general recovery finally showed up in economic statistics. By 2147 the Gross World Product had dwindled to 7% of its level six years earlier. Unemployment in the developed nations averaged 35%; in some of the undeveloped nations the combination of unemployed and under-employed amounted to 90% of the population. It is estimated that as many as one hundred million people starved to death during the awful year of 2142 alone, when a great drought and concomitant famine girdled the world in the tropical regions. The combination of an astronomical death rate from many causes and a minuscule birth rate (for who wanted to bring a child into such a hopeless world) caused the world's population to drop by almost a billion in the decade ending in 2150.

The experience of the Great Chaos left a permanent scar on an entire generation. As the years passed, and the children born after its conclusion reached adolescence, they were confronted by parents who were cautious to the point of phobia. Life as a teenager in the 2160s and even the 2170s was very strict. The memories of the terrible traumas of their youth during the Chaos haunted the adult generation and made them extremely rigid in their application of parental discipline. To them life was not a joyride at an amusement park. It was a deadly serious affair and only through a combination of solid values, self-control, and a steady commitment to a worthwhile goal was there a chance to achieve happiness.

The society that emerged in the 2170s was therefore dramatically different from the freewheeling laissez-faire-ism of fifty years earlier. Many very old, established institutions, among them the nation-state, the Roman Catholic church, and the British monarchy, had enjoyed a renaissance during the half century interim. These institutions had prospered because they had adapted quickly and taken leadership positions in the restruc-turing that followed the Chaos.

By the late 2170s, when a semblance of stability had

returned to the planet, interest in space began to build again. A new generation of observation and communication satellites was launched by the reconstituted International Space Agency, one of the administrative arms of the Council of Governments. At first the space activity was cautious and the ISA's budgets were very small. Only the developed nations participated actively. When piloted flights recommenced and were successful, a modest schedule of missions was planned for the decade of the 2190s. A new Space Academy to train cosmonauts for those missions opened in 2188 and had its first graduates four years later.

On Earth, growth was achingly slow but regular and predictable for most of the twenty years preceding the discovery of the second Raman spaceship in 2196. In a technological sense, mankind was at approximately the same overall level of development in 2196 as it had been seventy years earlier, when the first extraterrestrial craft had appeared. Recent spaceflight experience was much less, to be certain, at the time of the second encounter; however, in certain critical technical areas like medicine and information management, the human society of the last decade of the twenty-second century was considerably more advanced than it had been in 2130. In one other component the civilisations encountered by the two Raman spacecraft were markedly different – many of the human beings alive in 2196, especially those who were older and held the policy-making positions in the governing structure, had lived through some of the very painful years of the Great Chaos. They knew the meaning of the word fear. And that powerful word shaped their deliberations as they debated the priorities that would guide a human mission to rendezvous with Rama II.

6

La Signora Sabatini

'So you were working on your doctorate in physics at SMU when your husband made his famous prediction about supernova 2191a?'

Elaine Brown was sitting in a large soft chair in her living room. She was dressed in a stark brown suit, sexless, with a high collar blouse. She looked stiff and anxious, as if she were ready for the interview to be completed.

'I was in my second year and David was my dissertation adviser,' she said carefully, her eyes glancing furtively at her husband. He was across the room, watching the proceedings from behind the cameras. 'David worked very closely with his graduate students. Everybody knew that. It was one of the reasons why I chose SMU for my graduate work.'

Francesca Sabatini looked beautiful. Her long blonde hair was flowing freely over her shoulders. She was wearing an expensive white silk blouse, trimmed by a royal blue scarf neatly folded around her neck. Her lounging pants were the same colour as the scarf. She was sitting in a second chair next to Elaine. Two coffee cups were on the small table between them.

'Dr Brown was married at the time, wasn't he? I mean during the period when he was your adviser.'

Elaine reddened perceptibly as Francesca finished her question. The Italian journalist continued to smile at her, a disarmingly ingenuous smile, as if the question she had just asked was as simple and straightforward as two plus two. Mrs Brown hesitated, drew a breath, and then stammered slightly in giving her response. 'In the beginning, yes, I believe that he still was,' she answered. 'But his divorce was final before I finished my degree.' She stopped again and then her face brightened. 'He gave me an engagement ring for a graduation present,' she said awkwardly.

Francesca Sabatini studied her subject. *I could easily tear you apart on that reply*, she thought rapidly. *With just a couple more questions. But that would not serve my purpose.*

'Okay, cut,' Francesca said suddenly. 'That's a wrap. Let's take a look and then you can put all the equipment back in the truck.' The lead cameraman walked over to the side of robot camera #1, which had been programmed to stay in closeup on Francesca, and entered three commands into the miniature keyboard on the side of the camera housing. Meanwhile, because Elaine had risen from her seat, robot camera #2 was automatically backing away on its tripod legs and retracting its zoom lens. Another cameraman motioned to Elaine to stand still until he was able to disconnect the second camera.

Within seconds the director had programmed the automatic monitoring equipment to replay the last five minutes of the interview. The output of all three cameras was shown simultaneously, split screen, the composite picture of both Francesca and Elaine occupying the centre of the monitor with the tapes from the two closeup cameras on either side. Francesca was a consummate professional. She could tell quickly that she had the material she needed for this portion of the show. Dr David Brown's wife Elaine was young, intelligent, earnest, plain, and not comfortable with the attention being focused on her. And it was all clearly there on tape.

While Francesca was wrapping up the details with her crew and arranging to have the annotated interview composite delivered to her hotel at the Dallas Transportation Complex before her flight in the morning, Elaine Brown came back into the living room with a standard robot server, two different kinds of cheese, bottles of wine, and plenty of glasses for everyone. Francesca glimpsed a frown on David Brown's face as Elaine announced that there would now be 'a small party' to celebrate the end of the interview. The crew and Elaine gathered around the robot and the wine. David excused himself and walked out of the living room into the long hall that connected the back of the house, where all the bedrooms were, with the living quarters in the front. Francesca followed him.

'Excuse me, David,' she said. He turned around, his impatience clear. 'Don't forget that we still have some unfinished business. I promised an answer to Schmidt and Hagenest upon my return to Europe. They are anxious to proceed with the project.'

'I haven't forgotten,' he replied. 'I just want to make certain first that your friend Reggie is finished interviewing my children.' He heaved a sigh. 'There are times when I wish I was a total unknown in the world.'

Francesca walked up close to him. 'I don't believe that for a minute,' she said, her eyes fixed on his. 'You're just nervous today because you can't control what your wife and children are saying to Reggie and me. And nothing is more important to you than control.'

Dr Brown started to reply but was interrupted by a shriek of '*Mommeee*' reverberating down the hall from its origin in a distant bedroom. Within seconds a small boy, six or seven years old, swept past David and Francesca and raced pell mell into the arms of his mother, who was now standing in the doorway connecting the hall and the living room. Some of Elaine's wine sloshed out of her glass from the force of the collision with her son; she unconsciously licked it off her hand as she sought to comfort the little boy.

'What is it, Justin?' she asked.

'That black man broke my dog,' Justin whined between sobs. 'He kicked it in the butt and now I can't make it work.'

The little boy pointed back down the hall. Reggie Wilson and a teenage girl, tall, thin, very serious, were walking toward the rest of the group. 'Dad,' said the girl, her eyes imploring David Brown for help, 'Mr Wilson was talking to me about my pin collection when that damned robot dog came in and bit him on the leg. After peeing on him first. Justin had programmed him to make mischief –'

'She's lying,' the crying little boy interrupted her with a shout. 'She doesn't like Wally. She's never liked Wally.'

Elaine Brown had one hand on the back of her nearly hysterical son and the other firmly around the stem of her wine glass. She would have been unsettled by the scene even if she hadn't noticed the disapproval that she was receiving from her husband. She quaffed the wine and put the glass on a nearby bookshelf. 'There, there, Justin,' she said, looking embarrassingly at the others, 'calm down and tell Mom what happened.'

'That black man doesn't like me. And I don't like him. Wally knew it, so he bit him. Wally always protects me.'

The girl Angela became more agitated. 'I knew something like this would happen. When Mr Wilson was talking to me, Justin kept coming into my room and interrupting us, showing Mr Wilson his games, his pets, his trophies, and even his clothes. Eventually Mr Wilson had to speak sharply to him. Next thing we know Wally is running wild and Mr Wilson has to defend himself.'

'She's a liar, Mom. A big liar. Tell her to stop –'

Dr David Brown interrupted him angrily. '*Elaine*,' he shouted above the din, 'get ... *him* ... out of here.' He turned to his daughter as his wife pulled the weeping little boy through the door into the living room. 'Angela,' he said, his rage now raw and unconcealed, 'I thought I told you not to fight with Justin today under any circumstances.'

The girl recoiled from her father's attack. Tears welled up in her eyes. She started to say something but Reggie Wilson walked between her and her father. 'Excuse me, Dr Brown,' Reggie interceded, 'Angela really didn't do anything. Her story is basically correct. She –'

'Look, Wilson,' David Brown said sharply, 'if you

don't mind, I can handle my own family.' He paused a moment to calm his anger. 'I'm terribly sorry for all this confusion,' he continued in a subdued tone, 'but it will all be finished in another minute or so.' The look he gave his daughter was cold and unkind. 'Go back to your room, Angela. I'll talk to you later. Call your mother and tell her that I want her to pick you up before dinner.'

Francesca Sabatini watched with great interest as the entire scene unfolded. She saw David Brown's frustration, Elaine's lack of self-confidence. *This is perfect*, Francesca thought. *Even better than I might have hoped. He will be very easy.*

The sleek silver train cruised through the North Texas countryside at two hundred and fifty kilometres per hour. Within minutes the lights from the Dallas Transportation Complex appeared on the horizon. The DTC covered a mammoth area, almost twenty-five square kilometres. It was part airport, part train station, part small city. Originally constructed in 2185 both to handle the burgeoning long distance air traffic and to provide an easy nexus for transferring passengers to the high speed train system, it had grown, like other similar transportation centres around the world, into an entire community. More than a thousand people, most of whom worked at the DTC and found life easier when there was no need to commute, lived in the apartments that formed a semicircle around the shopping centre south of the main terminal. The terminal itself housed four major hotels, seventeen restaurants, and over a hundred different shops, including a branch of the chic Donatelli fashion chain.

'I was nineteen at the time,' the young man was saying to Francesca as the train approached the station, 'and had had a very sheltered upbringing. I learned more about love and sex in that ten weeks, watching your series on television, than I had learned in my whole life before. I just wanted to thank you for that programme.'

Francesca accepted the compliments gracefully. She was accustomed to being recognised when she was in public. When the train stopped and she descended on to the platform, Francesca smiled again at the young man and his date. Reggie Wilson offered to carry her camera equipment as they walked toward the people mover that would take them to the hotel. 'Does it ever bother you?' he asked. She looked at him quizzically. 'All the attention, being a public figure?' he added in explanation.

'No,' she answered, 'of course not.' She smiled to herself. *Even after six months this man still does not understand me. Maybe he's too engrossed with himself to figure out that some women are as ambitious as men.*

'I knew that your two television series had been popular,' Reggie was saying, 'before I met you during the personnel screening exercises. But I had no idea that it would be impossible to go out to a restaurant or to be seen in a public place without running into one of your fans.'

Reggie continued to chat as the people mover eased out of the train station and into the shopping centre. Near the track at one end of the enclosed mall a large group of people were milling around outside a theatre. The marquee proclaimed that the production inside was *In Any Weather*, by the American playwright Linzey Olsen.

'Did you ever see that play?' Reggie idly asked Francesca. 'I saw the movie when it first came out about five years ago,' he continued without waiting for her to answer. 'Helen Caudill and Jeremy Temple. Before she was really big. It's a strange story, about two people who have to share a hotel room during a snowstorm in Chicago. They're both married. They fall in love while talking about their failed expectations. As I said, a weird play.'

Francesca was not listening. A boy who reminded her of her cousin Roberto had climbed into the car just in front of them at the first stop in the shopping centre. His skin and hair were dark, his features handsomely chiselled. *How long has it been since I have seen Roberto,* she wondered. *Must be three years now. It was down in Positano with his wife Maria.* Francesca sighed and remembered earlier days, long ago. She could see herself laughing and running on the streets of Orvieto. She was nine or ten, still innocent and unspoiled. Roberto was fourteen. They were playing with a football in the piazza in front of Il Duomo. She had loved to tease her cousin. He was so gentle, so unaffected. Roberto was the only good thing from her childhood.

The people mover stopped outside the hotel. Reggie was looking at her with a fixed stare. Francesca knew intuitively that he had just asked her a question. 'Well?' he said, as they descended from their car.

'I'm sorry, dear,' she answered. 'I was daydreaming again. What did you say?'

'I didn't realise I was that boring,' Reggie said without humour. He turned dramatically to ensure that she was paying attention. 'What choice did you make for dinner tonight? I had narrowed it down to Chinese or Cajun.'

At that particular moment, the thought of having dinner with Reggie did not appeal to Francesca. 'I'm very tired tonight,' she said. 'I think I'll just eat by myself in the room and do a little work afterwards.' She could have predicted the hurt look on his face. She reached up and kissed him lightly on the lips. 'You can come by my room for a nightcap about ten.'

Once inside her hotel suite, Francesca's first action was to activate her computer terminal and check for messages. She had four altogether. The printed menu told her the originator of each message, the time of its transmission, the duration of the message, and its urgency priority. The Urgency Priority System was a new innovation of International Communications, Inc., one of the three surviving communications companies which were finally flourishing again after massive consolidation during the middle years of the century. A UPS user entered his daily schedule early in the morning and identified what priority messages could interrupt which activities. Francesca had chosen to accept forwarding of only Priority One (Acute Emergency) messages to the terminal at David Brown's house; the

taping of David and his family had to be accomplished in
one day and she had wanted to minimise the chances of an
interruption and delay.

She had a single Priority Two message, three minutes
long, from Carlo Bianchi. Francesca frowned, entered the
proper codes into the terminal, and turned on the video
monitor. A suave middle-aged Italian dressed in après-ski
clothes, sitting on a couch with a burning fireplace behind
him, came into view. 'Buon giorno, cara,' he greeted her.
After allowing the video camera to pan around the living
room at his new villa in Cortina d'Ampezzo, Signor
Bianchi came right to the point. Why was she refusing to
appear in the advertisements for his summer line of
sportswear? His company had offered her an incredible
amount of money and had even tailored the advertising
campaign to pick up on the space theme. The spots would
not be shown until after the Newton mission would be
over, so there was no conflict with her ISA agreements.
Carlo acknowledged that they had had some differences in
the past, but according to him they were many years ago.
He needed an anwer in a week.

Screw you, Carlo, Francesca thought, surprised at the
intensity of her reactions. There were few people in the
world who could upset Francesca, but Carlo Bianchi was
one of them. She entered the necessary commands to
record a message to her agent, Darrell Bowman, in
London. 'Hi Darrell. It's Francesca in Dallas. Tell that
weasel Bianchi I wouldn't do his ads even if he offered me
ten million marks. And by the way, since I understand
that his main competition these days is Donatelli, why
don't you find their advertising director, Gabriela something or other, I met her once in Milano, and let her know
that I would be happy to do something for them after
Project Newton is over. April or May.' She paused for a
moment. 'That's it. Back in Rome tomorrow night. My
best to Heather.'

Francesca's longest message was from her husband
Alberto, a tall, greying, distinguished executive about
sixty years old. Alberto ran the Italian division of Schmidt
and Hagenest, the multimedia German conglomerate that

owned, among other things, over one-third of the free newspapers and magazines in Europe as well as the leading commercial television networks in both Germany and Italy. In his transmission Alberto was sitting in the den in their home, wearing a rich charcoal suit and sipping a brandy. His tone was warm, familiar, but more like a father than a husband. He told Francesca that her long interview with Admiral Otto Heilmann had been on the news throughout Europe that day, that he had enjoyed her comments and insights as always, but that he had thought Otto came across as an egomaniac. *Not surprising*, Francesca mused when she heard her husband's comment, *since he absolutely is. But he is often useful to me.*

Alberto showed some good news about one of his children (Francesca had three stepchildren, all of whom were older than she) before telling her that he missed her and was looking forward to seeing her the next night. *Me too*, Francesca thought before responding to his message. *It is comfortable living with you. I have both freedom and security.*

Four hours later Francesca was standing outside on her balcony, smoking a cigarette in the cold Texas December air. She was wrapped tightly in the thick robe supplied to the rooms by the hotel. *At least it's not like California*, she said to herself as she pulled a deep drag into her lungs. *At least in Texas some of the hotels do have smoking balconies. Those zealots on the American west coast would make smoking a felony if they could.*

She walked over to the side of the railing so that she would have a better view of a supersonic airliner approaching the airport from the west. In her mind's eye she was inside the plane, as she would be the next day on her flight home to Rome. She imagined that this particular flight had come from Tokyo, the undisputed economic capital of the world before the Great Chaos. After being devastated by their lack of raw materials during the lean years in the middle of the century, the Japanese were now prosperous again as the world

returned to a free market. Francesca watched the plane
land and then looked up at the sky full of stars above her.
She took another pull on her cigarette, her gaze following
the exhaled smoke as it drifted slowly away into the air.

And so Francesca, she reflected, *now comes what may be
your greatest assignment. A chance to become immortal? At
least I should be remembered a long time as one of the
Newton crew.* Her mind turned to the Newton mission
itself and briefly conjured up images of fantastic
creatures who might have created the pair of gargantuan
spaceships and sent them to visit the solar system. But
her thoughts jumped back quickly to the real world, to
the contracts that David Brown had signed just before
she had left his home that afternoon.

*That makes us partners, my esteemed Dr Brown. And
completes the first phase of my plan. And unless I miss my
guess, that was a gleam of interest in your eyes today.*
Francesca had given David a perfunctory kiss when they
had finished discussing and signing the contracts. They
had been alone together in his study. For a moment she
had thought that he was going to return the kiss with a
more meaningful one.

Francesca finished her cigarette, stubbed it out in the
ashtray, and went back into her hotel room. As soon as
she opened the door she could hear the sound of heavy
breathing. The oversized bed was in disarray and a naked
Reggie Wilson was lying across it on his back, his regular
snores disturbing the silence of the suite. *You have great
equipment, my friend,* she commented silently, *both for life
and for lovemaking. But neither is an athletic contest. You
would be more interesting if there were some subtlety, perhaps
even a little finesse.*

7

Public Relations

The solitary eagle soared high above the marshes in the early morning light. It banked on a gust of wind coming from the ocean and turned north along the coast. Far below the eagle, starting at the light brown and white sands beside the ocean and continuing through the collection of islands and rivers and bays that stretched for miles toward the western horizon, an intermittent complex of diverse buildings connected by paved roads broke up the grassland and swamp. Seventy-five years earlier, the Kennedy Spaceport had been one of half a dozen locations on the Earth where travellers could disembark from their high speed trains and aeroplanes to catch a shuttle flight up to one of the LEO (Low Earth Orbit) space stations. But the Great Chaos had changed the spaceport into a ghostly reminder of a once flourishing culture. Its portals and connecting passageways were abandoned for years to the grasses, water birds, alligators, and ubiquitous insects of Central Florida.

In the 2160s, after about twenty years of complete atrophy, the spaceport had gradually been reactivated. It was used first as an airport and then had evolved again into a general transportation centre serving the Florida Atlantic coast. When space launches recommenced in the mid-2170s, it was natural that the old Kennedy launch pads would be recommissioned. By December 2199 more than half of the old spaceport had been refurbished to handle the steadily growing traffic between Earth and space.

From one of the windows of his temporary office Valeriy Borzov watched the magnificent eagle glide gracefully back to its nest high in one of the few tall trees within the centre. He loved birds. He had been fascinated by them for years, beginning in his early boyhood in China. In his most vivid recurring dream General Borzov was living on an amazing planet where the skies swarmed with flying creatures. He could still remember asking his father if there had been any flying biots inside the first Rama spacecraft and then being acutely disappointed with the reply.

General Borzov heard the sound of a large transport vehicle and looked out his west-facing window. Across the way, in front of the test facility, the propulsion module that would be used by both Newton vehicles was emerging from its test complex, on a huge platform moving on multiple tracks. The repaired module, sent back to the subsystem test area because of a problem with its ion controller, would be placed that afternoon inside a cargo shuttle and transferred to the spacecraft assembly facility at space station LEO-2, where it would be retrofitted prior to the final integrated vehicle tests just before Christmas. Both of the Newton flight spacecraft were currently undergoing final checkout and test at LEO-2. All the simulation exercises for the cosmonauts, however, were conducted over at LEO-3 with the backup equipment. The cosmonauts would only use the actual flight systems at LEO-2 during the last week before launch.

On the south side of the building, an electric bus pulled to a stop outside the offices and discharged a small handful of people. One of the passengers was a blonde woman wearing a long-sleeved yellow blouse with vertical black stripes and a pair of black silk pants. She walked with an effortless grace over to the building entrance. General Borzov admired her from a distance, reminding himself that Francesca had been a successful model before becoming a television journalist. He wondered what it was that she wanted and why she had insisted on seeing him privately before the medical briefing this morning.

A minute later he greeted her at the door to his office.

'Good morning, Signora Sabatini,' he said.

'Still so formal, General?' she replied, laughing. 'Even when there's only the two of us? You and the two Japanese men are the only members of the team who refuse to call me Francesca.' She noticed that he was staring strangely at her. She looked down at her clothing to see if something was wrong. 'What's the matter?' she asked him after a momentary hesitation.

'It must be your blouse,' General Borzov answered with a start. 'For just a moment I had the distinct impression that you were a tiger poised to pounce on a hapless antelope or gazelle. Maybe it's old age. Or my mind has started playing tricks on me.' He invited her to come into his office.

'I have had men tell me before that I resemble a cat. But never a tiger.' Francesca sat down in the chair beside the general's desk. She meowed with a mischievous smile. 'I'm just a harmless tabby housecat.'

'I don't believe that for a moment,' Borzov chuckled. 'Many adjectives can be used to describe you, Francesca, but harmless would never be one of them.' He suddenly became very businesslike. 'Now what can I do for you? You said that you had something very important to discuss with me that absolutely could not wait.'

Francesca pulled a large sheet of paper out of her soft briefcase and handed it to General Borzov. 'This is the press schedule for the project,' she said. 'I reviewed it in detail only yesterday with both the public information office and the world television networks. Notice that of the in-depth personal interviews with the cosmonauts, only five have already been completed. Four more were originally scheduled for this month. But notice also that when you added that extra three-day simulation to this coming set of exercises, you wiped out the time that had been allotted to interview Wakefield and Turgenyev.'

She paused for a moment to make sure he was following her. 'We can still catch Takagishi next Saturday and will tape the O'Tooles on Christmas Eve in Boston. But both Richard and Irina say that they now have no time for their interviews. In addition, we still have an old problem: neither you nor Nicole is scheduled at all....'

'You insisted on a meeting at 7:30 this morning to discuss this *press* schedule,' Borzov interrupted, his voice clearly conveying the relative importance that he assigned to such activities.

'Among other things,' Francesca answered nonchalantly. She ignored the implied criticism in his comment. 'Of the people on this mission,' she continued, 'the polls show that the public has the greatest interest in you, me, Nicole des Jardins, and David Brown. So far, I have been unable to pin you down on a date for your personal interview and Madame des Jardins says that she 'does not intend' to have one at all. The networks are unhappy. My prelaunch coverage is going to be incomplete. I need some help from you.'

Francesca looked directly at General Borzov. 'I am asking you to cancel the additional simulation, to set a definite time for your personal interview, and to talk to Nicole on my behalf.'

The general frowned. He was both angered and annoyed by Francesca's presumption. He was going to tell her that the scheduling of personal publicity interviews was not high on his priority list. But something held him back. Both his sixth sense and a lifetime of experience in dealing with people told him to hesitate, that there was more to this discussion than he had yet heard. He temporised by changing the subject.

'Incidentally, I must tell you that I am growing increasingly concerned about the lavish scope of this New Year's Eve party that your friends in the Italian government/business coalition are hosting. I know we agreed at the beginning of our training that we would participate, as a group, in that one social function. But I had no idea that it was going to be billed as "the party of the century", as it was called last week by one of those American personality magazines. You know all those people, can't you do something to downplay the party?'

'The gala was another item on my agenda,' Francesca replied, carefully avoiding the thrust of his comment. 'I need your assistance there as well. Four of the Newton cosmonauts now say that they do not plan to attend and two or three more have suggested that they may have other commitments – even though we all agreed to the party back in March. Takagishi and Yamanaka want to celebrate the holiday with their families in Japan and Richard Wakefield tells me that he has made reservations to go scuba diving in the Cayman Islands. And then there's that Frenchwoman again, who simply says that she's not coming and refuses to offer any kind of explanation.'

Borzov could not suppress a grin. 'Why are you having such a hard time with Nicole des Jardins? I would think that since both of you are women, you would be able to speak to her more easily than the others.'

'She is entirely unsympathetic with the role of the press in this mission. She has told me so several times. And she is very stubborn about her privacy.' Francesca shrugged her shoulders. 'But the public is absolutely fascinated with her. After all, not only is she a doctor and a linguist and a former Olympic champion, but also she is the daughter of a famous novelist and the mother of a fourteen-year-old daughter, despite never having been married....'

Valeriy Borzov was looking at his watch. 'Just for my information,' he interrupted, 'how many more items are on your agenda, as you call it? We are due in the auditorium in ten more minutes.' He smiled back at Francesca. 'And I feel compelled to remind you that Madame des Jardins went out of her way today to accommodate your request for press coverage of this briefing.'

Francesca studied General Borzov for several seconds. *I think he's ready now*, she thought to herself. *And unless I've misjudged him he will understand immediately.* She pulled a small cubic object out of her briefcase and handed it across the desk. 'This is the only other item on my agenda,' she said.

The Newton commander-in-chief seemed puzzled. He turned the cube over in his hands. 'A freelance journalist sold it to us,' Francesca said in a very serious tone. 'We were assured it was the only copy in existence.'

She paused a moment while Borzov loaded the cube into the appropriate part of his desk computer. He blanched noticeably when the first video segment from the cube appeared on the monitor. He watched the wild rantings of his daughter Natasha for about fifteen seconds. 'I wanted to keep this out of the hands of the tabloid press,' Francesca added softly.

'How long is the tape?' General Borzov asked quietly.

'Almost half an hour,' she replied. 'I'm the only one who has seen the entire thing.'

General Borzov heaved a sigh. This was the moment that his wife Petra had dreaded ever since it was first made official that he would be the commanding officer of the Newton. The institute director at Sverdlovsk had promised that no reporters would have access to his daughter. Now here was a videotape with a thirty minute interview with her. Petra would be mortified.

He stared out the window. In his mind he was assessing what would happen to the mission if his daughter's acute schizophrenia were paraded before the public. It would be embarrassing, he conceded, but the mission would not be damaged in any serious way ... General Borzov looked across at Francesca. He hated making deals. And he wasn't certain that Francesca herself had not commissioned the interview with Natasha. Nevertheless....

Borzov relaxed and forced a smile. 'I guess I could thank you,' he said, 'but somehow it doesn't seem appropriate.' He paused for a moment. 'I assume I'm expected to show some gratitude.'

So far so good, Francesca thought. She knew better than to say anything just yet.

'All right,' the general continued after the lengthy silence, 'I will cancel the extra simulation. Others have already complained about it.' He turned the data cube over in his hands. 'And Petra and I will come to Rome early, as you once suggested, for the personal interview. I will remind all the cosmonauts tomorrow about the party

on New Year's Eve and tell them that it is their duty to
attend. But neither I nor anyone else can require Nicole
des Jardins to talk to you about anything except her
work.' He stood up abruptly. 'Now it's time for us to go
to that biometry meeting.'

Francesca reached up and kissed him on the cheek.
'Thank you, Valeriy,' she said.

8
Biometry

The medical briefing had already begun when Francesca and General Borzov arrived. All the rest of the cosmonauts were present, as well as twenty-five or thirty additional engineers and scientists associated with the mission. Four newspaper reporters and a television crew completed the audience. At the front of the small auditorium stood Nicole des Jardins, wearing her grey flight outfit as always, and holding a laser pointer in her hand. To the side of her was a tall Japanese man in a blue dress suit. He was listening carefully to a question from the audience. Nicole interrupted him to acknowledge the new arrivals.

'Sumimasen, Hakamatsu-san,' she said. 'Let me introduce our commander, General Valeriy Borzov of the Soviet Union, as well as the journalist-cosmonaut Francesca Sabatini.'

She turned toward the latecomers. 'Dobriy Utra,' Nicole said to the general, quickly nodding a greeting in Francesca's direction as well. 'This is the esteemed Dr Toshiro Hakamatsu. He designed and developed the biometry system that we are going to use in flight, including the tiny probes which will be inserted into our bodies.'

General Borzov extended his hand. 'I am glad to meet you, Hakamatsu-san,' he said. 'Madame des Jardins has made us all very much aware of your outstanding work.'

'Thank you,' the man replied, bowing in the direction of Borzov after shaking his hand. 'It is an honour for me to be part of this project.'

Francesca and General Borzov took the two empty seats at the front of the auditorium and the meeting recommenced. Nicole aimed her pointer at a keyboard on the side of a small podium and a fullscale, multicoloured male model of the human cardiovascular system, with veins marked in blue and arteries in red, appeared as a three-dimensional holographic image in the front of the room. Tiny white markers circulating inside the flowing blood vessels indicated the direction and rate of flow. 'The Life Sciences Board of the ISA just last week gave final approval to the new Hakamatsu probes as our key health monitoring system for the mission,' Nicole was saying. 'They withheld their approval until the last minute so that they could properly assess the results of the stress testing, in which the new probes were asked to perform in a wide variety of off-nominal situations. Even under those conditions there was no sign that any rejection mechanisms were triggered in any of the test subjects.

'We are fortunate that we will be able to use this system, for it will make life much easier both for me, as your life science officer, and for you. During the mission you will not be subjected to the routine injection/ scanning techniques that have been used on previous projects. These new probes are injected once, maybe twice at the most, during our one-hundred-day mission, and they do not need to be replaced.'

'How did the longterm rejection problem get solved?' A question from another doctor in the audience interrupted Nicole's train of thought.

'I will discuss that in detail during our splinter session this afternoon,' she replied. 'For now, it should be sufficient for me to mention that since the key chemistry governing rejection focuses on four or five critical parameters, including acidity, the probes are coated with chemicals that adapt to the local chemistry at the implantation site. In other words, once the probe arrives at its destination, it non-invasively samples its ambient biochemical environment and then exudes a thin coating for itself that is designed to be consistent with the chemistry of the host and thereby avoid rejection.

'But I am getting ahead of myself,' Nicole said, turning to face the large model showing blood circulation in the human being. 'The family of probes will be inserted here, in the left arm, and the individual monitors will disperse according to their prescribed guidance programs to thirty-two distinct locales in the body. There they will embed themselves in the host tissue.' The inside of the holographic model became animated as she spoke and the audience watched as thirty-two blinking lights started from the left arm and scattered throughout the body. Four went to the brain, three more to the heart, four to the primary glands of the endocrine system, and the remaining twenty-one monitors spread out to assorted locations and organs ranging from the eyes to the fingers and toes.

'Each of the individual probes contains both an array of microscopic sensors to sample important health parameters and a fancy data system that first stores and then transmits the recorded information upon receipt of an enabling command from the scanner. In practice, I would expect to scan each of you and dump all your health telemetry once a day, but the recorders can handle data covering up to four days if necessary.' Nicole stopped and looked at the audience. 'Are there any questions so far?' she asked.

'Yes,' said Richard Wakefield in the front row. 'I see how this system gathers trillions of bits of data. But that's the easy part. There's no way you or any other human being could look at all that information. How does the data get synthesised or analysed so that you can tell if anything irregular is happening?'

'You'd make a great straight man, Richard,' Nicole smiled. 'That's my next subject.' She held up a small, flat thin object with a keyboard on it. 'This is a standard programmable scanner which permits the monitored information to be sampled in many different ways. I can call for a full dump from any and/or all channels, or I can request transmission only of warning data....'

Nicole saw many confused looks in her audience. 'I'd better back up and start this part of the explanation again,' she said. 'Each measurement made by each instrument has an "expected range" – one that will vary of course from individual to individual – and a much wider "tolerance range" used to identify a true emergency. If a particular measurement only exceeds the expected range, it is entered in the warning file and that specific channel is marked with an alarm identifier. One of my options using the scanner is to read out only these warning lists. If an individual cosmonaut is feeling fine, my normal procedure would be just to see if there are any entries in the warning buffer.'

'But if you have a measurement outside the tolerance range,' Janos Tabori interjected, 'then watch out. The monitor turns on its emergency transmitter and uses all its internal power to send out a "beep, beep" noise that is frightening. I know. It happened to me during a short test with what turned out to be improper tolerance values. I thought I was dying.' Janos was the backup life science officer. His comment caused general laughter. The image of little Janos walking around emitting a high-pitched beep was amusing.

'No system is foolproof,' Nicole continued, 'and this one is only as good as the set of values that are entered to trigger both the warnings and the emergencies. So you can see why calibration data is essential. We have examined each of your medical histories with extreme care and entered initial values in the monitors. But we must see actual results with the real probes inserted in your bodies. That's the reason for today's activity. We will insert your probe set today, monitor your performance during the four final simulation exercises that begin on Thursday, and then update the trigger values, if necessary, before we actually launch.'

There was some involuntary squirming as each cosmonaut thought about the prospect of tiny medical laboratories embedded indefinitely in their body. They were accustomed to the regular investigative probes that were placed in the body to obtain some specific information, like the amount of plaque blocking the arteries, but these probes were always temporary. The thought of permanent electronic invasion was to say the least disquieting. General Michael O'Toole asked two questions that were bothering most of the crew.

'Nicole,' he enquired in his usual earnest manner, 'can you tell us how you make sure that the probes actually go to the right places. Even more important, what happens if one malfunctions?'

'Of course, Michael,' she answered pleasantly. 'Remember these things will be inside me as well and I had to ask the same questions.' Nicole des Jardins was in her middle thirties. Her skin was a shiny copper brown, her eyes dark brown and almond-shaped, her hair a luxurious jet black. There was an unmistakable self-confidence radiating from her that was sometimes interpreted as arrogance. 'You won't leave the clinic today until we have verified that all the probes are properly positioned,' she continued. 'Based on recent past experience, one or two of you may have a monitor wander off course. It is an easy matter to track it with the lab equipment and then send over-ride commands as necessary to move it to the proper spot.

'As far as the malfunction issue is concerned, there are several levels of fault protection. First, each specific monitor tests its own battery of sensors more than twenty times a day. Any individual instrument failing a test is turned off immediately by the executive software in its own monitor. In addition, each of the probe packages undergoes a full and rigorous self-test twice a day. Failure of self-test is one of many fault conditions that causes the monitor to secrete chemicals causing self-destruction, with eventual harmless absorption by the body. Lest you become unduly concerned, we have rigorously verified all these fault paths with test subjects during the past year.'

Nicole wound up her presentation and stood quietly in front of her colleagues. 'Any questions?' she asked. After a few seconds' hesitation she continued, 'Then I need a volunteer to walk up here beside the robot nurse and be inoculated. My personal probe set was injected and verified last week. Who wants to be next?'

Francesca stood up. 'All right, we'll start with la bella signora Sabatini,' Nicole said. She gestured to the television personnel. 'Focus those cameras on the tracer simulation. It's quite a show when these electronic bugs swarm through the bloodstream.'

9

Diastolic Irregularity

Through the window Nicole could barely discern the Siberian snow fields in the oblique December light. They were more than fifty thousand feet below her. The supersonic plane was slowing now as it moved south toward Vladivostok and the islands of Japan. Nicole yawned. After only three hours of sleep, it would be a fight all day to keep her body awake. It was almost ten in the morning in Japan but back home at Beauvois, in the Loire Valley not far from Tours, her daughter Genevieve still had four more hours of sleep until her alarm would awaken her at seven o'clock.

The video monitor in the back of the seat in front of Nicole automatically turned on and reminded her that it was only fifteen minutes until the plane would land at the Kansai Transportation Centre. The lovely Japanese girl on the screen suggested that now would be an excellent time to make or confirm ground transportation and housing arrangements. Nicole activated the communication system in her seat and a thin rectangular tray with a keyboard and small display area slid in front of her. In less than a minute Nicole arranged both her train ride to Kyoto and her electric trolley passage from there to her hotel. She used her Universal Credit Card to pay for all transactions, after first correctly identifying herself by indicating that her mother's maiden name was Anawi Tiasso. When she was finished a small printed schedule listing her train and trolley identifiers, along with the times of arrival and transit (she would reach her hotel at

11:14 am Japanese time), popped out of one end of the tray.

As the plane prepared for its landing, Nicole thought about the reason for her sudden trip one-third of the way around the world. Just twenty-four hours ago she had been planning to spend this day around her home, following some office work in the morning with language practice for Genevieve in the afternoon. It was the beginning of the holiday break for the cosmonauts and, except for that stupid party in Rome at the end of the year, Nicole was supposedly free until she had to report to LEO-3 on January 8. But while she had been sitting in her office at home the previous morning, routinely checking the biometry from the final set of simulations, Nicole had come across a curious phenomenon. She had been studying Richard Wakefield's heart and blood pressure during a variable gravity test and had not understood a particularly rapid surge in his pulse rate. She had then decided to check Dr Takagishi's detailed heart biometry for comparison, since he had been engaged in a strenuous physical activity with Richard at the time of the pulse surge.

What she had found when she had examined a full dump of Takagishi's heart information had been an even bigger surprise. The Japanese professor's diastolic expansion was decidedly irregular, maybe even patho- logical. But no warnings had been issued by the probe and no data channels had been alarmed. What was going on? Had she detected a malfunction in the Hakamatsu system?

An hour's worth of detective work had resulted in the identification of more peculiarities. During the full set of simulations, there had been four separate intervals in which Takagishi's problem had occurred. The abnormal behaviour was sporadic and intermittent. Sometimes the extra long diastole, reminiscent of a valve problem during the filling of the heart with blood, would not appear for as long as thirty-eight hours. However, the fact that it did recur four different times suggested that there was definitely an abnormality of some kind.

What has mystified Nicole was not the raw data itself – it was the failure of the system to trigger the proper alarms in the presence of the wildly irregular observations. As part of her analysis, she had traced laboriously through the Takagishi medical history, paying special attention to the cardiology report. She had found no hint of any kind of abnormality, so had convinced herself that she was seeing a sensor error and not a true medical problem.

So if the system were working correctly, she had reasoned, *the onset of the long diastole should have immediately sent the heart monitor outside the expected range and triggered an alarm. But it didn't. Neither the first time nor subsequently. Is it possible that we have a double failure here? If so, how did the unit continue to pass self-test?*

At first Nicole had thought about phoning one of her assistants in the life science office at ISA to discuss the anomaly she had found, but she decided instead, since it was a holiday for ISA, to telephone Dr Hakamatsu in Japan. That phone call to him had completely bewildered her. He had told her flatly that the phenomenon she had observed must have been in the patient, that no combination of component failures in his probe could have produced such strange results. 'But then why were there no entries in the warning file?' she had asked the Japanese electronics designer.

'Because no expected range values were exceeded,' he answered confidently. 'For some reason an extremely wide expected range must have been entered for this particular cosmonaut. Have you looked at his medical history?'

Later on in the conversation, when Nicole told Dr Hakamatsu that the unexplained data had actually come from the probes inside one of his countrymen, namely cosmonaut-scientist Takagishi, the usually restrained engineer had actually shouted into the phone. 'Wonderful,' he had said. 'Then I'll be able to clear up this mystery in a hurry. I'll contact Takagishi-san over at Kyoto University and let you know what I find.'

Three hours later Nicole's video monitor had revealed

the sombre face of Dr Shigeru Takagishi. 'Madame des Jardins,' he had said very politely, 'I understand that you have been talking with my colleague Hakamatsu-san about my biometry output during the simulations. Would you be kind enough to explain to me what you have found?'

Nicole had then presented all the information to her fellow cosmonaut, concealing nothing and expressing her personal belief that the source of the erroneous data had indeed been a probe malfunction.

A long silence followed Nicole's explanation. At length the worried Japanese scientist had spoken again. 'Hakamatsu-san just visited me here at the university and checked out the probe set inside me. He will report that he found no problems with his electronics.' Takagishi had then paused, seemingly deep in thought. 'Madame des Jardins,' he had said a few seconds later, 'I would like to ask you a favour. It is a matter of the utmost importance to me. Could you possibly come to see me in Japan in the very near future? I would like to talk with you personally and explain something that may be related to my irregular biometry data.'

There had been an earnestness in Takagishi's face that Nicole could neither overlook nor misintrepret. He was clearly imploring her to help him. Without asking any more questions, she had agreed to visit him immediately. A few minutes later she had reserved a seat on the overnight supersonic flight from Paris to Osaka.

'It was never bombed during the great war with America,' Takagishi said, waving his arms at the city of Kyoto spread out below them, 'and it suffered almost no damage when the hoodlums took over for seven months in 2141. I admit that I am prejudiced,' he said smiling, 'but to me Kyoto is the most beautiful city in the world.'

'Many of my countrymen feel that way about Paris,' Nicole answered. She pulled her coat tightly around her. The air was cold and damp. It felt as if it might snow at any moment. She was wondering when her associate was going to start talking about their business. She had not flown five thousand miles for a tour of the city, although she did admit that this Kiyomizu Temple set among the trees on a hillside overlooking the city was certainly a magnificent spot.

'Let's have some tea,' Takagishi said. He led her to one of the several outside tearooms flanking the main part of the old Buddhist temple. *Now*, Nicole said to herself as she stifled a yawn, *he's going to tell me what this is all about.* Takagishi had met her at the hotel when she had arrived. He had suggested that she have some lunch and a short nap before he returned. After he had picked her up at three o'clock, they had come directly to this temple.

He poured the thick Japanese tea into two cups and waited for Nicole to take a sip. The hot liquid warmed her mouth even though she didn't care for the bitter taste. 'Madame,' Takagishi began, 'you are doubtless wondering why I have asked you to come all the way to Japan on such short notice. You see –' he spoke slowly but with great intensity – 'all my life I have dreamed that perhaps another Rama spacecraft would return while I was still alive. During my studies at the university and during my many years of research I was preparing myself for one single event, the return of the Ramans. On that March morning in 2197 when Alastair Moore called me to say that the latest images from Excalibur indicated that we had another extraterrestrial visitor, I nearly wept with joy. I knew immediately that the ISA would mount a mission to visit the spaceship. I resolved to be part of that mission.'

The Japanese scientist took a drink from his tea and looked to his left, out across the manicured green trees and the slopes above the city. 'When I was a boy,' he continued, his careful English barely audible, 'I would climb these hills on a clear night and stare into the sky, searching for the home of the special intelligence that had created that incomparable giant machine. Once I came with my father and we huddled together in the cold night air, looking at the stars, while he told me what it had been like in his village during the days of the first Rama encounter twelve years before I was born. I believed on that night –' he turned to look at Nicole and she could again see the passion in his eyes – 'and I still believe today, that there was some reason for that visit, some purpose for the appearance of that awesome spaceship. I have studied all the data from that first encounter, hoping to find a clue that would explain why it came. Nothing has been conclusive. I have developed several theories on the subject, but I do not have enough evidence to support any of them.'

Again Takagishi stopped talking to drink some of his tea. Nicole had been both surprised and impressed by the depth of feeling he had exhibited. She sat patiently and said nothing while she waited for him to continue. 'I knew that I had a good chance of being selected as a cosmonaut,' he said, 'not only because of my publications, including the *Atlas*, but also because one of my closest associates, Hisanori Akita, was the Japanese representative on the selection board. When the number of scientists remaining in the competition had been reduced to eight and I was one of them, Akita-san suggested to me that it looked as if the two leading contenders were myself and David Brown. You'll recall that up until that time no physical examinations of any kind had been conducted.'

That's right, Nicole remembered. *The potential crew was first reduced to forty-eight and then we were all taken to Heidelberg for the physicals. The German doctors in charge insisted that each of the candidates must pass every single medical criterion. The Academy graduates were the first group tested and five out of twenty failed. Including Alain Blamont.*

'When your countryman Blamont, who had already flown half a dozen major missions for the ISA, was disqualified from consideration because of that trivial heart murmur – and the Cosmonaut Selection Board subsequently upheld the doctors by denying his appeal – I completely panicked.' The proud Japanese physicist was now staring directly into Nicole's eyes, entreating her to understand. 'I was afraid that I was going to lose the most important opportunity of my career because of a minor physical problem that had never before affected any part of my life.' He paused to choose his words carefully. 'I know that what I did was wrong and dishonourable, but I convinced myself at the time it was all right, that my chance to decipher the greatest puzzle in man's history should not be blocked by a group of smallminded doctors defining acceptable health only in terms of numerical values.'

Dr Takagishi told the rest of his story without embellishment or obvious emotion. The passion he had fleetingly demonstrated during his discussion of the Ramans had vanished, his monotonic recital was crisp and clear. He explained how he had cajoled his family physician into falsifying his medical history and providing him with a new drug that would prevent the occurrence of his diastolic irregularity during the two days of his physical at Heidelberg. Although there had been some risk of deleterious side effects from the new drug, everything went according to plan. Takagishi passed the rigorous physical and was ultimately selected as one of the two mission scientists, along with Dr David Brown. He had never thought again about the medical issue until about three months ago, when Nicole had first explained to the cosmonauts that she was planning to recommend the usage of the Hakamatsu probe system during the mission instead of the standard temporary probe scans once every week.

'You see,' Takagishi explained, his brow now starting to furrow, 'under the old mission technique I could have used that same drug once a week and neither you nor any other life science officer would ever have seen my irregularity. But a permanent monitoring system cannot be fooled – the drug is much too dangerous for constant use.'

So you somehow worked out a deal with Hakamatsu, Nicole jumped ahead of him in her own mind. *Either with or without his explicit knowledge. And you input expected value ranges that would not trigger in the presence of your abnormality. You hoped that nobody analysing the tests would call for a full biometry dump*. Now she understood why he had summoned her urgently to Japan. *And you want me to keep your secret.*

'Watakushi no dõryõ wa, wakarimasu,' Nicole said kindly, changing into Japanese to show her sympathy for her colleague's anguish. 'I can tell how much distress this is causing you. You need not explain in detail how you tampered with the Hakamatsu probes.' She paused and watched his face relax. 'But if I understand you correctly, what you want is for me to become an accomplice to your deception. You recognise of course that I cannot even consider preserving your secret unless I am absolutely convinced that your minor physical problem, as you call it, represents no possible threat to the mission. Otherwise I would be forced....'

'Madame des Jardins,' Takagishi interrupted her, 'I have the utmost respect for your integrity. I would never, *never* ask you to keep my heart irregularity out of the record unless you agreed that it really was an insignificant problem.' He looked at her in silence for several seconds. 'When Hakamatsu phoned me this evening,' he continued quietly, 'I thought originally that I would call a press conference and then resign from the project. But while I was thinking about what I would say in my resignation, I kept seeing this image of Professor Brown. He is a brilliant man, my American counterpart, but he is also, in my opinion, too certain of his own infallibility. The most likely replacement for me would be Professor Wolfgang Heinrich from Bonn. He has published many fine papers about Rama but he, like Brown, believes that these celestial visits represent random events, totally without connection to us and our planet.' The intensity and passion had returned to his eyes. 'I cannot quit now. Unless I have no choice. Both Brown and Heinrich might miss the clue.'

Behind Takagishi, on the path that led back to the main wooden building of the temple, three Buddhist monks walked briskly past. Despite the cold, they were dressed lightly in their usual charcoal grey smocks, their feet exposed to the cold in open sandals. The Japanese scientist was proposing to Nicole that they spend the rest of the day at the office of his personal physician, where they could study his complete and uncensored medical history dating back to his childhood. If she would be willing, he added, they would give her a data cube containing all the information for her to take back to France and study at her leisure.

Nicole, who had been listening intently to Takagishi for almost an hour, momentarily diverted her attention to the three monks now purposefully climbing the stairs in the distance. *Their eyes are so serene,* she thought. *Their lives so free of contradiction. Onemindedness can be a virtue. It makes all the answers easy.* For just a moment she was envious of the monks and their ordered existence. She wondered how well they would handle the dilemma with which Dr Takagishi was presenting her. *He is not one of the space cadets,* she was now thinking, *so his role is not absolutely critical to mission success. And in a sense he is right. The doctors on the project have been too strict. They never should have disqualified Alain. It would be a shame if....*

'Daijōbu,' she said before he had finished talking. 'I will go with you to see your doctor and if I don't find anything that bothers me, I will take the entire file home with me to study during the holidays.' Takagishi's face lit up. 'But let me warn you again,' she added, 'if there is anything in your history that I find questionable, or if I have the slightest shred of evidence that you have withheld any information from me, then I will ask you to resign immediately.'

'Thank you, thank you so much,' Dr Takagishi replied, standing and bowing to his female colleague. 'Thank you so much,' he repeated.

10

The Cosmonaut and the Pope

General O'Toole could not have slept more than two hours altogether. The combination of excitement and jet lag had kept his mind active all night long. He had studied the lovely bucolic mural on the wall opposite the bed in his hotel room and counted all the animals twice. Unfortunately, he had remained wide awake after he had finished both counts.

He took a deep breath, hoping that it would help him relax. *So why all this nervousness?* he asked himself. *He is just a man like all the rest on earth. Well, not exactly.* O'Toole sat up straight in his chair and smiled. It was ten o'clock in the morning and he was sitting in a small anteroom inside the Vatican. He was about to have a private audience with the Vicar of Christ, Pope John-Paul V.

During his childhood, Michael O'Toole had often dreamed of someday becoming the first North American pope. 'Pope Michael', he had called himself during the long Sunday afternoons when he had studied his catechism alone. As he had repeated the words of his lessons over and over and committed them to memory, he had imagined himself, maybe fifty years in the future, wearing the cassock and papal ring, celebrating mass for thousands in the great churches and stadia of the world. He would inspire the poor, the hopeless, the downtrodden. He would show them how God could lead them to a better life.

As a young man Michael O'Toole had loved all

learning, but three subjects had especially intrigued him.
He could not read enough about religion, history, and
physics. Somehow his facile mind found it easy to jump
between these different disciplines. It never bothered
him that the epistemologies of religion and physics were
one hundred and eighty degrees apart. Michael O'Toole
had no difficulty recognising which questions in life
should be answered by physics and which ones by
religion.

All three of his favourite scholastic subjects merged in
the study of creation. It was, after all, the beginning of
everything, including religion, history, and physics.
How had it happened? Was God present, as the referee
perhaps, for the kickoff of the universe eighteen billion
years ago? Wasn't it He who had provided the impetus
for the cataclysmic explosion known as the Big Bang that
produced all matter out of energy: Hadn't He foreseen
that those original pristine hydrogen atoms would
coalesce into giant clouds of gas and then collapse under
gravitation to become the stars in which would be
manufactured the basic chemical building blocks of life?

And I have never lost my fascination with creation,
O'Toole said to himself as he waited for his papal
audience. *How did it all happen? What is the significance of
the particular sequence of events?* He remembered his
questions of the priests when he was a teenager. *I
probably decided not to become a priest because it would have
limited my free access to scientific truth. The church has never
been as comfortable as I am with the apparent
incompatibilities between God and Einstein.*

An American priest from the Vatican state department
had been waiting at his hotel in Rome the previous
evening when O'Toole had returned from his day as a
tourist. The priest had introduced himself and
apologised profusely for not having responded to the
letter that General O'Toole had written from Boston in
November. It would have 'facilitated the process', the
priest had remarked in passing, if the general had
pointed out in his letter that he was *the* General O'Toole,
the Newton cosmonaut. Nevertheless, the priest had

continued, the papal schedule had been juggled and the Holy Father would be delighted to see O'Toole the next morning.

As the door to the papal office swung open, the American general instinctively stood up. The priest from the night before walked into the room, looking very nervous, and quickly shook O'Toole's hand. They both glanced toward the doorway where the pope, wearing his normal white cassock, was concluding a conversation with a member of his staff. John-Paul V came forward into the anteroom, a pleasant smile on his face, and extended his hand toward O'Toole. The cosmonaut automatically dropped to one knee and kissed the papal ring.

'Holy Father,' he murmured, astonished at the excited pounding of his heart, 'thank you for seeing me. This is indeed a great honour for me.'

'For me as well,' the pope replied in lightly accented English. 'I have been following the activities of you and your colleagues with great interest.'

He gestured toward O'Toole and the American general followed the church leader into a grand office with high ceilings. A very large, dark wood desk stood on one side of the room under a lifesized portrait of John-Paul IV, the man who had become pope during the darkest days of the Great Chaos and had provided both the world and the church with twenty years of energetic and inspirational leadership. The gifted Venezuelan, a poet and historical scholar in his own right, had demonstrated to the world between 2139 and 2158 how positive a force the organised church could be at a time when virtually every other institution was collapsing and was, therefore, unable to give any succour to the bewildered masses.

The pope sat down on a couch and motioned for O'Toole to sit next to him. The American priest left the room. In front of O'Toole and the pope were great windows that opened onto a balcony overlooking the Vatican gardens some twenty feet below. In the distance O'Toole could see the Vatican museum where he had spent the previous afternoon.

'You wrote in your letter,' the Holy Father said, without referring to any notes, 'that there were some "theological issues" that you would like to discuss with me. I assume these are in some way related to your mission.'

O'Toole looked at the seventy-year-old Spaniard who was the spiritual leader of a billion Catholics. The pope's skin was olive, his features sharp, his thick black hair now mostly grey. His brown eyes were soft and clear. *He certainly doesn't waste any time*, O'Toole thought, recalling an article in a Catholic magazine in which one of the leading cardinals in the Vatican administration had praised John-Paul V for his management efficiency.

'Yes, Holy Father,' O'Toole said. 'As you know, I am about to embark on a journey of the utmost significance for humankind. As a Catholic, I have some questions that I thought it might be helpful for me to discuss with you.' He paused for a moment. 'I certainly don't expect you to have all the answers. But maybe you can guide me a little with your accumulated wisdom.'

The pope nodded and waited for O'Toole to continue. The cosmonaut took a deep breath. 'The issue of redemption is one that's bothering me, even though I guess it's just a part of a bigger concern that I have in reconciling the Ramans with our faith.'

The pope's brow furrowed and O'Toole could tell that he was not communicating very well. 'I have no trouble whatsoever,' the general added as an explanation, 'with the concept of God creating the Ramans, that's easy to comprehend. But did the Ramans follow a similar pattern of spiritual evolution and therefore need to be redeemed, at some point in their history, like human beings on Earth? And if so, did God send Jesus, or perhaps his Raman equivalent, to save them from their sins? Do we humans thus represent an evolutionary paradigm that has been repeated over and over throughout the universe?'

The pope's smile broadened almost into a grin. 'Goodness, General,' he said with humour, 'you have romped over a vast intellectual territory very quickly.

You must know that I do not have fast answers to such profound questions. The church has had its scholars addressing the issues raised by Rama for almost seventy years and, as you would expect, our research has recently intensified because of the discovery of the second spacecraft.'

'But what do you personally believe, your holiness?' O'Toole persisted. 'Did the creatures who made these two incredible space vehicles commit some original sin and also need a saviour sometime in their history? Is the story of Jesus unique for us here on Earth, or is it just one small chapter in a book of nearly infinite length that covers all sentient beings and a general requirement for redemption to achieve salvation?'

'I'm not certain,' the Holy Father replied after several seconds. 'Sometimes it is nearly impossible for me to fathom the existence of other intelligence in any form out there in the rest of the universe. Then, as soon as I acknowledge that it certainly wouldn't look like us, I struggle with images and pictures that sidetrack my thinking from the kinds of theological questions that you have raised this morning.' He paused for a moment, reflecting. 'But most of the time I imagine that the Ramans too had lessons to learn in the beginning, that God did not create them perfect either, and that at some time in their development He must have sent them Jesus....'

The pope interrupted himself and looked intently at General O'Toole. 'Yes,' he continued softly, 'I said Jesus. You asked me what I believed personally. To me Jesus is both the true saviour and the only son of God. It would be He who would be sent to the Ramans also, albeit in a different guise.'

O'Toole's face had brightened at the end of the pontiff's remarks. 'I agree with you, Holy Father,' he said excitedly. 'And therefore all intelligence is united, everywhere throughout the universe, by a similar spiritual experience. In a very, very real sense, assuming that the Ramans and the Others have also been saved, we are all brothers. After all, we are made from the same basic chemicals. That means that Heaven will not be limited just to humans but will encompass all beings everywhere who have understood His message.'

'I can see where you might come to that conclusion,' John-Paul replied. 'But it is certainly not one that is universally accepted. Even within the church there are those who have an altogether different view of the Ramans.'

'You mean the group that uses quotations from St Michael of Siena for support?'

The pope nodded.

'For myself,' General O'Toole said, 'I find their narrow homocentric interpretation of St Michael's sermon on the Ramans much too confining. In saying that the extraterrestrial spacecraft might have been a herald, like Elijah or even Isaiah, foretelling the second coming of Christ, Michael was not restricting the Ramans to having only that particular role in our history and no other function or existence. He was simply explaining one possible view of the event from a human spiritual perspective.'

Again the pontiff was smiling. 'I can tell that you have spent considerable time and energy thinking about all this. My advance information about you was only partially correct. Your devotion to God, the church, and your family were all cited in your dossier. But there is little mention of your active intellectual interest in theology.'

'I consider this mission to be by far the most important assignment of my life. I want to make certain that I properly serve both God and mankind. So I am trying to prepare myself in every possible way, including discovering whether or not the Ramans may have a spiritual component. It could affect my actions on the mission.'

O'Toole paused a few seconds before continuing. 'By the way, your holiness, have your researchers found any evidence of possible Raman spirituality, based on their analysis of the first rendezvous?'

John-Paul V shook his head. 'Not really. However,

one of my most devout archbishops, a man whose religious zeal sometimes overshadows his logic, insists that the structural order inside the first Raman craft – you know, the symmetries, geometric patterns, even the repetitive redundant designs based on the number three – is suggestive of a temple. He could be right. We just don't know. We don't see any evidence either way about the spiritual nature of the beings who created that first spaceship.'

'Amazing!' said General O'Toole. 'I had never thought of that before. Imagine if it really was created as some kind of a temple. That would stagger David Brown.' The general laughed. 'Dr Brown insists,' he said in explanation, 'that we poor ignorant human beings would not have any chance of ever determining the purpose of such a spaceship, for the technology of its builders is so far advanced beyond our comprehension that it would be impossible for us ever to understand any of it. And, according to him, of course there could be no Raman religion. In his opinion they would have left all the superstitious mumbo-jumbo behind eons before they developed the capability to construct such a fabulous interstellar spacecraft.'

'Dr Brown is an atheist, isn't he?' the pope asked.

O'Toole nodded. 'An outspoken one. He believes that all religious thinking impairs the proper functioning of the brain. He regards anyone who doesn't agree with his point of view as an absolute idiot.'

'And the rest of the crew? Are they as strongly opinionated on the subject as Dr Brown?'

'He is the most vocal atheist, although I suspect Wakefield, Tabori, and Turgenyev all share his basic attitudes. Strangely enough, my intuitive sense tells me that Commander Borzov has a soft spot in his heart for religion. That's true of most of the survivors of the Chaos. Anyway, Valeriy seems to enjoy asking me questions about my faith.'

General O'Toole stopped for a moment as he mentally completed his survey of the religious beliefs of the Newton crew. 'The European women, des Jardins and

Sabatini, are nominally Catholic, although they would not be considered devout by any stretch of the imagination. Admiral Heilmann is a Lutheran on Easter and Christmas. Takagishi meditates and studies Zen. I don't know about the other two.'

The pontiff stood up and walked over to the window. 'Somewhere out there a strange and wonderful space vehicle, created by beings from another star, is headed toward us. We are sending a crew of a dozen to rendezvous with it.' He turned toward General O'Toole. 'This spaceship may be a messenger from God, but probably only you will be able to recognise it as such.'

O'Toole did not reply. The pope stared out the window again and was quiet for almost a minute. 'No, my son,' he finally said softly, as much to himself as to General O'Toole. 'I do not have the answers to your questions. Only God has them. You must pray that He will provide the answers when you need them.' He faced the general. 'I must tell you that I am delighted to find you so concerned with these issues. I am confident that God also has purposely selected you for this mission.'

General O'Toole could tell that the audience was coming to an end. 'Holy Father,' he said, 'thank you again for seeing me and sharing this time. I feel deeply honoured.'

John-Paul V smiled and walked over to his guest. He embraced him in the European manner and escorted General O'Toole out of his office.

11

St Michael of Siena

The exit from the subway station was opposite the entrance to the International Peace Park. As the escalator deposited General O'Toole on the upper level and he walked out into the afternoon light, he could see the domed shrine to his right, not more than two hundred yards away. To his left, at the other end of the park, the top of the ancient Roman Colosseum was visible behind a complex of administrative buildings.

The American general walked briskly into the park and turned right on the pavement leading to the shrine. He passed a lovely small fountain, part of a monument to the children of the world, and stopped to watch the animated, sculptured figures playing in the cold water. O'Toole was full of anticipation. *What an incredible day*, he was thinking. *First I have an audience with the pope. And now I finally visit the shrine of St Michael.*

When Michael of Siena was canonised in 2188, fifty years after his death (and, perhaps more significantly, three years after John-Paul V had been elected as the new pope), there had been an immediate consensus that the perfect place to locate a major shrine in his honour would be in the International Peace Park. The great park stretched from the Piazza Venezia to the Colosseum, wandering around and among those few ruins from the old Roman fora that had somehow survived the nuclear holocaust. Choosing the exact spot for the shrine had been a delicate process. The Memorial to the Five Martyrs, honouring those courageous men and women who had dedicated themselves to the restoration of order in Rome during the months immediately following the disaster, had been the feature attraction of the park for years. There was considerable feeling that the new shrine to St Michael of Siena must not be allowed to overshadow the dignified, open, marble pentagon that had occupied the southeast corner of the park since 2155.

After much debate it was decided that St Michael's shrine should be located in the opposite, northwest corner of the park, its foundation symbolically centred on the actual epicentre of the blast, only ten yards from the place where Trajan's column had stood until it was instantaneously vaporised by the intense heat at the core of the fireball. The first floor of the round shrine was entirely for meditation and worship. There were twelve alcoves or chapels attached to the central nave, six with sculpture and artwork following classical Roman Catholic motifs and the other six each honouring one of the world's major religions. This eclectic partition of the ground floor was purposely designed to provide comfort for the many non-Catholics who made pilgrimages to the shrine to pay their respects to the memory of the beloved St Michael.

General O'Toole did not spend much time on the first level. He knelt and said a prayer in the chapel of St Peter, and looked briefly at the famous wood sculpture of Buddha in the nook beside the entrance, but like most tourists he could not wait to see the frescoes on the second floor. O'Toole was overwhelmed by both the size and the beauty of the famous paintings the moment he stepped out of the elevator. Directly in front of him was a lifesized portrait of a lovely girl of eighteen with long blonde hair. She was bending down in an old church in Siena on Christmas Eve in 2115 and leaving behind a curly-haired baby, wrapped in a blanket and placed in a basket, on the cold church floor. This painting represented the night of St Michael's birth and was the first in a sequence of twelve panels of frescoes that completely circled the shrine and told the story of the saint's life.

General O'Toole walked over to the small kiosk beside the elevator and rented a forty-five minute audio tour cassette. Ten centimetres square, it fitted easily in his coat pocket. He picked up one of the tiny disposable receivers and clipped it into his ear. After choosing English as his language, he pushed the button marked 'Introduction' and listened as a feminine British voice explained what he was about to see.

'Each of the twelve frescoes is six metres high,' the woman was saying as the general was studying the features of the baby Michael in the first panel. 'The lighting in the room is a combination of natural light from the outside, coming through filtered skylights, and artificial illumination from the electronic arrays in the dome. Automatic sensors determine the ambient conditions and mix the natural with the artificial light so that the viewing of the frescoes is always perfect.

'The twelve panels on this level correspond to the twelve alcoves on the floor below. The arrangement of the frescoes themselves, which follow the life of the saint in a chronological order, flows in a clockwise direction. Thus the final painting, commemorating Michael's canonisation ceremony at Rome in 2188, is right next to the painting of his birth in the Siena cathedral seventy-two years earlier.

'The frescoes were designed and implemented by a team of four artists, including the master Feng Yi from China, who arrived suddenly in the spring of 2190 without any prior warning. Despite the fact that very little was known outside China of his skill, the other three artists, Rosa da Silva from Portugal, Fernando Lopez from Mexico, and Hans Reichwein from Switzerland, immediately welcomed Feng Yi to their team on the strength of the superb sketches that he had brought with him.'

O'Toole glanced around the circular room as he listened to the lyrical voice on the cassette. On this last day of 2199, there were more than two hundred people on the second floor of St Michael's shrine, including three tour groups. The American cosmonaut progressed slowly around the circle, stopping in front of each panel to study the artwork and listen to the discussion on the cassette.

The major events of St Michael's life were depicted in detail in the frescoes. The second, third, fourth and fifth panels featured his days as a Franciscan novitiate in Siena, his factfinding tour around the world during the Great Chaos, the beginning of his religious activism when he returned to Italy, and Michael's use of the church resources to feed the hungry and house the homeless. The sixth painting showed the tireless saint inside the television studio donated by a wealthy American admirer. Here Michael, who spoke eight languages, repeatedly proclaimed his message of the fundamental unity of all humanity and the requirement for the wealthy to care for the less fortunate.

The seventh fresco was Feng Yi's portrait of the confrontation in Rome between Michael and the old and dying pope. It was a masterpiece of contrast. Using colour and light brilliantly, the painting conveyed the image of an energetic, vibrant, and vital young man being wrongly censured by a world-weary prelate anxious to live out his final days in peace and quiet. In Michael's facial expression could be seen two distinctly different reactions to what he was being told: obedience to the papacy and disgust that the church was more concerned with style and order than substance.

'Michael was sent to a monastery in Tuscany by the pope,' the audio guide continued, 'and it was there that the final transformations in his character took place. The eighth panel depicts God's appearance to Michael during this period of solitude. According to the saint, God spoke to him twice, the first time in the middle of a thunderstorm and the second time when a magnificent rainbow filled the sky. It was during the long and violent storm that God shouted out, on the claps of thunder, the new 'Laws of Life' which Michael later proclaimed at his Easter sunrise service at Bolsena. On His second visitation God informed the saint that his message would be spread to the ends of the rainbow and that He would 'give the faithful a sign' during the Easter mass.

'That most famous miracle of Michael's life, one that was watched on television by over a billion people, is shown in the ninth panel. The painting presents Michael preaching Easter mass to the multitudes gathered around the shores of Lake Bolsena. A vigorous spring shower is drenching the crowd, most of whom are dressed in the familiar blue robes that had become associated with his following. But while the rain falls all around St Michael, not a drop ever falls on the pulpit or on the sound equipment being used to amplify his voice. A perpetual radiant spotlight from the sun bathes the young saint's face as he announces God's new laws to the world. It was this crossover from being a purely religious leader....'

General O'Toole switched off the cassette as he walked toward the tenth and eleventh paintings. He was familiar with the rest of the story. After the mass at Bolsena, Michael was beset by a flock of troubles. His life abruptly changed. Within two weeks most of his cable television licences were rescinded. Stories of corruption and immorality among his young devotees, whose numbers had grown into the hundreds of thousands in the Western world alone, were constantly in the press. There was an assassination attempt, which was foiled at the last minute by his staff. There were also baseless reports in the media that Michael had proclaimed himself the second Christ.

And so the leaders of the world became afraid of you. All of them. You were a threat to everyone with your laws of life. And they never understood what you meant by the final evolution. O'Toole stood in front of the tenth fresco. It was a scene he knew by heart. Almost every other educated person in the world would also recognise it instantly. The television replays of the last seconds before the terrorist bomb exploded were shown every year on June 28, the first day of the Feast of St Peter and St Paul and the anniversary of the day that Michael Balatresi and almost a million others had perished in Rome on a fateful early summer morning in 2138.

You had called them to come to Rome to join you. To show

the world that everyone was united. And so they came. The tenth painting showed Michael in his blue robes, standing high on the steps of the Vittorio Emmanuel Monument next to the Piazza Venezia. He was in the middle of a sermon. Around him in all directions, spilling over into the Roman fora from the jam-packed Via dei Fori Imperiali leading to the Colosseum, was a sea of blue. And faces. Eager, excited faces, mostly young, looking up and around the monuments of the ancient city to catch a glimpse of the boy-man who dared to suggest that he had a way, God's way, out of the despair and hopelessness that had engulfed the world.

Michael Ryan O'Toole, a fifty-seven-year-old American Catholic from Boston, fell on his knees and wept, like thousands before him, when he looked at the eleventh panel in the sequence. This painting depicted the same scene as the previous panel, but the time was more than an hour later, an hour *after* the seventy-five-kiloton nuclear bomb hidden in a sound truck near Trajan's column had exploded and sent its hideous mushroom-shaped cloud into the skies above the city. Everything within two hundred metres of the epicentre had been instantly vaporised. There was no Michael, no Piazza Venezia, no huge Vittorio Emmanuel Monument. In the centre of the fresco was nothing but a hole. And around the perimeter of that hole, where the vaporisation had not been quite as complete, were scenes of agony and horror that would shatter the complacency of even the most self-protected individuals.

Dear God, General O'Toole said through his tears, *help me to comprehend the message in Saint Michael's life. Help me to understand how I can contribute, in whatever small way, to your overall plan for us. Guide me as I prepare to be your emissary to the Ramans.*

12
Ramans and Romans

'So, what do you think?' Nicole des Jardins stood up and turned around slowly in front of the camera beside the monitor. She was wearing a form-fitting white dress made from one of the new stretch fabrics. The hem of the dress was cut just below her knees and the long sleeves were marked by one black stripe that passed under her elbow as it ran from the shoulder to the wrist. The wide, jet-black belt matched both the colour of the stripe and the comb at the back of her head and then left to tumble freely almost to her waist. Her only jewellery was a gold tennis bracelet containing three rows of small diamonds that she was wearing around her left wrist.

'You look beautiful, Maman,' her daughter Genevieve answered her from the screen. 'I've never seen you both dressed up and with your hair down. What happened to your normal sweatsuit?' The fourteen-year-old grinned. 'And when does the party start?'

'At nine-thirty,' Nicole replied. 'Very fashionably late. We probably won't have dinner until an hour after that. I'm going to eat something in the hotel room before I leave so that I won't starve.'

'Maman, now don't forget your promise. Last week's *Aujourd'hui* said my favourite singer, Julien LeClerc, would definitely be one of the guest entertainers. You have to tell him that your daughter thinks he's absolutely *divine*!'

Nicole smiled at her daughter. 'I will, darling, for you. Although it will probably be misinterpreted. From what

81

I have heard your Monsieur LeClerc thinks that every woman in the world is in love with him.' She paused for a moment. 'Where's your grandfather? I thought you said he would be joining you in a few minutes.'

'Here I am,' Nicole's father said as his weathered, friendly face appeared on the screen next to his grand-daughter. 'I was just finishing up a section of my novel on Peter Abelard. I didn't expect you to call this early.' Pierre des Jardins was now sixty-six years old. A successful historical novelist for many years, his life since the early death of his wife had been blessed by fortune and accomplishment. 'You look stunning!' he exclaimed after seeing his daughter in her evening wear. 'Did you buy that dress in Rome?'

'Actually, Papa,' Nicole said, again turning around so that her father could see the entire outfit, 'I bought this for Françoise's wedding three years ago. But of course I never had a chance to wear it. Do you think it's too simple?'

'Not at all,' Pierre replied. 'In fact, I think it's just perfect for this kind of extravaganza. If it's like the big fêtes that I used to attend, every woman there will be wearing her fanciest and most expensive clothing and jewellery. You will stand out in your "simple" black and white. Particularly with your hair down like that. You look perfect.'

'Thanks,' Nicole said. 'Even though I know you're prejudiced, I still like to hear your compliments.' She looked at her father and daughter, her only two close companions for the last seven years. 'I'm really surprisingly anxious. I don't think I'll be this nervous on the day we encounter Rama. I often feel out of my element at big parties like this and tonight I have a peculiar sense of foreboding that I can't explain. You remember, Papa, the way I felt the day before our dog died when I was a child.'

Her father's face became serious. 'Maybe you'd better consider staying in the hotel. Too many of your premonitions have been accurate in the past. I remember your telling me that something was wrong with your mother two days before we received that message....'

'It's not that strong a feeling,' Nicole interrupted. 'And

besides, what would I give as an excuse? Everyone's expecting me, especially the press, according to Francesca Sabatini. She's still annoyed with me for refusing to have a personal interview with her.'

'Then I guess you should go. But try to have some fun. Don't take things so seriously for this one night.'

'And remember to say hello to Julien LeClerc for me,' Genevieve added.

'I'll miss you both when midnight comes,' Nicole said. 'It will be the first time I've been away from you on New Year's Eve since 2194.' Nicole paused for a moment, remembering their family celebrations together. 'Take care, both of you. You know I love you very much.'

'I love you, too, Maman,' Genevieve shouted. Pierre waved good-bye.

Nicole switched off the videophone and checked her watch. It was eight o'clock. She still had an hour before she was supposed to meet her driver in the lobby. She walked over to the computer terminal to order something to eat. With a few commands she requested a bowl of minestrone and a small bottle of mineral water. The computer monitor told her to expect them both in between sixteen and nineteen minutes.

I really am highly strung tonight, Nicole thought as she leafed through the magazine *Italia* and waited for her food. The feature story in *Italia* was an interview with Francesca Sabatini. The article covered ten full pages and must have had twenty different photographs of 'la bella signora'. The interviewer discussed both of Francesca's highly successful documentary projects (the first on modern love and the second on drugs), stressing the point, in the middle of some questions about the drug series, that Francesca repeatedly smoked cigarettes during the conversation.

Nicole perused the article in a hurry, noting as she read that there were facets to Francesca she had never considered. *But what motivates her?* Nicole wondered to herself. *What is it that she wants?* Near the end of the magazine story, the interviewer had asked Francesca her opinion of the other two women in the Newton crew. 'I

feel that I'm actually the only woman on the mission,'
Francesca had answered. Nicole slowed down to read the
rest of the paragraph. 'The Russian pilot Turgenyev
thinks and acts like a man and the French-African
princess Nicole des Jardins has purposely suppressed her
femininity, which is sad because she could be such a
lovely woman.'

Nicole was only slightly angered by Francesca's glib
comments. More than anything, she was amused. She
felt a brief competitive surge but then chided herself for
such a childish reaction. *I'll ask Francesca about this
article at just the right time*, Nicole thought with a smile.
*Who knows? Maybe I'll even ask her if seducing married
men qualifies her as feminine.*

The forty-minute drive from the hotel to the party at
Hadrian's Villa, which was located on the outskirts of the
Roman suburbs not far from the resort town of Tivoli,
was passed in total silence. The other passenger in
Nicole's car was Hiro Yamanaka, the most taciturn of all
the cosmonauts. In her television interview two months
earlier with Yamanaka, a frustrated Francesca Sabatini,
after ten minutes of two and three word, monosyllabic
responses to all her questions, had asked Hiro if the
rumour about his being an android were true.

'What?' Hiro Yamanaka had asked.

'Are you an android?' Francesca had repeated with a
mischievous smile.

'No,' the Japanese pilot had responded, his features
remaining absolutely expressionless while the camera
zoomed in on his face.

When the car turned off the main road between Rome
and Tivoli to drive the final mile to the Villa Adriani, the
traffic became congested. Progress was very slow, not
only because of the many cars carrying people to the gala,
but also because of the hundreds of curious onlookers
and paparazzi who were lining the narrow single
carriageway road.

Nicole took a deep breath as the automobile finally
pulled into a circular drive and stopped. Outside her

tinted window she could see a bevy of photographers and
reporters, poised to pounce on whoever climbed out of
the car. Her door opened automatically and she stepped
out slowly, pulling her black suede coat around her and
trying to be careful not to catch her heels.

'Who's that?' she heard a voice say.

'Franco, over here, quick –it's cosmonaut des Jardins.'

There was a smattering of applause and the flash of
many cameras. A kindly-looking Italian gentleman came
forward and took Nicole by the hand. People milled
around her, several microphones were stuck in her face,
and it seemed as if she were being given a hundred
simultaneous questions and requests in four or five
different languages.

'Why have you refused all personal interviews?'

'Please open your coat so we can see your dress.'

'Do the other cosmonauts respect you as a doctor?'

'Stop a moment. Please smile.'

'What is your opinion of Francesca Sabatini?'

Nicole said nothing as the security men held back the
crowd and led her to a covered electric cart. The
four-passenger cart moved slowly up a long hill, leaving
the crowd behind, as a pleasant Italian woman in her
mid-twenties explained in English to Nicole and Hiro
Yamanaka what they were seeing around them. Hadrian,
who had ruled the Roman empire between 117 and 138
AD, had built this immense villa, she told them, for his
own enjoyment. The architectural masterpiece represented a blending of all the building styles that Hadrian had
seen on his many journeys to the distant provinces and
was designed by the emperor himself on three hundred
acres of plain at the foot of the Tiburtini Hills.

The initial cart ride past the ancient assortment of
buildings was apparently an integral part of the evening's
festivities. The lighted ruins themselves were only
vaguely suggestive of their previous glory, for roofs were
mostly missing, the decorative statuary had all been
removed, and the rough stone walls were bare of
adornment. But by the time the cart wound past the
ruins of the Canopus, a monument built around a

rectangular pool in the Egyptian style (it was the fifteenth or sixteenth building in the complex – Nicole had lost count), a general sense of the huge extent of the villa had definitely emerged.

This man died over two thousand years ago, Nicole thought to herself, remembering her history. *One of the cleverest humans who ever lived. Soldier, administrator, linguist.* She smiled as she recalled the story of Antinous. *Lonely most of his life. Except for one brief, all-consuming passion that ended in tragedy.*

The cart came to a stop at the end of a short walkway. The guide finished her monologue. 'To honour the great Pax Romana, an extended time of world peace two millennia ago, the Italian government, helped by generous donations from the corporations listed underneath the statue over there on your right, decided in 2189 to construct a perfect replica of Hadrian's Maritime Theatre. You may recall that we passed the ruins of the original at the beginning of the ride. The goal of the reconstruction project was to show what it would have been like to have visited a part of this villa during the emperor's lifetime. The building was finished in 2193 and has been used for state events ever since.'

The guests were met by formally clad young Italian men, uniformly tall and handsome, who escorted them along the walkway, up to and through Philosopher's Hall, and finally into the Maritime Theatre. There was a brief security check at the actual entrance and then the guests were free to roam as they pleased.

Nicole was enchanted by the building. It was basically round in shape, about forty metres in diameter. An annulus of water separated an inner island, on which was located a large house with five rooms and a big yard, from the wide portico with its fluted columns. There was no roof above the water or the inner part of the portico, the open skies giving the entire theatre a wonderful feeling of freedom. Around the building the guests mixed and talked and drank; advanced robot waiters rolled around carrying large trays of champagne and wine and other alcoholic spirits. Across the two small bridges that connected the island with its house and yard to the portico and the rest of the building, Nicole could see a dozen people, all dressed in white, working to set up the dinner buffet.

A heavy blonde woman and her pint-sized, jocular husband, a bald man wearing an old-fashioned pair of spectacles, were rapidly approaching Nicole from about thirty feet away. Nicole prepared for the coming onslaught by taking a small sip of the champagne and cassis cocktail that had been handed to her by a strangely insistent robot a few minutes before.

'Oh, Madame des Jardins,' the man said, waving at her and closing in with great speed. 'We just have to talk to you. My wife is one of your biggest fans.' He walked up beside Nicole and gestured to his wife. 'Come on, Cecelia,' he shouted, 'I've got her.'

Nicole took a deep breath and forced a wide smile. *It's going to be one of those evenings*, she said to herself.

Finally, Nicole was thinking, *maybe I'll have a few minutes of peace and quiet*. She was sitting by herself, her back deliberately toward the door, at a small table in the corner of the room. The room was at the rear of the island house in the middle of the Maritime Theatre. Nicole finished the last few bites of her food and washed them down with some wine.

She sighed, trying without success to remember even half the people she had met in the last hour. She had been like a prized photograph, passed from person to person and praised by everyone. She had been embraced, kissed, hugged, pinched, flirted with (by both men and women), and even propositioned by a rich Swedish ship builder who had invited her to his 'castle' outside the city of Göteborg. Nicole had hardly said a word to any of them. Her face ached from polite smiling and she was a trifle tipsy from the wine and champagne cocktails.

'Well, as I live and breathe,' she heard a familiar voice behind her say, 'I believe the lady in the white dress is none other than my fellow cosmonaut, the ice princess herself, Madame Nicole des Jardins.' Nicole turned and saw Richard Wakefield staggering toward her. He bounced off a table, reached out to stabilise himself on a chair, and nearly fell in her lap.

'Sorry,' he grinned, managing to seat himself beside her. 'I'm afraid I've had too much gin and tonic.' He took a big gulp from the glass that had miraculously remained unspilled in his right hand. 'And now,' he said with a wink, 'if you don't mind, I'm going to take a nap before the dolphin show.'

Nicole laughed as Richard's head hit the wooden table with a splat and he feigned unconsciousness. After a moment she leaned over playfully and forced one of his eyelids open. 'If you don't mind, comrade, could you not pass out until after you explain to me the bit about the dolphin show.'

With great effort Richard sat up and began rolling his eyes. 'You mean you don't know? You, who always know *all* the schedules and *all* the procedures? That's impossible.'

Nicole finished her wine. 'Seriously, Wakefield. What are you talking about?'

Richard opened one of the small windows and stuck his arm through it, pointing at the pool of water that encircled the house. 'The great Dr Luigi Bardolini is here with his intelligent dolphins. Francesca is going to introduce him in about fifteen minutes.' He stared at Nicole with wild abandon. 'Dr Bardolini is going to prove, here and tonight,' he shouted, 'that his dolphins can pass our university entrance exams.'

Nicole pulled back and looked carefully at her colleage. *He really is drunk*, she thought to herself. *Maybe he feels as out of place as I do.*

Richard was now gazing intently out the window. 'This party is really a zoo, isn't it?' Nicole said after a long silence. 'Where did they find....'

'That's it,' Wakefield interrupted her suddenly, giving the table a triumphant pounding. 'That's why this place has seemed familiar to me since the moment we walked in.' He glanced at Nicole, who was eyeing him as if he had lost his mind. 'It's miniature Rama, don't you see?'

He jumped up, unable to contain his happiness at his discovery. 'The water surrounding this house is the Cylindrical Sea, the porticoes represent the Central Plain, and we, lovely lady, are sitting in the city of New York.'

Nicole was beginning to comprehend but could not keep up with the racing thoughts of Richard Wakefield. 'And what does similarity of design prove?' he conjectured out loud. 'What does it mean that human architects two thousand years ago constructed a theatre with some of the same guiding principles of design as those used in the Raman ship? Similarity of nature? Similarity of culture? Absolutely not.'

He stopped, now aware that Nicole was staring fixedly at him. 'Mathematics,' he said emphatically. A quizzical expression told him that she still didn't understand completely. 'Mathematics,' he said again, surprisingly lucid all of a sudden. 'That's the key. The Ramans almost certainly didn't look like us and clearly evolved on a world far different from the Earth. But they must have understood the same mathematics as the Romans.'

His face brightened. 'Hah,' he shouted again, causing Nicole to jump. He was pleased with himself. 'Ramans and Romans. That's what tonight is all about. And at some level of development in between is modern day Homo sapiens.'

Nicole shook her head as Richard exulted in the joy of his wit. 'You don't understand, lovely lady?' he said, extending his hand to help her up from her seat. 'Then perhaps you and I should go to watch a dolphin show and I will speak to you of Ramans there and Romans here, of cabbages and kings, of dum-de-dum and sealing wax, and whether pigs have wings.'

13
Happy New Year

After everyone had finished eating and all the plates had been cleared, Francesca Sabatini appeared in the centre of the yard with a microphone and spent ten minutes thanking all the gala sponsors. Then she introduced Dr Luigi Bardolini, suggesting that the techniques he had pioneered to communicate with the dolphins might prove extremely useful when humans try to talk to any extraterrestrials.

Richard Wakefield had disappeared just before Francesca had started speaking, ostensibly to find the rest room and obtain another drink. Nicole had caught sight of him briefly five minutes later, immediately after Francesca had finished with her introduction. He had been surrounded by a pair of buxom Italian actresses, both of whom were laughing heartily at his jokes. He had waved at Nicole and winked, pointing at the two women as if his actions were self-explanatory.

Good for you, Richard, Nicole had thought, smiling to herself. *At least one of us social misfits is having a good time.* She now watched Francesca walk gracefully across the bridge and start to move the crowd back from the water so that Bardolini and his dolphins would have plenty of room. Francesca was wearing a tight black dress, bare on one shoulder, with a starburst of gold sequins in the front. A gold scarf was tied around her waist. Her long blonde hair was braided and pinned against her head.

You really belong here, Nicole thought, truthfully admiring Francesca's ease in large crowds. Dr Bardolini began the first segment of his dolphin show and Nicole turned her attention to the circular pool of water. Luigi Bardolini was one of those controversial scientists whose work is brilliant but never quite as exceptional as he himself wants others to believe. It was true that he had developed a unique way of communicating with the dolphins and had isolated and identified the sounds of thirty to forty action verbs in their portfolio of squeaks. But it was not true, as he so often claimed, that two of his dolphins could pass a university entrance exam. Unfortunately, the way the twenty-second century international scientific community operated, if your most outrageous or advanced theories could not be substantiated, or were held up to ridicule, then your other discoveries, no matter how solid, were often disparaged as well. This behaviour had induced an endemic conservatism in science that was not altogether healthy.

Unlike most scientists, Bardolini was a brilliant showman. In the final segment of his show he had his two most famous dolphins, Emilio and Emilia, take an intelligence test in a realtime competition against two of the villa guides, one male and one female, who had been selected at random that evening. The construction of the competitive test was enticingly simple. On two of the four large electronic screens (one pair of screens was in the water and another pair was in the yard), a three by three matrix was shown with a blank in the lower right hand corner. The other eight elements were filled with different pictures and shapes. The dolphins and humans taking the test were supposed to discern the changing patterns moving from left to right and top to bottom in the matrix, and then correctly pick out, from a set of eight candidates displayed on the companion screen, the element that should be placed in the blank lower right corner. The competitors had one minute to make their choice on each problem. The dolphins in the water, like the humans on the land above them, had a control panel of eight buttons that they could push (the dolphins used their snouts) to indicate their selection.

The first few problems were easy, both for the humans

and for the dolphins. In the first matrix, a single white ball
was in the upper left corner, two white balls in the second
column of the first row, and three white balls in the matrix
element corresponding to row one and column three.
Since the first element of the second row was a single ball
as well, half white and half black, and since the beginning
element of the third row was another single ball, now fully
black, it was easy to read the entire matrix quickly and
determine that what belonged in the blank lower right
corner was three black balls.

Later problems were not so easy. With each successive
puzzle, more complications were added. The humans
made their first error on the eighth matrix, the dolphins on
the ninth. Altogether Dr Bardolini exhibited sixteen
matrices, the last one so complicated that at least ten
separate changing patterns had to be recognised properly
to identify what should be entered as the last element. The
final score was a tie, Humans 12, Dolphins 12. Both pairs
took a bow and the audience applauded.

Nicole had found the exercise fascinating. She wasn't
certain if she believed Dr Bardolini's assertion that the
competition was fair and unrehearsed, but it didn't matter
to her. What she thought was interesting was the nature of
the competition itself, the idea that intelligence could be
defined in terms of an ability to identify patterns and
trends. *Is there a way that synthesis can be measured?* she
thought. *In children. Or even adults for that matter*.

Nicole had participated in the test along with the human
and dolphin contestants and had correctly answered the
first thirteen, missing the fourteenth because of a careless
assumption, and just finishing the fifteenth accurately
before the buzzer sounded the end of the allocated time.
She had had no idea where to begin on the sixteenth. *And
what about you Ramans?* she was wondering, as Francesca
returned to the microphone to introduce Genevieve's
heart-throb Julien LeClerc. *Would you have been able to
answer all sixteen correctly in one tenth the time? One
hundredth?* She gulped, as she realised the full range of
possibilities. *Or maybe even one millionth?*

*

'I never lived, 'til I met you ... I never loved, 'til I saw you....' The soft melody of the old recorded song swam in Nicole's memory and brought back an image from fifteen years before, from another dance with another man when she had still believed that love could conquer everything. Julien LeClerc misread her body signals and pulled her closer to him. Nicole decided not to fight it. She was already very tired and, if the truth were known, it felt good being held tightly by a man for the first time in several years.

She had honoured her agreement with Genevieve. When Monsieur LeClerc had finished his short set of songs, Nicole had approached the French singer and given him the message from her daughter. As she had anticipated, he had interpreted her approach to mean something entirely different. They had continued talking while Francesca had announced to the partygoers that there would be no more formal entertainment until after midnight and that all the guests were free to drink or eat or dance to the recorded music until then. Julien had offered his arm to Nicole and the two of them had walked back over to the portico, where they had been dancing ever since.

Julien was a handsome man, in his early thirties, but he was not really Nicole's type. First of all, he was too conceited for her. He talked about himself all the time and did not pay any attention when the conversation switched to other topics. Although he was a gifted singer, he had no other particularly outstanding characteristics. *But*, Nicole reasoned as their continued dancing brought stares from the other guests, *he's all right as a dancer and it beats standing around twiddling my thumbs*.

At a break in the music Francesca came over to talk to them. 'Good for you, Nicole,' she said, her open smile appearing genuine. 'I'm glad to see that you're enjoying yourself.' She extended a small tray with half a dozen dark chocolate balls lightly sprayed with white, possibly a sugar confection. 'These are fantastic,' Francesca said. 'I made them especially for the Newton crew.'

Nicole took one of the chocolates and popped it into

her mouth. It was delicious. 'Now I have a favour to ask,' Francesca continued after several seconds. 'Since I was never able to schedule a personal interview with you and our mail indicates that there are millions of people out there who would like to find out more about you, do you think that you could come over to our studio here and give me ten or fifteen minutes before midnight?'

Nicole stared intently at Francesca. A voice inside her was sending out a warning, but her mind was somehow garbling the message.

'I agree,' Julien LeClerc said while the two women looked at each other. 'The press always talks about the "mysterious lady cosmonaut" or refers to you as "the ice princess". Show them what you've shown me tonight, that you're a normal, healthy woman like everybody else.'

Why not? Nicole finally decided, suppressing her interior voice. *At least by doing it here I don't have to involve Papa and Genevieve.*

They had started to walk toward the makeshift studio on the other side of the portico when Nicole saw Shigeru Takagishi across the room. He was leaning against a column and talking to a trio of Japanese businessmen dressed in formal attire. 'Just a minute,' Nicole said to her companions, 'I'll be right back.'

'Tanoshii shinnen, Takagishi-san,' Nicole greeted him. The Japanese scientist turned, startled at first, and smiled as he saw her approach. After he had formally introduced Nicole to his associates, and they had all bowed to acknowledge her presence and accomplishments, Takagishi started a polite conversation.

'O genki desu ka?' he asked.

'O kage same de,' she replied. Nicole leaned across to her Japanese colleague and whispered in his ear. 'I only have a minute. I wanted to tell you that I have carefully examined all your records and I am in complete agreement with your personal physician. There is no reason to say anything about your heart anomaly to the medical committee.'

Dr Takagishi looked as if he had just been told that his

wife had given birth to a healthy son. He started to say something personal to Nicole but remembered he was in the midst of a group of his countrymen. 'Dõmõ arigatõ gozaimasu,' he said to the retreating Nicole, his warm eyes conveying the depth of his thanks.

Nicole felt wonderful as she waltzed into the studio between Francesca and Julien LeClerc. She posed willingly for the still photographers while Signora Sabatini ensured that all the television equipment was in working order for the interview. She sipped some more champagne and cassis, making intermittent small talk with Julien. Finally she took a seat beside Francesca underneath the klieg lights. *How great*, Nicole kept thinking about the earlier interaction with Takagishi, *to be able to help that brilliant little man.*

Francesca's first question was innocent enough. She asked Nicole if she was excited about the coming launch. 'Of course,' Nicole answered. She then gave a lively summary of the training exercises that the cosmonaut crew had been undergoing while waiting for the opportunity to rendezvous with Rama II. The entire interview was conducted in English. The questions flowed in an orderly pattern. Nicole was asked to describe her role in the mission, what she expected to discover ('I don't really know, but whatever we find will be extremely interesting'), and how she happened to go to the Space Academy in the first place. After about five minutes, Nicole was feeling at ease and very comfortable; it seemed to her that she and Francesca had fallen into a complementary rhythm.

Francesca then asked three personal questions, one about her father, a second about Nicole's mother and the Senoufo tribe in the Ivory Coast, the third about her life with Genevieve. None of them were difficult. So Nicole was totally unprepared for Francesca's last question.

'It is obvious from your daughter's photographs that her skin is considerably lighter than yours,' Francesca said in the same tone and manner that she had used for all the other questions. 'Genevieve's skin colour suggests that her father was probably white. Who was the father of your daughter?'

Nicole felt her heart rate surge as she listened to the question. Then time seemed to stand still. A surprising flood of powerful emotions engulfed Nicole and she was afraid she was going to cry. A brilliant hot image of two entwined bodies reflected in a large mirror burst into her mind and made her gasp. She momentarily looked down at her feet, trying to regain her composure.

You stupid woman, she said to herself as she struggled to calm the combination of anger and pain and remembered love that had crashed upon her like a tidal wave. *You should have known better*. Again the tears threatened and she fought them. She looked up at the lights and Francesca. The gold sequins on the front of the Italian journalist's dress had grouped into a pattern, or so it seemed to Nicole. She saw a head in the sequins, the head of a large cat, its eyes gleaming and its mouth with sharp teeth just beginning to open.

At last, after what seemed to be forever, Nicole felt that she again had her emotions under control. She stared angrily at Francesca. 'Non voglio parlare di quello,' Nicole said quietly in Italian. 'Abbiamo terminato questa intervista.' She stood up, noticed that she was trembling, and sat down again. The cameras were still rolling. She breathed deeply for several seconds. At length Nicole rose from her chair and walked out of the temporary studio.

She wanted to flee, to run away from everything, to go somewhere where she could be alone with her private feelings. But it was impossible. Julien grabbed her as she departed from the interview. 'What a bitch!' he said, waving an accusing finger in Francesca's direction. There were people all around Nicole. All of them were talking at the same time. She was having trouble focusing her eyes and ears in all the confusion.

In the distance Nicole heard some music that she vaguely recognised but the song was more than half over before she realised it was 'Auld Lang Syne'. Julien had his arm around her back and was singing lustily. He was also leading the group of twenty or so people clustered around them in singing the final words. Nicole mouthed the last bar mechanically and tried to maintain her equilibrium. Suddenly a moist pair of lips was pressed against hers and an active tongue was trying to pry open her mouth and force its way inside. Julien was kissing her feverishly, photographers were snapping pictures all around, there was an incredible amount of noise. Nicole's head began to spin and she felt as if she were going to faint. She struggled hard, finally succeeding in freeing herself from Julien's grasp.

Nicole staggered backward and bumped into an angry Reggie Wilson. He pushed her aside in his haste to grab a couple sharing a deep New Year's kiss in the flashing lights. Nicole watched him disinterestedly, as if she were in a movie theatre, or even in one of her own dreams. Reggie pulled the pair apart and raised his right arm as if he were going to slug the other man. Francesca Sabatini restrained Reggie as a confused David Brown retreated from her embrace.

'Keep your hands off her, you bastard,' Reggie shouted, still threatening the American scientist. 'And don't think for one minute that I don't know what you're doing.' Nicole could not believe what she was seeing. Nothing made any sense. Within seconds the room was full of security guards.

Nicole was one of many people ushered summarily away from the fracas while order was being restored. As she left the studio area she happened to pass Elaine Brown, sitting by herself in the portico with her back against a column. Nicole had met Elaine and enjoyed her company when she had gone to Dallas to talk to David Brown's family physician about his allergies. At the moment Elaine was obviously drunk and in no mood to talk to anybody. 'You shit,' Nicole heard her mutter, 'I never should have shown you the results until after I had published them myself. Then everything would have been different.'

Nicole left the gala as soon as she was able to arrange her transportation back to Rome. Francesca, unbelievably, tried to escort her out to the limousine as if nothing had happened. Nicole curtly rejected her fellow cosmonaut's offer and walked out alone.

It started to snow during the ride back to the hotel. Nicole concentrated on the falling snowflakes and was eventually able to clear her mind enough to assess the evening. Of one thing she was absolutely certain. There had been something unusual and very powerful in that chocolate ball she had eaten. Nicole had never before come so close to losing complete control of her emotions. *Maybe she gave one to Wilson too,* Nicole thought. *And that partially explains his eruption. But why?* she asked herself again. *What is she trying to accomplish?*

Back at the hotel she prepared quickly for bed. But just as she was ready to turn out the lights, Nicole thought she heard a soft knock on the door. She stopped and listened, but there was no sound for several seconds. She had almost decided that her ears were playing tricks on her when she heard the knock again. Nicole pulled the hotel robe around her and approached the locked door very cautiously. 'Who's there?' she said forcefully but not convincingly. 'Identify yourself.'

She heard a sound of scraping and a piece of folded paper was thrust under the door. Nicole, still wary and frightened, picked up the paper and opened it. On it were written, in the original Senoufo script of her mother's tribe, three simple words – *Ronata. Omeh. Here.* Ronata was Nicole's name in Senoufo.

A mixture of panic and excitement caused Nicole to open the door without first checking on the monitor to see who was outside. Standing ten feet away from the door, his amazing old eyes already locked on hers, was an ancient, wisened man with his face painted in green and white horizontal streaks. He was wearing a full length, bright green tribal costume, similar to a robe, on which were gold swiggles and a collection of line drawings of no apparent meaning.

'Omeh!' Nicole said, her heart threatening to jump out of her chest. 'What are you doing here?' she added in Senoufo.

The old black man said nothing. He was holding out a stone and a small vial of some kind, both in his right hand. After several seconds he stepped deliberately forward into the room. Nicole backpedalled with each of his steps. His gaze never wavered from her. When they were in the centre of her hotel room and only three or four feet apart, the old man looked up at the ceiling and began to chant. It was a ritual Senoufo song, a general blessing and spell invocation used by the tribal shaman for hundreds of years to ward off evil spirits.

When he had finished the chant the old man Omeh stared again at his great-granddaughter and began to speak very slowly. 'Ronata,' he said, 'Omeh has sensed strong danger in this life. It is written in the tribal chronicles that the man of three centuries will chase the evil demons away from the woman with no companion. But Omeh cannot protect Ronata after Ronata leaves the kingdom of Minowe. Here,' he said, taking her hand and placing the stone and vial therein, 'these stay with Ronata always.'

Nicole looked down at the stone, a smooth, polished oval about eight inches long and four inches in each of the other two dimensions. The stone was mostly creamy white with a few strange brown lines wriggling across its surface. The small green vial that he had given her was no bigger than a travelling bottle of perfume.

'The water from the Lake of Wisdom can help Ronata,' Omeh said. 'Ronata will know the time to drink.' He tilted his head back and earnestly repeated the earlier chant, this time with his eyes closed. Nicole stood beside him in puzzled silence, the stone and the vial in her right hand. When he was finished singing, Omeh shouted three words that Nicole did not understand. Then he abruptly turned around and walked quickly toward the open door. Startled, Nicole ran out into the hall just in time to see his green gown disappear into the elevator.

14

Goodbye Henry

Nicole and Genevieve walked arm in arm up the hill through the light snow. 'Did you see the look on that American's face when I told him who you were?' Genevieve laughed. She was very proud of her mother.

Nicole shifted her skis and poles over to the other shoulder as they approached the hotel. 'Guten Abend,' an old man who would have made a perfect Santa Claus mumbled as he ambled by. 'I wish you wouldn't be so quick to tell people,' Nicole said, not really chastising her daughter. 'Sometimes it's nice not to be recognised.'

There was a small shed for the skis beside the entrance to the hotel. Nicole and Genevieve stopped and placed their equipment in a locker. They exchanged their ski boots for soft snow slippers and walked back out into the fading light. Mother and daughter stood together for a moment and looked back down the hill toward the village of Davos. 'You know,' said Nicole, 'there was a time today, during our race down that back piste toward Klosters, when I found it impossible to believe that I will actually be way out there –' she gestured at the sky – 'in less than two weeks, headed for a rendezvous with a mysterious alien spacecraft. Sometimes the human mind balks at the truth.'

'Maybe it's only a dream,' her daughter said lightly.

Nicole smiled. She loved Genevieve's sense of play. Whenever the day-to-day drudgery of hard work and tedious preparation began to overwhelm Nicole, she could always count on her daughter's easy nature to lighten her mood. They were very much a trio, the three of them who lived at Beauvois. Each of them was immensely dependent on the other two. Nicole did not like to think how the hundred-day separation might affect their harmonious accord.

'Does it bother you that I will be gone so long?' Nicole asked Genevieve as they entered the hotel lobby. A dozen people were sitting around a roaring fire in the middle of the room. An inconspicuous but efficient Swiss waiter was serving hot drinks to the après-ski crew. There would be no robots in a Morosani hotel, not even for room service.

'I don't think of it that way,' her cheerful daughter responded. 'After all, I'll be able to talk with you almost every night on the videophone. The delay time will even make it fun. And challenging.' They walked past the old-fashioned registration desk. 'Besides,' Genevieve added, 'I'll be the centre of attention at school for the whole mission. My class project is already set; I'm going to draw a psychological portrait of the Ramans based on my conversations with you.'

Nicole smiled again and shook her head. Genevieve's optimism was always infectious. It was a shame –

'Oh, Madame des Jardins.' A voice interrupted her thought. The hotel manager was beckoning to her from the desk. Nicole turned around. 'There's a message for you,' the manager continued. 'I was told to deliver it to you personally.'

He handed her a small plain envelope. Nicole opened it and saw just the tiniest portion of a crest on the note card. Her heart raced into overdrive as she closed the envelope again. 'What is it, Mother?' Genevieve enquired. 'It must be special to be hand-delivered. Nobody does things like that these days.'

Nicole tried to hide her feelings from her daughter. 'It's a secret memo about my work,' she lied. 'The delivery man made a terrible mistake. He should never have given it even to Herr Graf. He should have put it in my hands only.'

'More confidential medical data about the crew?'

Genevieve asked. She and her mother had often discussed the delicate role of the life science officer on a major space mission.

Nicole nodded. 'Darling,' she said to her daughter, 'why don't you run upstairs and tell your grandfather that I'll be along in a few minutes. We'll still plan dinner for seven-thirty. I'll read this message now and see if any urgent response is required.'

Nicole kissed Genevieve and waited until her daughter was on the elevator before walking back outside into the light snow. She stood under the street light and opened the envelope with her cold hands. She had difficulty controlling her trembling fingers. *You fool*, she thought, *you careless fool. After all this time. What if the girl had seen....*

The crest was the same as it had been on that afternoon, fifteen-and-a-half years ago, when Darren Higgins had handed her the dinner invitation outside the Olympic press area. Nicole was surprised by the strength of her emotions. She steeled herself and finally looked at the rest of the note below the crest.

'Sorry for the last minute notice. Must see you tomorrow. Noon exactly. Warming hut #8 on the Weissfluhjoch. Come alone. Henry.'

The next morning Nicole was one of the first in line for the cable car that carried skiers to the top of the Weissfluhjoch. She climbed into the polished glass car with about twenty others and leaned against the window while the door automatically shut. *I have seen him only once in these fifteen years,* she thought to herself, *and yet....*

As the cable car ascended, Nicole pulled her snow glasses down over her eyes. It was a dazzling morning, not unlike the January morning seven years earlier when her father had called for her from the villa. They had had a rare snowfall at Beauvois the night before and, after much pleading, she had let Genevieve stay home from school to play in the snow. Nicole was working at the hospital in Tours at the time and was waiting to hear about her application to the Space Academy.

She had been showing her seven-year-old daughter how to make a snow angel when Pierre had called a second time from the house. 'Nicole, Genevieve, there's something special in our mail,' he had said. 'It must have come during the night.' Nicole and Genevieve had run to the villa in their snowsuits while Pierre posted the full text of the message on the wall videoscreen.

'Most extraordinary,' Pierre had said. 'It seems we've all been invited to the English coronation, including the private reception afterwards. This is extremely unusual.'

'Oh, Grandpapa,' Genevieve said excitedly, 'I want to go. Can we go? Do I get to meet a real king and queen?'

'There is no queen, darling,' her grandfather replied, 'unless you mean the queen mother. This king has not yet married.'

Nicole read the invitation several times without saying anything. After Genevieve had calmed down and left the room, her father had put his arms around Nicole.

'I want to go,' she had said quietly.

'Are you certain?' he had asked, pulling away and regarding her with an inquisitive stare.

'Yes,' she had answered affirmatively.

Henry had never seen her until that evening, Nicole was thinking as she checked first her watch and then her equipment in preparation for her ski run down from the summit. *Father had been wonderful. He had let me disappear at Beauvois and almost nobody knew I had a baby until Genevieve was almost a year old. Henry never even suspected. Not until that night at Buckingham Palace.*

Nicole could still see herself waiting in the reception line. The king had been late. Genevieve had been fidgety. At last Henry had been standing opposite her. 'The honourable Pierre des Jardins of Beauvois, France, with his daughter Nicole and granddaughter Genevieve.' Nicole had bowed very properly and Genevieve had curtsied.

'So this is Genevieve,' the king had said. He had bent down for only a moment and put a hand under the child's chin. When the girl had lifted up her face he had seen something that he recognised. He had turned to look at

Nicole, a trace of questioning in his glance. Nicole had revealed nothing with her smile. The crier was calling out the names of the next guests in the line. The king had moved on.

So you sent Darren to the hotel, Nicole thought as she schussed a short slope, aimed for a small jump, and was airborne for a second or two. *And he hummed and ha'ed and finally asked me if I would come and have tea*. Nicole dug her edges into the snow and came to an abrupt stop. 'Tell Henry I can't,' she remembered saying to Darren in London seven years earlier.

She looked again at her watch. It was only eleven o'clock, too early to ski to the hut. She eased over to one of the lifts and took another ride to the summit.

It was two minutes past noon when Nicole arrived at the small chalet on the edge of the woods. She took off her skis, stuck them in the snow, and walked toward the front door. She ignored the conspicuous signs all around her that said EINTRITT VERBOTEN. From out of nowhere came two burly men, one of whom actually jumped between Nicole and the door to the hut. 'It's all right,' she heard a familiar voice say, 'we're expecting her.' The two guards vanished as quickly as they had appeared and Nicole saw Darren, smiling as always, occupying the doorway to the chalet.

'Hi there, Nicole,' he said in his normal friendly fashion. Darren had aged. There were a few flecks of grey around his temples and some salt with the pepper in his short beard. 'How are you?'

'I'm fine, Darren,' she answered, aware that despite all her lectures to herself, she was already starting to feel nervous. She reminded herself that she was now a professional, as accomplished in her own way as this king she was about to see. Nicole then strode forcefully into the chalet.

It was warm inside. Henry was standing with his back to a small fireplace. Darren closed the door behind her and left the two of them alone. Nicole self-consciously removed her scarf and opened her parka. She took off her snow glasses. They stared at each other for twenty, maybe thirty seconds, neither saying a word, neither wanting to interrupt the powerful flow of emotions that was carrying each of them back to two magnificent days fifteen years before.

'Hello, Nicole,' the king said finally. His voice was soft and tender.

'Hello, Henry,' she replied. He started to walk around the couch, to come close to her, perhaps to touch her, but there was something in her body language that stopped him. He leaned upon the side of the couch.

'Won't you sit down?' he invited.

Nicole shook her head. 'I'd prefer to stand, if it's all right with you.' She waited a few more seconds. Their eyes again locked in a deep communication. She felt herself being drawn to him despite her strong internal warnings. 'Henry,' she blurted out suddenly, 'why did you summon me here? It must be important. It's not normal for the King of England to spend his days sitting in a chalet on the side of a Swiss ski mountain.'

Henry walked toward the corner of the room. 'I brought you a present,' he said as he bent down with his back to Nicole, 'in honour of your thirty-sixth birthday.'

Nicole laughed. Some of the tension was easing. 'That's tomorrow,' she said. 'You're a day early. But why....'

He extended a data cube toward her. 'This is the most valuable gift I could find for you,' he said seriously, 'and it has taken many marks from the royal treasury to compile it.'

She looked at him quizzically.

'I have been worried for some time about this mission of yours,' Henry said, 'and in the beginning I could not understand why. But about four months ago, one night when I was playing with Prince Charles and Princess Eleanor, I realised what was bothering me. My intuitive sense tells me that this crew of yours will have problems. I know it sounds crazy, particularly coming from me, but I'm not worried about the Ramans. That megalomaniac Brown is probably right, the Ramans couldn't care less about us Earthlings. But you're about to spend a hundred days in confined quarters with eleven other....'

He could tell that Nicole was not following him. 'Here,' he said, 'take this cube. I had my intelligence agents put together full and complete dossiers on every member of the Newton dozen, including you.' Nicole's brow furrowed. 'The information, most of which is not available in the official ISA files, confirmed my personal view that the Newton team contains quite a few unstable elements. I didn't know what to do with –'

'This is none of your business,' Nicole interrupted angrily. She was affronted by Henry's involvement in her professional life. 'Why are you meddling....'

'Hey, hey, calm down, will you,' the king replied. 'I assure you my motives were all good. Look,' he added, 'you probably won't even need all this information, but I thought that maybe it could be useful. Take it. Throw it away if you like. You're the life science officer. You can treat it however you want.'

Henry could tell that he had botched the meeting. He walked away and sat down in a chair facing the fire. His back was toward Nicole.

'Take care of yourself, Nicole,' he mumbled.

She thought for a long moment, put the data cube inside her parka, and walked over behind the king. 'Thank you, Henry,' she said. Nicole let her hand fall on his shoulder. He didn't turn around. He reached up with his hand and very slowly wrapped his fingers around hers. They remained in that position for almost a minute.

'There was some data that eluded even my investigators,' he said in a low voice. 'One fact in particular in which I was extremely interested.'

Nicole could hear her heart amidst the crackle of the logs in the fireplace. A voice inside her shouted *Tell him, tell him*. But another voice, full of wisdom, counselled silence.

She slowly withdrew her fingers from his. He turned around to look at her. She smiled. Nicole walked over to the door. She put her scarf back on her head and zipped her parka before going outside. 'Goodbye, Henry,' she said.

15

Encounter

The combined Newton spacecraft had manoeuvred so that Rama filled the expanded view port in the control centre. The alien spaceship was immense. Its surface was a dull, drab grey, and its long body was a geometrically perfect cylinder. Nicole stood beside Valeriy Borzov in silence. For each of them, this first sight of the entire Rama vehicle in the sunlight was a moment to savour.

'Have you detected any differences?' Nicole said at length.

'Not yet,' Commander Borzov replied. 'It looks as if the two of them came off the same assembly line.' They were quiet again.

'Wouldn't you love to see that assembly line?' Nicole asked.

Valeriy Borzov nodded. A small flying craft, like a bat or a hummingbird, zoomed past the view port in the near field and headed off in the direction of Rama. 'The exterior drones will confirm the similarities. Each of them has a stored set of images from Rama I. Any variations will be logged and reported within three hours.'

'And if there are no unexplained variations?'

'Then we proceed as planned,' General Borzov answered with a smile. 'We dock, open up Rama, and release the interior drones.' He glanced at his watch. 'All of which should take place about twenty-two hours from now, provided the life science officer asserts that the crew is ready.'

'The crew is in fine shape,' Nicole reported. 'I've just finished looking at a synopsis of the cruise health data again. It's been surprisingly regular. Except for hormonal abnormalities in all three women, which were not totally unexpected, we have seen no significant anomalies in forty days.'

'So physically we're all ready to go,' the commander said thoughtfully, 'but what about our psychological readiness? Are you troubled by this recent spate of arguments? Or can we chalk it up to tension and excitement?'

Nicole was silent for a moment. 'I agree these four days since the docking have been a little rough. Of course, we knew about the Wilson-Brown problem even before launch. We partially solved it by having Reggie on your ship during most of the cruise, but now that we've joined the two spacecraft and the team is all together again, those two seem to be at each other at every opportunity. Particularly if Francesca is around.'

'I tried to talk to Wilson twice while the two ships were separated,' Borzov said in a frustrated tone. 'He wouldn't discuss it. But it's clear that he is very angry about something.'

General Borzov walked over to the control panel and started fiddling with the keyboards. Sequencing information appeared on one of the monitors. 'It must involve Sabatini,' he continued. 'Wilson didn't do much work during cruise, but his log indicates that he spent an inordinate amount of time on the videophone with her. And he was always in a foul mood. He even offended O'Toole.' General Borzov turned and looked intently at Nicole. 'As my life science officer, I want to know if you have any "official" recommendations about the crew, especially with respect to interactions among the team members.'

Nicole had not expected this. When General Borzov had scheduled this final 'crew health assessment' with her, she had not thought that the meeting would extend to the mental health of the Newton dozen as well. 'You're asking for a professional psychological evaluation also?' she asked.

'Certainly.' General Borzov emphasised his earlier statement. 'I want an A5401 from you that attests to both the physical and psychological readiness of every one of the crew members. The procedure clearly states that the commanding officer, before each sortie, should request crew certification from the life science officer.'

'But during the simulations you asked only for physical health data.'

Borzov smiled. 'I can wait, Madame des Jardins,' he said, 'if you'd like time to prepare your report.'

'No, no,' Nicole said after some reflection. 'I can give my opinions now and then officially document them later tonight.' She hesitated several more seconds before continuing. 'I wouldn't put Wilson and Brown together as crew members on any subteam, at least not in the first sortie. And I'd even have some qualms, although this opinion is certainly not as strong, about combining Francesca in a group with either of the two men. I would place no other limitations of any kind on this crew.'

'Good. Good.' The commander grinned broadly. 'I appreciate your report, and not just because it confirms my own opinions. As you can understand, these matters can sometimes be fairly delicate.' General Borzov abruptly changed the subject. 'Now I have another question of an altogether different nature to ask you.'

'What's that?'

'Francesca came to me this morning and suggested that we have a party tomorrow night. She contends that the crew is tense and in need of some kind of release before the first sortie inside Rama. Do you agree with her?'

Nicole reflected for a moment. 'It's not a bad idea,' she replied. 'The strain has been definitely showing ... But what kind of party did you have in mind?'

'A dinner all together, here in the control room, some wine and vodka, maybe even a little entertainment.' Borzov smiled and put his arm on Nicole's shoulder. 'I'm asking your professional opinion, you understand, as my life science officer.'

'Of course.' Nicole laughed. 'General,' she added, 'if

you think it's time for the crew to have a party, then I'd
be delighted to lend a hand....'

Nicole finished her report and transferred the file by data
line over to Borzov's computer in the military ship. She
had been very careful in her language to identify the
problem as a 'personality conflict' rather than any kind of
behavioural pathology. To Nicole, the problem between
Wilson and Brown was straightforward: jealousy, pure
and simple, the ancient green-eyed monster itself.

She was certain that it was wise to prevent Wilson and
Brown from working closely together during sorties
inside Rama. Nicole chastised herself for not having
raised the issue with Borzov on her own. She realised that
her mission portfolio included mental health as well, but
somehow she had difficulty thinking of herself as the
crew psychiatrist. *I avoid it because it's not an objective
process,* she thought. *We have no sensors yet to measure good
or bad mental health.*

Nicole walked down the hall of the living area. She was
careful to keep one foot on the floor at all times; she was
so accustomed to the weightless environment that it was
almost second nature. Nicole was glad that the Newton
design engineers had worked so hard to minimise the
differences between being in space and on the Earth. It
made the job of being a cosmonaut much simpler by
allowing the crew to concentrate on the more important
elements of their work.

Nicole's room was at the end of the corridor. Although
each of the cosmonauts had private quarters (the result of
heated arguments between the crew and the system
engineers, the latter having insisted that sleeping in pairs
was a more efficient use of the space), the rooms were
very small and confining. There were eight bedrooms on
this larger vehicle, called the 'scientific' ship by the crew
members. The military ship had four more small
bedrooms. Both spacecraft also had exercise rooms and
'lobbies', common rooms where there was more
comfortable furniture as well as some entertainment
options not available in the bedrooms.

As Nicole passed Janos Tabori's room on her way to the exercise area, she heard his unmistakable laugh. His door was open as usual. 'Did you really expect me,' Janos was saying, 'to trade bishops and leave your knights in command of the centre of the board? Come on, Shig, I may not be a master, but I do learn from my mistakes. I fell for that one in an earlier game.'

Tabori and Takagishi were involved in their usual postprandial chess match. Almost every 'night' (the crew had stayed on a twenty-four hour day that coincided with Greenwich Mean Time) the two men played for an hour or so before sleeping. Takagishi was a ranked chess master but he was also softhearted and wanted to encourage Tabori. So in virtually every game, after establishing a solid position, Takagishi would allow his edge to be eroded.

Nicole stuck her head in the door. 'Come in, beautiful,' Janos said with a grin. 'Watch me destroy our Asiatic friend in this pseudo-cerebral endeavour.' Nicole had started to explain that she was going to the exercise room when a strange creature, about the size of a big mouse, scurried through her legs and into Tabori's room. She jumped back involuntarily as the toy, or whatever it was, headed for the two men.

'The ousel cock, so black of hue
with orange-tawny bill,
the throstle, with his note so true,
the wren with little quill....'

The robot was singing as it skipped toward Janos. Nicole dropped down on her knees and examined the curious newcomer. It had the lower body of a human and the head of a donkey. It continued to sing. Tabori and Takagishi stopped their game and both laughed at the bewildered expression on Nicole's face.

'Go on,' said Janos, 'tell him that you love him. That's what the fairy queen Titania would do.'

Nicole shrugged her shoulders. The little robot was

temporarily quiet. As Janos urged again, Nicole mumbled 'I love you' to the twenty centimetre robot.

The miniature Bottom turned to Nicole. 'Methinks, mistress, you should have little reason for that. And yet, to say the truth, reason and love keep little company together nowadays.'

Nicole was amazed. She reached out to pick up the tiny figure but stopped herself when she heard another voice.

'Lord, what fools these mortals be. Now where is that player I changed into an ass. Bottom, where art thou?'

A second small robot, this one dressed as an elf, leaped into the room. When he saw Nicole, he jumped up from the floor and hovered at eye level for several seconds, his tiny back wings beating at a frantic pace. 'I be Puck, fair lass,' he said. 'I've not seen thee before.' The robot dropped to the ground and was silent. Nicole was dumbfounded.

'What in the world....' she started to say.

'Shh....' Janos said, motioning for her to be quiet. He pointed at Puck. Bottom was sleeping in the corner near the edge of Janos's bed. Puck had now found Bottom and was spraying him with a fine light dust from a small pouch. As the three human beings watched, Bottom's head began to change. Nicole could tell that the small plastic and metal pieces making up the ass's head were simply rearranging themselves, but even she was impressed by the scope of the metamorphosis. Puck scampered off just as Bottom awakened with his new human head and started talking.

'I have had a most rare vision,' Bottom said. 'I have had a dream, past the wit of man to say what dream it was. Man is but an ass if he go about to expound this dream.'

'Bravo, Bravo.' Janos shouted as the creature fell silent.

'O medetõ,' Takagishi added.

Nicole sat down in the single unoccupied chair and looked at her companions. 'And to think,' she said, shaking her head, 'that I actually told the commander you two were psychologically sound.' She paused two or three seconds. 'Would one of you please tell me what is going on here?'

'It's Wakefield,' Janos said. 'The man is absolutely brilliant and, unlike some geniuses, also very clever. In addition he's a Shakespeare fanatic. He has a whole family of these little guys, although I think Puck is the only one that flies and Bottom's the only one that changes shape.'

'Puck doesn't fly,' Richard Wakefield said, coming into the room. 'He is barely capable of hovering, and only for a short period.' Wakefield seemed embarrassed. 'I didn't know you were going to be here,' he said to Nicole. 'Sometimes I entertain these two in the middle of their chess game.'

'One night,' Janos added as Nicole remained speechless, 'I had just conceded defeat to Shig when we heard what we thought was a fracas in the hall. Moments later, Tybalt and Mercutio entered the room, swearing and slashing their swords at each other.'

'This is a hobby of yours?' Nicole asked after several seconds, indicating the robots with a wave of her hand.

'My lady,' Janos interrupted before Wakefield could answer, 'never, *never* mistake a passion for a hobby. Our esteemed Japanese scientist does not play chess as a hobby. And this young man from the Bard's home town of Stratford-upon-Avon does not create these robots as a hobby.'

Nicole glanced at Richard. She was trying to imagine the amount of energy and work that was necessary for the creation of sophisticated robots like the ones she had just seen. Not to mention talent and, of course, passion. 'Very impressive,' she said to Wakefield.

His smile acknowledged her compliment. Nicole excused herself and started to leave the room. Puck zoomed around her and stood in the doorway.

'If we shadows have offended,
Think but this, and all is mended,
That you have but slumbered here,
While these visions did appear.'

Nicole was laughing as she stepped over the sprite and waved good night to her friends.

Nicole stayed in the exercise room longer than she expected. Ordinarily thirty minutes of hard bicycling or running in place was enough to release her tensions and relax her body for sleep. On this evening, however, with the goal of their mission now so close at hand, it was necessary for her to work out longer to calm her hyperactive system. Part of her difficulty was her residual concern about the report she had filed recommending that Wilson and Brown be separated on all important mission activities.

Was I too hasty? she asked herself. *Did I let General Borzov sway my opinion?* Nicole was very proud of her professional reputation and often constructively second-guessed her major decisions. Toward the end of her exercise she convinced herself again that she had filed the proper report. Her tired body told her that it was ready to sleep.

When she returned to the living area in the spacecraft, it was dark everywhere except in the hallway. As she started to turn left into the corridor that led to her room, she happened to glance beyond the lobby, in the direction of the small room where she kept all the medical supplies. *That's strange*, she thought, straining her eyes in the dim light. *It looks as if I left the supply room door open.*

Nicole walked across the lobby. The supply door was indeed ajar. She had already activated the automatic lock and had started to close the door when she heard a noise inside the dark room. Nicole reached in and turned on the light. She surprised Francesca Sabatini, who was sitting in the corner at a computer terminal. There was information displayed on the monitor in front of her and Francesca was holding a thin bottle in one of her hands.

'Oh, hello Nicole,' Francesca said nonchalantly, as if it were normal for her to be sitting in the dark at the computer in the medical supply room.

Nicole walked slowly over to the computer. 'What's

going on?' she said casually, her eyes scanning the information on the screen. From the coded headings, Nicole could tell that Francesca had requested the inventory subroutine to list the birth control devices available on board the spacecraft.

'What is this?' Nicole now asked, pointing at the monitor. There was a trace of irritation in her voice. All the cosmonauts knew that the medical supply room was off limits to everyone but the life science officer.

When Francesca still did not reply, Nicole became angry. 'How did you get in here?' she demanded. The two women were only a few centimetres apart in the small alcove next to the desk. Nicole suddenly reached over and grabbed the bottle out of Francesca's hand. While Nicole was reading the label, Francesca pushed her way through the narrow space and headed for the door. Nicole discovered that the liquid in her hand was for inducing abortions and quickly followed Francesca into the lobby.

'Are you going to explain this?' Nicole asked.

'Just give me the bottle, please,' Francesca said finally.

'I can't do that,' answered Nicole, shaking her head. 'This is a very strong medicine with serious side-effects. What did you think you were going to do? Steal it and have it pass unnoticed? As soon as I completed an inventory comparison I would know that it was gone.'

The two women stared at each other for several seconds. 'Look, Nicole,' Francesca said at length, managing a smile, 'this is really a very simple matter. I have discovered recently, much to my chagrin, that I am in the very early stages of pregnancy. I wish to abort the embryo. It's a private matter and I did not want to involve you or any of the rest of the crew.'

'You can't be pregnant,' Nicole replied quickly. 'I would have seen it in your biometry data.'

'I'm only four or five days. But I'm certain. I can already feel the changes in my body. And it's the right time of the month.'

'You know the proper procedures for medical problems,' Nicole said after some hesitation. 'This might have been very simple, to use your phrase, if you had first come to me. Most likely I would have respected your request for confidentiality. But now you've given me a dilemma....'

'Will you stop with the bureaucratic lecture,' Francesca interrupted sharply. 'I'm really not interested in the goddamn rules. A man has made me pregnant and I intend to remove the foetus. Now are you going to give me the bottle, or must I find another way?'

Nicole was outraged. 'You are amazing,' she responded to Francesca. 'Do you really expect me to hand you this bottle and walk away? Without asking any questions? You may be that cavalier about your life and health, but I certainly am not. I have to examine you first, check your medical history, determine the age of the embryo – only then would I even *consider* prescribing this medicine for you. Besides, I would feel compelled as well to point out to you that there are moral and psychological ramifications....'

Francesca laughed out loud. 'Spare me your ramifications, Nicole. I don't need your upper-class Beauvois morality passing judgment on my life. Congratulations to you for raising a child as a single parent. My situation is much different. The father of this baby purposely stopped taking his pills, thinking my being pregnant would rekindle my love for him. He was wrong. This baby is unwanted. Now, should I be more graphic....'

'That's enough,' Nicole interrupted, pursing her lips in disgust. 'The details of your personal life are really none of my business. I must decide what is best for you and for the mission.' She paused. 'In any event, I must insist on a proper examination, including the normal pelvic internal image set. If you refuse, then I won't authorise the abortion. And of course I'd be forced to make a complete report....'

Francesca laughed. 'You don't need to threaten me. I am not *that* stupid. If it will make you feel better to stick your fancy equipment between my legs, then be my guest. But let's do it. I want this baby out of me before the sortie.'

Nicole and Francesca hardly exchanged a dozen words

during the next hour. They went together to the small infirmary where Nicole used her sensitive instruments to verify the existence and size of the embryo. She also tested Francesca for her suitability to receive the abortion liquid. The foetus had been growing inside Francesca for five days. *Who might you be?* Nicole thought as she looked on the monitor at the microscopic image of the tiny sac embedded in the walls of the uterus. Even in the microscope on the probe there was no way to tell that the collection of cells was a living thing. *But you are already alive. And much of your future is already programmed by your genes.*

Nicole made the printer list for Francesca what she could expect physically once she had ingested the medicine. The foetus would be swept away, rejected by her body, within twenty-four hours. There could possibly be some slight cramping with the normal menstruation that would follow immediately.

Francesca drank the liquid without hesitation. As her patient was dressing, Nicole thought back to the time when she had first suspected her own pregnancy. *Never once did I consider ... and not just because her father was a prince. No. It was a question of responsibility. And love.*

'I can tell what you're thinking,' Francesca said when she was ready to leave. She was standing by the infirmary door. 'But don't waste your time. You have enough problems of your own.'

Nicole did not reply. 'So tomorrow the little bastard will be gone,' Francesca said coldly, her eyes tired and angry. 'It's a damn good thing. The world doesn't need another half-black baby.' Francesca didn't wait for Nicole's response.

16
Rama, Rama, Burning Bright

The touchdown near the entry port to Rama was smooth and without incident. Following the precedent of Commander Norton seventy years earlier, General Borzov instructed Yamanaka and Turgenyev to guide the Newton to a contact point just outside the hundred-metre circular disc centred on the spin axis of the giant cylinder. A set of low, pillbox-shaped structures temporarily held the spacecraft from Earth in place against the slight centrifugal force created by the spinning Rama. Within ten minutes strong attachments anchored the Newton firmly to its target.

The large disc was, as anticipated, the outer seal of the Raman air lock. Wakefield and Tabori departed from the Newton in their EVA gear and started searching for an embedded wheel. The wheel, which was the manual control for the air lock, was in exactly the predicted place. It turned as expected and exposed an opening in the outer shell of Rama. Since nothing about Rama II had yet varied from its predecessor in any way, the two cosmonauts continued with the entry procedure.

Four hours later, after considerable shuttling back and forth in the half kilometre of corridors and tunnels that connected the great hollow interior of the alien spaceship to the external air lock, the two men had finished opening the three redundant cylindrical doors. They had also deployed the Newton to the inside of Rama. This ferry had been designed by the engineers on Earth to slide along the parallel grooves the Ramans had cut into the walls of the outer tunnels unknown ages ago.

After a short break for lunch, Yamanaka joined
Wakefield and Tabori and the three of them constructed
the planned Alpha communications relay station at the
inner end of the tunnel. The patterns of the arrayed
antennae had been carefully engineered so that, if the
second Raman vehicle was identical to the first, two-way
communication would be possible between cosmonauts
located anywhere on the stairways or in the northern half
of the Central Plain. The master communication plan
called for the establishment of another major relay
station, to be called Beta, near the Cylindrical Sea; the
pair of stations would provide strong links everywhere in
the Northern Hemicylinder and would even extend to
the island of New York.

Brown and Takagishi took their positions in the
control centre once the operation of the Alpha relay
station was verified. The countdown to interior drone
deployment proceeded. Takagishi was obviously both
nervous and excited as he finished his preflight tests with
his drone. Brown seemed relaxed, even casual, as he
completed his final preparations. Francesca Sabatini was
sitting in front of the multiple monitors, ready to select
the best images for realtime transmission to the Earth.

General Borzov himself announced the major events in
the sequence. He paused for a dramatic breath before
issuing the command to activate the two drones. The
drones then flew away into the dark emptiness of Rama.
Seconds later the main screen in the control centre,
whose picture came directly from the drone being
commanded by David Brown, was flooded with light as
the first flare ignited. When the light became more
manageable, the outline of the first wide-angle shot could
be seen. It had always been planned that this initial
picture would be a composite of the Northern
Hemicylinder, covering all the territory from the
bowl-shaped end where they had entered down to the
Cylindrical Sea at the midpoint of the artificial world.
The sharp image that was eventually frozen on the screen
was overwhelming. It was one thing to read about Rama

and to conduct simulations inside its replica; it was quite another to be anchored to the gigantic spaceship near the orbit of Venus, and to be taking a first look inside....

That the vista was familiar barely lessened the wonder of the image. In the end of the crater-shaped bowl, starting from the tunnels, a complex of terraces and ramps fanned out until they reached the main body of the spinning cylinder. Trisecting this bowl were three wide ladders, resembling broad railway tracks, each of which later expanded into enormous stairways with more than thirty thousand steps each. The ladder/stairway combinations resembled three equally spaced ribs of an umbrella and provided a way to ascend (or descend) from the flat bottom of the crater to the vast Central Plain wrapped round the wall of the spinning cylinder.

The northern half of the Central Plain spread out to fill most of the picture on the screen. The huge expanse was broken into rectangular fields which had irregular dimensions except immediately around the 'cities'. The three cities in the wide-angle image – clusters of tall slim objects, resembling man-made buildings, which were connected by what looked like highways running along the edges of the fields – were immediately recognised by the crew as the Paris, Rome, and London named by the first Raman explorers. Equally striking in the image were the long straight grooves or valleys of the Central Plain. These three linear trenches, ten kilometres long and a hundred metres wide, were equally spaced around the curve of Rama. During the first Raman encounter these valleys had been the sources of the light that had filled the worldlet shortly after the melting of the Cylindrical Sea.

The strange sea, a body of water running completely around the huge cylinder, was at the far edge of the image. It was still frozen, as expected, and in its centre was the mysterious island of towering skyscrapers that had been called New York since its original discovery. The skyscrapers stretched off the end of the picture, the looming towers beckoning to be visitied.

The entire crew stared silently at the image for almost

a minute. Then Dr David Brown started hooting. 'All right, Rama,' he said in a proud voice. 'You see, all you disbelievers,' he shouted, loudly enough for everyone to hear, 'it is *exactly* like the first one.' Francesca's video camera turned to record Brown's exultation. Most of the rest of the crew were still speechless, transfixed by the details on the monitor.

Meanwhile, Takagishi's drone was transmitting narrow-angle photos of the area just under the tunnel. These images were featured on the smaller screens around the control centre. The pictures would be used to reverify the designs of the communication and transportation infrastructure to be established inside Rama. This was the real 'job' of this phase of the mission – comparing the thousands of pictures that would be taken by these drones to the existing camera mosaics from Rama I. Although most of the comparisons could be done digitally (and therefore automatically), there would always be differences that would require human explanation. Even if the two spaceships were identical, the differing light levels at the times the images were taken would create some artificial miscompares.

Two hours later the last of the drones returned to the relay station and an initial summary of the photographic survey was complete. There were no major structural differences between Rama II and the earlier space vehicle, down to a scale of a hundred metres. The only significant region of miscompares at that resolution was the Cylindrical Sea itself, and ice reflectivity was a notoriously difficult phenomenon to handle with a straightforward digital comparison algorithm. It had been a long and exciting day. Borzov announced that crew assignments for the first sortie would be posted in an hour and that a 'special dinner' would be served in the control centre two hours later.

'You cannot do this,' an angry David Brown shouted, bursting into the commander's office without knocking and brandishing a hard copy printout of the first sortie assignments.

'What are you talking about?' General Borzov responded. He was annoyed by Dr Brown's rude entrance.

'There must be some kind of mistake,' Brown continued in a loud voice. 'You can't really expect me to stay here on the Newton during the first sortie.' When there was no response from General Borzov, the American scientist changed tactics. 'I want you to know that I don't accept this. And the ISA management won't like it either.'

Borzov stood up behind his desk. 'Close the door, Dr Brown,' he said calmly. David Brown slammed the sliding door. 'Now *you* listen to me for a minute,' the general continued. 'I don't give a damn who you know. I am the commanding officer of this mission. If you continue to act like a prima donna, I'll see to it that you *never* set foot inside Rama.'

Brown lowered his voice. 'But I demand an explanation,' he said with undisguised hostility. 'I am the senior scientist on this mission. I am also the leading spokesman for the Newton project among the media. How can you possibly justify leaving me on board the Newton while nine other cosmonauts go inside Rama?'

'I don't have to justify my actions,' Borzov replied, for the moment enjoying his power over the arrogant American. He leaned forward. 'But for the record, and because I anticipated this childish outburst of yours, I will tell you why you're not going on the first sortie. There are two major purposes for our first visit: to establish the communications/transportation infrastructure and to complete a detailed survey of the interior, confirming that this spaceship is exactly like the first one....'

'That's already been confirmed by the drones,' Brown interrupted.

'Not according to Dr Takagishi,' Borzov rebutted. 'He says that –'

'Shit, General, Takagishi won't be satisfied until every square centimetre of Rama has been shown to be exactly the same as the first ship. You saw the results of the drone survey. Do you have any doubt in your mind....'

David Brown stopped himself in mid-sentence. General Borzov was drumming on his desk with his fingers and regarding Dr Brown with a cold stare. 'Are you going to let me finish now?' Borzov said at length. He waited a few more seconds. 'Whatever you may think,' the commander continued, 'Dr Takagishi is considered to be the world expert on the interior of Rama. You cannot argue even for a minute that your knowledge of the details approaches his. I need all five of the space cadets for the infrastructure work. The two journalists must go inside, not only because there are two separate tasks, but also because world attention is focused on us at this time. Finally, I believe it is important for my subsequent management of this mission that I myself go inside at least once, and I choose to do it *now*. Since the procedures clearly state that at least three members of the crew must remain outside Rama during the early sorties, it is not difficult to figure out –'

'You don't fool me for a minute,' David Brown interrupted nastily. 'I know what this is all about. You've concocted an apparently logical excuse to hide the real reason for my exclusion from the first sortie team. You're jealous, Borzov. You can't stand the fact that I am regarded by most people as the real leader of this mission.'

The commander stared at the scientist for over fifteen seconds without saying anything. 'You know, Brown,' he said finally, 'I feel sorry for you. You are remarkably talented, but your talent is exceeded by your own opinion of it. If you weren't such a....' This time it was Borzov's turn to stop himself in mid-sentence. He looked away. 'Incidentally, since I know that you will go back to your room and immediately whine to the ISA, I should probably tell you that the life science officer's fitness report explicitly recommends against your sharing any mission duties with Wilson – because of the personal animosity that both of you have demonstrated.'

Brown's eyes narrowed. 'Are you telling me that Nicole des Jardins actually filed an official memorandum citing Wilson and me by name?'

Borzov nodded.

'The bitch,' Brown muttered.

'It's always someone else who is at fault, isn't it, Dr Brown?' General Borzov said, smiling at his adversary.

David Brown turned around and stalked out of the office.

For the banquet, General Borzov ordered a few precious bottles of wine to be opened. The commanding officer was in an excellent mood. Francesca's suggestion had been a good one. There was a definite feeling of camaraderie among the cosmonauts as they brought the small tables together in the control centre and anchored them to the floor.

Dr David Brown did not come to the banquet. He remained in his room while the other eleven crew members feasted on game hens and wild rice. Francesca awkwardly reported that Brown was 'feeling under the weather', but when Janos Tabori playfully volunteered to go and check the American scientist's health, Francesca hurriedly added that Dr Brown wanted to be left alone. Janos and Richard Wakefield, each of whom had several glasses of wine, bantered with Francesca at one end of the table while Reggie Wilson and General O'Toole engaged in an animated discussion about the coming baseball season at the opposite end. Nicole sat between General Borzov and Admiral Heilmann and listened to their reminiscences of peacekeeping activities in the early post-Chaos days.

When the meal was over, Francesca excused herself. She and Dr Takagishi disappeared for several minutes. When they returned Francesca asked the cosmonauts to turn their chairs to face the large screen. Then, with the lights out, she and Dr Takagishi projected a full exterior view of Rama on the monitor. Except that this was not the dull grey cylinder everyone had seen before. No, this Rama had been cleverly coloured, using image processing subroutines, and was now a black cylinder with yellow-gold stripes. The end of the cylinder looked almost like a face. There was a momentary quiet in the room before Francesca began to recite.

'Tyger, tyger, burning bright,
In the forests of the night,
What immortal hand or eye
Could frame thy fearful symmetry?'

Nicole des Jardins felt a cold chill run up her spine as she listened to Francesca begin the next verse.

'In what distant deeps or skies,
Burnt the fire of thine eyes …'

That is the real question after all, Nicole was thinking. *Who made this gargantuan spacecraft? That's much more important for our ultimate destiny than why.*

'What the hammer? What the chain?
In what furnace was thy brain?
What the anvil? What dread grasp
Dare its deadly terrors clasp? …'

Across the table General O'Toole was also mesmerised by Francesca's recitation. His mind was again struggling with the same fundamental questions that had been bothering him since he originally applied for the mission. *Dear God*, he was wondering, *how do these Ramans fit into Your universe? Did You create them first, before us? Are they our cousins in some sense? Why have You sent them here at this time?*

'When the stars threw down their spears
And water'd heaven with their tears,
Did He smile His work to see?
Did He who made the Lamb make thee?'

When Francesca finished the short poem there was a brief silence and then spontaneous applause. She

graciously mentioned that Dr Takagishi had provided all
the image processing intelligence and the likeable
Japanese cosmonaut took an embarrassed bow. Then
Janos Tabori stood at his chair. 'I think I speak for all of
us, Shig and Francesca, in congratulating you on that
original and thought-provoking performance,' he said
with a grin. 'It almost, but not quite, made me feel
serious about what we are doing tomorrow.'

'Speaking of which,' General Borzov said, rising at the
head of the table with his recently opened bottle of
Ukrainian vodka, from which he had already taken two
strong swigs, 'it is now time for an ancient Russian
tradition – the toasts. I brought along only two bottles of
this national treasure and I propose to share them both
with you, my comrades and colleagues, on this very
special evening.'

He placed both bottles in General O'Toole's hands and
the American adroitly used the liquid dispenser to
channel the vodka into small covered cups that were
passed around the table. 'As Irina Turgenyev knows,' the
commander continued, 'there is always a small worm in
the bottom of a bottle of Ukrainian vodka. Legend has it
that he who eats the worm will be endowed with special
powers for twenty-four hours. Admiral Heilmann has
marked two of the cup bottoms with an infrared cross.
The two people who drink from the marked cups will
each be allowed to eat one of the vodka-saturated
worms.'

'Yeuch,' said Janos a moment later, as he passed the
infrared scanner to Nicole. He had first verified that he
had no cross on the bottom of his cup. 'This is one
contest I am glad to lose.'

Nicole's cup did have a marking on the bottom. She
was one of the two lucky cosmonauts who would be able
to eat a Ukrainian worm for dessert. She found herself
wondering, *Must I do this?* and then answering her own
question affirmatively as she saw the earnest look on her
commanding officer's face. *Oh well*, she thought, *it
probably won't kill me. Any parasites have probably been
rendered harmless by the alcohol.*

General Borzov himself had the second cup with a cross on the bottom. The general smiled, placed one of the two tiny worms in his own cup and the other in Nicole's, and raised his vodka toward the ceiling of the spacecraft.

'Let us all drink to a successful mission,' he said. 'For each of us, these next few days and weeks will be the greatest adventure of our lives. In a real sense, we dozen are human ambassadors to an alien culture. Let us each resolve to do our best to represent our species properly.'

He took the cover off his cup, being careful not to jiggle it, and then drank it all in one gulp. He swallowed the worm whole. Nicole also ate the worm quickly, commenting to herself that the only thing she had ever eaten that tasted worse than the worm was that awful tuber during her Poro ceremony in the Ivory Coast.

After several more short toasts the lights in the room began to dim. 'And now,' General Borzov announced with a grand gesture, 'direct from Stratford, the Newton proudly presents Richard Wakefield and his talented robots.' The room became dark except for a square metre to the left of the table that was spotlit from above. In the middle of the light was a cutaway of an old castle. A female robot, twenty centimetres high and dressed in a robe, was walking around in one of the rooms. She was reading a letter at the beginning of the scene. After a few steps, however, she dropped her hands to her sides and began to speak.

'Glamis thou art, and Cawdor; and shalt be
What thou art promised. Yet do I fear thy nature:
It is too full o'th'milk of human kindness
To catch the nearest way. Thou wouldst be great....'

'I know that woman,' Janos said with a grin to Nicole. 'I have met her somewhere before.'

'Shh,' replied Nicole. She was fascinated by the precision in the movements of Lady Macbeth. *That Wakefield really is a genius,* she was thinking. *How is he able to design such extraordinary detail into those little things?* Nicole was astonished by the range of expressions on the robot's face.

As she concentrated, the tiny stage began to swim in Nicole's mind. She momentarily forgot she was watching robots in a miniature performance. A messenger came in and told Lady Macbeth both that her husband was drawing near and that King Duncan would be spending the night in their castle. Nicole watched Lady Macbeth's face explode with ambitious anticipation as soon as the messenger had departed.

> !…Come you Spirits
> That tend on mortal thoughts. Unsex me here
> And fill me, from the crown to the toe, top-full
> of direst cruelty! Make thick my blood....'

My God, Nicole thought, blinking her eyes to make certain they were not playing tricks on her, *she's changing!* Indeed she was. As the words 'Unsex me here' came from the robot, her (or its) shape began to change. The impression of the breasts against the metal gown, the roundness of the hips, even the softness of the face all disappeared. An androgynous robot played on as Lady Macbeth.

Nicole was spellbound and floating in a fantasy induced both by her wild imagination and by the sudden intake of alcohol. The new face on the robot was vaguely reminiscent of someone she knew. She heard a disturbance to her right and turned to see Reggie Wilson talking avidly with Francesca. Nicole glanced back and forth quickly from Francesca to Lady Macbeth. *That's it*, she said to herself, *this new Lady Macbeth resembles Francesca.*

A burst of fear, a premonition of tragedy, suddenly overwhelmed Nicole and plunged her into terror. *Something terrible is going to happen*, her mind was saying. She took several deep breaths and tried to calm herself but the eerie feeling would not go away. On the little stage King Duncan had just been greeted by his gracious hostess for the evening. To her left Nicole saw Francesca offer General Borzov the last sips of the wine. Nicole could not quell her panic.

'Nicole, what's the matter?' Janos asked. He could tell that she was distressed.

'Nothing,' she said. She gathered all her strength and rose to her feet. 'Something I ate must have disagreed with me. I think I'll go to my room.'

'But you'll miss the movie after dinner,' Janos said humorously. Nicole forced a painted smile. He helped her to stand up. Nicole heard Lady Macbeth berating her husband for his lack of courage and one more wave of premonitory fear surged through her. She waited until the adrenaline burst had subsided and then excused herself quietly from the group. She walked slowly back to her room.

17
Death of a Soldier

In her dream Nicole was ten years old again and playing in the woods behind her home in the Paris suburb of Chilly-Mazarin. She had a sudden feeling that her mother was dying. The little girl panicked. She ran toward the house to tell her father. A small snarling cat blocked her path. Nicole stopped. She heard a scream. She left the path and went through the trees. The branches scraped her skin. The cat followed her. Nicole heard another scream. When she awakened a frightened Janos Tabori was standing over her. 'It's General Borzov,' Janos said. 'He's in excruciating pain.'

Nicole jumped swiftly out of bed, threw her robe around her, grabbed her portable medical kit, and followed Janos into the corridor. 'It looks like appendicitis,' he mentioned as they hurried into the lobby. 'But I'm not certain.'

Irina Turgenyev was kneeling beside the commander and holding his hand. The general himself was stretched out on a couch. His face was white and there was sweat on his brow. 'Ah, Doctor des Jardins has arrived.' He managed to smile. Borzov tried to sit up, winced from the pain, and let himself lie back down. 'Nicole,' he said quietly, 'I am in agony. I've never felt anything like this in my life, not even when I was wounded in the army.'

'How long ago did it start?' she asked. Nicole had pulled out her scanner and biometry monitor to check all his vital statistics. Meanwhile Francesca and her video camera had moved over right behind Nicole's shoulder to film the doctor performing the diagnosis. Nicole impatiently motioned for her to back away.

'Maybe two or three minutes ago,' General Borzov said with effort. 'I was sitting here in a chair watching the movie, laughing heartily as I recall, when there was an intense, sharp pain, here on my lower right side. It felt as if something was burning me from the inside.'

Nicole programmed the scanner to search through the last three minutes of detailed data recorded by the Hakamatsu probes inside Borzov. She located the onset of the pain, easily identifiable in terms of both heart rate and endocrine secretions. She next requested a full dump over the time period of interest from all channels. 'Janos,' she said to her colleague, 'go over to the supply room and bring me the portable diagnostician.' She handed Tabori the code card for the door.

'You have a slight fever, suggesting your body is fighting some infection,' Nicole told General Borzov. 'All the internal data confirms that you are feeling severe pain.' Cosmonaut Tabori returned with a small electronic array shaped like a box. Nicole extracted a small data cube from the scanner and inserted it into the diagnostician. In about thirty seconds the little monitor blinked and the words 94% LIKELY APPENDICITIS appeared. Nicole pressed a key and the screen displayed the other possible diagnoses, including hernia, internal muscle tear, and drug reaction. According to the diagnostician, none was more than two percent probable.

I have two choices at this juncture, Nicole was thinking rapidly as General Borzov winced again from the pain. *I can send all the data down to earth for a complete diagnostic, per the procedure* … She glanced at her watch and quickly computed twice the round trip light time plus the minimum duration of a physician's conference after the electronic diagnosis was complete. *By which time it might be too late.*

'What does it say, Doctor?' the general was asking. His eyes were entreating her to end the pain as quickly as possible.

'Most likely diagnosis is appendicitis,' Nicole

answered.

'Damnit,' General Borzov responded. He looked around at all the others. Everyone was there except Wilson and Takagishi, both of whom had skipped the movie. 'But I won't make the project wait. We'll go ahead with the first and second sorties while I'm recuperating.' Another sharp pain jolted him and his face contorted.

'Whoa,' said Nicole. 'It's not certain yet. We need a little more data first.' She repeated the earlier data dump, now using the extra two minutes of information that had been recorded since she arrived in the lobby. This time the diagnosis read 92% LIKELY APPENDICITIS. Nicole was about to check the alternative diagnoses when she felt the commander's strong hand on her arm.

'If we do this quickly, before too much poison builds up in my system, then this is a straightforward operation for the robot surgeon, isn't it?'

Nicole nodded.

'And if we spend the time to obtain a diagnostic concurrence from the Earth – *ouch*! – then my body may be in deeper trauma?'

He is reading my mind, Nicole thought at first. Then she realised that the general was only displaying his thorough knowledge of the Newton procedures.

'Is the patient trying to give the doctor a suggestion?' Nicole asked, smiling despite Borzov's obvious pain.

'I wouldn't be that presumptuous,' the commander answered with just a trace of a twinkle in his eye.

Nicole glanced back at the monitor. It was still blinking 92% LIKELY APPENDICITIS. 'Do you have anything to add?' she said to Janos Tabori.

'Only that I have seen an appendicitis before,' the little Hungarian answered, 'once, when I was a student, in Budapest. The symptoms were exactly like this.'

'All right,' Nicole said. 'Go prepare RoSur for the operation. Admiral Heilmann, will you and cosmonaut Yamanaka help General Borzov to the infirmary, please?' She turned around to Francesca. 'I recognise that this is big news. I will allow you in the operating room on three conditions. You will scrub like all the surgical staff. You will stand quietly over against the wall with your camera. And you will absolutely obey any order that I give you.'

'Good enough,' Francesca nodded. 'Thank you.'

Irina Turgenyev and General O'Toole were still waiting in the lobby after Borzov left with Heilmann and Yamanaka. 'I'm certain that I speak for both of us,' the American said in his usual sincere manner. 'Can we help in any way?'

'Janos will assist me while RoSur performs the operation. But I could use one more pair of hands, as an emergency backup.'

'I would like to do that,' O'Toole said. 'I have some hospital experience from my charity work.'

'Fine,' replied Nicole. 'Now come with me to clean up.'

RoSur, the portable robot surgeon that had been brought along on the Newton mission for just this kind of situation, was not in the class, in terms of medical sophistication, of the fully autonomous operating rooms at the advanced hospitals on Earth. But RoSur was a technological marvel in its own right. It could be packed in a small suitcase and weighed only four kilograms. Its power requirements were low. And there were more than a hundred configurations in which it could be used.

Janos Tabori unpacked RoSur. The electronic surgeon didn't look like much in its stowed configuration. All its spindly joints and appendages were neatly arranged for easy storage. After Janos rechecked his RoSur User's Guide, he picked up the central control box of the robot surgeon and affixed it, as suggested, to the side of the infirmary bed where General Borzov was already lying. His pain had only subsided a little. The impatient commander was urging everyone to hurry.

Janos entered the code word identifying the operation. RoSur automatically deployed all its limbs, including its extraordinary scalpel/hand with four fingers, in the configuration needed to remove an appendix. Nicole then entered the room, her hands in gloves and her body covered with the white gown of the surgeon.

'Have you finished the software check?' she said.

Janos nodded.

'I'll complete all the pre-operation tests while you scrub,' she said to him. She motioned for Francesca and General O'Toole, both of whom were standing right outside the door, to enter the small room. 'Any better?' she said to Borzov.

'Not much,' he grumbled.

'That was a light sedative I administered. RoSur will give you the full anaesthetic as the first step in the operation.' Nicole had done all her memory refreshing in her room while she was dressing. She knew this operation inside out; it had been one of the surgical procedures they had performed during the test simulations. She entered Borzov's personal data file into RoSur, hooked up the electronic lines that would bring patient monitor information to RoSur during the appendectomy, and verified that all the software had passed self-test. As her last check, Nicole carefully tuned the pair of tiny stereo cameras that worked in concert with the surgical hand.

Janos came back into the room. Nicole pressed a button on the robot surgeon's control box and two hard copies of the operations sequence were quickly printed. Nicole took one and handed the other to Janos. 'Is everyone ready?' she asked, her eyes on General Borzov. The commanding officer of the Newton shook his head up and down. Nicole activated RoSur.

One of the robot surgeon's four hands gunned an anaesthetic into the patient and in one minute Borzov was unconscious. As Francesca's camera recorded every move of this historic operation (she was whispering occasional comments into her ultrasensitive microphone), the scalpel hand of RoSur, aided by its twin eyes, made the incisions necessary to isolate the suspect organ. No human surgeon had ever been so swift or deft. Armed with a battery of sensors checking hundreds of parameters every microsecond, RoSur had folded back all the requisite tissue and laid the appendix bare within two minutes. Programmed into the automatic sequence was a thirty second inspection time before the robot surgeon would continue with the removal of the organ.

Nicole bent over the patient to check the exposed appendix. It was neither swollen nor inflamed. 'Look at this, quick, Janos,' she said, her eye on the digital clock counting down the inspection period. 'It looks perfectly healthy.' Janos leaned over from the opposite side of the operating table. *My God*, Nicole thought, *we're going to remove* ... The digital clock read 00:08. 'Stop it,' she shouted. 'Stop the operation.' Nicole and Janos both reached for the robot surgeon control box at the same time.

At that instant the entire Newton spacecraft lurched sideways. Nicole was thrown backward, against the wall. Janos fell forward, smacking his head against the operating table. His outstretched fingers landed on the control box and then slowly released as he slumped to the floor. General O'Toole and Francesca were both thrown against the far wall. A *beep! beep!* from one of the inserted Hakamatsu probes indicated that someone in the room was in serious trouble physically. Nicole checked briefly to see that O'Toole and Sabatini were all right and then struggled against the continuing torque to regain her position next to the operating table. With great effort she pulled herself across the room on the floor, using the anchored legs of the table. When she was beside the table she steadied herself, still holding on to the legs, and stood up.

Blood spattered Nicole as her head crossed the plane of the operating table. She stared with disbelief at Borzov's body. The entire incision was full of blood and RoSur's scalpel/hand was buried inside, apparently still cutting away. It was Borzov's probe set that was going *beep! beep!*, despite the fact that Nicole had inserted, by command, significantly wider emergency values just before the operation.

A wave of fear and nausea swept through Nicole as she realised that the robot had not aborted its surgical activities. Holding on tight against the powerful force trying to push her against the wall again, she somehow

managed to reach over to the control box and switch off
the power. The scalpel withdrew from the pool of blood
and restowed itself against a stanchion. Nicole then tried
to stop the massive haemorrhaging.

Thirty seconds later the unexplained force vanished as
suddenly as it had appeared. General O'Toole clambered
to his feet and came over beside the now desperate
Nicole. The scalpel had done too much damage. The
commander was bleeding to death before her eyes. 'Oh,
no. Oh, God,' O'Toole said as he surveyed the wreckage
of his friend's body. The insistent beeping continued.
Now the life system alarms around the table sounded as
well. Francesca recovered in time to record the final ten
seconds of Valeriy Borzov's life.

It was a very long night for the entire Newton crew. In
the two hours immediately after the operation, Rama
went through a sequence of three more manoeuvres,
each, like the first one, lasting one or two minutes. The
Earth eventually confirmed that the combined
manoeuvres had changed the attitude, spin rate, and
orbit of the alien spaceship. Nobody could ascertain the
exact purpose of the set of manoeuvres; they were just
'orientation changes' that had altered the inclination and
line of apsides of the Rama orbit. However, the energy of
the trajectory had not been changed significantly – Rama
was still on a hyperbolic escape path with respect to the
Sun.

Everyone on board the Newton and on Earth was
stunned by the sudden death of General Borzov. He was
eulogised by the press of all nations and his many
accomplishments were lauded by his peers and
associates. His death was reported as an accident,
attributed to the untimely motion of the Rama spacecraft
that had taken place during the middle of a routine
appendectomy. But within eight hours after his death,
knowledgeable people everywhere were asking tough
questions. Why had the Rama spacecraft moved at
exactly that time? Why had RoSur's fault protection
system failed to stop the operation? Why were the human

medical officers presiding over the procedure not able to switch off the power before it was too late?

Nicole des Jardins was asking herself the same questions. She had already completed the documents required when a death occurs in space and had sealed Borzov's body in the vacuum coffin at the back of the military ship's huge supply depot. She had quickly prepared and filed her report on the incident; O'Toole, Sabatini, and Tabori had all done the same. There was only one significant discrepancy in the reports. Janos failed to mention that he had reached for the control box during the Raman manoeuvre. At the time Nicole did not think his omission was important.

The required teleconferences with ISA officials were extremely painful. Nicole was the person who bore the brunt of all the inane and repetitious questioning. She had to reach deep inside herself for extra reserves to keep from losing her temper several times. Nicole had expected that Francesca might hint at incompetence on the part of the Newton medical staff in her teleconference, but the Italian journalist was even-handed and fair in her reportage.

After a short interview with Francesca, in which Nicole discussed how horrified she had been at the moment she had first seen Borzov's incision filled with blood, the life science officer retired to her room, ostensibly to rest and/or sleep. But Nicole did not allow herself the luxury of resting. Over and over again she reviewed the critical seconds of the operation. Could she have done anything to change the outcome? What could possibly explain RoSur's failure to stop itself automatically?

In Nicole's mind there was little or no probability that RoSur's fault protection algorithms had a design flaw; they wouldn't have passed all the rigourous prelaunch testing if they contained errors. So somewhere there must have been a human error, either negligence (had she and Janos, in their haste, forgotten to initialise some key fault protection parameter?) or an accident during those chaotic seconds following the unexpected torque.

Her fruitless searching for an explanation and her almost total fatigue made her extremely depressed when she finally fell asleep. To her, one part of the equation was very clear. A man had died and she had been responsible.

18
Post Mortem

As expected, the day after General Borzov's death was full of turmoil. The ISA investigation into the incident expanded and most of the cosmonauts were subjected to another long cross-examination. Nicole was interrogated about her sobriety at the time of the operation. Some of the questions were ugly and Nicole, who was trying to husband her energy for her own investigation of the events surrounding the tragedy, lost her patience twice with the interrogators.

'Look,' she exclaimed at one point, 'I have now explained four times that I had two glasses of wine and one glass of vodka three hours before the operation. I have admitted that I would not have drunk any alcohol prior to surgery, *if* I had known that I was going to operate. I have even acknowledged, in retrospect, that perhaps one of the two life science officers should have remained completely sober. But that's all hindsight. I repeat what I said earlier. Neither my judgment nor my physical abilities were in any way impaired by alcohol at the time of the operation.'

Back in her room, Nicole focused her attention on the issue of why the robot surgeon proceeded with the operation when its own internal fault protection should have aborted all activities. Based upon the User's Guide to RoSur, it was evident that at least two separate sensor systems should have sent error messages to the central processor in the robot surgeon. The accelerometer package should have informed the processor that the environmental conditions were outside acceptable limits because of the untoward lateral force. And the stereo cameras should have transmitted a message indicating that the observed images were at variance with the predicted images. But for some reason neither sensor set was successful in interrupting the ongoing operation. What had happened?

It took Nicole almost five hours to rule out the possibility of a major error, either software or hardware, in the RoSur system itself. She verified that the loaded software and data base had been correct by doing a code comparison with the benchmark standard version of the software tested extensively during prelaunch. She also isolated the stereo imaging and accelerometer telemetry from the few seconds right after the spacecraft lurched. These data were properly transmitted to the central processor and should have resulted in an aborted sequence. But they didn't. Why not? The only possible explanation was that the software had been changed by manual command between the time of loading and the performance of the appendectomy.

Nicole was now out of her league. Her software and system engineering knowledge had been stretched to the limit in satisfying herself that there had been no error in the loaded software. To determine whether and when commands might have changed the code or parameters after they were installed in RoSur required someone who could read machine language and carefully interrogate the billions of bits of data that had been stored during the entire procedure. Nicole's investigation was stalled until she could find someone to help her. *Maybe I should give this up?* a voice inside her said. *How could you?* another voice replied, *until you know for certain the cause of General Borzov's death.* At the root of Nicole's desire to know the answer was a desperate yearning to prove for certain that his death had not been her fault.

She turned away from her terminal and collapsed on her bed. As she was lying there, she remembered her surprise during the thirty second inspection period when Borzov's appendix had been in plain view. *He definitely didn't have appendicitis*, she thought. Without having any particular motive, Nicole returned to her terminal and accessed the second set of data that she had had evaluated by the electronic diagnostician, just prior to her decision to operate. She glanced only briefly at the 92% LIKELY APPENDICITIS on the first screen, moving instead to the backup diagnoses. This time DRUG REACTION was listed as the second most likely cause, with a four percent probability. Nicole now called for the data to be displayed in another way. She asked a statistical routine to compute the likely cause of the symptoms, *given* the fact that it could not be an appendicitis.

The results flashed up on the monitor in seconds. Nicole was astonished. According to the data, if the biometry information input from Borzov's probe set was analysed under the assumption that the cause for the abnormalities could *not* be appendicitis, then there was a 62% chance that it was due to a drug reaction. Before Nicole was able to complete any more analysis, there was a knock on her door.

'Come in,' she said, continuing to work at her terminal. Nicole turned and saw Irina Turgenyev standing in the doorway. The Soviet pilot said nothing for a moment.

'They asked me to come for you,' Irina said haltingly. She was very shy around everyone except her fellow Eastern Europeans Tabori and Borzov. 'We're having a meeting of the crew down in the lobby.'

Nicole saved her temporary data files and joined Irina in the corridor. 'What sort of meeting is it?' she asked.

'An organisational meeting,' Irina answered. She said nothing more.

There was a heated exchange between Reggie Wilson and David Brown in progress when the two women reached the lobby. 'Am I to understand then,' Dr Brown was saying sarcastically, 'that you believe the Rama spacecraft *purposely* decided to manoeuvre at precisely that moment? Would you like to explain to all of us *how* this asteroid of dumb metal happened to know that General Borzov was having an appendectomy at that very minute? And while you're at it, will you explain why this supposedly malevolent spaceship has allowed us to attach ourselves and has done nothing to dissuade us from continuing our mission?'

Reggie Wilson glanced around the room for support. 'You're logic-chopping again, Brown,' he said, his frustration obvious. 'What you say always sounds logical on the surface. But I'm not the only member of this crew who found the coincidence unnerving. Look, here's Irina Turgenyev. She's the one who suggested the connection to me in the first place.'

Dr Brown acknowledged the arrival of the two women. There was an authority in the way he was asking the questions that suggested he was in control of the gathering. 'Is that right, Irina?' David Brown asked. 'Do you feel, like Wilson, that Rama was trying to send us some specific message by performing its manoeuvre during the general's operation?'

Irina and Hiro Yamanaka were the two cosmonauts who spoke least during crew meetings. With all eyes turned toward her, Irina mumbled 'no' very meekly.

'But when we were discussing it last night....' Wilson insisted to the Soviet pilot.

'That's enough on that subject,' David Brown interrupted imperiously. 'I think we have a consensus, shared by our mission control officers on Earth, that the Raman manoeuvre was coincidence and not conspiracy.' He looked at the fuming Reggie Wilson. 'Now we have other more important issues to discuss. I would like to ask Admiral Heilmann to tell us what he has learned about the leadership problem.'

Otto Heilmann stood up on cue and read from his notes. 'According to the Newton procedures, in the event of the death or the incapacity of the commanding officer, the crew is expected to complete all sequences then underway in accordance with previous directions. However, once those 'in process' activities are finished, the cosmonauts are supposed to wait for the Earth to name a new commanding officer.'

David Brown jumped back into the conversation.

'Admiral Heilmann and I started discussing our situation about an hour ago and we quickly realised that we had valid reasons for being concerned. ISA are wrapped up in their investigations of General Borzov's death. They have not even begun to think about his replacement. Once they do start, it may take them weeks to decide. Remember, this is the same bureaucracy that was never able to select a deputy for Borzov, so they eventually decided that he didn't need one.' He paused several seconds to allow the rest of the crew members to consider what he was saying.

'Otto suggested that maybe we should not wait for the Earth to decide,' Dr Brown continued. 'It was his idea that we should develop our own management structure, one that is acceptable to all of us here, and then send it to ISA as a recommendation. Admiral Heilmann thinks they will accept it because it will avoid what could be a protracted debate.'

'Admiral Heilmann and Doctor Brown came to see me with this idea,' Janos Tabori now chimed in, 'and emphasised how important it is for us to get started with our mission inside Rama. They even laid out a strawman organisation that made sense to me. Since none of us has the broad experience of General Borzov, they suggested that maybe we should now have two leaders, possibly Admiral Heilmann and Dr Brown themselves. Otto would cover the military and spacecraft engineering issues; Dr Brown would lead the Rama exploration effort.'

'And what happens when they disagree or their areas of responsibility overlap?' asked Richard Wakefield.

'In that case,' Admiral Heilmann responded, 'we would submit the item in question to a vote of all the cosmonauts.'

'Isn't this cute?' said Reggie Wilson. He was still angry. He had been taking notes on his keyboard but now he stood up to address the rest of the cosmonauts. 'Brown and Heilmann just happened to be worrying about this critical problem and they just happened to have developed a new leadership structure in which all the power and responsibility are divided between them. Am I the only one here who smells something fishy?'

'Now come on, Reggie,' Francesca Sabatini said forcefully. She dropped her video camera to her side. 'There is sound logic in the strawman proposal. Dr Brown is our senior scientist. Admiral Heilmann has been a close colleague of Valeriy Borzov's for many years. None of us has a solid overall command of all aspects of the mission. To split the duties would be –'

It was difficult for Reggie Wilson to argue with Francesca. Nevertheless, he did interrupt her before she was finished. 'I disagree with this plan,' he said in a subdued tone. 'I think we should have a single leader. And based on what I have observed during my time with this crew, there's only one cosmonaut that we could all easily follow. That's General O'Toole.' He waved in the direction of his fellow American. 'If this is a democracy, I nominate him as our new commanding officer.'

There was a general uproar as soon as Reggie sat down. David Brown tried to restore order. 'Please, please,' he shouted, 'let's work one issue at a time. Do we want to decide our own leadership and then hand it to ISA as a fait accompli? Once we handle that question, then we can settle who those leaders should be.'

'I had not thought about any of this before the meeting,' Richard Wakefield said. 'But I agree with the idea of cutting the Earth out of the loop. They have not lived with us on this mission. More importantly, they are not on board a spaceship affixed to an alien creation somewhere just inside the orbit of Venus. We are the ones who will suffer if a bad decision is made; we should decide our own organisation.'

It was clear that everyone, with the possible exception of Wilson, preferred the idea of defining the leadership structure and then presenting it to the ISA. 'All right,' Otto Heilmann said a few minutes later, 'we must now choose our leaders. One strawman proposal has been advanced, suggesting a leadership split between myself and Dr Brown. Reggie Wilson has nominated General Michael O'Toole as the new commanding officer. Are there any other suggestions or discussion?'

The room was silent for about ten seconds. 'Excuse me,' General O'Toole then said, 'but I would like to make a few observations.' Everyone listened to the American general. Wilson was correct. Despite O'Toole's known preoccupation with religion (which he didn't force anyone else to share), he had the respect of the entire cosmonaut crew. 'I think we must be careful at this point not to lose the team spirit that we have worked so hard to develop during the past year. A contested election at this point could be divisive. Besides, it's not all that important or necessary. Regardless of who becomes our nominal leader, or leaders, each of us is trained to perform a specific set of functions. We will do them under any circumstances.'

Heads were nodding in agreement around the lobby. 'For myself,' General O'Toole continued, 'I must admit that I know little or nothing about the inside-Rama aspects of this mission. I have never trained to do anything except manage the two Newton spacecraft, assess any potential military threat, and act as a communications nexus on board. I'm not qualified to be the commanding officer.' Reggie Wilson started to interrupt but O'Toole continued without a pause. 'I'd like to recommend that we adopt the plan offered by Heilmann and Brown and move on with our primary task – namely the exploration of this alien leviathan that has come to us from the stars.'

At the conclusion of the meeting the two new leaders informed the rest of the cosmonauts that a rough draft of the first sortie scenario would be ready for review the following morning. Nicole headed for her room. On the way she stopped and knocked on the door of Janos Tabori. At first there was no response. When she knocked a second time, she heard Janos yell, 'Who is it?'

'It's me. Nicole,' she answered.

'Come in,' he said.

He was lying on his back on the small bed with an uncharacteristic frown on his face.

'What's the matter?' Nicole asked.

'Oh, nothing,' Janos answered. 'I just have a headache.'

'Did you take something?' Nicole enquired.

'No. It's not that serious.' He still didn't smile. 'What can I do for you?' he asked, in an almost unfriendly tone.

Nicole was puzzled. She approached her subject cautiously. 'Well, I was rereading your report on Valeriy's death –'

'Why were you doing that?' Janos interrupted brusquely.

'To see if there was anything we might have done differently,' Nicole responded. It was obvious to her that Janos did not want to discuss the subject. After waiting a few seconds, Nicole spoke again. 'I'm sorry, Janos. I'm imposing on you. I'll come back another time.'

'No. No,' he said. 'Let's get this over with now.'

That's a curious way of putting it, Nicole was thinking as she formulated her question. 'Janos,' she said, 'nowhere in your report did you mention reaching for RoSur's control box right before the manoeuvre. And I could have sworn I saw your fingers on the keyboard panel as I was being swept over against the wall.'

Nicole stopped. There was no expression of any kind on Cosmonaut Tabori's face. It was almost as if he were thinking of something else. 'I don't remember,' he said at length, without emotion. 'You may be right. Perhaps my hitting my head erased part of my memory.'

Stop now, Nicole said to herself as she studied her colleague. *There's nothing more you can learn here.*

19
Rite of Passage

Genevieve suddenly broke into tears. 'Oh, Maman,' she said. 'I love you so much and this is absolutely awful.'

The teenager hurriedly moved out of the camera frame and was replaced by Nicole's father. Pierre looked off to his right for a few seconds, to make certain that his granddaughter was out of earshot, and then turned toward the monitor. 'These last twenty-four hours have been especially hard on her. You know how she idolises you. Some of the foreign press have been saying that you bungled the surgery. There was even a suggestion this evening from an American television reporter that you were drunk during the operation.'

He paused. The strain was showing on her father's face as well. 'Both Genevieve and I know that neither of these allegations is true. We love you completely and send all our support.'

The screen went dark. Nicole had initiated the videophone call and had, at first, been cheered by talking to her family. After her second transmission, however, when her father and daughter had reappeared on the screen twenty minutes later, it had been obvious that the events on board the Newton had unsettled life at Beauvois as well. Genevieve had been particularly distraught. She had cried intermittently while talking about General Borzov (she had met him several times and the avuncular Russian had always been especially nice to her) and had barely managed to compose herself before breaking into tears again right before the end of the call.

So I have embarrassed you as well, Nicole thought as she sat down on her bed. She rubbed her eyes. She was extremely tired. Slowly, without being aware of how depressed she had become, she undressed for bed. Her mind was plagued with pictures of her daughter at school in Luynes. Nicole winced as she imagined one of Genevieve's friends asking her about the operation and Borzov's death. *My darling daughter*, she thought, *you must know how much I love you. If only I could spare you from this pain.* Nicole wanted to reach out and comfort Genevieve, to hold her close, to share one of those mother-daughter caresses that chase away the demons. But it could not be. Genevieve was a hundred million kilometres away.

Nicole lay in bed on her back. She closed her eyes but did not sleep. She was aware of a deep and profound loneliness, a sense of isolation more acute than any she had felt before in her life. She knew that she was longing for some sympathy, for some human being who would tell her that her feelings of inadequacy were overblown and not consistent with reality. But there was nobody. Her father and daughter were back on Earth. Of the two Newton crew members she knew best, one was dead and the other was behaving suspiciously.

I have failed, Nicole was thinking as she was lying on her bed. *On my most important assignment I have failed.* She recalled another feeling of failure, when she was only sixteen. At that time Nicole had competed for the role of Joan of Arc in a huge national contest associated with the 750th anniversary of the death of the Maid. If she had won, Nicole would have portrayed Joan in a series of pageants lasting over two years. She had thrown herself totally into the contest, reading every book she could find about Joan and watching scores of video presentations. Nicole had scored at the top in virtually every test category except 'suitability'. She should have won, but she didn't. Her father had consoled her by telling Nicole that France was not ready for its heroines to have dark skin.

But that was not exactly a failure, the Newton life

science officer told herself. *And anyway I had my father to comfort me.* An image of her mother's funeral came into Nicole's mind. She had been ten years old at the time. Her mother had gone to the Ivory Coast by herself to visit their African relatives. Anawi had been in Nidougou when a virulent epidemic of Hogan fever had swept through the village. Nicole's mother had died quickly.

Five days later Anawi had been cremated as a Senoufo queen. Nicole had wept while Omeh chanted her mother's soul through the nether world and into the Land of Preparation, where beings rested while waiting to be selected for another life on Earth. As the flames had mounted the pyre and her mother's regal dress had begun to burn, Nicole had felt an overpowering sense of loss. And loneliness. *But that time also my father was there beside me,* she recalled. *He held my hand as we watched mother disappear. Together it was easier to bear. I was much more lonely during the Poro. And more frightened.*

She could still remember the mixture of terror and helplessness that had filled her seven-year-old body at the Paris airport on that spring morning. Her father had caressed her very tenderly. 'Darling, darling Nicole,' he had said. 'I will miss you very much. Come back safely to me.'

'But why must I go, Papa?' she had replied. 'And why are you not coming with us?'

He had bent down beside her. 'You are going to become part of your mother's people. All Senoufo children go through the Poro at the age of seven.'

Nicole had started crying. 'But Papa, I don't want to go. I'm French, not African. I don't like all those strange people and the heat and the bugs....'

Her father had placed his hands firmly on her cheeks. 'You must go, Nicole. Your mother and I have agreed.' Anawi and Pierre had indeed discussed it many times. Nicole had lived in France all her life. All she knew of her African heritage was what her mother had taught her and what she had learned from two month-long visits to the Ivory Coast with her family.

It had not been easy for Pierre to agree to send his beloved daughter off to the Poro. He knew that it was a primitive ceremony. He also knew that it was the cornerstone of the Senoufo traditional religion and that he had promised Omeh, at the time of his marriage to Anawi, that all their children would return to Nidougou for at least the first cycle of the Poro.

The hardest part for Pierre was staying behind. But Anawi was right. He was an outsider. He would not be able to participate in the Poro. He would not understand it. His presence would distract the little girl. There was an ache in his heart as he kissed his wife and daughter and put them on to the plane to Abidjan.

Anawi was also apprehensive about the rite of passage ceremony for her only child, her little girl of barely seven years. She had prepared Nicole as well as she could. The child was a gifted linguist and had picked up the rudiments of the Senoufo language very easily. But there was no doubt that she was at a severe disadvantage with respect to the rest of the children. All of the others had lived their whole lives in and around the native villages. They were familiar with the area. To alleviate the orientation problem a little, Anawi and Nicole arrived in Nidougou a week ahead of time.

The fundamental idea of the Poro was that life was a succession of phases or cycles and that each transition should be carefully marked. Each cycle lasted seven years. There were three Poros in every normal Senoufo life, three metamorphoses that were necessary before the child could be transformed into an adult in the tribe. Despite the fact that many of the tribal customs faded away with the arrival of modern telecommunications devices in the Ivory Coast villages in the twenty-first century, the Poro remained an integral part of Senoufo society. In the twenty-second century, tribal practices enjoyed a renaissance of sorts, especially after the Great Chaos proved to most of the African leaders that it was dangerous to depend too much on the outside world.

Anawi kept a good acting smile upon her face during the afternoon when the tribal priests came to take Nicole away for the Poro. She didn't want her fear or anxiety to be transferred to her daughter. Nevertheless, Nicole could tell that her mother was troubled. 'Your hands are cold and sweaty, Maman,' she whispered in French as she hugged Anawi before departing. 'Don't worry. I'll be all right.' In fact, Nicole, the only brown face among the dozen dark black girls climbing into the carts, seemed almost cheery and expectant, as if she were going to an amusement park or a zoo.

There were four carts altogether, two carrying the little girls and two that were covered and unexplained. Nicole's friend from four years earlier, Lutuwa, who was actually one of Nicole's cousins, explained to the rest of the girls that the other wagons contained the priests and the 'instruments of torture'. There was a long silence before one of the little girls had the courage to ask Lutuwa what she was talking about.

'I dreamed it all two nights ago,' Lutuwa said matter-of-factly. 'They are going to burn our nipples and stick sharp objects in all our holes. And as long as we don't cry, we won't feel any pain.' The other five girls in Nicole's cart, including Lutuwa, hardly said a word for the next hour.

By sunset they had travelled a long way east, past the abandoned microwave station, into the special area known only to the tribal religious leaders. The half-dozen priests threw up temporary shelters and started building a fire. When it was dark, food and drink were served to the initiates, who sat cross-legged in a wide circle around the fire. After dinner the costumed dancing began. Omeh narrated the four dances, each of which featured one of the indigenous animals. Music for the dances came from tambourines and crude xylophones, the rhythm being maintained by the monotonic beat of the tom-tom. Occasionally, an especially meaningful point in the story would be punctuated by a blast on the oliphant, the ivory hunting horn.

Just before bedtime Omeh, still wearing the great mask and headdress identifying him as chieftain, handed each of the girls a large kit made of antelope hide and told them to study its contents very carefully. There was a flask of water, some dried fruit and nuts, two chunks of native bread, a cutting implement, some rope, two different kinds of unguents, and a tuber from an unknown plant.

'Tomorrow morning each child will be removed from this camp,' Omeh said, 'and placed in a specific location not too far away. The child will have only the gifts in the antelope hide. The child is expected to survive on her own and return to the same spot by the time the sun is full in the sky on the following day.

'The hide contains everything that is needed except for wisdom, courage, and curiosity. The tuber is something very special. Eating the fleshy root will terrify the child, but may also give abnormal powers of strength and vision.'

20

Blessed Slumber

The little girl had been alone for almost two hours before she really understood what was happening to her. Omeh and one of the younger priests had placed Nicole right near a small, brackish pond, surrounded on all sides by the high grasses of the savanna. They had reminded her that they would return in the middle of the next day. Then they were gone.

At first Nicole had reacted as if the entire experience were a great game. She had taken out her kit made of antelope hide and carefully inventoried the contents. She had mentally divided the food into three parts, planning what she would eat for dinner, breakfast, and midmorning snack. There was not excessive food, but little Nicole judged that it would be enough. On the other hand, when she had visually measured the flask to determine the adequacy of her water supply, she had concluded that it was marginal. It would be good if she could find a spring or some pure running water that could be used in an emergency.

Nicole's next activity had been to create a mental map of her location, paying special attention to any landmarks that would help her identify the brackish pond from a distance. She was an extremely organised little girl and, back at Chilly-Mazarin, often played by herself in a wooded vacant lot very close to her house. In her room at home Nicole had maps of the wood that she had carefully drawn by hand, her secret hiding places marked with stars and circles.

It was when she came upon four striped antelope, grazing calmly under the steady afternoon sun, that Nicole first understood how utterly isolated she was. Her first instinct was to look for her mother, to show Anawi the beautiful animals she had found. *But Mother is not here,* the little girl thought, her eyes scanning the horizon. *I am all alone.* The last word echoed through her mind and she felt an inchoate despair. She fought against the despair and looked off into the distance to see if she could find any indication of civilisation. There were birds all around and some more grazing animals on the horizon at the limit of her vision, but no sign of any human beings. *I am all alone,* Nicole said to herself again, a slight shiver of fear running through her body.

She remembered that she wanted to find another source of water and walked off in the direction of a large grove of trees. The little girl had no idea about distances in the open savanna. Although she did carefully stop every thirty minutes or so to ensure that she could still find her way back to the pond, it amazed her that the distant grove did not appear to be coming any closer. She walked on and on. As the afternoon waned, she became tired and thirsty. She stopped to drink some of her water. The tsetse flies surrounded her, buzzing her face as she tried to drink. Nicole took out the two unguents, smelled them both, and applied the worse smelling of the two to her face and arms. Her choice was apparently correct; the flies also found the unguent noisome and kept their distance.

She reached the trees about an hour before dark. She was delighted to find that she had fortuitously stumbled upon a small oasis in the middle of the great stretch of savanna. There was a strong spring in the grove where the water rushed out of the ground and formed a circular pool about ten metres in diameter. The excess water in turn trickled out of one edge of the pool and became a creek that ran from the oasis back into the savanna. Nicole was exhausted and sweaty from her long walk. The water in the pool was inviting. Without thinking she pulled off her clothes, except for her underpants, and jumped in for a swim.

The water invigorated and soothed her tired little body. With her head underwater and her eyes closed, she swam and swam and fantasised that she was in the community pool in her suburb near Paris. In her imagination she had gone to the *piscine*, as she generally did once a week, and was playing water sports with her friends. The memory comforted her. After a long time Nicole rolled over on her back and took a few strokes. She opened her eyes and looked at the trees above her. The rays from the late afternoon sun were making magic as they cut through the branches and the leaves.

Seven-year-old Nicole stopped swimming and trod water for several seconds, looking around the edge of the pool for her clothes. She didn't see them. Puzzled, she scanned the perimeter of the pool more carefully. Still she saw nothing. In her mind she reconstructed all the scenes of her arrival in the grove and conclusively remembered exactly where she had placed both her clothes and the kit made from antelope hide. She climbed out of the water and examined the spot more closely. *This is definitely the place*, she thought. *And my clothes and the kit are gone.*

There was no way to quell the panic. It overpowered her in an instant. Her eyes flooded with tears, a wail broke from her throat. She closed her eyes and wept, hoping that this was all a bad dream and that she would wake up in the next few seconds and see her mother and father. But when she opened her eyes again, the same scene was still there. A half-naked little girl was alone in the wilds of Africa with no food, no water, and no hope of rescue before the middle of the next day. And it was almost dark.

With great effort Nicole managed at last to control both her fright and her tears. She decided to look for her clothes. Where they had been before, she found fresh prints of some kind. Nicole had no way of knowing what kind of animal might have made the tracks, so she assumed that it was one of the gentle antelope that she had seen that afternoon in the savanna. *That would make sense*, the little girl thought logically. *This is probably the best water hole in the area. They stopped here and were curious about my things. My splashing must have scared them away.*

As the light faded she followed the tracks along a tiny pathway through the trees. After a short trek she found the antelope hide, or rather what was left of it, discarded on the side of the path. The kit was torn completely open. All the food was gone, the water flask was mostly drained, and everything else had fallen out except the unguents and the tuber. Nicole finished the water that was left in the flask and put it with the tuber in her right hand. She discarded the messy unguents. She was about to continue following the path when she heard a sound, halfway between a yelp and a cry. The sound was very close. The path opened into the savanna about fifty metres ahead. Nicole strained her eyes and thought she saw motion, but she couldn't make out anything specific. Then she heard the yelp again, louder this time. She dropped down on her stomach and crawled slowly along the path.

There was a small rise fifteen metres before the end of the grove. From that vantage point little Nicole saw the source of the yelp. Two lion cubs were playing with her green dress. Their watchful mother was on the opposite side, staring out into the savanna twilight. Nicole froze in terror as she comprehended that she was not visiting a zoo, that she was out in the wild and a real African lioness was only twenty metres away. Trembling with fear, she inched back along the path, very slowly, very quietly, lest she call attention to her presence.

Back near the pool she resisted the urge to jump up and run pell mell into the savanna. *Then the lioness will see me for certain*, she thought. But where to spend the night? *I'll find a ditch among the trees*, she reasoned, *away from the path. And lie still. Then maybe I'll be safe.* Still clutching the flask and the tuber, Nicole walked softly over to the spring. She took a drink and filled her flask. Next she crawled into the grove and found her ditch. Then, convinced that she was as safe as she could possibly be under the circumstances, the exhausted little girl fell asleep.

She woke up suddenly with a sensation that bugs were crawling all over her. She reached down and rubbed her bare stomach. It was covered with ants. Nicole screamed, and then she realised what she had done. In a flash she heard the lioness crashing through the brush, searching for the creature that had made the noise. The little girl shuddered and scraped the ants off with a stick. Then she saw the lioness staring at her, the feral eyes piercing the dark. Nicole was near collapse. In her fright she somehow remembered what Omeh had said about the tuber. She put the dirt-covered root into her mouth and chewed vigorously. It tasted awful. She forced herself to swallow.

A moment later Nicole was rushing through the trees with the lioness chasing her. Branches and leaves cut her face and chest. She slipped once and fell. When she reached the pool she did not stop. Nicole ran across the water, her feet barely touching the top. She flapped her arms. They had changed to wings, white wings. She was no longer touching the water. She was a great white heron soaring up, up into the night sky. She turned and looked at the puzzled lioness far below her. Laughing to herself Nicole intensified her wing motion and rose above all the trees. The great savanna unfolded below her. She could see for over a hundred kilometres.

She flew across to the brackish pond, turned west, and spotted a campfire. She zoomed toward it, her bird shrieks piercing the calm of the night. Omeh awakened with a start, saw the solitary bird spread out against the sky, and made a loud bird cry of his own. 'Ronata?' his voice seemed to ask. But Nicole did not answer. She wanted to fly higher, even above the clouds.

On the other side of the clouds the moon and stars were clear and bright. They beckoned to her. She thought she heard music in the distance, a tinkling like crystal bells, as she soared higher and higher. She tried to flap her wings. They would barely move. They had changed into control surfaces, which now extended to increase the lift in the ultra-thin air. Her aft rockets began to fire. Nicole was now a silver shuttle, thin and sleek, leaving the Earth behind.

The music was louder out in orbit. There it was

magnificent symphony, in complete harmony with the majestic Earth below her. She heard her name being called. From where? Who could be calling way out here? The sound came from beyond the moon. She changed her heading, pointed toward the void of deep space, and fired her rockets again. She swept past the moon, heading away from the sun. Her speed was still increasing exponentially. Behind her the sun was growing smaller and smaller. It became a tiny light and then disappeared altogether. There was blackness all around. She held her breath and came to the surface of the water.

The lioness was prowling back and forth on the edge of the pool. Nicole could vividly see all the muscles in her powerful shoulders and read the expression on her face. *Please leave me alone*, Nicole said, *I won't hurt you or your babies.*

'I recognise your smell,' the lioness answered. 'My cubs were playing with that smell.'

I too am a cub, Nicole continued, *and I want to return to my mother. But I am afraid.*

'Come out of the water,' the lioness replied. 'Let me see you. I do not believe that you are what you say.'

Summoning all her courage, her eyes riveted on the lioness, the little girl walked slowly out of the water. The lioness didn't move. When the water was only waist deep, Nicole shaped her arms into a cradle and began to sing. It was a simple, peaceful melody, the one she remembered from the beginning of her life, when her mother or father would kiss her good night, put her down in the crib, and then turn out the light. The little animals in the mobile would go around and around while a woman's soft voice sang the Brahms lullaby.

'Lay thee down, now and rest ... May thy slumber be blessed.'

The lioness rocked back on her haunches and threatened to pounce. The girl, still softly singing, continued walking toward the animal. When Nicole was completely out of the water and only about five metres away, the lioness jumped aside and leaped back into the grove. Nicole kept walking, the soothing song giving her both comfort and strength. In a few minutes she was back out at the edge of the savanna. By sunrise she had reached the pond, where she lay down among the grasses and fell fast asleep. Omeh and the Senoufo priests found her lying there, half naked and still asleep, when the sun was high in the sky.

She could remember it all as if it were yesterday. *Almost thirty years ago now*, she recalled as she lay still awake in her small bed on the Newton, *and the lessons I learned have never stopped being valuable.* Nicole thought about the little seven-year-old girl who had been stranded in a completely alien world and had managed to survive. *So why am I feeling sorry for myself now?* she thought. *That was a much tougher situation.*

Immersing herself in her childhood experience had given her unexpected strength. Nicole was no longer depressed. Her mind was working overtime again, trying to formulate a plan that would give her the critical answers to what had happened during the operation on Borzov. She had pushed her loneliness aside.

Nicole realised that she would have to stay on board the Newton during the first sortie if she wanted to do a thorough analysis of all aspects of the Borzov incident. She resolved to bring up the issue with Brown or Heilmann in the morning.

At length the exhausted woman fell asleep. As she was drifting into the twilight world that separates waking and sleeping, Nicole was humming a tune to herself. It was Brahm's Lullaby.

21
Pandora's Cube

Nicole could see David Brown sitting behind the desk. Francesca was leaning over him, pointing at something on a large chart that was spread out in front of the two of them. Nicole knocked on the door to the commander's office.

'Hello, Nicole,' Francesca said, as she opened the door. 'What can we do for you?'

'I came to see Dr Brown,' Nicole replied. 'About my assignment.'

'Come on in,' Francesca said.

Nicole shuffled in slowly and sat in one of the two chairs opposite the desk. Francesca sat in the other. Nicole looked at the walls of the office. They had definitely changed. General Borzov's photographs of his wife and children, along with his favourite painting, a picture of a solitary bird with outstretched wings soaring above the Neva River in Leningrad, had been replaced by huge sequencing charts. The charts, each one headed by a different name (First Sortie, Second Sortie, etc), covered the side bulletin boards from one end of the wall to the other.

General Borzov's office had been warm and personal. This room was definitely sterile and intimidating. Dr Brown had hung laminated replicas of two of his most prestigious international scientific awards on the wall behind his desk. He had also raised the height of his chair so that he looked down on anyone else in the room who might be sitting.

'I have come to see you about a personal matter,' Nicole said. She waited several seconds, expecting David Brown to ask Francesca to leave the room. He said nothing. Finally Nicole glanced in Francesca's direction to make her concern obvious.

'She has been helping me with my administrative duties,' Dr Brown explained. 'I find that her feminine insight often detects signals that I have missed altogether.'

Nicole sat silently for another fifteen seconds. She had been prepared to talk to David Brown. She had not expected that it would be necessary also for her to explain everything to Francesca. *Maybe I should just leave*, Nicole thought fleetingly, somewhat surprised to find that she was irritated about Francesca's being there.

'I have read the assignments for the first sortie,' Nicole said eventually in a formal tone, 'and I would like to make a request. My duties, as outlined in the sequence, are minimal. Irina Turgenyev, it seems to me, is also underworked for the three-day sortie. I recommend that you give my non-medical tasks to Irina and I will stay on board the Newton with Admiral Heilmann and General O'Toole. I will follow the progress of the mission carefully and can be available immediately if there is any significant medical problem. Otherwise Janos can handle the life science responsibilities.'

Again there was silence in the room. Dr Brown stared at Nicole and then at Francesca. 'Why do you want to stay on board the Newton?' Francesca responded at length. 'I would have thought that you couldn't wait to see the inside of Rama.'

'As I said, it's mostly personal,' Nicole answered vaguely. 'I'm still extremely tired from the Borzov ordeal and I have a lot of paperwork to finish. The first sortie should be straightforward. I would like to be fully rested and prepared for the second.'

'It's a highly irregular request,' David Brown said, 'but under the circumstances, I think we can do it.' He glanced again at Francesca. 'But we'd like to ask a favour of you. If you're not going into Rama, then perhaps you'd be willing to spell O'Toole as communications officer from time to time? Then Admiral Heilmann could go inside....'

'Certainly,' Nicole answered before Brown had finished.

'Good. Then I guess we're all agreed. We'll change the manifests for the first sortie. You will remain on board the Newton.' After Dr Brown had finished talking Nicole still made no move to leave her chair. 'Was there something else?' he asked impatiently.

'According to our procedures, the life science officer prepares certification memoranda on the cosmonauts prior to each sortie. Should I give a copy to Admiral –'

'Give all those memos to me,' Dr Brown interrupted her. 'Admiral Heilmann is not concerned with personnel matters.' The American scientist looked directly at Nicole. 'But you don't need to prepare new reports for the first sortie. I've read all the documents you wrote for General Borzov. They are quite adequate.'

Nicole did not let herself be cowed by the man's penetrating gaze. *So you know what I wrote about you and Wilson,* she thought, *and you think I should feel guilty or embarrassed. Well, I don't. My opinions have not changed just because you are now nominally in charge.*

That night Nicole continued with her investigation. Her detailed analysis of the biometry data from General Borzov showed that he had had extraordinary levels of two strange chemicals in his system just before his death. Nicole could not work out where they had come from. Had he been taking medication without her knowledge? Could these chemicals, which were known to trigger pain (they were used, according to her medical encyclopedia, to test pain sensitivity in neurologically distressed patients), somehow have been manufactured internally in some kind of allergic reaction?

And what about Janos? Why couldn't he remember reaching for the control box? Why had he been reticent and withdrawn since Borzov's death? Just after midnight she stared at the ceiling of her small bedroom. *Today the crew enters Rama and I will be here alone. I should wait until then to continue my analysis.* But she couldn't wait. She was unable to push aside all the questions that were flooding her mind. *Could there be a connection between Janos and the drugs in Borzov? Is it possible that his death was not completely accidental?*

Nicole took her personal briefcase out of the tiny closet. She opened it hastily and the contents spilled into the air. She grabbed a group of family photographs that were floating above her bed. Then she gathered up most of the rest of the. items and returned them to her briefcase. Nicole retained in her hand the data cube that King Henry had given her in Davos.

She hesitated before inserting the cube. At last she took a deep breath and placed it into the reader. Eighteen menu items were immediately displayed on the monitor. She could choose any of the twelve individual dossiers on the cosmonauts or six different compilations of crew statistics. Nicole called for the dossier on Janos Tabori. There were three submenus for his biography: Personal Data, Chronological Summary, and Psychological Assessment. She could tell from the listed file sizes that the Chronological Summary contained most of the details. Nicole accessed Personal Data first to gain familiarity with the format of the dossiers.

The brief chart did not tell her much that she didn't already know. Janos was forty-one and single. When he was not on duty for the ISA, he lived alone in an apartment in Budapest, only four blocks away from where his twice-divorced mother lived by herself. He had received an honours engineering degree from the University of Hungary in 2183. In addition to mundane items like height, weight, and number of siblings, the chart listed two other numbers: IE (for Intelligence Evaluation) and SC (for Socialisation Coefficient). Tabori's numbers were +3.37 for IE and 64 for SC.

Nicole returned to the main menu and called up the Glossary to refresh her memory about the definitions of IE and SC. The IE numbers supposedly represented a composite measure of overall intelligence, based on a comparison with a similar worldwide student population. All students took a set of standardised tests at specified times between the ages of twelve and twenty. The index was actually an exponent in a decimal measuring system. An IE number of zero was average. An IE index of +1.00 meant the individual was above 90% of the population; +2.00 was above 99% of the population; +3.00 above 99.9%, etc. Negative IE indices indicated below average intelligence. Janos's score of +3.37 placed him in the middle of the upper one-tenth of one percent of the population in intelligence.

The SC numbers had a more straightforward explanation. They too were based on a battery of standardised tests administered to all students between the ages of twelve and twenty, but the interpretation here was easier to understand. The highest SC score was 100. A person scoring close to 100 was liked and respected by virtually everybody, would fit into most any group, was almost never quarrelsome or moody, and was very dependable. A footnote to the explanation of the SC scores acknowledged that written tests could not accurately measure personality traits in all cases, so the numbers should be used with discretion.

Nicole reminded herself to do a comparison sometime of all the cosmonaut IE and SC scores. Then she accessed the Chronological Summary file for Janos Tabori. The next sixty minutes were an eye-opening experience for Nicole. As the life science officer, she had of course studied the official ISA personnel files for the entire crew. But if the information about Janos Tabori on the cube given to her by King Henry was correct (and she had no way of knowing one way or the other), then the ISA files were woefully incomplete.

Nicole had known previously that Janos had twice been selected as the outstanding engineering student at the University of Hungary; she had not known that he had been president for two years of the Gay Students Association of Budapest. She was aware that he had entered the Space Academy in 2192 and had graduated in only three years (because of his previous experience with

major Soviet engineering projects); she had never been
told that he had applied to the Academy twice previously
and been rejected both times. Despite sensational
entrance scores, he had twice failed his personal interview.
Both times the interview committee had been headed by
General Valeriy Borzov. Janos had been active in various
gay organisations until 2190. Subsequently he had resig-
ned from them all and never rejoined or participated in
any organised gay activities. None of this information had
been in his ISA file.

Nicole was stunned by what she had learned. It wasn't
that Janos had been (or was) gay that disturbed her; she
was free of prejudices where sexual orientation was concerned. What bothered her the most was the likelihood
that his official file had been deliberately censored to
remove all references both to his homosexuality and to his
earlier interactions with General Borzov.

The last entries in the Tabori Chronological Summary
were also surprising for Nicole. According to the dossier,
Janos had purportedly signed a contract with Schmidt and
Hagenest, the German publishing conglomerate, in the
last week of December, just before launch. His task was to
perform unspecified 'consulting' for a wide variety of
post-Newton media endeavours in support of what was
referred to as the Brown-Sabatini project. Cosmonaut
Tabori was paid an initial fee of three hundred thousand
marks for signing. Three days later his mother, who had
been waiting almost a year for one of the new artificial
brain implants that reversed the damage from Alzheimer's
disease, entered the Bavarian Hospital in Munich for
neurological surgery.

Her eyes weary and burning, Nicole finished reading the
extensive dossier on Dr David Brown. During the hours
that she had been studying his Chronological Summary,
she had created a special subfile for herself of those items
in the summary that were of particular interest to her.
Before trying again to sleep, Nicole scrolled through this
special subfile one more time.

Summer 2161: Brown, eleven, enrolled in Camp Longhorn by father over strenuous objections of mother. Typical outdoor summer camp in hill country of Texas for upper-class boys, featuring athletics of all kinds, rifle-shooting, crafts, and hiking. Boys lived ten to a barracks. Brown was extremely unpopular immediately. On fifth day bunkmates seized him coming out of shower and painted his genitals black. Brown refused to move from bed until Mother had travelled almost two hundred miles to pick him up and take him home. Father apparently ignored son altogether after this incident.

September 2166: After being valedictorian from private high school, Brown enrolled as freshman in physics at Princeton. Remained in New Jersey only eight weeks. Completed undergraduate work at SMU while living at home.

June 2173: Awarded PH.D in physics and astronomy by Harvard. Dissertation advisor Wilson Brownwell called Brown 'an ambitious, diligent student'.

June 2175: Brown completed post-doctorate research on the evolution of stars with Brian Murchison at Cambridge.

April 2180: Married Jeannette Hudson of Pasadena, California. Ms Hudson had been graduate student in astronomy at Stanford. Only child, daughter Angela, born in December 2184.

November 2181: Refused tenure in astronomy department at Stanford because two members of evaluation committee believed Brown had falsified scientific data in several of his many scholarly publications. Issue was never resolved.

January 2184: Appointed to first ISA Advisory Committee. Prepared comprehensive plans for series of major new astronomical telescopes on far side of the moon.

May 2187: Brown named chairman of Department of Physics and Astronomy at SMU in Dallas, Texas.

February 2188: Fistfight with Wendell Thomas, Princeton professor, in atrium outside AAAS meeting in Chicago. Thomas insisted that Brown had stolen and published ideas they had discussed together.

April 2190: Electrified scientific world by not only publishing breakthrough models of supernova process, but also predicting nearby supernova to occur in mid-March 2191. Research done in collaboration with SMU doctoral student, Elaine Bernstein of New York. Strong suggestion from graduate associates of Ms Bernstein that she was actually one with the new insights. Brown catapulted to fame as a result of his bold and correct prediction.

June 2190: Brown divorced wife, from whom he had been separated for eighteen months. Separation had started three months after Elaine Bernstein had begun graduate work.

December 2190: Married Ms Bernstein in Dallas.

March 2191: Supernova 2191a filled night sky with light, as predicted by Brown et al.

June 2191: Brown signed two year science reporting contract with CBS. Jumped to UBC in 2194 and then, at recommendation of agent, to INN in 2197.

December 2193: Brown awarded top ISA medal for Distinguished Scientific Achievement.

November 2199: Signed exclusive multimillion mark, multiyear contract with Schmidt and Hagenest to 'exploit' all possible commercial applications of Newton mission, including books, videos, and educational material. Teamed with Francesca Sabatini as other principal, cosmonauts Heilmann and Tabori as consultants. Signing bonus of two million marks deposited in secret account in Italy.

Her alarm awakened her after she had been asleep for only two hours. Nicole dragged herself out of bed and freshened up in the retractable wash basin. She moved slowly into the corridor and turned toward the lobby. The other four space cadets were gathered around David Brown in the control centre, excitedly reviewing the details of the initial sortie.

'All right,' Richard Wakefield was saying, 'first priorities are the lightweight individual chairlifts by the right and left stairways and one heavy load elevator from the hub to the Central Plain. Then we set up a temporary control centre at the edge of the plain and assemble and test the three rovers. Crude campsite tonight, base camp at the Beta site near the edge of the Cylindrical Sea tomorrow. We will leave the assembly and deployment of the two helicopters for tomorrow, the icemobiles and motorboats for Day Three.'

'That's an excellent summary,' Dr Brown replied. 'Francesca will go with the four of you while you're setting up the infrastructure this morning. When the lightweight lifts are installed and operational, Admiral Heilmann and I will join you along with Dr Takagishi and Mr Wilson. We'll all sleep inside Rama tonight.'

'How many long duration flares do you have?' Janos Tabori asked Irina Turgenyev.

'Twelve,' she answered. 'That should be plenty for today.'

'And tonight, when we go to sleep in there, it will be the darkest night that any of us have ever seen,' Dr Takagishi said. 'There will be no moon and no stars, no reflection off the ground, nothing but blackness all around.'

'What will the temperature be?' Wakefield asked.

'We don't know for certain,' the Japanese scientist answered. 'The initial drones carried only cameras. But the temperature in the region around the end of the tunnel was the same as in Rama I. If that's any indication, then it should be about ten degrees below freezing at the campsites.' Takagishi paused for a moment. 'And getting warmer,' he continued. 'We're now inside the orbit of Venus. We expect the lights to come on in another eight or nine days, and the Cylindrical Sea to melt from the bottom soon thereafter.'

'Hey,' kidded David Brown. 'It sounds as if you're becoming converted. You no longer qualify *all* your statements, just some of them.'

'With each datum that indicates this spaceship is like its predecessor seventy years ago,' Takagishi replied, 'the probability that they are identical increases. Thus far, if we ignore the exact timing of the correction manoeuvre, everything about the two vehicles has been the same.'

Nicole approached the group. 'Well, look who's here,' Janos said with his usual grin. 'Our fifth and final space cadet.' He noticed her swollen eyes. 'And our new commander was right. You do look as if you might benefit from some rest.'

'I, for one,' Richard Wakefield interjected, 'am disappointed that my rover assembly assistant will now be Yamanaka instead of Madame des Jardins. At least our life science officer talks. I may have to recite Shakespeare to myself to stay awake.' He elbowed Yamanaka in the ribs. The Japanese pilot almost smiled.

'I wanted to wish you all good luck,' Nicole said. 'As I'm sure Dr Brown has told you, I felt I was still too tired to be very helpful. I should be fresh and ready by the second sortie.'

'Well,' Francesca Sabatini remarked impatiently after her camera had panned around the room and captured one final closeup of each face. 'Are we finally ready?'

'Let's go,' said Wakefield. They headed toward the airlock at the front of the Newton spacecraft.

22
Dawn

Richard Wakefield worked quickly in the near darkness. He was halfway down the Alpha stairway, where the gravity due to the centrifugal force created by the spin of Rama had grown to more than a quarter of a gee. The light from his headgear illuminated the near field. He was almost finished with another pylon.

He checked his air supply. It was already below the midpoint. By now they should have been deeper into Rama, closer to where they could breathe the ambient air. But they had underestimated how long it would take them to install the lightweight chairlifts. The concept was extremely simple and they had practised it several times in the simulations. The upper part of the job, when they had been in the vicinity of the ladders and virtually weightless, had been relatively straightforward. But at this level the installation of each pylon was a different process because of the increasing and changing gravity.

Exactly a thousand steps above Wakefield, Janos Tabori finished wrapping anchor lines around the metal bannisters that lined the stairway. After almost four hours of tedious, repetitive work, he was becoming fatigued. He remembered the argument the engineering director had advanced when he and Richard had recommended a specialised machine for the installation of the lifts. 'It's not cost-effective to create a robot for non-recurring uses,' the man had said. 'Robots are only good for recurring tasks.'

Janos glanced below him but could not see as far as the

next pylon, two hundred and fifty steps down the stairway. 'Is it time for lunch yet?' he said to Wakefield on his commpak.

'Could be,' was the response. 'But we're way behind. We didn't send Yamanaka and Turgenyev over to Gamma stairway until 10:30. At the rate we're going, we'll be lucky to finish these lightweight lifts and the crude campsite today. We'll have to postpone the heavy load elevator and the rovers until tomorrow.'

'Hiro and I are already eating,' they both heard Irina say from the other side of the bowl. 'We were hungry. We finished the chair rack and the upper motor in half an hour. We're down to Pylon #12.'

'Good work,' Wakefield said. 'But I'll warn you that you're in the easy part, around the ladders and the top of the stairway. Working weightless is a snap. Wait until the gravity is measurably different at each location.'

'According to the laser range finder, Cosmonaut Wakefield is exactly 8.13 kilometres away from me,' everyone heard Dr Takagishi interject.

'That doesn't tell me anything, professor, unless I know where the hell you are.'

'I'm standing on the ledge just outside our relay station, near the bottom of the Alpha stairway.'

'Come on, Shig, won't you Orientals ever go along with the rest of the world? The Newton is parked on the *top* of Rama and you are at the *top* of the stairway. If we can't agree on up and down, how can we ever hope to communicate our innermost feelings? Much less play chess together.'

'Thank you, Janos. I am at the *top* of the Alpha stairway. By the way, what are you doing? Your range is increasing rapidly.'

'I'm sliding down the bannisters to meet Richard for lunch. I don't like eating fish and chips by myself.'

'I'm also coming down for lunch,' Francesca said. 'I just finished filming an excellent demonstration of the Coriolis force using Hiro and Irina. It will be great for elementary physics classes. I should be there in five minutes.'

'Say, signora –' it was Wakefield again – 'do you think we could talk you into some honest-to-goodness work. We stop what we're doing to accommodate your filming – maybe we can make a trade with you.'

'I'm willing,' answered Francesca. 'I'll help after lunch. But what I would like now is some light. Could you use one of your flares and let me capture you and Janos having a picnic on the Stairway of the Gods?'

Wakefield programmed a flare for a delayed ignition and climbed eighty steps to the nearest ledge. Cosmonaut Tabori arrived at the same spot half a minute before the light flooded them. From two kilometres above, Francesca panned across the three stairways and then zoomed in on the two figures sitting cross-legged on the ledge. From that perspective, Janos and Richard looked like two eagles nesting in a high mountain eyrie.

By late afternoon the Alpha chairlift was finished and ready for testing. 'We'll let you be the first customer,' Richard Wakefield said to Francesca, 'since you were good enough to help.' They were standing in full gravity at the foot of the incredible stairway. Thirty thousand steps stretched into the darkness of the artificial heavens above them. Beside them on the Central Plain the ultralight motor and the self-contained portable power station for the chairlift were already in operation. The cosmonauts had transported the electrical and mechanical subsystems in unassembled pieces on their backs and assembly had required less than an hour.

'The little chairs are not permanently connected to the cables,' Wakefield explained to Francesca. 'At each end there is a mechanism that attaches or detaches the chairs. That way it's not necessary to have an almost infinite number of seats.'

Francesca hesitantly sat down in the plastic structure that had been pulled away from a group of similar baskets hanging from a side cable. 'You're certain this is safe?' she said, staring at the darkness above her.

'Of course,' laughed Richard. 'It's exactly like the simulation. And I'll be in the next chair behind you, only

one minute or four hundred metres below. Altogether
the ride takes forty minutes from bottom to top. Average
speed is twenty-four kilometres per hour.'

'And I don't do anything,' Francesca remembered,
'except sit tight, hold on, and activate my breathing
system about twenty minutes from the summit.'

'Don't forget to fasten your seat belt,' Wakefield
reminded her with a smile. 'If the cable were to slow
down or stop near the top, where you are weightless,
your momentum could cause you to sail out into the
Raman void.' He grinned. 'But since the entire chairlift
runs beside the stairway, in the event of any emergency,
you could always climb out of your basket and walk back
up to the hub along the stairs.'

Richard nodded and Janos Tabori switched on the
motor. Francesca was lifted off the ground and soon
disappeared above them. 'I'll go right over to Gamma
after I'm certain you're on your way,' Richard said to
Janos. 'The second system should be easier. With all of
us working together, we should be finished by 19:00 at
the latest.'

'I'll have the campsite ready by the time you reach the
summit,' Janos remarked. 'Do you think we're still going
to stay down here tonight?'

'That doesn't make much sense,' David Brown said
from above. He or Takagishi had monitored all
cosmonaut communications throughout the day. 'The
rovers aren't ready yet. We had hoped to do some
exploring tomorrow.'

'If we each bring down a few subsystems,' Wakefield
replied, 'Janos and I could assemble one rover tonight
before we go to sleep. The second rover will probably be
operational before noon tomorrow if we don't encounter
any difficulties.'

'That's a possible scenario,' Dr Brown responded.
'Let's see how much progress we have made and how
tired everyone is three hours from now.'

Richard climbed into his tiny chair and waited for the
automatic loading algorithm in the processor to attach his
seat to the cable. 'By the way,' he said as he started his

ascent, 'thanks a lot for your good humour today. I might not have made it without the jokes.'

Janos smiled and waved at his friend. Looking upward from his moving chair, Richard Wakefield could barely make out the light from Francesca's headgear. *She's more than a hundred floors above me*, he thought. *But only two and a half percent of the distance from here to the hub. This place is immense.*

He reached in his pocket and pulled out the portable meteorological station that Takagishi had asked him to carry. The professor wanted a careful profile of all the atmospheric parameters in the North Polar bowl of Rama. Of particular importance for his circulation models were the density and temperature of the air versus the distance below the airlock.

Wakefield watched the pressure readings, which started at 1.05 bars, fall below Earth levels and continue their steady, monotonic decline. The temperature held fixed at a cold −8 degrees Celsius. He leaned back and closed his eyes. It was a strange feeling, riding a basket upward, ever upward in the dark. Richard turned down the volume of one channel on his commpak; the only ongoing conversation was between Yamanaka and Turgenyev and neither of them ever had very much to say. He increased the volume on Beethoven's Sixth Symphony, which was playing in the background on another channel.

As he listened to the music, Richard was surprised at how his interior visions of brooks and flowers and green fields on Earth evoked a powerful feeling of homesickness. It was almost impossible for him to fathom the miraculous concatenation of events that had carried him from his boyhood home in Stratford to Cambridge to the Space Academy in Colorado and finally here, to Rama, where he was riding a chairlift in the dark along the Stairway of the Gods.

No, Prospero, he said to himself, *no magician could ever have conceived of such a place*. He remembered seeing *The Tempest* for the first time as a boy and being frightened by the portrayal of a world whose mysteries might be beyond our comprehension. *There is no magic*, he had said at the time. *There are only natural concepts that we cannot yet explain.* Richard smiled. *Prospero was not a mage; he was only a frustrated scientist.*

A moment later Richard Wakefield was stupefied by the most amazing sight he had ever seen. As his chair was sailing soundlessly upward, parallel to the stairway, dawn burst upon Rama. Three kilometres below him, cut into the Central Plain, the long straight valleys that ran from the edge of the bowl to the Cylindrical Sea suddenly exploded with light. The six linear suns of Rama, three in each hemicylinder, were carefully designed to produce a balanced illumination throughout the alien world. Wakefield's first feelings were of vertigo and nausea. He was suspended in air by a thin cable, thousands of metres above the ground. He closed his eyes and tried to maintain his bearings. *You will not fall*, he said to himself.

'Aieee,' he heard Hiro Yamanaka yell.

From the ensuing conversation he could tell that Hiro, startled by the burst of light, had lost his footing near the middle of the Gamma stairway. He had apparently fallen twenty or thirty metres before he had adroitly (and luckily) managed to grab part of the bannisters.

'Are you all right?' David Brown asked.

'I think so,' Yamanaka answered breathlessly.

With the short crisis over, everyone started talking at once. 'This is fantastic!' Dr Takagishi was shouting. 'The light levels are phenomenal. And this is all happening *before* the thawing of the sea. It's different. It's altogether different.'

'Have another module ready for me as soon as I reach the top,' Francesca said. 'I'm almost out of film.'

'Such beauty. Such indescribable beauty,' General O'Toole added. He and Nicole des Jardins were watching the monitor on board the Newton. The realtime picture from Francesca's camera was being transmitted to them through the relay station at the hub.

Richard Wakefield said nothing. He simply stared, entranced by the world below him. He could barely discern Janos Tabori, the chairlift apparatus, and the half-completed campsite down at the bottom of the stairway. Nevertheless the distance to them gave him some measure of this alien world. As he looked out across the hundreds of square kilometres of the Central Plain, he saw fascinating shapes in every direction. There were two features, however, that overwhelmed his imagination and vision: the Cylindrical Sea and the massive, pointed structures in the southern bowl opposite him, fifty kilometres away.

As his eyes grew more accustomed to the light, the gigantic central spire in the southern bowl seemed to grow larger and larger. It had been called Big Horn by the first explorers. *Can it really be eight kilometres tall?* Wakefield asked himself. The six smaller spires, surrounding the Big Horn in a hexagonal pattern and connected both to it and to the walls of Rama by enormous flying buttresses, were each larger than anything made by man on Earth. Yet they were dwarfed by this neighbouring prominence originating from the very centre of the bowl and growing straight along the spin axis of the cylinder.

In the foreground, halfway between Wakefield's position near the north pole and that mammoth construction in the south, a band of bluish white ringed the cylindrical world. The frozen sea seemed illogical and out of place. It could never melt, the mind wanted to say, or all the water would fall toward the central axis. But the Cylindrical Sea was held in its banks by the centrifugal force of Rama. None knew better than the Newton crew that on its shore a human being would have the same weight as he would standing beside a terrestrial ocean.

The island city in the middle of the Cylindrical Sea was Rama's New York. To Richard its skyscrapers had not been too imposing in the views that had been offered by the light from the flares. But under the light of the Raman suns, it was clear that this city held centre stage. The eyes were drawn to New York from any point inside Rama – the dense oval island of buildings was the only break in the orderly annulus that formed the Cylindrical Sea.

'Just look at New York!' Dr Takagishi was gushing

excitedly into his commpak. 'There must be almost a thousand buildings over two hundred metres tall.' He paused only a second. 'That's where *they* live. I know it. New York must be our target.'

After the initial outbursts there was a protracted silence while each of the cosmonauts privately integrated the sunlit world of Rama into his own consciousness. Richard could now clearly see Francesca, four hundred metres above him, as his chair crossed the transition between the stairways and the ladders and closed in on the hub.

'Admiral Heilmann and I have just had a quick conversation,' David Brown broke the silence, 'with some advice from Dr Takagishi. There seems to be no obvious reason to change our plans for this sortie, at least not the early part. Unless something else unexpected occurs, we will go forward with Wakefield's suggestion. We will finish the two chairlifts, carry the rover down for assembly later this evening, and all sleep in the campsite at the foot of the stairway as planned.'

'Don't forget me,' Janos shouted into his commpak. 'I'm the only one who doesn't have much of a view.'

Richard Wakefield unfastened his seat belt and stepped out on to the ledge. He looked down to where the stairway disappeared from view. 'Roger, Cosmonaut Tabori. We have arrived back at Station Alpha. Whenever you give the signal, we will hoist you up to join us.'

23
Nightfall

'... Considering the regular abuse that he received from his neurotic father and the emotional scars that must remain from his youthful marriage to British actress Sarah Tydings, Cosmonaut Wakefield is remarkably well-adjusted. He underwent two years of professional therapy after his celebrated divorce, concluding a year before he entered the Space Academy in 2192. His scholastic record at the Academy is still unequalled to this day; his professors in electrical engineering and computer sciences all insist that by the time of his graduation, Wakefield knew more than any member of the faculty....

'... Except for a wariness where intimacy is concerned (particularly with women – he has apparently had no sustained emotional involvements since the breakup of his marriage), Wakefield exhibits none of the antisocial behaviour usually found in abused children. Although his SC was low as a youth, he has grown less arrogant as he has matured and is now less likely to force his brilliance upon others. His honesty and character are unassailable. Knowledge, not power or money, seems to be his goal....'

Nicole finished reading the Psychological Assessment for Richard Wakefield and rubbed her eyes. It was very late. She had been studying the dossiers ever since the crew inside Rama had settled down to sleep. They would be awakening for their second day in that strange world in less than two hours. Her six-hour shift as communications officer would start in another thirty minutes. *So out of this entire bunch*, Nicole was thinking, *there are only three who are beyond question. Those four with their illegal media contract have already compromised themselves. Yamanaka and Turgenyev are unknowns. Wilson is marginally stable and has his own agenda anyway. That leaves O'Toole, Takagishi, and Wakefield.*

Nicole washed her face and hands and sat down again at the terminal. She exited from the Wakefield dossier and returned to the main menu of the data cube. She scanned the comparative statistics available and keyed a pair of displays to appear side by side on the screen. On the left hand side was the ordered set of IE scores for each member of the crew; opposite, for comparison, Nicole had displayed the SC indices for the Newton dozen.

IE		SC	
Wakefield	+ 5.58	O'Toole	86
Sabatini	+ 4.22	Borzov	84
Brown	+ 4.17	Takagishi	82
Takagishi	+ 4.02	Wilson	78
Tabori	+ 3.37	des Jardins	71
Borzov	+ 3.28	Heilmann	68
des Jardins	+ 3.04	Tabori	64
O'Toole	+ 2.92	Yamanaka	62
Turgenyev	+ 2.87	Turgenyev	60
Yamanaka	+ 2.66	Wakefield	58
Wilson	+ 2.48	Sabatini	56
Heilmann	+ 2.24	Brown	49

Although Nicole had glanced very quickly through most of the information in the dossiers earlier, she had not read all the charts on all the crew members. Some of the indices she now saw for the first time. She was particularly surprised by the very high intelligence rating for Francesca Sabatini. *What a waste*, Nicole thought immediately. *All that potential being used for such ordinary pursuits.*

The overall intelligence level of the crew was quite

impressive. Every cosmonaut was in the top one percent of the population. Nicole was 'one in a thousand' and she was only in the middle of the dozen. Wakefield's intelligence rating was truly exceptional and placed him in the 'super-genius' category; Nicole had never before personally known someone with such high scores on the standardised tests.

Although her training in psychiatry had taught her to distrust attempts to quantify personality traits, Nicole was intrigued by the SC indices as well. She herself would intuitively have placed O'Toole, Borzov, and Takagishi at the top of the list. All three men seemed confident, balanced, and sensitive to others. But she was astonished by Wilson's high socialisation coefficient. *He must have been an altogether different person before he became involved with Francesca.* Nicole wondered for a brief moment why her own SC index was no higher than a 71; then she remembered that as a young woman she had been more withdrawn and self-centred.

So what about Wakefield? she asked herself, realising that he was the only viable candidate to help her understand what had happened inside the RoSur software during Borzov's operation. Could she trust him? And could she enlist Richard's help without revealing some of her farfetched suspicions? Again the thought of abandoning her investigation altogether seemed very appealing. *Nicole*, she said to herself. *If this conspiracy idea of yours turns out to be a waste of time....*

But Nicole was convinced that there were enough unanswered questions to warrant continuing her investigation. She resolved to talk to Wakefield. After determining that she could add her own files to the king's data cube, she created a new file, a nineteenth file, simply called NICOLE. She called in her word processing subroutine and wrote a brief memorandum:

3-3-00 – Have determined for certain that RoSur malfunction during Borzov procedure due to external manual command after initial load and verification. Enlisting Wakefield for support.

Nicole pulled a blank data cube from the supply drawer adjacent to her computer. She copied on to it both her memorandum and all the information stored on the cube that she had been given by King Henry. When she dressed for her work shift in her flight suit, she put the duplicate cube in her pocket.

General O'Toole was dozing in the Command and Control Complex of the military spacecraft when Nicole arrived to give him a break. Although the visual displays in the smaller vehicle were not quite as breathtaking as those in the scientific ship, the layout of the military CCC as a communications centre was far superior, especially from a human engineering point of view. All the controls could easily be handled by a single cosmonaut.

O'Toole apologised for not being awake. He pointed to the three monitors that showed three different views of the same scene – the remainder of the crew fast asleep inside the crude campsite at the foot of Alpha stairway. 'This last five hours has not been what you would call exciting,' he said.

Nicole smiled. 'General, you don't need to apologise to me. I know you've been on duty for almost twenty-four hours.'

General O'Toole stood up. 'After you left,' he summarised, checking his electronic log on one of the six monitors in front of him, 'they finished dinner and then they started the assembly of the first rover. The automatic navigation program failed its self-test, but Wakefield found the problem – a software bug in one of the subroutines that was changed in the last delivery – and fixed it. Tabori took the rover for a test drive before the crew prepared for sleep. At the end of the day Francesca did a stirring short piece for transmission to the Earth.' He paused for a moment. 'Would you like to see it?'

Nicole nodded. O'Toole activated the far right television monitor and Francesca appeared in a closeup outside the enclosed campsite. The frame showed a portion of the bottom of the stairway and the equipment for the chairlift as well. 'It is time to sleep in Rama,' she intoned. She looked up and around her. 'The lights in this amazing world came on unexpectedly about nine hours ago, showing us in more detail the elaborate handiwork of our intelligent cousins from across the stars.' A montage of still photographs and short videos, some taken by the drones and some taken by Francesca herself on that day, punctuated her tour of the artificial 'worldlet' that the crew was 'about to explore'. At the end of the brief segment the camera was fixed on Francesca.

'Nobody knows why this second spacecraft in less than a century has invaded our little domain at the edge of the galaxy. Perhaps this magnificent creation has no explanation that would be even remotely comprehensible to us human beings. But perhaps somewhere in this vast and precise world of metal we will find some keys that will unlock the mysteries enshrouding the creatures who constructed this vehicle.' She smiled and her nostrils flared dramatically. 'And if we do, then perhaps we will have moved one step closer to an understanding of ourselves ... and maybe our Gods as well.'

Nicole could tell that General O'Toole was moved by Francesca's oratory. Despite her personal antipathy for the woman, Nicole grudgingly acknowledged again that Francesca was talented. 'She captures my feelings about this venture so well,' O'Toole enthused. 'I just wish I could be that articulate.'

Nicole sat down at the console and entered the handover code. She followed the listed procedure on the monitor and checked out all the equipment. 'All right, General,' she said as she turned around in her chair, 'I believe I can handle it from here.'

O'Toole lingered behind her. It was obvious that he wanted to talk. 'I had a long discussion with Signora Sabatini three nights ago,' he said. 'About religion. She told me that she had become an agnostic before finally coming back to the church. She told me that thinking about Rama had made her a Catholic again.'

There was a long silence. For some reason, the fifteenth-century church in the old village of Sainte

Etienne de Chigny, eight hundred metres down the road from Beauvois, came into Nicole's mind. She remembered standing inside the church with her father on a beautiful spring day and being fascinated by the light scattering through the stained glass windows.

'Did God make the colours?' Nicole had asked her father.

'Some say so,' he had answered laconically.

'And what do you think, Papa?' she had then asked.

'I must admit,' General O'Toole was saying as Nicole forced herself to return to the present, 'that this entire voyage has been spiritually uplifting for me. I feel closer to God now than I have ever felt before. There's something about contemplating the vastness of the universe that humbles you and makes you....' He stopped himself. 'I'm sorry,' he started to apologise, 'I have imposed....'

'No,' Nicole answered. 'No, you haven't. I find your religious certitude very refreshing.'

'Nevertheless, I hope I haven't offended you in any way. Religion is a very private matter.' He smiled. 'But sometimes it's hard not to share your feelings, particularly since both you and Signora Sabatini are Catholics as well.'

As O'Toole left the control complex, Nicole wished him a sound sleep during his nap. When he had gone, she removed the duplicate data cube from her pocket and placed it in the CCC cube reader. *At least this way*, she said to herself, *I have backed up my information sources*. Into her mind came a picture of Francesca Sabatini listening intently while General O'Toole waxed philosophical about the religious significance of Rama. *You're an amazing woman*, Nicole thought. *You do whatever it takes. Even immorality and hypocrisy are acceptable.*

Dr Shigeru Takagishi stared in rapt silence at the towers and spheres of New York four kilometres away. From time to time he would walk over to the telescope that he had temporarily set up on the cliff overlooking the Cylindrical Sea and study a particular feature in that alien landscape.

'You know,' he said at length to Cosmonauts Wakefield

and Sabatini, 'I don't believe the reports the first crew gave on New York are entirely accurate. Or else this is a different spaceship.' Neither Richard nor Francesca responded. Wakefield was engrossed in the last stages of assembly of the icemobile and Francesca, as usual, was busy video-recording Wakefield's efforts.

'It looks as if there are certainly three identical parts to the city,' Dr Takagishi continued, talking primarily to himself, 'and three subdivisions within each of those parts. But all nine sections are not *absolutely* the same. There appear to be subtle differences.'

'There,' said Richard Wakefield, standing up with a satisfied smile. 'That ought to do it. A full day ahead of schedule. I'll just quickly test all the important engineering functions.'

Francesca glanced at her watch. 'We're almost half an hour behind the revised timeline. Are we still going to take a fast look at New York before dinner?'

Wakefield shrugged his shoulders and looked at Takagishi. Francesca walked over to the Japanese scientist. 'What do you say, Shigeru? Shall we take a quick run across the ice and give the people on Earth a closeup view of the Rama version of New York?'

'By all means,' Takagishi answered. 'I can't wait....'

'Only if you will be back at camp by 19:30 at the latest,' David Brown interrupted. He was in the helicopter with Admiral Heilmann and Reggie Wilson. 'We need to do some serious planning tonight. We may want to revise the deployments for tomorrow.'

'Roger,' said Wakefield. 'If we forget about the pulley system for now and have no problem carrying the icemobile down the stairs, we should be able to cross the sea in ten minutes each way. That would get us back to camp in plenty of time.'

'We've overflown many of the features of the Northern Hemicylinder this afternoon,' Brown said. 'No biots anywhere. The cities look like duplicates of each other. There were no surprises anywhere in the Central Plain. I personally think that maybe we should attack the mysterious south tomorrow.'

'New York,' Takagishi shouted. 'A detailed recon-
naissance of New York should be our goal for tomorrow.'
Brown didn't answer. Takagishi walked out to the edge
of the cliff and stared down at the ice fifty metres below.
To his left the unimposing narrow stairway cut in the
cliff descended in short steps. 'How heavy is the
icemobile?' Takagishi asked.

'Not very,' Wakefield answered. 'But it's bulky. Are
you certain you don't want to wait for me to install the
pulleys? We can always go across tomorrow.'

'I can help carry it,' Francesca interjected. 'If we don't
at least see New York, we will not be able to make
educated inputs at the planning meeting tonight.'

'All right,' Richard replied, shaking his head in
amusement at Francesca. 'Anything for journalism. I'll
go first, so that most of the lifting is on my back.
Francesca, get in the middle. Dr Takagishi at the top.
Watch out for the runners. They are sharp on the edges.'

The climb down to the surface of the Cylindrical Sea
was uneventful. 'Goodness,' Francesca Sabatini said as
they prepared to cross the ice, 'that was easy. Why is a
pulley system needed at all?'

'Because sometimes we may be carrying something
else or, perish the thought, we may need to defend
ourselves during ascent or descent.'

Wakefield and Takagishi sat in the front of the
icemobile. Francesca was in the back with her video
camera. Takagishi became more and more animated as
they drew closer to New York. 'Just look at that place,' he
said when the icemobile was about five hundred metres
from the opposite shore. 'Can there be any doubt that
this is the capital of Rama?'

As the trio approached the shore, the breathtaking
sight of the strange city spread out before their eyes
inhibited all conversation. Everything about its complicated structure spoke of order and purposeful creation by
intelligent beings; yet the first set of cosmonauts, seventy
years earlier, had found it as empty of life as the rest of
Rama. Was this vast complex broken into nine sections
indeed an enormously complicated machine, as the first

visitors had suggested, or was the long thin island (ten kilometres by three) actually a city whose denizens had long ago disappeared?

They parked the icemobile on the edge of the frozen sea and walked along a path until they found a stairway leading to the ramparts of the wall surrounding the city. The excited Takagishi loped along about twenty metres in front of Wakefield and Sabatini. As they ascended, more and more of the details of the city became apparent.

Richard was immediately intrigued by the geometrical shapes of the buildings. In addition to the normal tall, thin skyscrapers, there were scattered spheres, rectangular solids, even an occasional polyhedron. And they were definitely arranged in some kind of a pattern. *Yes*, he thought to himself as his eyes scanned the fascinating complex of structures, *over there is a dodecahedron, there a pentahedron....*

His mathematical ruminations were interrupted when all the lights were suddenly extinguished and the entire interior of Rama was plunged into darkness.

24

Sounds in the Darkness

At first Takagishi could see absolutely nothing. It was as if he had suddenly been struck blind. He blinked twice and stood motionless in the total darkness. The momentary silence on the commlinks erupted into hopeless noise as all the cosmonauts began to talk at the same time. Calmly, fighting against his growing fear, Takagishi tried to remember the scene that had been in front of his eyes at the moment that the lights were extinguished.

He had been standing on the wall overlooking New York, about a metre from the dangerous edge. In the final second he had been looking off to the left and had just glimpsed a staircase descending into the city about two hundred metres away. Then the scene had vanished....

'Takagishi,' he heard Wakefield calling his name, 'are you all right?'

He turned around to acknowledge the question and noticed that his knees had become weak. In the complete darkness he had lost his orientation. How many degrees had he turned? Had he been facing the city directly? Again he recalled the last image. The elevated wall was twenty or thirty metres above the floor of the city. A fall would be fatal.

'I'm here,' he said tentatively. 'But I'm too close to the edge.' He dropped down on all fours. The metal was cold against his hands.

'We're coming,' Francesca said. 'I'm trying to find the light on my video camera.'

Takagishi turned down the volume on his commpak and listened for the sound of his companions. A few seconds later he saw a light in the distance. He could barely make out the forms of his two associates.

'Where are you, Shigeru?' Francesca asked. The light from her camera illuminated only the area immediately around her.

'Up here. Up here.' He waved before he realised that they could not see him.

'I want complete quiet,' David Brown shouted over the communications system, 'until everyone is accounted for.' The conversations ceased after a few seconds. 'Now,' he continued, 'Francesca, what's going on down there?'

'We're climbing the stairway up the wall, on the New York side, David, about a hundred metres from where we parked the icemobile. Dr Takagishi was ahead of us, already at the top. We have the light from my camera. We're going to meet him.'

'Janos,' Dr Brown said next, 'where are you in rover #2?'

'About three kilometres from camp. The headlights are working fine. We could return in ten minutes or so.'

'Go back there and man the navigation console. We'll stay airborne until you verify that the homing system is operational from your side ... Francesca, be careful, but come back to camp as fast as you can. And give us a report every two minutes or so.'

'Roger, David,' she said. Francesca switched off her commpak and called for Takagishi again. Despite the fact that he was only thirty metres away, it took Francesca and Richard over a minute to find him in the dark.

Takagishi was relieved to touch his colleagues. They sat down beside him on the wall and listened to the renewed chatter on the commpak. O'Toole and des Jardins verified that there had been no other observed changes inside Rama at the time the lights had gone out. The half-dozen portable scientific stations that had already been deployed in the alien spaceship had exhibited no meaningful perturbations. Temperatures, wind velocities and directions, seismic readings, and near field spectroscopic measurements were all unchanged.

'So the lights went out,' Wakefield said. 'I admit that it was scary, but it was no big deal. Probably –'

'Shh,' said Takagishi abruptly. He reached down and turned off both his and Wakefield's commpak. 'Do you hear that noise?'

To Wakefield the sudden silence was nearly as unnerving as the total darkness had been a few minutes before. 'No,' he said in a whisper, after listening for several seconds, 'but my ears are not very –'

'Shh.' Now it was Francesca's turn. 'Are you talking about that distant, high-pitched, scraping sound?' she whispered.

'Yes,' said Takagishi, quietly but excitedly. 'Like something is brushing against a metallic surface. It suggests movement.'

Wakefield listened again. Maybe he could hear something. Maybe he was imagining it. 'Come on,' he said to the others, 'let's go back to the icemobile.'

'Wait,' said Takagishi as Richard stood up. 'It seemed to stop just as you spoke.' He leaned over to Francesca. 'Turn off the light,' he said softly. 'Let's sit here in the darkness and see if we can hear it again.'

Wakefield sat back down beside his companions. With the camera light off it was absolutely black around them. The only sound was their breathing. They waited a full minute. They heard nothing. Just as Wakefield was about to insist that they leave, he heard a sound from the direction of New York. It was like hard brushes dragging across metal, but there was also an embedded high frequency noise, as if a tiny voice were singing very fast, that punctuated the nearly constant scraping. The sound was definitely louder. And eerie. Wakefield felt his spine tingle.

'Do you have a tape recorder?' Takagishi whispered to Francesca. The scraping stopped at the sound of Takagishi's voice. The trio waited another fifteen seconds.

'Hey there, hey there,' they heard David Brown's loud voice on the emergency interrupt channel. 'Is everybody all right? You're way overdue for a report.'

'Yes, David,' Francesca replied. 'We're still here. We heard an unusual sound coming from New York.'

'Now's not the time for dilly-dallying. We have a major crisis on our hands. All our new plans have assumed that Rama would be constantly lit. We need to regroup.'

'All right,' Wakefield responded. 'We're leaving the wall now. If all goes well we should be back to the campsite in less than an hour.'

Dr Shigeru Takagishi was reluctant to leave New York with the mystery of the strange sound unresolved. But he understood completely that now was not the appropriate time for a scientific foray into the city. As the icemobile raced across the frozen Cylindrical Sea, the Japanese scientist smiled to himself. He was happy. He knew that he had heard a new sound, something decidedly different from any of the sounds catalogued by the first Rama team. This was a good beginning.

Cosmonauts Tabori and Wakefield were the last two to ride up the chairlift beside the Alpha stairway. 'Takagishi was really quite irritated with Dr Brown, wasn't he?' Richard was saying to Janos as he helped the little Hungarian disembark from the chair. They glided along the ramp toward the ferry.

'I've never seen him so angry,' Janos replied. 'Shig is a consummate professional and he has great pride in his knowledge of Rama. For Brown to discount the noise you guys heard in such an offhand manner suggests an absence of respect for Takagishi. I don't blame Shig for being irritated.'

They climbed on board the ferry and activated the transportation module. The vast darkness of Rama retreated behind them as they eased through the lighted corridor toward the Newton.

'It was a very strange sound,' Richard said. 'It really gave me the chills. I have no idea if it was a new sound, or if maybe Norton and his team heard the same thing seventy years ago. But I do know that I had a bad case of the willies while I was standing there on the wall.'

'Even Francesca was pissed off with Brown at first. She wanted to do a feature interview with Shig for her nightly report. Brown talked her out of it, but I'm not certain he completely convinced her that strange noises are not news. Luckily she had enough of a story with just the lights going out.'

The two men descended from the ferry and approached the air lock. 'Whew,' said Janos. 'I'm bushed. It has been a couple of long and hectic days.'

'Yeah,' Richard agreed. 'We thought we would be spending the next two nights at the campsite. Instead we're back up here. I wonder what surprises are in store for us tomorrow.'

Janos smiled at his friend. 'You know what's funny about all this?' he said. He did not wait for Wakefield to answer. 'Brown really believes he's in charge of this mission. Did you see how he reacted when Takagishi suggested that we could explore New York in the dark? Brown probably thinks it was *his* decision for us to return to the Newton and abort the first sortie.'

Richard looked at Janos with a quizzical smile. 'It wasn't, of course,' Janos continued. 'Rama made the decision for us to leave. And Rama will decide what we do next.'

25

A Friend in Need

In his dream he was lying on a futon in a
seventeenth-century ryokan. The room was very large,
nine tatami mats in all. To his left, in the yard on the
other side of the open screen, was a perfect miniaturised
garden with tiny trees and a manicured stream. He was
waiting for a young woman.

'Takagishi-san, are you awake?'

He stirred and reached out for the communicator.
'Hello,' he said, his voice betraying his grogginess. 'Who
is it?'

'Nicole des Jardins,' the voice said. 'I'm sorry to call
you so early, but I need to see you. It's urgent.'

'Give me three minutes,' Takagishi said.

There was a knock on his door exactly three minutes
later. Nicole greeted him and entered the room. She was
carrying a data cube. 'Do you mind?' she said, pointing
to the computer console. Takagishi shook his head.

'Yesterday there were half a dozen separate incidents,'
Nicole said gravely, pointing at some blips on the
monitor, 'including the two largest aberrations I have
ever seen in your heart data.' She looked at him. 'Are you
certain that you and your doctor provided me with
complete historical records?'

Takagishi nodded.

'Then I have reason for concern,' she continued. 'The
irregularities yesterday suggest that your chronic
diastolic abnormality has worsened. Perhaps the valve
has sprung a new leak. Perhaps the long periods of

weightlessness –'

'Or perhaps,' Takagishi interrupted with a soft smile, 'I became overly excited and my extra adrenaline aggravated the problem.'

Nicole stared at the Japanese scientist. 'That's possible, Dr Takagishi. One of the major incidents occurred just after the lights went out. I guess it was when you were listening to your "strange sound".'

'And the other, by chance, could it have been during my argument with Dr Brown in the campsite? If so, that would support my hypothesis.'

Cosmonaut des Jardins touched several keys on the console and her software entered a new subroutine. She studied the data displayed on two sides of a split screen. 'Yes,' she said, 'it looks right. The second incident took place twenty minutes before we started leaving Rama. That would have been toward the end of the meeting.' She moved away from the monitor. 'But I can't dismiss the bizarre behaviour of your heart just because you were excited.'

They stared at each other for several long seconds. 'What are you trying to tell me, doctor?' Takagishi said softly. 'Are you going to confine me to my quarters on the Newton? Now, at the most significant moment in my professional career?'

'I'm considering it,' Nicole answered directly. 'Your health is more important to me than your career. I've already lost one member of the crew. I'm not certain that I could forgive myself if I lost another.'

She saw the entreaty in her colleague's face. 'I know how critical these sorties into Rama are to you. I'm trying to find some kind of rationalisation that will allow me to overlook yesterday's data.' Nicole sat down at the far end of the bed and looked away. 'But as a doctor, not a Newton cosmonaut, it's very very tough.'

She heard Takagishi approach and felt his hand gently on her shoulder. 'I know how difficult it has been for you these last few days,' he said. 'But it was not your fault. All of us are aware that General Borzov's death was unavoidable.'

Nicole recognised the respect and friendship in Takagishi's gaze. She thanked him with her eyes. 'I very much appreciate what you did for me before launch,' he continued. 'If you feel compelled to limit my activities now, I will not object.'

'Damnit,' said Nicole, standing up quickly, 'it's not that simple. I've been studying your overnight data for almost an hour. Look at this. Your chart for the last ten hours is perfectly normal. There's not a trace of any anomaly. And you had had no incidents for weeks. Until yesterday. What is it with you, Shig? Do you have a bad heart? Or just a weird one?'

Takagishi smiled. 'My wife told me once that I had a strange heart. But I think she was referring to something altogether different.'

Nicole activated her scanner and displayed the data on the monitor in realtime. 'There we are again.' She shook her head. 'The signature of a perfectly healthy heart. No cardiologist in the world would argue with my conclusion.' She moved toward the door.

'So what's the verdict, doc?' Takagishi asked.

'I haven't decided,' she answered. 'You could help. Have another one of your incidents in the next few hours and make it easy for me.' She waved goodbye. 'See you at breakfast.'

Richard Wakefield was coming out of his room as Nicole headed down the hall after leaving Takagishi. She made a spontaneous decision to talk to him about the RoSur software.

'Good morning, princess,' he said as he approached. 'What are you doing awake at this hour? Something exciting, I hope.'

'As a matter of fact,' Nicole replied in the same playful tone, 'I was coming to talk to you.' He stopped to listen. 'Do you have a minute?'

'For you, Madame Doctor,' he answered with an exaggerated smile, 'I have *two* minutes. But no more. Mind you, I'm hungry. And if I am not fed quickly when I'm hungry, I turn into an awful ogre.' Nicole laughed.

'What's on your mind?' he added lightly.

'Could we go into your room?' she asked.

'I knew it. I knew it,' he said, spinning around and sliding quickly toward his door. 'It's finally happened, just like in my dreams. An intelligent, beautiful woman is going to declare her undying affection....'

Nicole could not suppress a chortle. 'Wakefield,' she interrupted, still grinning, 'you are hopeless. Are you never serious? I have some business to discuss with you.'

'Oh, darn,' Richard said dramatically. 'Business. In that case I'm going to limit you to the two minutes I allocated you earlier. Business also makes me hungry ... and grumpy.'

Richard Wakefield opened the door to his room and waited for Nicole to enter. He offered her the chair in front of his computer monitor and sat down behind her on the bed. She turned around to face him. On the shelf above his bed were a dozen tiny figurines similar to the ones she had seen before in Tabori's room and at the Borzov banquet.

'Allow me to introduce you to some of my menagerie,' Richard said, noticing her curiosity. 'You've met Lord and Lady Macbeth, Puck, and Bottom. This matched pair is Tybalt and Mercutio from *Romeo and Juliet*. Next to them are Iago and Othello, followed by Prince Hal, Falstaff, and the wonderful Mistress Quickly. The last one on the right is my closest friend, the Bard, or TB for short.'

As Nicole watched, Richard activated a switch near the head of his bed and TB climbed down a ladder from the shelf to the bed. The twenty-centimetre-high robot carefully navigated the folds in the bed coverings and came over to greet Nicole.

'And what be your name, fair lady?' TB said.

'I am Nicole des Jardins,' she replied.

'Sounds French,' the robot said immediately. 'But you don't look French. At least not Valois.' The robot appeared to be staring at her. 'You look more like a child of Othello and Desdemona.'

Nicole was astonished. 'How did you do that?' she asked.

'I'll explain later,' Richard said with a wave of his hand. 'Do you have a favourite Shakespearean sonnet?' he now inquired. 'If you do, recite a line, or give TB a number.'

'Full many a glorious morning ...' recalled Nicole.

'...have I seen,' the robot added,

'Flatter the mountain tops with sovereign eye,
Kissing with golden face the meadows green,
Gilding pale streams with heavenly alchemy....'

The little robot recited the sonnet with fluid head and arm movements as well as a wide range of facial expressions. Again Nicole was impressed by Richard Wakefield's creativity. She remembered the key four lines of the sonnet from her university days and mumbled them along with TB,

'Even so my sun one early morn did shine,
With all-triumphant splendour on my brow;
But, out alack, he was but one hour mine,
The region cloud hath masked him from me now....'

After the robot finished the final couplet, Nicole, who was moved by the almost forgotten words, found herself applauding. 'And he can do all the sonnets?' she asked.

Richard nodded. 'Plus many, many of the more poetic dramatic speeches. But that's not his most outstanding capability. Remembering passages from Shakespeare only requires plenty of storage. TB is also a very intelligent robot. He can carry on a conversation better than....'

Richard stopped himself in mid-sentence. 'I'm sorry, Nicole. I'm not monopolising the time. You said you had some business to discuss.'

'But you've already used my two minutes,' she said with a twinkle in her eye. 'Are you certain that you won't die of starvation if I take five more minutes of your time?'

Nicole quickly summarised her investigation into the RoSur software malfunction, including her conclusion that the fault protection algorithms must have been disabled by manual commands. She indicated that she could go no further with her own analysis and that she would like some help from Richard. She did not discuss her suspicions.

'Should be a snap,' he said with a smile. 'All I have to do is find the place in memory where the commands are buffered and stored. That could take a little time, given the size of the storage, but these memories are generally designed with logical architectures. However, I don't understand why you're doing all this detective work. Why don't you simply ask Janos and the others if they input any commands?'

'That's the problem,' Nicole replied. 'Nobody recalls commanding RoSur at any time after the final load and verify. When Janos hit his head during the manoeuvre, I thought his fingers were on the control box. He doesn't remember and I can't be certain.'

Richard's brow furrowed. 'It would be very unlikely that Janos just happened to toggle the fault protection enable switch with a random command. That would mean the overall design was stupid.' He thought for a moment. 'Oh, well,' he continued, 'there's no need to speculate. Now you've aroused my curiosity. I'll look at the problem as soon as I have –'

'Break break. Break break.' They both heard Otto Heilmann's voice on the communicator. 'Will everyone come immediately to the science control centre for a meeting. We have a new development. The lights inside Rama just came on again.'

Richard opened the door and followed Nicole into the corridor. 'Thanks for your help,' Nicole said. 'I appreciate it very much.'

'Thank me after I do something,' Richard said with a grin. 'I'm notorious for promises ... Now what do you think is the meaning of all these games with the lights?'

26
Second Sortie

David Brown had placed a single large sheet of paper on the table in the middle of the control centre. Francesca had divided it into partitions, representing hours, and was now busy writing down whatever he told her. 'The damn mission planning software is too inflexible to be useful in a situation like this,' Dr Brown was saying to Janos Tabori and Richard Wakefield. 'It's only good when the sequence of activities being planned is consistent with one of the preflight strategies.'

Janos walked over to one of the monitors. 'Maybe you can use it better than I can,' Dr Brown continued, 'but I have found it much easier this morning to rely on pencil and paper.' Janos called up a software program for mission sequencing and began to key in some data.

'Wait a minute,' Richard Wakefield interjected. Janos stopped typing on the keyboard and turned to listen to his colleague. 'We're getting all worked up over nothing. We don't need to plan the entire next sortie at this moment. In any case, we know the first major job must be setting up our base. That will take another ten or twelve hours. The rest of the sortie design can be done in parallel.'

'Richard's right,' Francesca added. 'We're trying to do everything too fast. Let's send the space cadets into Rama to finish setting up. While they're gone we can work out the details of the sortie.'

'That's impractical,' Dr Brown replied. 'The academy graduates are the only ones who know how long each of the various engineering activities should take. We can't make meaningful timelines without them.'

'Then one of us will stay here with you,' Janos Tabori said. He grinned. 'And we can use Heilmann or O'Toole inside, as an extra worker. That shouldn't slow us down too much.'

A consensus decision was reached in half an hour. Nicole would stay on board the Newton again, at least until the infrastructure was completed, and represent the cadets in the mission planning process. Admiral Heilmann would go into Rama with the four other professional cosmonauts. They would finish the remaining three infrastructure tasks: the assembly of the rest of the vehicles, the deployment of another dozen portable monitoring stations in the Northern Hemicylinder, and the construction of the Beta campsite/communications complex on the north side of the Cylindrical Sea.

Richard Wakefield was in the process of reviewing all the detailed subtasks with his small team when Reggie Wilson, who had been virtually silent during the entire morning, suddenly jumped up from his chair. 'This is all bullshit,' he shouted. 'I can't believe all the nonsense I'm hearing.'

Richard stopped his review. Doctors Brown and Takagishi, who had already started discussing the sortie design, were suddenly silent. All eyes were focused on Reggie Wilson.

'A man died here four days ago,' he said, 'killed, most likely, by whoever or whatever is operating that gigantic spacecraft. But we went inside exploring anyway. Next the lights go on and off unexpectedly.' Wilson looked around the room at the rest of the crew. His eyes were wild. His forehead was sweating. 'And what do we all do? Huh? How do we respond to this warning from alien creatures far superior to us? We sit down calmly and plan the rest of our exploration of their vehicle. Don't any of you get it? They don't want us in there. They want us to *leave*, to go home to Earth.'

Wilson's outburst was greeted by an uncomfortable silence. At length General O'Toole walked over beside

Reggie Wilson. 'Reggie,' he said quietly, 'we were all upset by General Borzov's death. But none of the rest of us see any connection –'

'Then you're blind, man, you're blind. I was up in that goddamn helicopter when the lights went out. One minute it was bright as a summer day and the next, poof, it was pitch black. It was fucking weird, man. Somebody turned out *all* the lights. In this discussion never once have I heard anybody ask *why* the lights went out. What's the matter with you people? Are you too smart to be afraid?'

Wilson ranted for several minutes. His recurring theme was always the same. The Ramans had planned Borzov's death, they were sending a warning with the lights going on and off, there would be more disasters if the crew insisted on continuing with the exploration.

General O'Toole stood beside Reggie during the entire episode. Dr Brown, Francesca, and Nicole had a hurried discussion on the side and then Nicole approached Wilson. 'Reggie,' she said informally, interrupting his diatribe, 'why don't you and General O'Toole come with me? We can continue this conversation without delaying the rest of the crew.'

He looked at her suspiciously. 'You, doctor? Why should I come with you? You weren't even in there. You haven't seen enough to know anything.' Wilson moved over in front of Wakefield. 'You were there, Richard,' he said. 'You saw that place. You know what kind of intelligence and power it would take to make a space vehicle that large and then launch it on a trip between the stars. Hey, man, we're *nothing* to them. We're less than ants. We haven't got a chance.'

'I agree with you, Reggie,' Richard Wakefield said calmly after a moment's hesitation. 'At least where our comparative capabilities are concerned. But we have no evidence they're hostile. Or even care about whether or not we explore their craft. On the contrary, the very fact that we are alive –'

'*Look*,' shouted Irina Turgenyev suddenly. 'Look at the monitor.'

A solitary image was frozen on the giant screen in the control centre A crablike creature filled the entire frame. It had a low, flat body, about twice as long as it was wide. Its weight was supported on six triple-jointed legs. Two scissor-like claws extended in front of the body and a whole row of manipulators, which looked uncannily like tiny human hands at first glance, nestled close to some kind of opening in the carapace. On closer inspection the manipulators were a veritable hardware store of capabilities – there were pincers, probes, rasps, and even something that resembled a drill.

Its eyes, if that was what they were, were deeply recessed in protective hoods and raised like periscopes above the top of the shell. The eyeballs themselves were crystal or jelly, vivid blue in colour, and utterly expressionless.

From the legend on the side of the image it was clear that the photograph had been taken just moments before, by one of the long range drones, at a spot roughly five kilometres south of the Cylindrical Sea. The frame, filmed with a telescopic lens, covered an area roughly six metres square.

'So we have company in Rama,' said Janos Tabori. The rest of the cosmonauts stared at the monitor in amazement.

All the crew later agreed that the image of the crab biot on the giant screen would not have been so frightening if it had not occurred at that precise moment. Although Reggie's behaviour was definitely aberrant, there was enough sense in what he was saying to remind each of them of the dangers in their expedition. None of the crew was completely free from fear. All of them had, in some private moment, confronted the disquieting fact that the super-advanced Ramans might not be friendly.

But most of the time they pushed aside their fears. It was part of their job. Like the early space shuttle astronauts in America, who knew that every so often the vehicle would crash or explode, the Newton cosmonauts accepted that there were uncontrollable risks associated with their mission. Healthy denial caused the group to avoid discussion of the unsettling issues, most of the time, and to focus on the more bounded (and therefore more controllable) items, such as the sequence of events for the following day.

Reggie's outburst and the simultaneous appearance of the crab biot on the monitor triggered one of the few serious group discussions that ever occurred on the project. O'Toole staked out his position early. Although he was fascinated by the Ramans, he did not fear them. God had seen fit to place him on this mission and, if He so chose, could decide that this extraordinary adventure would be O'Toole's last. In any case, whatever happened would be God's will.

Richard Wakefield articulated a point of view that was apparently shared by several of the other crew members. To him, the entire project was both a challenging voyage of discovery and a test of personal mettle. The uncertainties were there, to be sure, but they produced excitement as well as danger. The intense thrill of new learning, together with the possible monumental significance of this extraterrestrial encounter, more than compensated for the risks. Richard had no qualms about the mission. He was certain that this was the apotheosis of his life; if he didn't live beyond the end of the project, it would still have been worth it. He would have done something important during his brief existence on Earth.

Nicole listened attentively to the discussion. She didn't say much herself, but she found her own opinions crystallising as she followed the flow of the conversation. She enjoyed watching the responses, both verbal and nonverbal, from the other cosmonauts. Shigeru Takagishi was clearly in the Wakefield camp. He was vigorously nodding his head the entire time that Richard was talking about the excitement of participating in such a significant effort. Reggie Wilson, now subdued and probably embarrassed by his earlier tirade, did not say much. He commented only when asked a direct question. Admiral Heilmann looked uncomfortable from the beginning to the end. His entire contribution was to remind everyone of the passage of time.

Surprisingly, Dr David Brown did not add much to the philosophical discussion. He made several short comments, and once or twice seemed on the verge of launching into a long, amplifying explanation. But he never did. His true beliefs about the nature of Rama were not revealed.

Francesca Sabatini initially acted as a kind of moderator or interlocutor, asking questions of clarification and keeping the conversation on an even keel. Toward the end of the discussion, however, she offered several personal, candid comments of her own. Her philosophical view of the Newton mission was altogether different from that expressed by O'Toole and Wakefield.

'I think you're making this entire thing much too complex and intellectual,' she said after Richard had delivered a long panegyric on the joys of knowledge. 'There was no need for me to do any deep soul-searching before I applied to be a Newton cosmonaut. I approached the issue the same way I do all my major decisions. I did a risk/reward tradeoff. I judged that the rewards – considering all the factors, including fame, prestige, money, even adventure – more than warranted the risks. And I absolutely disagree with Richard in one respect. If I die on this mission I will not be at all happy. For me, most of the rewards from this project are delayed; I cannot benefit from them if I do not return to Earth.'

Francesca's comments aroused Nicole's curiosity. She wanted to ask the Italian journalist some more questions, but Nicole didn't think it was the proper time or place. After the meeting was over, she was still intrigued by what Francesca had said. *Can life really be that simple to her?* Nicole said to herself. *Can everything be evaluated in terms of risks and rewards?* She remembered Francesca's lack of emotion when she drank the abortion liquid. *But what about principles or values? Or even feelings?* As the meeting broke up Nicole admitted to herself that Francesca was still very much a puzzle.

Nicole watched Dr Takagishi carefully. He was handling himself much better today. 'I have brought a printout of the Sortie Strategy, Dr Brown,' he was saying, waving a four-inch-thick set of papers in his hand, 'to remind us of the fundamental tenets of sortie design that resulted from over a year of unhurried mission planning. May I read from the summary?'

'I don't think you need to do that,' David Brown responded. 'We're all familiar with –'

'I'm not,' interrupted General O'Toole. 'I would like to hear it. Admiral Heilmann asked me to pay close attention and brief him on the issues.'

Dr Brown waved for Takagishi to continue. The diminutive Japanese scientist was borrowing a page from Brown's own portfolio. Even though he knew that David Brown personally favoured going after the crab biots on the second sortie, Takagishi was still attempting to convince the other cosmonauts that the top priority activity should be a scientific foray into the city of New York.

Reggie Wilson had excused himself an hour earlier and had gone to his room for a nap. The remaining five crew members on board the Newton had spent most of the afternoon struggling, without success, to reach an agreement on the activities for the second sortie. Since the two scientists, Brown and Takagishi, had radically different opinions on what should be done, no consensus was possible. Meanwhile, behind them on the large monitor, there had been intermittent views of the space cadets and Admiral Heilmann working inside Rama. The current picture showed Tabori and Turgenyev at the campsite adjoining the Cylindrical Sea. They had just finished assembling the second motorboat and were checking its electrical subsystems.

'…The sequence of sorties has been carefully designed,' Takagishi was reading, 'to be consistent with the Mission Policies and Priorities Document, ISA-NT-0014. The primary goals of the first sortie are to establish the engineering infrastructure and to examine the interior on at least a superficial level. Of particular importance will be the identification of any characteristics of this second Rama spacecraft that are in any way different from the first.

'Sortie #2 is designed to complete the mapping of the inside of Rama, focusing particularly on regions unexplored seventy years ago, as well as the collections of buildings called cities and any interior differences identified on the first sortie. Encounters with biots will be *avoided* on the second sortie, although the presence and location of the various kinds of biots will be part of the mapping process.

'Interaction with the biots will be delayed until the third sortie. Only after careful and *prolonged* observation will any attempt be made –'

'That's enough, Dr Takagishi,' David Brown interrupted. 'We all have the gist of it. Unfortunately that sterile document was prepared months before launch. The situation we face now was never contemplated. We have the lights going on and off. And we have located and are tracking a herd of six crab biots just beyond the southern edge of the Cylindrical Sea.'

'I disagree,' said the Japanese scientist respectfully. 'You said yourself that the unpredicted lighting profile did not represent a fundamental difference between the two spacecraft. We are not facing an unknown Rama. I submit that we should implement the sorties in accordance with the original mission plan.'

'So you favour dedicating this entire second sortie to mapping, including or perhaps even featuring a detailed exploration of New York?'

'Exactly, General O'Toole. Even if one takes the position that the 'strange sound' heard by cosmonauts Wakefield, Sabatini, and myself does not constitute an official 'difference', the careful mapping of New York is clearly one of the highest priority activities. And it is vital that we accomplish it on this sortie. The temperature in the Central Plain has already risen to −5 degrees. Rama is carrying us closer and closer to the Sun. The spacecraft is heating from the outside in. I predict the Cylindrical Sea will begin to melt from the bottom in three or four more days –'

'I have never said that New York was not a legitimate target for exploration,' David Brown interrupted again,

'but I have maintained from the very beginning that the
biots are the true scientific treasure of this voyage. Look at
these amazing creations,' he said, filling the centre screen
with a film of the six crab biots moving slowly across a
bland region in the Southern Hemisphere. 'We may never
have another opportunity to capture one. The drones have
almost finished reconnoitring the whole hemicylinder and
no other biots have been spotted.'

The rest of the crew members, including Takagishi,
looked at the monitor with rapt attention. The bizarre
assemblage of aliens, arranged in a triangular formation
with a slightly larger specimen in the lead, approached a
jumbled mound of loose metal. The lead crab moved
directly into the obstacle, paused a few seconds, and then
used its claws to chop the elements of the mound into still
smaller pieces. The two crabs in the second row transferred the metal fragments on to the backs of the remaining
three members of the troop. This new material increased
the size of the small piles already on the tops of the shells of
the three crab biots in the back row.

'They must be the Raman garbage crew,' Francesca
said. Everyone laughed.

'But you can see why I want to move quickly, David
Brown continued. 'Right now the short film we just saw is
on its way to all the television networks on Earth. Over a
billion of our fellow men and women will watch it today
with the same mixture of fear and fascination that all of
you just felt. Imagine what kind of laboratories we will be
able to build to study such a creature. Imagine what we
will learn....'

'What makes you think you can capture one?' General
O'Toole asked. ' They look as if they could be quite
formidable.'

'We are certain that these creatures, although they
appear to be biological, are actually robots. Hence the
name "biots", which became popular during and after the
first Rama expedition. Based on all the reports from
Norton and the other Rama I cosmonauts, each of these
biots is designed to perform a singular function. They
have no intelligence as we know it. We should be able to

outsmart them ... and capture them.'

A camera closeup of the scissor-like claws appeared on the giant screen. They were obviously very sharp. 'I don't know,' said General O'Toole. I'd be inclined to follow Dr Takagishi's suggestion and observe them for quite a while before trying to catch one.'

'I disagree,' said Francesca. 'Speaking as a journalist, no story could be bigger than the attempted capture of one of those things. Everyone on Earth will watch. We may never have another chance like this.' She paused for a moment. 'The ISA has been pushing us for some upbeat news. The Borzov incident didn't exactly convince the taxpayers of the world that their space money is being wisely spent.'

'Why can't we do both tasks on the same sortie?' General O'Toole asked. 'One subteam could explore New York and the other would go after a crab.'

'No way,' replied Nicole. 'If the goal of this sortie is to seize a biot, then all of our resources should be applied in that direction. Remember, we are limited in both manpower and time.'

'Unfortunately,' David Brown now said with a wan smile, 'we can't make this decision by committee. Since we don't have complete agreement, I must make the choice ... Therefore, the purpose of the next sortie will be to capture a crab biot. I presume that Admiral Heilmann will agree with me. If he doesn't, we will submit the issue to a vote of the crew.'

The meeting broke up slowly. Dr Takagishi wanted to offer one more argument, to point out that the majority of the biot species seen by the first Rama explorers did not materialise until *after* the thawing of the Cylindrical Sea. But nobody wanted to listen any more. Everyone was tired.

Nicole approached Takagishi and clandestinely activated her biometry scanner. The warning file was empty. 'Clean as a whistle,' she said with a smile.

Takagishi looked at her very seriously. 'Our decision is a mistake,' he said sombrely. 'We should be going into New York.'

27
To Catch a Biot

'Be very careful,' Admiral Heilmann said to Francesca. 'It makes me nervous to see you leaning out like that.'

Signora Sabatini had hooked her ankles underneath the seats of the helicopter and was now stretching out beyond the plane of the door. She was holding a small video camera in her right hand. Three or four metres below her, apparently oblivious of the whirring machine overhead, the six crab biots plodded methodically along. They were still in their phalanx formation, arrayed like the first three rows of a set of bowling pins.

'Move out over the sea,' Francesca shouted to Hiro Yamanaka. 'They're coming to the edge and will be turning again.'

The helicopter veered sharply to the left and flew over the side of the five hundred metre cliff that separated the Southern half of Rama from the Cylindrical Sea. The bank here was ten times higher than its northern counterpart. David Brown gasped as he looked down at the frozen sea half a kilometre below him.

'This is ridiculous, Francesca,' he said. 'What do you hope to accomplish? The automatic camera in the nose of the copter will take adequate pictures.'

'This camera was specifically designed for zoom action,' she said. 'Besides, a little jitter gives the images more verisimilitude.' Yamanaka steered back toward the bank. The biots were now about thirty metres directly ahead. The lead biot came up to within half a body-length of the edge, paused for a fraction of a second, and then turned abruptly to its right. Another quick ninety-degree right turn completed the manoeuvre and left the biot heading in the exactly opposite direction. The other five crabs followed their leader, executing their turns row by row with military precision.

'I got it that time,' Francesca said happily, pulling herself back into the helicopter. 'Head on and full frame. And I think I caught a glimmer of movement in the leader's blue eye just before it turned.'

The biots were now ambling away from the cliff at their normal speed of ten kilometres per hour. Their movement caused a slight indentation in the loamy soil. Their heading was along a path parallel to their last previous sweep toward the sea. From above, the whole region looked like a suburban garden in which part of the grass had been mown – on one side the ground was neat and packed, while in the territory not yet covered by the biots there was no orderly pattern in the soil markings.

'This could get boring,' Francesca said, playfully reaching up and putting her arms around David Brown's neck. 'We may have to amuse ourselves with something else.'

'We'll only watch them one more strip. Their pattern is fairly simple.' He ignored Francesca's light tickling on his neck. It seemed as if he were going through some kind of checklist in his mind. At length Brown spoke into the communicator. 'What do you think, Dr Takagishi? Is there anything else we should do at this time?'

Back in the scientific control centre on the Newton, Dr Takagishi was following the progression of the biots on the monitor. 'It would be extremely valuable,' he said, 'if we could find out more about their sensory capabilities before we try to capture one of them. So far they have not responded to noises or to distant visual stimuli. In fact, they have apparently not even noticed our presence. As I'm sure you would agree, we don't have enough data yet to come to any definitive conclusions. If we could expose them to an entire range of electromagnetic frequencies and calibrate their responses, then we might have a better idea....'

'But that would take *days*,' Dr Brown interrupted. 'And in the final analysis we would still have to take our chances. I can't imagine what we might learn that would materially alter our plans.'

'If we found out more about them first,' Takagishi argued, 'then we could design a better, safer capture procedure. It might even occur that we would learn something that would dissuade us altogether....'

'Unlikely,' was David Brown's abrupt response. As far as he was concerned, this particular discussion was over. 'Hey there, Tabori,' he now shouted. 'How are you guys coming with the huts?'

'We're almost finished,' the Hungarian answered. 'Another thirty minutes at the most. Then I'll be ready for a nap.'

'Lunch comes first,' Francesca interjected. 'You can't go to sleep on an empty stomach.'

'What are you cooking, beautiful?' Tabori said in a bantering tone.

'Osso buco alla Rama.'

'That's enough,' Dr Brown said. He paused for a couple of seconds. 'O'Toole,' he then continued, 'can you handle the Newton all by yourself? At least for the next twelve hours?'

'Affirmative,' was the response.

'Then send down the rest of the crew. By the time we all meet at the new campsite, it should be ready for occupancy. We'll have some lunch and a brief nap. Then we'll plan our biot hunt.'

Below the helicopter the six crablike creatures continued their relentless march across the barren soil. The four human beings watched them encounter a distinct boundary, where the floor changed from dirt and small rocks into a fine wire mesh. As soon as they touched the narrow lane dividing the two sections, the biots executed a U-turn. They then headed back toward the sea along a parallel line adjacent to their last track. Yamanaka banked the helicopter, increased his altitude, and headed for the Beta campsite ten kilometres across the Cylindrical Sea.

★

They were all correct, Nicole was thinking. *Seeing it on the monitor is nothing by comparison.* She was descending on the chairlift into Rama. Now that she was beyond the halfway point, she had a breathtaking view in every direction. She remembered a similar feeling once, when she had been standing on the Tonto Plateau in the Grand Canyon National Park. *But that was made by nature and took over a billion years*, she said to herself. *Rama was actually built by somebody. Or something.*

The chair stopped momentarily. Shigeru Takagishi climbed off a kilometre below her. Nicole couldn't see him, but she could hear him talking to Richard Wakefield on the communicator. 'Hurry up,' she heard Reggie Wilson shout. 'I don't like sitting here in the middle of nowhere.' Nicole enjoyed being suspended on the chairlift. The amazing scene around her was temporarily static and she could study at her leisure any feature that was particularly interesting.

After one more stop for Wilson to disembark, Nicole was at last approaching the bottom of the Alpha chairlift herself. She watched, fascinated, as the resolution of her eyes improved quickly during the last three hundred metres of her descent. What had been a jumble of indistinct images resolved itself into a rover, three people, some equipment, and a small surrounding camp. After a few more seconds she could identify each of the three men. She had a quick flashback to another chairlift ride, this one in Switzerland some two months before. An image of King Henry flitted momentarily through her mind. It was replaced by the smiling face of Richard Wakefield just below her. He was giving her instructions on how best to ease herself out of the chair.

'It will never come to a complete stop,' he was saying, 'but it will slow down a lot. Unfasten your belt and then hit the ground walking, as if you were coming off a moving walkway.'

He grabbed her by the waist and lifted her off the platform. Takagishi and Wilson were already in the back seat of the rover. 'Welcome to Rama,' Wakefield said.

'All right, Tabori,' he continued into the communicator. 'We're all here and ready to go. We're switching now to the listen-only mode for our drive.'

'Hurry,' Janos urged him. 'We're having a hard time not eating your lunch … By the way, Richard, will you bring Tool Box C when you come? We've been talking about nets and cages and I may need a wider variety of gadgets.'

'Roger,' Wakefield replied. He jogged over to the campsite and entered the only large hut. He emerged with a long rectangular metal box that was obviously very heavy. 'Shit, Tabori,' he said into the radio, 'what in the world is in here?'

They all heard a laugh. 'Everything you could possibly need to catch a crab biot. And then some.'

Wakefield switched off the transmitter and climbed in the rover. He started driving away from the stairway in the direction of the Cylindrical Sea. 'This biot hunt is the stupidest goddamn idea I've ever heard,' Reggie Wilson groused. 'Somebody is going to get hurt.'

There was quiet in the rover for almost a minute. To the right, at the limit of their vision, the cosmonauts could barely see the Raman city of London. 'Well, how does it feel to be part of the second team?' Wilson said to nobody in particular.

After an awkward silence, Dr Takagishi turned to address him. 'Excuse me, Mr Wilson,' he said politely, 'are you talking to me?'

'Sure I am,' Wilson replied, nodding his head up and down. 'Didn't anyone ever tell you that you were the number *two* scientist on this mission? I guess not,' Wilson continued after a short pause. 'But that's not surprising. Down on Earth I never knew that I was the number two journalist.'

'Reggie, I don't think –' Nicole said before she was interrupted.

'As for you, doctor –' Wilson leaned forward in the rover – 'you may be the only member of the *third* team. I overheard our glorious leaders Heilmann and Brown talking about you. They'd like to leave you on the Newton permanently. But since we may need your skills –'

'That's enough,' Richard Wakefield broke in. There was a threatening edge in his voice. 'You can stop being so unpleasant.' Several tense seconds passed before Wakefield spoke again. 'By the way, Wilson,' he said in a friendlier tone, 'if I remember correctly, you're a racing fanatic. Would you like to drive this buggy?'

It was the perfect suggestion. A few minutes later Reggie Wilson was in the driver's seat beside Wakefield, laughing wildly as he accelerated the rover around a tight circle. Cosmonauts des Jardins and Takagishi were bumping around in the back seat.

Nicole was observing Wilson very carefully. *He's erratic again,* she was thinking. *That's at least three times in the last two days.* Nicole tried to recall when she had last done a full scan on Wilson. *Not since the day after Borzov died. I've checked the cadets twice in the interim ... damnit,* she said to herself, *I let my preoccupation with the Borzov incident make me careless.* She made a mental note to scan everyone as soon as possible after she arrived at the Beta campsite.

'Incidentally, my good professor,' Richard Wakefield said once Wilson had finally straightened out and was heading for camp, 'I have a question for you.' He turned around and faced the Japanese scientist. 'Have you worked out our "strange sound" from the other day? Or has Dr Brown convinced you that it was just a figment of our collective imagination?'

Dr Takagishi shook his head. 'I told you at the time that it was a new noise.' He stared off into the distance, across the unexplained mechanical fields of the Central Plain. 'This is a different Rama. I know it. The chequerboard squares in the south are laid out in an entirely new pattern and no longer extend to the shore of the Cylindrical Sea. The lights now go on before the sea melts. And they go off abruptly, without dimming for several hours as the first Rama explorers reported. The crab biots now appear in herds instead of individually.' He paused, still looking out across the fields. 'Dr Brown says that all these differences are trivial, but I think they mean something. It's just possible,' Takagishi said softly, 'that Dr Brown is wrong.'

'It's also possible that he's a complete son of a bitch,'

said Wilson bitterly. He accelerated the rover to its maximum speed. 'Beta campsite, here we come!'

28

Extrapolation

Nicole completed her lunch of pressed duck, reconstituted broccoli, and mashed potatoes. The rest of the cosmonauts were still eating and it was temporarily quiet at the long table. In the corner, by the entrance, a monitor tracked the location of the crab biots. Their pattern had not changed. The blip representing the crabs would move in one direction for slightly more than ten minutes and then reverse itself.

'What happens after they finish this parcel?' Richard Wakefield asked. He was looking at a computer map of the area that was posted on a temporary bulletin board.

'Last time they followed one of those lanes between the chequerboard partitions until they came to a hole,' Francesca responded from the other end of the table. 'Then they dumped their garbage in it. They haven't picked up anything in this new territory, so what they will do when they finish is anybody's guess.'

'Everyone is convinced that our biots are in fact garbage men?'

'The evidence is fairly strong,' David Brown said. 'A similar solitary crab biot encountered by Jimmy Park inside the first Rama was also believed to be a garbage collector.'

'We flatter ourselves,' Shigeru Takagishi interjected. He finished chewing his last bite and swallowed. 'Dr Brown himself was the one who first said it was unlikely we human beings could comprehend what Rama was about. Our conversation reminds me of that old Hindu proverb about the blind men who felt the elephant. They all described it differently, for each of them touched only a small part of the animal. None of them was correct.'

'You don't think our crabs work for the Rama Sanitation Department?' Janos Tabori inquired.

'I didn't say that,' Takagishi replied. 'I merely suggested that it's hubris on our part to conclude so quickly that those six creatures have no purpose except cleaning up the garbage. Our observational data is woefully inadequate.'

'Sometimes it is necessary to extrapolate,' Dr Brown rejoined testily, 'and even speculate, based on minimal amounts of data. You know yourself that new science is based on maximum likelihood rather than certainty.'

'Before we become involved in an esoteric discussion about science and its methodology,' Janos interrupted with a grin, 'I have a sporting proposition for you all.' He stood up at his place. 'Actually it was Richard's idea originally, but I've figured out how to make it into a game. It has to do with the lights.'

Janos took a quick drink of water from his cup. 'Since we first arrived here in Ramaland,' he intoned formally, 'there have been three transitions in the illumination state.'

'Boo. Hiss,' shouted Wakefield. Janos laughed.

'Okay, you guys –' the little Hungarian then continued in his normal offhand way – 'what's the deal with the lights? They've come on, gone off, and now come on again. What's going to happen in the future? I propose that we have a pool and contribute, say, twenty marks apiece. Each of us will make a prediction about the behaviour of the lights for the rest of the mission and whoever is closest will win the pot.'

'Who will judge the winner?' Reggie Wilson inquired sleepily. He had yawned several times during the preceding hour. 'Despite the impressive set of brains around this table, I don't think anyone has figured out Rama yet. My personal belief is that the lights will not follow any pattern. They will go on and off at random times to keep us guessing.'

'Write it down and send it on the modem to General O'Toole. Richard and I agreed that he would make a perfect judge. When the mission is over, he'll compare the predictions with actuality and someone will win a lucky dinner for two.'

Dr David Brown pushed his chair back from the table. 'Are you finished with your game, Tabori?' he asked. 'If so,' he added, without waiting for an answer, 'perhaps we can clean up this lunch mess and get on with our schedule.'

'Hey, skipper,' Janos replied, 'I'm just trying to loosen things up. Everybody's getting tense....'

Brown walked out of the hut before Cosmonaut Tabori had finished his sentence.

'What's bothering him?' Richard asked Francesca.

'I guess he's anxious about the hunt,' Francesca answered. 'He has been in a bad mood since this morning. Maybe he's feeling all the responsibility.'

'Maybe he's just a jerk,' said Wilson. He too rose from his seat. 'I'm going to take a nap.'

As Wilson was leaving the large hut Nicole remembered that she wanted to check everyone's biometry before the hunt. It was a simple enough task. All she needed was to stand close to each cosmonaut for about forty-five seconds with her activated scanner and then read the critical data off the monitor. If there were no entries in the warning files, the entire procedure was quite straightforward. On this particular check everyone was clean, including Takagishi. 'Nice going,' Nicole said to her Japanese colleague very quietly.

She walked outside to look for David Brown and Reggie Wilson. Dr Brown's hut was at the far end of the campsite. Like the rest of the individual dwellings, his hut resembled a tall thin hat sitting on the ground. All the huts were off-white in colour, about two and a half metres tall, with a circular base just under two metres in diameter. They were manufactured with super-lightweight, flexible materials which combined easy packing and storage with formidable strength. Nicole remarked to herself that the huts looked something like native American Indian teepees.

David Brown was in his hut, sitting cross-legged on the ground in front of a portable computer monitor. On the screen was text from the chapter on biots in Takagishi's *Atlas of Rama*. 'Excuse me, Dr Brown,' Nicole said as she stuck her head in his door.

'Yes,' he said, 'what is it?' He made no attempt to hide his annoyance at the interruption.

'I need to check your biometry data,' Nicole said. 'You haven't been dumped since just before the first sortie.'

Brown gave her an irritated glance. Nicole held her ground. The American shrugged his shoulders, half-grunted, and turned back to the monitor. Nicole knelt beside him and activated her scanner.

'There are some folding chairs over in the supply hut,' Nicole offered as Dr Brown shifted his weight uncomfortably on the ground. He ignored her comment. *Why is he so rude to me?* Nicole found herself wondering. *Is it because of that report on Wilson and him? No*, she answered her own question, *it's because I have never been properly deferential.*

Data began to appear on Nicole's screen. She carefully keyed in several inputs which permitted a synopsis of the warning data to be shown. 'Your blood pressure has been too high for intermittent intervals during the last seventy-two hours, including almost all of today,' she said without emotion. 'This particular kind of pattern is usually associated with stress.'

Dr Brown stopped reading about biots and turned to face his life science officer. He looked at the displayed data without understanding it. 'This graph shows the amplitudes and durations of your out-of-tolerance excursions,' Nicole said, pointing at the screen. 'None of the individual occurrences would be serious by itself. But the overall pattern is cause for concern.'

'I have been under some pressure,' he mumbled. David Brown watched while Nicole called up other displays showing data that corroborated her original statements. Many of Brown's warning files were overflowing.

The lights continued to flash on the monitor. 'What's the worst case scenario?' he inquired.

Nicole eyed her patient. 'A stroke with paralysis or death,' she replied. 'If the condition persists or worsens.'

He whistled. 'What should I do?'

'In the first place,' Nicole answered, 'you must start by getting more sleep. Your metabolic profile shows that since the death of General Borzov you have only had a total of eleven hours of solid rest. Why didn't you tell me you were having trouble sleeping?'

'I thought it was just excitement. I even took a sleeping pill one night and it had no effect.'

Nicole's brow furrowed. 'I don't remember giving you any sleeping pills.'

Dr Brown smiled. 'Shit,' he said, 'I forgot to tell you. I was talking to Francesca Sabatini about my insomnia one night and she offered me a pill. I took it without thinking.'

'Which night was that?' Nicole asked. She changed displays again on her monitor and called for more data from the storage buffers.

'I'm not certain,' Dr Brown said after some hesitation. 'I think it was –'

'Oh, here it is,' Nicole said. 'I can see it in the chemical analysis. That was 3 March, the second night after Borzov's death. The day you and Heilmann were selected as joint commanders. From the breakout in this spectrometry data, I would guess that you took a single medvil.'

'You can tell *that* from my biometry data?'

'Not exactly,' Nicole smiled. 'The interpretation is not unique. What was it you said at lunch? Sometimes it's necessary to extrapolate ... and speculate.'

Their eyes met for a moment. *Could that be fear?* Nicole wondered as she tried to interpret what she was seeing in his gaze. Dr Brown looked away. 'Thank you, Doctor des Jardins,' he said stiffly, 'for your report on my blood pressure. I will try to relax and get plenty of sleep. And I apologise for not informing you about the sleeping pill.' He dismissed her with a wave of his hand.

Nicole started to protest her dismissal but decided against it. *He wouldn't follow my advice anyway*, she said to herself as she walked toward Wilson's hut. *And his blood pressure was certainly not dangerously high.* She thought about the strained final two minutes of their conversation, after she had astonished Dr Brown by correctly identifying the type of sleeping pill. *There's something not quite right here. What is it that I am missing?*

She could hear Reggie Wilson snoring before she arrived at the door of his tent. After a brief debate with herself, Nicole decided that she would scan him after his nap. She then returned to her own hut and quickly fell asleep. 'Nicole. Nicole des Jardins.' The voice intruded in her dream and awakened her. 'It's me. Francesca. I need to tell you something.'

Nicole sat up slowly on her cot. Francesca had already entered the hut. The Italian was wearing her friendliest smile, the one that Nicole had thought was always saved for the camera.

'I was talking to David just a few minutes ago,' Francesca said as she approached the cot, 'and he told me about your conversation after lunch.' Francesca kept talking as Nicole yawned and swung her legs around to the floor. 'I was, of course, very concerned to learn about his blood pressure – don't worry, he and I have already agreed that I won't use it – but what really bothered me was he reminded me that we never told you about the sleeping pill. I'm so embarrassed. We should have told you immediately.'

Francesca was talking too fast for Nicole. Just moments before she had been in a deep sleep, dreaming of Beauvois, and now all of a sudden she was expected to listen to a staccato confession from the Italian cosmonaut.

'Could you wait a minute until I wake up?' Nicole asked crossly. She leaned around Francesca to a makeshift table and took a cup of water. She drank slowly.

'Now am I to understand,' Nicole said, 'that you have awakened me to tell me that you gave Dr Brown a sleeping pill? Something I already know?'

'Yes,' smiled Francesca. 'I mean, that's part of it. But I realised that I had forgotten to tell you about Reggie also.'

Nicole shook her head. 'I'm not following you, Francesca. Are you talking about Reggie Wilson now?'

Francesca hesitated for a second. 'Yes,' she said. 'Didn't you check him with your scanner right after lunch?'

Nicole shook her head again. 'No, he was already asleep.' She looked at her watch. 'I had planned to scan him before the meeting started. Maybe an hour from now.'

Francesca was flustered. 'Well,' she said, 'when David told me that the medvil showed up in his biometry data, I thought....' She stopped herself in mid-sentence. She seemed to be collecting her thoughts. Nicole waited patiently.

'Reggie started complaining of headaches over a week ago,' Francesca eventually continued, 'after the two Newton ships joined for the rendezvous with Rama. Since he and I have been close friends and he knew about my knowledge of drugs – you know, from all that work on my documentary series – he asked me if I would give him something for headaches. I refused at first, but finally, after he kept badgering me, I gave him some nubitrol.'

Nicole frowned. 'That's a very strong medicine for a simple headache. There are still doctors who believe it should never be prescribed unless everything else has failed....'

'I told him all that,' Francesca said. 'He was adamant. You don't know Reggie. Sometimes you can't reason with him.'

'How much did you give him?'

'Eight pills altogether, a total of two hundred milligrams.'

'No wonder he's been acting so strangely.' Nicole leaned over and picked up her pocket computer sitting on the end table. She accessed her medical data base and read the short entry about nubitrol. 'Not much here,' she said. 'I'll have to ask O'Toole to transmit the full entry from the medical encyclopedia. But if I remember correctly, wasn't there a controversy about nubitrol remaining in the system for weeks?'

'I don't recall,' Francesca replied. She looked at the monitor in Nicole's hand and quickly read the text. Nicole was irritated. She started to lambast Francesca verbally but at the last moment changed her mind. *So you gave drugs to both David and Reggie*, she was thinking. Out of her memory came a vague recollection of Francesca handing Valeriy Borzov a glass of wine several hours before he died. A strange chill ran through Nicole's body. Could her intuition be correct?

Nicole turned around and fixed Francesca with a cold stare. 'Now that you have confessed to playing doctor and pharmacist for both David and Reggie, is there anything else you want to tell me?'

'What do you mean?' Francesca asked.

'Have you given drugs to any other member of the crew?'

Nicole felt her heart race as Francesca blanched, ever so slightly, and hesitated before replying.

'No. No, of course not,' was her answer.

29
The Hunt

The helicopter very slowly dropped the rover to the ground. 'How much farther?' Janos Tabori asked over the communicator.

'About ten metres,' Richard Wakefield replied from below. He was standing in a spot about a hundred metres south of the edge of the Cylindrical Sea. Above him the rover dangled at the end of two long cables. 'Be careful to let it down gently. There are some delicate electronics in the chassis.'

Hiro Yamanaka commanded the helicopter into its tightest possible altitude control loop while Janos electronically extended the cables a few centimetres at a time. 'Contact,' shouted Wakefield. 'On the rear wheels. The front needs to come down another metre.'

Francesca Sabatini raced around to the side of the rover to record its historic touchdown in the Southern Hemicylinder of Rama. Fifty metres farther from the cliff, in the neighbourhood of a hut that was serving as a temporary headquarters, the rest of the cosmonauts were preparing for the hunt to begin. Irina Turgenyev was checking the installation of the cable snare in the second helicopter. David Brown was by himself a few metres away from the hut, talking on the radio with Admiral Heilmann back at the Beta campsite. The two men were reviewing the details of the capture plan. Wilson, Takagishi, and des Jardins were watching the conclusion of the rover landing operation.

'Now we know who's really the boss of this outfit,'

Reggie Wilson was saying to his two companions. He pointed at Dr Brown. 'This damn hunt is more like a military operation than anything we've done, yet our senior scientist is in charge and our ranking officer is manning the phones.' He spat on the ground. 'Christ, do we have enough equipment here? Two helicopters, a rover, three different kinds of cages – not to mention several large boxes of electrical and mechanical shit. Those poor bastard crabs don't have a chance.'

Dr Takagishi put the laser binoculars to his eyes. He found the target quickly. Half a kilometre to the east the crab biots were nearing the edge of the cliff again. Nothing about their motion had changed. 'We need all the equipment because of the uncertainty,' Takagishi said quietly. 'Nobody really knows what is going to happen.'

'I hope the lights go out,' Wilson laughed.

'We're prepared for that,' David Brown interjected tersely as he walked up to join the other three cosmonauts. 'The shells of the crabs have been sprayed with a light fluorescent material and we have plenty of flares. While you were complaining about the length of our last meeting, we were finishing the contingency plans.' He stared truculently at his countryman. 'You know, Wilson, you could try –'

'Break break,' the voice of Otto Heilmann interrupted him. 'News. Hot news. I just received word from O'Toole that INN will be carrying our feed *live*, beginning twenty minutes from now.'

'Good work,' replied Brown. 'We should be ready by then. I see Wakefield headed this way in the rover.' He glanced at his watch. 'And the crabs should be turning again in another few seconds. Incidentally, Otto, do you still disagree with my suggestion to snare the lead biot?'

'Yes, David, I do. I think it's an unnecessary risk. What little we do know suggests that the lead crab has the most capability. Why take a chance? Any biot would be an incredible treasure to carry back to Earth, particularly if it's still functional. We can worry about the leader after we already have one in the bag.'

'Then I guess I'm outvoted on this one. Dr Takagishi and Tabori both agree with you. So does General O'Toole. We'll proceed with Plan B. The target biot will be number four, the back right biot as we approach from the rear.'

The rover carrying Wakefield and Sabatini arrived at the hut area at almost the same time as the helicopter. 'Good job, men,' Dr Brown said as Tabori and Yamanaka jumped down from the copter. 'Take a short breather, Janos. Then go over and make sure Turgenycv and the cable snare are both ready to go. I want you airborne in five minutes.'

'All right,' Brown said, turning to the others, 'this is it. Wilson, Takagishi, and des Jardins in the rover with Wakefield. Francesca, you come with me in the second helicopter with Hiro.'

Nicole started walking toward the rover but Francesca intercepted her. 'Have you ever used one of these?' The Italian journalist extended a video camera the size of a small book.

'Once,' Nicole answered, studying the camera in Francesca's hand, 'eleven or twelve years ago. I recorded one of Dr Delon's brain operations. I guess –'

'Look,' interrupted Francesca, 'I could use some help. I'm sorry I didn't discuss it with you earlier, but I didn't know ... Anyway, I need another camera, one on the ground, especially now that we're live on INN. I'm not asking for miracles. You're the only one who –'

'What about Reggie?' Nicole replied. 'He's the other journalist.'

'Reggie won't help,' Francesca said quickly. Dr Brown called for her to come to the helicopter. 'Will you do it, Nicole? Please? Or should I ask someone else?'

Why not? ran through Nicole's mind. *I have nothing else to do unless an emergency comes up.* 'Sure,' she replied.

'Thanks a million,' Francesca shouted as she handed Nicole the camera and dashed off to the waiting helicopter.

'Well, well,' said Reggie Wilson as Nicole approached the rover with the camera cradled in her hands. 'I see that our crew doctor has been recruited by the number one journalist. I hope you asked for the minimum wage.'

'Lighten up, Reggie,' Nicole replied. 'It doesn't bother me to help others when I have nothing specific to do myself.'

Wakefield switched on the rover and began to drive east toward the biots. The headquarters had been intentionally established in the area already 'cleaned' by the crabs. The packed soil made progress very easy for the rover. They were within a hundred metres of the biots in less than three minutes. Overhead the two helicopters circled around the crabs. They reminded Wilson of buzzards circling over a dying animal.

'What exactly do you want me to do?' Nicole called to Francesca on the rover transmitter.

'Try to move parallel to the biots,' Francesca answered. 'You can probably run alongside, at least for some of the time. The most important moment is when Janos tries to close the snare.'

'We're all ready here,' Tabori announced a few seconds later. 'Just give the word.'

'Are we on the air?' Brown asked Francesca. She nodded her head. 'All right,' he said to Janos. 'Go ahead.'

From out of one of the helicopters came a long, thick cable with what looked like an inverted basket on the end. 'Janos will try to centre the snare on the target biot,' Wakefield explained to Nicole, 'and let the sides drape naturally over the corner of the shell. Then he will increase the tension and pull the biot off the ground. We will cage the crab after we return it to the Beta campsite.'

'Let's see what they look like from down there,' Nicole heard Francesca say. The rover was now right next to the biots. Nicole climbed out and jogged beside them. She was frightened at first. For some reason she had not expected them to be so large or so strange looking. Their metallic sheen reminded her of the cold exterior of many of the new buildings in Paris. As she ran along on the soil, the biots were only about two metres away from her. With the automatic focusing and framing of the camera, it was not difficult for Nicole to take the proper pictures.

'Don't get in front of them,' Dr Takagishi warned her. He didn't need to worry. Nicole had not forgotten what they had done to that mound of metal.

'Your pictures are really very good.' Francesca's voice boomed on the rover receiver. 'Nicole, try to speed up to the lead biot and then fall back little by little, letting the camera pan across each of the ranks.' She waited while Nicole moved to the front of the biots. 'Wow. That's superb. Now I know why we brought an Olympic champion with us.'

On his first two attempts Janos missed with the snare. However, on the third try it landed perfectly on the number four crab's back. The edges of the net, or basket, spread out to the limit of the shell. Nicole was starting to sweat. She had been running already for four minutes. 'From now on,' Francesca said to her from the helicopter, 'focus on the single target crab. Move up as close as you dare.'

Nicole reduced her distance from the closest biot to about a metre. She nearly slipped once and a cold chill swept over her. *If I were to fall across their path*, she thought, *they'd make mincemeat out of me*. Her camera was fixed on the right rear crab as Janos tightened the cables.

'Now!' he shouted. The snare, with the biot entrapped, began to rise off the ground. Everything happened very fast. The target biot used its scissor-like claws to snap through one of the metal threads of the snare. The other five biots came to a brief halt, for perhaps one full second, and then immediately all attacked the snare with their claws. The metal net was completely shredded and the biot freed in five seconds.

Nicole was amazed by what she was seeing. Despite her pounding heart she continued to film. The lead biot now sat down on the ground. The other five surrounded it in an extremely tight circle. Each of the biots attached one claw to the crab in the centre and the other to its neighbour on the right. The formation was finished in less than five more seconds. The biots were locked and motionless.

Francesca was the first to speak. 'Absolutely

incredible,' she screamed in elation. 'We just made the hair stand up on every human being on Earth.'

Nicole felt Richard Wakefield beside her. 'Are you all right?' he asked.

'I think so,' she said. She was still shaking. The two of them glanced over at the biots. There was no movement.

'They're in a huddle,' Reggie Wilson said from the rover. 'The score is now Biots 7, Humans 0.'

'Since you're so convinced that there is no danger, I'll agree to go ahead. But I must confess that I myself am nervous about another attempt. Those things clearly communicate with each other. And I don't think they want to be captured.'

'Otto, Otto,' Dr Brown replied. 'This procedure is only a straightforward refinement of what we tried the first time. The line nexus will adhere to the shell of the crab and will wrap its thin cables tightly around the entire carapace. The other biots will not be able to use their claws. There will be no room between the line and the shell.'

'Admiral Heilmann, this is Dr Takagishi.' There was definite concern in his voice as he spoke into the communicator. 'I must register my strongest objection to proceeding with this hunt. We have seen already how little we understand about these creatures. As Wakefield said, our attempt to snare one of them has obviously triggered their main fault protection responses. We have no idea at all how they will react next.'

'We all understand that, Dr Takagishi,' David Brown interjected before Heilmann could respond. 'But there are extenuating factors that override the uncertainties. First, as Francesca pointed out, the entire Earth will again be watching if we go after the biots right away. You heard what Jean-Claude Revoir said twenty minutes ago – we have already done more for space exploration than anyone since the original Soviet and American cosmonauts back in the twentieth century. Secondly, we are prepared to complete the hunt now. If we abandon the attempt and return all our equipment to Beta, then we

will have wasted a huge amount of time and effort.
Finally, there is no obvious danger. Why do you insist on
making such dire predictions? All we saw the biots do
was engage in some kind of self-defence activity.'

'Professor Brown –' the eminent Japanese scholar tried
one last rational appeal – 'please look around you. Try to
imagine the capabilities of the creatures who made this
amazing vehicle. Try to appreciate the possibility that
perhaps, just perhaps, what we are trying to do might be
viewed as a hostile act and has somehow been
communicated to whatever intelligence is managing this
spacecraft. Suppose as a result that we, as representatives
of the human species, are condemning not only
ourselves, but also, in some larger sense, all of our
fellow –'

'Poppycock,' David Brown scoffed. 'How can anyone
ever accuse *me* of wild speculation ...?' He laughed
heartily. 'This is absurd. The evidence overwhelmingly
indicates that this Rama has the same purpose and
function as its predecessor and is completely oblivious of
our existence. The fact that one single subfamily of
robots bands together when threatened does not have
overwhelming significance.' He looked around at the
others. 'I say that's enough talk, Otto. Unless you object,
we're going out to capture a biot.'

There was a short hesitation from across the
Cylindrical Sea. Then the cosmonauts heard Admiral
Heilmann's affirmative reply. 'Go ahead, David. But
don't take any unnecessary chances.'

'Do you think we're really in danger?' Hiro Yamanaka
asked Dr Takagishi while the new capture tactics were
being reviewed by Brown, Tabori, and Wakefield. The
Japanese pilot was staring off in the distance at the
massive structures in the Southern bowl, thinking,
perhaps for the first time, of the vulnerability of their
position.

'Probably not,' his countryman replied, 'but it's insane
to take such –'

'Insane is a perfect word for it,' Reggie Wilson
interrupted. 'You and I were the only two vocal

opponents of continuing this stupidity. But our objections were made to sound foolish and even cowardly. Personally, I wish one of those goddamn things would challenge the esteemed Dr Brown to a duel. Or better still, a bolt of lightning would come shooting out of those spires over there.'

He pointed at the great horns which Yamanaka had been regarding earlier. Wilson's voice changed and there was a fearful edge to it. 'We are over our heads here. I can feel it in the air. We are being warned of danger by powers that none of us can begin to understand. But we are ignoring the warnings.'

Nicole turned away from her colleagues and glanced at the lively planning meeting taking place fifteen metres away from her. Engineers Wakefield and Tabori were definitely enjoying the challenge of outwitting the biots. Nicole wondered if perhaps Rama really was sending them some kind of a warning. *Poppycock*, she said to herself, repeating David Brown's expression. She shuddered involuntarily as she recalled the several seconds when the crab biots had devastated the metal snare. *I'm overreacting. And so is Wilson. There's no reason to be afraid.*

Yet, as she turned again and looked through the binoculars to study the biot formation half a kilometre away, there was a palpable fear in her that would not be assuaged. The six crabs had not moved in almost two hours. They were still locked in their original arrangement. *What are you really all about, Rama?* Nicole asked herself for the umpteenth time. Her next questions startled her. She had never verbalised it before. *And how many of us will make it back to Earth to tell your tale?*

For the second capture attempt Francesca wanted to be on the ground beside the biots. As before, Turgenyev and Tabori were up in the prime helicopter along with the most important equipment. Brown, Yamanaka, and Wakefield were in the other helicopter. Dr Brown had invited Wakefield to provide him with realtime advice; Francesca had of course persuaded Richard to take some aerial pictures for her to complement the automatic images from the helicopter system.

Reggie Wilson drove the ground-based cosmonauts to the biot site in the rover. 'Now here's a good job for me,' he said as they approached the location of the alien crabs. 'Chauffeur.' He gazed up at the distant ceiling of Rama. 'You hear that, you guys. I'm versatile. I can do many things.' He looked over at Francesca beside him in the front seat. 'By the way, Mrs Sabatini, were you planning to thank Nicole for her spectacular work? It was her action shots on the ground that captured the audience in your last transmission.'

Francesca was busy checking all her video equipment and at first ignored Reggie's comment. When he repeated his jibe, she responded, without looking up, 'May I remind Mr Wilson that I do not need his unsolicited advice on how to conduct my business?'

'There was a time,' Reggie mused to himself, shaking his head, 'when things were very different.' He glanced at Francesca. There was no indication that she was even listening. 'Back when I still believed in love,' he said in a louder voice. 'Before I knew about betrayal. Or ambition and its selfishness.'

He jerked the rover wheel vigorously to the left and brought it to a stop about forty metres west of the biots. Francesca jumped out without a word. Within three seconds she was chattering to David Brown and Richard Wakefield on the radio about the video coverage of the capture. The ever polite Dr Takagishi thanked Reggie Wilson for driving the rover.

'We're coming in,' Tabori shouted from above. He managed to position the dangling nexus properly on his second attempt. The nexus was a round, heavy sphere about twenty centimetres in diameter, with a dozen small holes or indentations on its surface. It was slowly dropped on to the centre of the shell of one of the outside biots. Next Janos, transmitting a barrage of commands from the hovering helicopter to the processor in the nexus, ordered the extension of the massed threads of metal rolled up inside the sphere. The crabs did not stir

as the threads wrapped themselves around the target
biot.

'What do you think, inspector?' Janos shouted at
Richard Wakefield in the other helicopter.

Richard surveyed the strange apparatus. The thick
cable was attached to a ring stanchion at the rear of the
helicopter. Fifteen metres below, the metal ball sat on
the back of the target biot, thin filaments extending from
inside the ball around the top and bottom of the
carapace. 'Looks fine,' Richard replied. 'Now there's
only the single question remaining. Is the helicopter
stronger than their collective grip?'

David Brown commanded Irina Turgenyev to lift the
prey. She slowly increased the speed of the blades and
tried to ascend. The tiny slack in the cable disappeared
but the biots barely moved. 'They're either very heavy or
they're holding on to the ground somehow,' Richard
said. 'Hit them with a sharp burst.'

The sudden jolt in the cable lifted the entire biot
formation momentarily skyward. The helicopter strained
as the biot mass dangled two or three metres off the
ground. The two crabs not attached to the target biot
dropped first, falling into a motionless heap seconds after
takeoff. The other three crabs lasted longer, ten seconds
altogether before they finally disengaged their claws from
their companion and fell to the ground below. There
were universal cries of joy and congratulations as the
helicopter climbed higher into the sky.

Francesca was filming the capture sequence from a
distance of about ten metres. After the last three biots,
including the leader, had released their grips on the
target crab and fallen on to the Raman soil, she leaned
back to record the helicopter as it headed for the banks of
the Cyclindrical Sea with its prey. It took her two or
three seconds to realise that everyone was shouting at
her.

The lead biot and its final two companion crabs had
not crumpled into a heap when they had hit the ground.
Although slightly damaged, they were active and on the
move within moments after landing. While Francesca

was filming the departure of the helicopter, the lead biot sensed her presence and headed toward her. The other two followed a step behind.

They were only four metres away when Francesca, still filming, finally understood that she was now the prey. She turned around and started to run. 'Run to the side,' Richard Wakefield screamed into the communicator, 'they can only go in straight lines.'

Francesca zigged and zagged but the biots continued to follow her. Her original burst of adrenaline enabled her to extend the distance separating her from the crabs to ten metres. But as she began to tire, the relentless biots began closing in on her. She slipped and almost fell. By the time Francesca regained her stride the lead biot was no more than three metres away.

Reggie Wilson had raced toward the rover as soon as it was clear that the biots were chasing Francesca. Once at the controls of the vehicle, he headed for her at top speed. His original intention was to pick her up and move her out of the way of the biot onslaught. They were too close to her, however, so Reggie decided to smash into the three crabs from the side. There was a crash of metal on metal as the lightweight vehicle rammed the biots. Reggie's plan worked. The momentum of the crash carried Reggie and the crabs several metres to the side. The threat to Francesca was over.

But the biots were not incapacitated. Far from it. Despite the fact that one of the follower crabs had lost a leg and the lead biot had a slightly damaged claw, within seconds all three of them were at work in the wreckage. They started slicing the rover into chunks with their claws, and then they used their fearful collection of probes and rasps to tear the chunks into still smaller pieces.

Reggie was momentarily stunned by the impact of the rover against the biots. The alien crabs had been heavier than he had anticipated and the damage to his vehicle was severe. As soon as he realised that the biots were still active, he started to jump out of the rover. But he couldn't. His legs were wedged underneath the collapsed dashboard.

His unmitigated terror lasted no longer than ten seconds. There was nothing anyone could do. Reggie Wilson's horrified shrieks echoed through the vastness of Rama as the biots chopped him apart exactly as if he were part of the rover. It was accomplished swiftly and systematically. Both Francesca and the automatic camera in the helicopter filmed the final seconds of his life. The pictures were transmitted live back to the Earth.

30

Post Mortem II

Nicole sat quietly in her hut at the Beta campsite. She could not erase from her mind the horrible image of Reggie Wilson's face, contorted in terror as he was being hacked to pieces. She tried to force herself to think of something else. *So what now*, she wondered. *What will happen to the mission now?*

Outside it was dark again in Rama. The lights had vanished abruptly three hours before, after a period of illumination thirty-four seconds less than the previous Raman day. The disappearance of the lights should have prompted much discussion and speculation. But it didn't. None of the cosmonauts wanted to talk about anything. The awful memory of Wilson's death weighed too heavily on everyone.

The normal crew meeting after dinner had been postponed until morning because David Brown and Admiral Heilmann were in an extended conference with ISA officials back on Earth. Nicole had not participated in any of the conversations, but it was not difficult for her to imagine their content. She realised that there was a very real possibility the mission would now be aborted. The hue and cry from the public might demand it. After all, they had witnessed one of the most gruesome scenes ...

Nicole thought of Genevieve sitting in front of the television at Beauvois, watching while Cosmonaut Wilson was being methodically subdivided by the biots. She shuddered. Then she chastised herself for being self-centred. *The real horror*, she said to herself, *must have been in Los Angeles*.

She had met the Wilson family twice during the early parties immediately after the crew selections were announced. Nicole remembered the boy particularly. Randy was his name. He was seven or eight, wide-eyed and beautiful. He loved sports. He had brought Nicole one of his prized possessions, a programme from the 2184 Olympics in nearly perfect condition, and had asked her to sign the page featuring the women's triple jump. She had tousled his hair as he had thanked her with a huge smile.

The image of Randy Wilson watching his father die on television was too much for her. Tears wedged themselves into the corners of her eyes. *What a nightmare this year has been for you, little boy*, she thought. *The roller-coaster of life. First the joy of having your father selected as a cosmonaut. Then all the Francesca nonsense and the divorce. Now this terrible tragedy.*

Nicole was becoming depressed and her mind was still too active for sleep. She decided that she wanted some company. She walked over to the next hut and knocked softly on the door.

'Is someone out there?' she heard from inside.

'Hai, Takagishi-san,' she replied. 'It's Nicole. May I come in?'

He walked over to the door and opened it. 'This is an unexpected surprise,' he said. 'Is the visit professional?'

'No,' she answered as she entered. 'Strictly informal. I was not ready to sleep. I thought....'

'You are welcome to visit me any time,' he said with a friendly smile. 'You do not need a reason.' He looked at her for several seconds. 'I am deeply disturbed by what happened this afternoon. I feel responsible. I don't think I did enough to stop –'

'Come on, Shigeru,' Nicole replied. 'Don't be ridiculous. You're not to blame. At least you spoke up. I'm the doctor and I didn't even say anything.'

Her eyes wandered aimlessly around Takagishi's hut. Beside his cot, sitting on a small piece of cloth on the floor, Nicole saw a curious white figurine with black markings. She walked over to it and bent down on her knees. 'What's this?' she asked.

Dr Takagishi was slightly embarrassed. He came over beside Nicole and picked up the tiny fat oriental man. He held it between his index finger and his thumb. 'It's a netsuke heirloom from my wife's family,' he said. 'It's made from ivory.'

He handed the little man to Nicole. 'He is the king of the gods. His companion, a similarly plump queen, rests on the table beside my wife's bed in Kyoto. Back before elephants became endangered, many people collected figures like this. My wife's family has a superb collection.'

Nicole studied the little man in her hand. He had a benign, serene smile on his face. She imaged the beautiful Machiko Takagishi back in Japan and for a few seconds she envied their marital bond. *It would make events like Wilson's death much easier to deal with*, she thought.

'Would you like to sit down?' Dr Takagishi was saying. Nicole positioned herself on a box next to the cot and they talked for twenty minutes. Mostly they shared memories of their families. They referred obliquely to the afternoon disaster several times, but they avoided detailed discussion of Rama and the Newton mission altogether. What they both needed were the comforting images of their daily lives on Earth.

'And now,' Takagishi said, finishing his cup of tea and putting it on the end table beside Nicole's, 'I have a strange request for Dr des Jardins. Would you please go over to your hut and bring back your biometry equipment? I would like to be scanned.'

Nicole started to laugh but noticed the seriousness in her colleague's face. When she returned with her scanner several minutes later, Dr Takagishi told her the reason for his request. 'This afternoon,' he said, 'I felt two very sharp pains in my chest. It was during the excitement, after Wilson crashed into the biots and I realised....' He did not complete his sentence. Nicole nodded and activated the scanning instrument.

Neither of them said anything for the next three

minutes. Nicole checked all the warning data, displayed graphs and charts of his cardiac performance, and shook her head regularly. When she was finished she faced her friend with a grim smile. 'You've had a slight heart attack,' she said to Dr Takagishi. 'Maybe two, very close together. And your heart has been irregular ever since.' She could tell that he had expected the news. 'I'm sorry,' she said. 'I have some medicine with me that I can give you, but it's only a stopgap measure. We must go back to the Newton immediately so we can treat this problem properly.'

'Well – ' he smiled wanly – ' if our predictions are correct, then it will be light again in Rama in about twelve hours. I assume we'll go then.'

'Probably,' she answered. 'I'll talk to Brown and Heilmann about it right away. My guess is that you and I will leave first thing in the morning.'

He reached out and took her hand. 'Thank you, Nicole,' he said.

She turned away. For the second time in an hour there were tears in the corner of her eyes. Nicole left Takagishi's hut and headed for the edge of camp to talk to David Brown.

'Ah, it *is* you,' she heard Richard Wakefield's voice in the dark. 'I thought for certain you were asleep. I have some news for you.'

'Hello Richard,' Nicole said as the figure holding the flashlight emerged from the darkness.

'I couldn't sleep,' he said. 'Too many grisly pictures in my head. So I decided to work on your problem.' He smiled. 'It was even easier than I thought. Would you like to come to my hut for an explanation?'

Nicole was confused. She had been preoccupied with what she was going to say to Brown and Heilmann about Takagishi. 'You do remember, don't you?' Richard enquired. 'The problem with the RoSur software and the manual commands.'

'You've been working on *that*?' she asked. 'Down here?'

'Certainly. All I had to do was have O'Toole transmit the data that I needed. Come on, let me show you.'

Nicole decided seeing Dr Brown could wait for a few more minutes. She walked beside Richard. He knocked on another hut as they went by. 'Hey, Tabori, guess what?' he shouted. 'I found out lovely lady doctor wandering around in the dark. Do you want to join us?'

'I explained some of it to him first,' Richard said to Nicole. 'Your hut was dark and I guessed you were asleep.'

Janos stumbled out of his door less than a minute later and acknowledged Nicole with a smile. 'All right, Wakefield,' he said, 'but let's not prolong it. I was finally drifting off.'

Back in Wakefield's hut, the British engineer recounted with evident enjoyment what had happened to the robot surgeon when the Newton had experienced the unexpected torque. 'You were right, Nicole,' he said, 'that there were manual commands input to RoSur. And these commands did indeed shut down the normal fault protection algorithms. But none of them was input until *during* the Raman manoeuvre.'

Wakefield smiled and continued, watching Nicole carefully to ensure that she was following his explanation. 'Apparently, when Janos fell and his fingers hit the control box, he generated three commands. At least that's what RoSur thought; it was told that there were three manual commands in its queue. Of course they were all garbage. But RoSur had no way of knowing this.

'Maybe now you can appreciate some of the nightmares that plague system software designers. There's just no way anybody could ever anticipate all possible contingencies. The designers had protected against *one* inadvertent garbage command – someone brushing the control box during an operation, for example – but not *several* bad commands. Manual commands were essentially considered to be emergencies by the overall system design. Hence they had the highest priority in the interrupt structure of the RoSur software and were always processed immediately. The design acknowledged, however, that there could be a single 'bad' manual command and had the capability of rejecting it and moving on to the next priority interrupts, which included fault protection.'

'Sorry,' said Nicole. 'You've lost me. How could a design be structured to disregard a single bad command, but not several? I thought this simple processor operated in series.'

Richard turned to his portable computer and, working from notes, called up on the monitor a mass of numbers arrayed in rows and columns. 'Here are the operations, instruction by instruction, that the RoSur software implemented after there were manual commands in its queue.'

'They repeat,' Janos observeed, 'every seven operations.'

'Exactly,' Richard replied. 'RoSur tried three times to process the first manual command, was unsuccessful in each attempt, and then went on to the next command. The software operated exactly as it was designed....'

'But why,' Tabori asked, 'did it go back to the first command afterwards?'

'Because the software designers never considered the possibility of *multiple* bad manual commands. Or at least never designed for the condition. The internal question the software asks after finishing with the processing of each command is whether or not there is another manual command in the buffer. If there is *not*, then the software rejects the first command and is free to handle another interrupt. If there *is*, however, the software is told to store the rejected command and process the next command. Now, if two commands in a row are rejected, the software *assumes* that the command processor *hardware* is broken, swaps to the redundant hardware set, and tries again to process the same manual commands. You can understand the reasonings. Suppose one....'

Nicole listened for several seconds as Richard and Janos talked about redundant subsystems, buffered commands, and queue structures. She had very little training in either fault protection or redundancy management and could not follow the exchange. 'Just a moment,' she interjected at length, 'you've lost me again. Remember, I'm not an engineer. Can't somebody give me a summary in normal English?'

Wakefield was apologetic. 'Sorry, Nicole,' he said. 'You know what an interrupt driven software system is?' She nodded. 'And you are familiar with the way priorities operate in such a system? Good. Then the explanation is simple. The fault protection interrupts based on the accelerometer and imaging data were lower priority than the manual commands inadvertently entered by Janos when he was falling. The system became locked in a software loop trying to process the bad commands and never had a chance to heed the fault signals from the sensor subsystems. That's why the scalpel kept cutting.'

For some reason Nicole was disappointed. The explanation was clear enough, and she had certainly not wanted the analysis to implicate Janos or any other member of the crew. But it was too simple. It had not been worth all her time and energy.

Nicole sat down on the cot in Richard Wakefield's hut. 'So much for my mystery,' she said.

Janos sat beside her. 'Cheer up, Nicole,' he said. 'This is good news. At least now we know for certain that we didn't foul up the initialisation process. There's a logical explanation for what happened.'

'Great,' she replied sarcastically. 'But General Borzov is still dead. And now Reggie Wilson is too.' Nicole thought about the American journalist's erratic behaviour over the last several days and remembered her earlier conversation with Francesca. 'Incidentally,' she said spontaneously, 'did either of you ever hear General Borzov complain of headaches or any other discomfort? Especially on the day of the banquet?'

Wakefield shook his head. 'No,' said Janos, 'why do you ask?'

'Well, I asked the portable diagnostician, based on Borzov's biometry data, to give me the possible causes of his symptoms, given that the general was *not* having an appendicitis. The most likely cause was listed as drug reaction. Sixty-two percent probable. I thought that maybe he might have had an adverse reaction to some medication.'

'Really?' Janos said, his curiosity piqued. 'Why have you never said anything about this to me before?'

'I was going to ... several times,' Nicole answered. 'But I didn't think you were interested. Remember when I stopped by your room on the Newton the day after General Borzov died? It was right after the crew meeting. From the way you responded I concluded that you didn't want to rehash –'

'Goodness.' Janos shook his head. 'How we humans fail to communicate. It was just a headache. Nothing more or less. I certainly didn't mean to give you the impression that I was unwilling to talk about Valeriy's death.'

'Speaking of communicating,' Nicole said, as she rose wearily from the cot, 'I must go to see Dr Brown and Admiral Heilmann before I go to bed.' She looked at Wakefield. 'Thanks a lot for your help, Richard. I wish I could say that I felt better now.'

Nicole walked over beside Janos. 'I'm sorry, friend,' she said. 'I should have shared my whole investigation with you. It probably would have been over much faster....'

'It's fine,' Janos replied. 'Don't worry about it.' He smiled. 'Come on, I'll walk with you as far as my suite.'

Nicole could hear the loud conversation inside before she knocked on the door to the hut. David Brown, Otto Heilmann, and Francesca Sabatini were arguing about how to reply to the latest directions from Earth.

'They're overreacting,' Francesca was saying. 'And they'll realise it as soon as they have some time to reflect. This is not the first mission to suffer a loss of human life.'

'But they have *ordered* us to return to the Newton as soon as possible,' Admiral Heilmann protested.

'So tomorrow we'll talk to them again and explain why

we want to survey New York first. Takagishi says the sea will start to melt in another day or two and we'll have to leave anyway. Besides, Wakefield and Takagishi and I did hear something that night, even if David doesn't believe us.'

'I don't know, Francesca,' Dr Brown was starting to respond when he finally heard Nicole's knock. 'Who's there?' he asked crossly.

'Cosmonaut des Jardins. I have some important medical information –'

'Look, des Jardins,' Brown interrupted quickly, 'we're very busy. Can't it wait until morning?'

All right, Nicole said to herself. *I can wait until morning.* She wasn't anxious to answer Dr Brown's questions about Takagishi's heart condition anyway. 'Roger,' she said out loud, laughing at herself for using the expression.

Within seconds Nicole could hear the discussion start again behind her. She walked slowly back to her hut. *Tomorrow has to be a better day*, she thought as she crawled on to her cot.

31
Orvieto Prodigy

'Good night, Otto,' David Brown said as the German admiral left his hut.

'See you in the morning.' Dr Brown yawned and stretched. He looked at his watch. It was a little more than eight hours until the lights should come on again.

He pulled off his flight suit and had a drink of water. He had just lain down on his cot when Francesca entered his hut. 'David,' she said, 'we have more problems.' She walked over and gave him a short kiss. 'I've been talking to Janos. Nicole suspects that Valeriy was drugged.'

'Whaaat?' he replied. He sat up on his cot. 'How could she? There was no way....'

'Apparently there was some evidence in his biometry data and she cleverly found it. She mentioned it to Janos tonight.'

'You didn't react when he told you, did you? I mean, we must be absolutely –'

'Of course not,' Francesca answered. 'Anyway, Janos would never suspect anything in a thousand years. He is a total innocent. At least where things like this are concerned.'

'Damn that woman,' David Brown said. 'And damn her biometry.' He rubbed his face with his hands. 'What a day. First that stupid Wilson tries to be a hero. Now this ... I told you we should have destroyed all the data from the operation. It would have been an easy matter to wipe out the central files. Then things would never –'

'She would still have his biometry records,' Francesca

countered. 'That's where the prime evidence is. You would have to be an absolute genius to take the data from the operation itself and deduce anything.' She sat down and cradled Dr Brown's head against her chest. 'Our big mistake was not when we failed to destroy the files. That would have aroused suspicion at the ISA. Our error was in underestimating Nicole des Jardins.'

Dr Brown shook free from the embrace and stood up. 'Damnit, Francesca, it's your fault. I never should have let you talk me into it. I knew at the time –'

'You knew at the time –' Francesca sharply interrupted her companion –' that you, Dr David Brown, were not going on the first sortie into Rama. You knew at the time that your future millions as the hero and perceived leader of this expedition would be seriously compromised if you stayed on board the Newton.' Brown stopped pacing and faced Francesca. 'You knew at the time,' she continued more softly, 'that I too had a vested interest in your going on the sortie. And that I could be counted on to provide you with support.'

She took his hands and pulled him back toward the cot. 'Sit down, David,' Francesca said. 'We've been over and over this. We did not kill General Borzov. We simply gave him a drug that created the symptoms of an appendicitis. We made the decision together. If Rama had not manoeuvred and the robot surgeon had not malfunctioned, then our plan would have worked perfectly. Borzov would be on the Newton today, recovering from his appendectomy, and you and I would be here leading the exploration of Rama.'

David Brown removed his hands from hers and started to wring them. 'I feel so ... so unclean,' he said. 'I've never done anything like this before. I mean, whether we like it or not, we are partially responsible for Borzov's death. Maybe even for Wilson's as well. We could be indicted.' He was shaking his head again. There was a forlorn expression on his face. 'I'm supposed to be a scientist,' he said. 'What has happened to me? How did I get mixed up in these things?'

'Spare me your righteousness,' Francesca said harshly.

'And don't try to kid yourself. Aren't you the man who stole the decade's most important astronomical discovery from a woman graduate student. And then married her to keep her quiet forever? Your integrity was compromised a long long time ago.'

'That's unfair,' Dr Brown said petulantly. 'I have mostly been honest. Except –'

'Except when it was important and worth a lot to you. What a pile of shit!' Francesca now stood up and paced around the hut herself. 'You men are so damn hypocritical. You preserve your lofty self-images with amazing rationalisations. You never admit to yourselves who you really are and what you really want. Most women are more honest. We acknowledge our ambitions, our desires, even our basest wants. We admit our weaknesses. We face ourselves as we are, not as we would like to be.'

She returned to the cot and took David's hands in hers again. 'Don't you see, darling?' she said earnestly, 'you and I are soulmates. Our alliance is based on the strongest bond of all – mutual self-interest. We are both motivated by the same goals – power and fame.'

'That sounds awful,' he said.

'But it's true. Even if you don't want to admit it to yourself. David, darling, can't you see that your indecisiveness comes from your failure to acknowledge your true nature? Look at me. I know exactly what I want and am never confused about what to do. My behaviour is automatic.'

The American physicist sat quietly beside Francesca for a long time. At length he turned and put his head on her shoulder. 'First Borzov, now Wilson,' he said with a sigh. 'I feel whipped. I wish none of this had happened.'

'You can't give up, David,' she said, stroking his head. 'We've come too far. And the big prize is now within our reach.'

Francesca reached across him and started to remove his shirt. 'It's been a long and trying day,' she said soothingly. 'Let's try to forget it.' David Brown closed his eyes as she caressed his face and chest.

Francesca bent over and kissed him slowly on the lips. A few moments later she abruptly stopped. 'You see,' she said, slowly removing her own clothes, 'as long as we are in this together, we can derive strength from each other.' She stood up in front of David, forcing him to open his eyes.

'Hurry,' he said impatiently, 'I was already....'

'Don't worry so much about it,' Francesca replied, lazily pulling down her pants, 'you've never had a problem with me.' Francesca smiled again as she pushed his knees apart and pressed his face against her breasts. 'Remember,' she said, tugging easily at his shorts with her free hand, 'I'm not Elaine.'

She studied David Brown as he slept beside her. The strain and anxiety that had dominated his face just minutes before had been replaced by the carefree smile of a boy. *Men are so simple*, Francesca was thinking. *Orgasm is the perfect pain reliever. I wish it were that easy for us.*

She slipped off the small cot and put her clothes on again. Francesca was very careful not to disturb her sleeping friend. *But you and I still have a real problem*, she said to herself as she finished dressing, *which we need to address quickly. And it will be more difficult because we are dealing with a woman.*

Francesca walked outside her hut, into the black of Rama. There were a few lights near the supplies at the other end of the camp, but otherwise the Beta campsite was dark. Everyone else was asleep. She switched on her small flashlight and walked away in a southerly direction, toward the Cylindrical Sea.

What is it that you want, Madame Nicole des Jardins? she thought as she walked along. And *where's your weakness, your Achilles heel?* For several minutes Francesca flipped through her entire memory bank on Nicole, attempting to find any personality or character flaw that could be exploited. *Money's not the answer. Sex isn't either, at least not with me.* She laughed involuntarily. *And certainly not with David. Your dislike for him is obvious.*

What about blackmail? Francesca asked herself as she drew near to the banks of the Cylindrical Sea. She remembered Nicole's strong reaction to her question about Genevieve's father. *Maybe*, she thought, *if I knew the answer to that question ... but I don't.*

Francesca was temporarily baffled. She could not work out any way to compromise Nicole des Jardins. By this time the lights from the campsite behind her were barely visible. Francesca extinguished her flashlight and very cautiously sat down to dangle her feet over the edge of the cliff.

Having her legs suspended above the frozen ice of the Cylindrical Sea brought back a suite of poignant memories from her childhood in Orvieto. At the age of eleven, despite the barrage of health warnings that assaulted her from every direction, the precocious Francesca had decided to start smoking cigarettes. Every day after school she would wind her way down the hill to the plain below the town and sit on the bank of her favourite stream. There she would smoke in silence, an act of solitary rebellion. On those lazy afternoons she would inhabit a fantasy world of castles and princes, millions of kilometres away from her mother and stepfather.

The memory of those adolescent moments produced an irresistible desire to smoke in Francesca. She had been taking her nicotine pills throughout the mission, but they satisfied only the physical addiction. She laughed at herself and reached into one of the special pockets of her flight suit. Francesca had hidden away three cigarettes in a special container that would preserve them in fresh condition. She had told herself before leaving the Earth that the cigarettes were there 'in case of emergency'....

Smoking a cigarette inside an extraterrestrial space vehicle was even more outrageous than smoking at the age of eleven. Francesca wanted to hoot with delight when she threw back her head and expelled the smoke into the Raman air. The act made her feel free, liberated. Somehow the threat represented by Nicole des Jardins did not seem so serious.

While she was smoking, Francesca recalled the acute loneliness of that young girl stealing down the slopes of old Orvieto. She also remembered the terrible secret that she had kept locked forever in her heart. Francesca had never told anyone about her stepfather, certainly not her mother, and she rarely told anyone about it any more. But as she sat on the banks of the Cylindrical Sea, the anguish of her childhood appeared to her in sharp relief.

It began right after my eleventh birthday, she thought, plunging back into the details of her life eighteen years before. *I had no idea what the bastard wanted at first.* She took another deep drag from her cigarette. *Even after he started bringing me gifts for no reason.*

He had been the principal of her new school. When she had taken her first full set of aptitude tests, Francesca had made the highest scores in the history of Orvieto. She was off the scale, a prodigy. Until then he had never noticed her. He had married her mother eighteen months before and fathered the twins almost immediately. Francesca had been a nuisance, another mouth to feed, nothing more than a part of her mother's furniture.

For several months he was especially nice to me. Then mother went to visit Aunt Carla for a few days. The painful memories came fast, rushing like a torrent through her mind. She remembered the smell of wine on her stepfather's breath, his sweat against her body, her tears after he had left her room.

The nightmare had lasted for over a year. He had forced himself upon her whenever her mother was not in the house. Then one evening, while he was putting on his clothes and looking in the other direction, Francesca had struck him on the back of the head with an aluminium baseball bat. Her stepfather had fallen to the floor, bloody and unconscious. She had dragged him into the living room and left him there.

He never touched me again, Francesca remembered, putting out her cigarette in the Raman dirt. *We were strangers in the same house. From then on I spent most of my time with Roberto and his friends. I was just waiting for my chance. I was ready when Carla came.*

Francesca was fourteen during the summer of 2184. She
spent most of her time that summer loitering around the
main square of Orvieto. Her older cousin Roberto had
just completed his certificate to be a tour guide for the
cathedral in the square. The old Duomo, the chief tourist
attraction of the town, had been built in phases, starting
in the fourteenth century. The church was an artistic and
architectural masterpiece. The frescoes by Luca Signorelli inside its San Brizio chapel were widely hailed as
the finest examples of imaginative fifteenth-century
painting outside the Vatican museum.

To have become an official Duomo guide was
considered quite an accomplishment, especially at the
age of nineteen. Francesca was very proud of Roberto.
She sometimes accompanied him on his tours, but only if
she agreed beforehand not to embarrass him with her
wisecracks.

One August afternoon, straight after lunch, a sleek
limousine pulled into the piazza around Il Duomo and
the chauffeur requested a guide from the tourist bureau.
The gentleman in the limousine had not made a
reservation and Roberto was the only guide available.
Francesca watched with great curiousity as a short,
handsome man, in his late thirties or early forties,
climbed out of the back of the car and introduced himself
to Roberto. Automobiles had been banned from upper
Orvieto, except by special permit, for almost a hundred
years, so Francesca knew the man must be an unusual
individual.

As he always did, Roberto began his tour with the
reliefs sculpted by Lorenzo Maitani on the outside
portals of the church. Still curious, Francesca stood just
off to the side, smoking quietly, while her cousin
explained the significance of the weird demonic figures at
the bottom of one of the columns. 'This is one of the
earliest representations of Hell,' Roberto said, pointing
at a group of Dantesque figures. 'The fourteenth-century
concept of Hell involved an extremely literal interpretation of the Bible.'

'Hah!' Francesca had suddenly interjected, dropping

her cigarette on the cobblestones and walking toward Roberto and the handsome stranger. 'It was also a very masculine concept of Hell. Notice that many of the demons have breasts and most of the sins depicted are sexual. Men have always believes that they were created perfect; it is women who have taught them to sin.'

The stranger was astonished by the appearance of this gangly teenager expelling smoke from her mouth. He immediately recognised her natural beauty and it was clear that she was very bright. Who was she?

'This is my cousin, Francesca,' Roberto said, obviously flustered by her interruption.

'Carlo Bianchi,' the man said, extending his hand. His hand was moist. Francesca looked up at his face and could see that he was interested. She could feel her heart pounding in her chest. 'If you listen to Roberto,' she said coyly, 'then all you'll get is the official tour. He leaves out the juicy bits.'

'And you, young lady –'

'Francesca,' she said.

'Yes, Francesca. Do you have a tour of your own?'

Francesca gave him her prettiest smile. 'I read a lot,' she said. 'I know all about the artists who worked on the cathedral, particularly the painter Luca Signorelli.' She paused for a moment. 'Did you know,' she continued, 'that Michelangelo came here to study Signorelli's nudes before he painted the ceiling at the Sistine Chapel?'

'No, I didn't.' Carlo laughed heartily. He was already fascinated. 'But I do now. Come. Join us. You can add to what your cousin Roberto says.'

She loved the way he kept staring at her. It was as if he were appraising her, as if she were a fine painting or a jewelled necklace, his eyes missing nothing as they roamed unabashedly over her figure. And his easy laughter spurred her on. Francesca's comments became increasingly outrageous and bawdy.

'You see that poor girl on the demon's back?' she said while they were gazing at the bewildering range of genius exhibited by Signorelli's frescoes inside the San Brizio chapel. 'She lookes like she's humping the demon from behind, right? You know who she is? Her face and naked body are portraits of Signorelli's girl friend. While he was slaving in here day after day, she became bored and decided to diddle a duke or two on the side. Luca was really pissed off. So he fixed her. He condemned her to ride a demon in perpetuity.'

When he stopped laughing. Carlo asked Francesca if she thought the woman's punishment was fair. 'Of course not,' the fourteen-year-old replied. 'It's just another example of the male chauvinism of the fifteenth century. The men could screw anybody they wanted and were called virile; but let a woman try to satisfy herself –'

'*Francesca*!', Roberto interrupted her. 'Really. This is too much. Your mother would kill you if she heard what you are saying....'

'My mother is irrelevant at this moment. I'm talking about a double standard that still exists today. Look at....'

Carlo Bianchi could hardly believe his good fortune. A rich clothes designer from Milano, one who had established an international reputation by the time he was thirty, he had just happened to decide, on a whim, to hire a car to take him to Rome instead of going on the usual high-speed train. His sister Monica had always told him about the beauty of Il Duomo in Orvieto. It had been another last-minute decision to stop. And now. My, my. The girl was such a splendid morsel.

He invited Francesca to dinner when the tour was over. But when they reached the entrance to the smartest restaurant in Orvieto, the young woman balked. Carlo understood. He took her to a store and bought her an expensive new dress with matching shoes and accessories. He was astonished by how beautiful she was. And only fourteen!

Francesca had never before drunk really fine wine. She drank it as if it were water. Each dish was so delicious that she positively squealed. Carlo was enchanted with his woman-child. He loved the way she let her cigarette dangle from the corner of her lips. It was so unspoiled, so perfectly gauche.

When the meal was over it was dark. Francesca walked

with him back to the limousine parked in front of Il
Duomo. As they went down a narrow alley, she leaned
over and playfully bit his ear. He spontaneously pulled
her to him and was rewarded with an explosive kiss. The
surge in his loins overwhelmed him.

Francesca had felt it too. She did not hesitate a second
when Carlo suggested they go for a ride in the car. By the
time the limousine had reached the outskirts of Orvieto,
she was sitting astride him in the back seat. Thirty
minutes later, when they finished making love the second
time, Carlo could not bear the thought of parting with
this incredible girl. He asked Francesca if she would like
to accompany him to Rome.

'Andiamo,' she replied with a smile.

So we went to Rome and then Capri, Francesca
remembered. *Paris for a week. In Milano you had me live
with Monica and Luigi. For appearances. Men are always
so worried about appearances.*

Francesca's long reverie was broken when she thought
she heard footsteps in the distance. She cautiously stood
up in the dark and listened. It was hard for her to hear
anything over her own breathing. Then she heard the
sound again, off to the left. Her ears told her the sound
was out on the ice. A burst of fear flooded her with an
image of bizarre creatures attacking their camp from
across the ice. She listened again very carefully, but
heard nothing.

Francesca turned back toward the camp. *I loved you
Carlo*, she said to herself, *if I ever loved any man. Even
after you began to share me with your friends.* More
long-buried pain came to the surface and Francesca
fought it with hard anger. *Until you started hitting me.
That ruined everything. You proved that you were a real
bastard.*

Francesca very deliberately pushed aside the memories. *Now where were we?* she thought as she approached
her hut. *Ah yes. The issue was Nicole des Jardins. How
much does she really know? And what are we going to do
about it?*

32
New York Explorer

The tiny bell on his wristwatch awakened Dr Takagishi from a deep sleep. For a few moments he was disoriented, unable to remember where he was. He sat up on his cot and rubbed his eyes. At length he recalled that he was inside Rama and that the alarm had been set to wake him up after five hours of sleep.

He dressed in the dark. When he was finished he picked up a large bag and fumbled around inside for several seconds. Satisfied with its contents, he threw the strap over his shoulder and walked to the door of his hut. Dr Takagishi peered out cautiously. He could not see lights in any of the other huts. He took a deep breath and tiptoed out the door.

The world's leading authority on Rama walked out of the camp in the direction of the Cylindrical Sea. When he reached the shore, he climbed slowly down to the icy surface on the stairs cut into the fifty-metre cliff. Takagishi sat on the bottom rung, hidden against the base of the cliff. He removed some special cleats from his bag and attached them to the bottom of his shoes. Before walking out on the ice, the scientist calibrated his personal navigator so that he would be able to keep a constant heading once he left the shoreline.

When he was about two hundred metres away from the shore, Dr Takagishi reached in his pocket to pull out his portable weather monitor. It dropped on the ice, making a short clacking sound in the quiet night. Takagishi picked it up a few seconds later. The monitor told him that the temperature was minus two degrees Centigrade and that a soft wind was blowing across the ice at eight kilometres per hour.

Takagishi inhaled deeply and was astonished by a peculiar but familiar odour. Puzzled, he inhaled again, this time concentrating on the smell. There was no doubt about it – it was cigarette smoke! He hurriedly extinguished his flashlight and stood motionless on the ice. His mind raced into overdrive, searching for an explanation. Francesca Sabatini was the only cosmonaut who smoked. Had she somehow followed him when he left the camp? Had she seen his light when he checked his weather monitor?

He listened for noises but heard nothing in the Raman night. Still he waited. When the cigarette smell had gone for several minutes, Dr Takagishi continued his trek across the ice, stopping every four or five steps to ensure that he was not being followed. Eventually he convinced himself that Francesca was not behind him. However, the cautious Takagishi did not turn on his flashlight again until he had walked more than a kilometre and had become worried that he might have drifted off course.

Altogether it took him forty-five minutes to reach the opposite edge of the sea and the island city of New York. When he was a hundred metres from the shore, the Japanese scientist took a larger flashlight from his bag and switched on its powerful beam. The ghostly silhouettes of the skyscrapers sent an exhilarating chill down his spine. At last he was here! At last he could seek the answers to his lifetime of questions unencumbered by someone else's arbitrary schedule.

Dr Takagishi knew exactly where he wanted to go in New York. Each of the three circular sections of the Raman city was further subdivided into three angular portions, like a pie divided into slices. At the centre of each of the three main sections was a core, or plaza, around which the rest of the buildings and streets were arranged. As a boy in Kyoto, after reading everything he could find about the first Raman expedition, Takagishi had wondered what it would be like to stand in the centre of one of those alien plazas and stare upward at buildings created by beings from another star. Takagishi felt certain not only that the secrets of Rama could be understood by studying New York, but also that its three plazas were the most likely locations for clues to the mysterious purpose of the interstellar vehicle.

The map of New York drawn by the earlier Raman explorers was as firmly etched in Takagishi's mind as the map of Kyoto where he was born and raised. But the first expedition had had only a limited time to survey New York. Of the nine functional units, only one had been mapped in detail; the earlier cosmonauts had simply assumed, on the basis of limited observations, that all the other units were identical.

As Takagishi's brisk pace carried him deeper and deeper into the foreboding quiet of one part of the central section, some subtle differences between this particular segment of Rama and the one studied by Norton's crew (they had surveyed an adjacent slice) began to emerge. The layout of the major streets in the two units was the same; however, as Dr Takagishi drew closer to the plaza, the smaller streets broke into a slightly different pattern from the one that had been reported by the first explorers. The scientist in Takagishi forced him to stop often and note all the variations on his pocket computer.

He entered the region immediately surrounding the plaza, where the streets ran in concentric circles. He crossed three avenues and found himself standing opposite a huge octahedron, about a hundred metres tall, with a mirrored exterior. His powerful flashlight beam reflected off its surface and then bounced from building to building around him. Dr Takagishi walked slowly around the octahedron, searching for an entrance, but he did not find one.

On the other side of the eight-sided structure, in the centre of the plaza, was a broad circular space without tall buildings. Shigeru Takagishi moved deliberately around the entire perimeter of the circle, studying the surrounding buildings as he walked. He gained no new insights about the purpose of the structures. When he turned inward at regular intervals to survey the plaza area itself, he saw nothing unusual or particularly noteworthy. Nevertheless, he did enter into his computer the location of the many low, nondescript metallic boxes that divided the plaza into partitions.

When he was again in front of the octahedron, Dr Takagishi reached into his bag and pulled out a thin hexagonal plate densely covered with electronics. He deployed the scientific apparatus in the plaza, three or four metres away from the octahedron, and then spent ten minutes verifying with his transceiver that all the scientific instruments were working properly. When the Japanese scientist had completed checking the payload, he quickly left the plaza area and headed for the Cylindrical Sea.

Takagishi was in the middle of the second concentric avenue when he heard a brief but loud popping noise behind him in the plaza. He turned around but didn't move. A few seconds later he heard a different sound. This one Takagishi recognised from his first sortie, both the dragging of the metal brushes and the embedded high frequency singing. He shone his flashlight in the direction of the plaza. The sound stopped. He switched off his flashlight and stood quietly in the middle of the avenue.

Several minutes later the brushdragging began again. Takagishi moved stealthily across the two avenues and started around the octahedron in the direction of the noise. When he was almost at the plaza, a beep-beep from his bag broke his concentration. By the time he turned off the alarm, which was indicating that the scientific package he had just deployed in the plaza had already malfunctioned, there was total quiet in New York. Again Dr Takagishi waited, but this time the sound did not recur.

He took a deep breath to calm himself and summoned all his courage. Somehow his curiosity won out over his fear and Dr Takagishi returned to the plaza opposite the octahedron to find out what had happened to the scientific payload. His first surprise was that the hexagonal package had vanished from the spot where he had left it. Where could it have gone? Who or what could have taken it?

Takagishi knew that he was on the verge of a scientific discovery of overwhelming importance. He was also terrified. Fighting a powerful desire to flee, he shone his large flashlight around the plaza, hoping to find an explanation for the disappearance of the science station. The beam reflected off a small piece of metal some thirty to forty metres closer to the centre of the plaza. Takagishi knew instinctively that the reflection was coming from the instrument package. He hurried over to it.

He bent down on his knees and examined the electronics. There was no obvious damage. He had just pulled out his transceiver to begin a methodical check of all the science instruments when he noticed a ropelike object about fifteen centimetres in diameter at the edge of the flashlight beam illuminating the science package. Dr Takagishi picked up his light and walked over to the object. It was striped, black and gold, and stretched off into the distance for twelve metres or so, disappearing behind an odd metal shed about three metres tall. He felt the thick rope. It was soft and fuzzy on the top. When he tried to turn it over to feel the bottom, the object began to move. Takagishi dropped it immediately and watched it slither slowly away from him toward the shed. The motion was accompanied by the sound of brushes dragging against metal.

Dr Takagishi could hear the sound of his own heartbeat. Again he fought the urge to run away. He remembered his dawn meditations as a college student in the garden of his Zen master. He would not be afraid. He ordered his feet to march in the direction of the shed.

The black and gold rope disappeared. There was silence in the plaza. Takagishi approached the shed with his light beam on the ground at the spot where the thick rope had last been visible. He came around the corner and thrust the beam into the shed. He could not believe what he saw. A mass of black and gold tentacles writhed underneath the light.

A high frequency whine suddenly exploded in his ears Dr Takagishi looked over his shoulder and was thunderstruck. His eyes bulged. His scream was lost as the noise intensified and three of the tentacles reached out to touch him. The walls of his heart gave way and he slumped, already dead, into the grasp of the amazing creature.

33
Missing Person

'Admiral Heilmann?'

'Yes, General O'Toole?'

'Are you by yourself?'

'Certainly. I just woke up a few minutes ago. My meeting with Dr Brown is not for another hour. Why are you calling so early?'

'While you were sleeping I received a coded top secret message from COG military headquarters. It's about Trinity. They wanted to know the status.'

'What do you mean, General?'

'Is this line secure, Admiral? Have you turned off the automatic recorder?'

'Now I have.'

'They asked two questions. Did Borzov die without telling anyone his RQ? Does anyone else on the crew know about Trinity?'

'You know the answers to both questions.'

'I wanted to be certain that you hadn't talked to Dr Brown. They insisted that I check with you before encoding my answer. What do you think this is all about?'

'I don't know, Michael. Maybe somebody down on Earth is getting nervous. Wilson's death probably scared them.'

'It certainly scared me. But not to the point that I would think about Trinity. I wonder if they know something that we don't?'

'Well, I guess we'll find out soon enough. All the ISA

officials have been insisting that we should evacuate
Rama at the first available opportunity. They didn't even
like our decision to rest the crew for several hours first.
This time I don't think they will change their minds.'

'Admiral, do you remember that hypothetical discussion we had with General Borzov during the cruise, about
the conditions under which we would activate Trinity?'

'Vaguely. Why?'

'Do you still disagree with his insistence that we must
know *why* the Trinity contingency is being called for?
You said at the time that if the Earth thought great
danger was imminent, you didn't personally need to
understand the rationale.'

'I'm afraid I'm not following you, General. Why are
you asking me these questions?'

'I would like your permission, Otto, when I encode the
response to COG military headquarters, to find out why
they are asking about the status of Trinity at this
particular time. If we are in danger, we have a right to
know.'

'You may request additional information, Michael, but
I would bet that their enquiry is strictly routine.'

Janos Tabori awakened while it was still dark inside
Rama. As he pulled on his flight suit, he made a mental
list of the activities that would be required to transport
the crab biot to the Newton. If the order to leave Rama
was confirmed, they would be departing soon after dawn.
Janos consulted the formal evacuation procedure stored
on his pocket computer and updated it by adding the new
tasks associated with the biot.

He checked his watch. Dawn was only fifteen minutes
away, assuming of course that the Rama diurnal cycle
was regular. Janos laughed to himself. Rama had
produced so many surprises already that there was no
certainty the lights would return on schedule. If they did,
however, Janos wanted to watch the Raman 'sunrise'. He
could eat his breakfast after dawn.

A hundred metres from his hut the caged crab biot was
immobile, as it had been since it was hoisted away from

its companions the previous day. Janos shone his
flashlight through the tough, transparent cage wall and
checked to see if there were any signs that the biot might
have moved during the night. After having established
that the biot had not changed position, Janos walked
away from the Beta campsite in the direction of the sea.

As he waited for the burst of light, he found himself
thinking about the very end of his conversation with
Nicole the night before. There was something not quite
right about her offhand revelation of the possible cause of
General Borzov's pain on the night that he died. Janos
remembered vividly the healthy appendix; there was no
doubt that the primary diagnosis had been incorrect. But
why had Nicole not talked to him about the backup drug
diagnosis? Especially if she was conducting an investigation into the issue....

Janos reached the inescapable conclusion that Dr des
Jardins had either lost faith in his ability or somehow
suspected that he might himself have administered the
drugs to General Borzov without consulting her. Either
way he should find out what she was thinking. A strange
idea, born from his own feelings of guilt, next crossed his
mind. Could it be, he mused, that Nicole somehow
knows about the Schmidt-Hagenest project and suspects
all four of us?

For the first time, Janos himself wondered if perhaps
Valeriy Borzov's pain had not been natural. He recalled
the chaotic meeting the four of them had had two hours
after David Brown had learned that he would be left on
board the Newton during the first sortie. 'You must talk
to him, Otto,' a frustrated Dr Brown had said to Admiral
Heilmann. 'You must convince him to change his mind.'

Otto Heilmann had then admitted it was unlikely
General Borzov would change the personnel assignments
based on his request. 'In that case,' Dr Brown had
replied angrily, 'we can say goodbye to all the incentive
awards in our contract.'

Throughout the meeting Francesca Sabatini had
remained quiet and seemingly unworried. As he was
leaving, Janos had overheard Dr Brown berating her.

'And why are you so calm?' he had said. 'You stand to lose as much as anyone else. Or do you have a plan I don't know about?'

Janos had glimpsed Francesca's smile for only a fraction of a second. But he had remarked to himself at the time that she had seemed oddly confident. Now, as Cosmonaut Tabori awaited dawn on Rama, that smile returned to haunt him. With Francesca's knowledge of drugs it would have been well within her capability to give General Borzov something that would induce appendicitis symptoms. But would she have done something so ... so blatantly dishonest, just to enhance the value of their post-mission media project?

Again Rama was instantaneously flooded with light. As always, it was a feast for the eyes. Janos turned around slowly, looking in all directions and studying both bowls of the immense structure. With the light now brightly shining, he resolved to talk to Francesca at the first opportunity.

It was Irina Turgenyev, strangely enough, who asked the question. The cosmonauts were almost finished with their breakfast. Dr Brown and Admiral Heilmann, in fact, had already left the table to conduct another of their interminable conference calls with ISA management. 'Where's Dr Takagishi?' she said innocently. 'He's the last member of the crew I would expect to be late for anything.'

'He must have slept through his alarm,' Janos Tabori answered, pushing his folding chair away from the table. 'I'll go check on him.'

When Janos returned a minute later he was perplexed. 'He wasn't there,' he said with a shrug of his shoulders. 'I guess he went out for a walk.'

Nicole des Jardins had an immediate sinking feeling in her stomach. She rose abruptly without finishing her breakfast. 'We should go and look for him,' she said, her concern undisguised, 'or he won't be ready when we leave.'

The other cosmonauts all noticed Nicole's agitation.

'What's going on here?' Richard Wakefield said good-naturedly. 'One of our scientists takes a little morning walk on his own and the company doctor goes into panic?' He switched on his radio. 'Hello, Dr Takagishi, wherever you are. This is Wakefield. Will you please let us know that you're all right so that we can finish our breakfast.'

There was a long silence. Every member of the crew knew that it was an absolutely mandatory requirement to carry a communicator at all times. You could choose to turn off the transmission capability, but you had to listen under any and all circumstances.

'Takagishi-san,' Nicole said next with an urgent edge in her voice. 'Are you all right? Please respond.' During the extended silence, the sinking feeling in Nicole's stomach turned into a large knot. Something terrible had happened to her friend.

'I've explained that to you twice, Dr Maxwell,' David Brown said in exasperation. 'It makes no sense to evacuate part of the crew. The most efficient way to search for Dr Takagishi is to use the entire staff. Once we find him we will clear out of Rama with great haste. And to answer your last question, no, this is not a ploy on the part of the crew to avoid compliance with the evacuation order.'

He turned to Admiral Heilmann and handed him the microphone. 'Damnit, Otto,' he muttered, 'you talk to that bureaucratic nincompoop. He thinks he can command this mission better than we can, even though he's a hundred million kilometres away.'

'Dr Maxwell, this is Admiral Heilmann. I am in complete agreement with Dr Brown. Anyway, with such long delay times we really can't afford to argue. We are going to proceed with our plan. Cosmonaut Tabori will stay here with me at Beta and pack all the heavy equipment, including the biot. I will coordinate the search. Brown, Sabatini, and des Jardins will cross the ice to New York, the most likely destination if the professor went under his own power. Wakefield,

Turgenyev, and Yamanaka will look for him in the helicopters.'

He paused for a moment. 'There's no need for you to respond to this transmission in a hurry. The search will already have begun before your next message arrives.'

Back in her hut, Nicole very carefully packed her medical supplies. She criticised herself for not foreseeing that Takagishi might try one last time to visit New York. *You made another mistake*, Nicole said to herself. *The least you can do is make certain you're prepared when you find him.*

She knew the personal packing procedure by heart. Nevertheless, she skimped on her own supplies of food and water to ensure that she had whatever an injured or sick Takagishi might need. Nicole had mixed emotions about her two companions on the quest to find the Japanese scientist, but it never occurred to her that the grouping might have been deliberately planned. Everyone knew Takagishi's fascination with New York. Given the circumstances, it was not surprising that Brown and Sabatini were accompanying her to the primary search area.

Just before Nicole left the hut, she saw Richard Wakefield at her door. 'May I come in?' he asked.

'Certainly,' she replied.

He walked in with uncharacteristic uncertainty, as if he were confused or embarrassed. 'What is it?' Nicole asked after an awkward silence.

He smiled. 'Well,' he said sheepishly, 'it seemed like a good idea a few minutes ago. Now it strikes me as a little stupid – maybe even childish.' Nicole noticed he was holding something in his right hand. 'I brought you something,' he continued. 'A good luck charm, I guess. I thought you might take it with you to New York.'

Cosmonaut Wakefield opened his hand. Nicole recognised the figurine of Prince Hal. 'You can say what you will about valour and discretion and all that, but sometimes a little luck is more important.'

Nicole was surprisingly touched. She took the little

figurine from Wakefield and studied its intricate detail with admiration. 'Does the prince have any special qualities I need to know about?' she asked with a smile.

'Oh, yes,' Richard brightened. 'He loves to spend witty evenings in pubs with fat knights and other unsavoury characters. Or battle renegade dukes and earls. Or court beautiful French princess.'

Nicole blushed slightly. 'If I'm lonely and want the prince to amuse me, what do I do?' she asked.

Richard came over beside Nicole and showed her a tiny keyboard just above Prince Hal's buttocks. 'He'll respond to many commands,' Richard said, handing her a very small baton the size of a pin. 'This will fit perfectly into any of the key slots. Try 'T' for talk or 'A' for action if you want him to show you his stuff.'

Nicole put the little prince and the baton in the pocket of her flight suit. 'Thank you, Richard,' she said. 'This is very sweet.'

Wakefield was flustered. 'Well, you know, it's no big deal. It's just that we've had a spate of bad luck and I thought, I mean, maybe –'

'Thanks again, Richard,' Nicole interrupted him. 'I appreciate your concern.' They walked out of her hut together.

34
Strange Companions

Dr David Brown was the kind of abstract scientist who neither liked nor trusted machines. Most of his published papers were written about theoretical subjects because he abhorred the formality and detail of empirical science. Empiricists had to contend with instrumentation and, even worse, engineers. Dr Brown considered all engineers to be nothing more than glorified carpenters and plumbers. He tolerated their existence only because some of them were necessary if his theories were ever to be proved by actual data.

When Nicole innocently asked Dr Brown some simple questions about the workings of the icemobile, Francesca could not restrain a cackle. 'He has absolutelty no idea,' the Italian journalist responded, 'and he couldn't care less. Would you believe that the man doesn't even know how to drive an electric cart? I've seen him stare at a simple food-processing robot for over thirty minutes, trying without success to figure out how to use it. He would starve to death if nobody helped him.'

'Come on, Francesca,' Nicole replied as the two women climbed into the front seat of the icemobile, 'he can't be that bad. After all, he has to use all the crew computers and communication devices, as well as the image processing system on board the Newton. So you must be exaggerating.'

The tenor of the conversation was light and harmless. Dr David Brown slumped in the back seat and heaved a sigh. 'Surely you two exceptional women have something more important to discuss. If not, perhaps you could explain to me why a lunatic Japanese scientist takes off from our camp in the middle of the night.'

'According to Maxwell's assistant, that obsequious cipher Mills, many people on Earth think our good Japanese doctor was kidnapped by the Ramans.'

'Come on, Francesca. Be serious. Why would Dr Takagishi decide to strike out on his own?'

'I have an idea,' Nicole said slowly, 'that he was impatient with the scheduled exploration process. You know how fervently he believes in the importance of New York. After the Wilson incident ... well, he was fairly certain that an evacuation would be ordered. By the time we come back inside, *if we* come back, the Cylindrical Sea may have melted and it will be more difficult to reach New York.'

Nicole's natural honesty was urging her to tell Brown and Sabatini about Takagishi's heart problems. But her intuitive sense told her not to trust her two companions. 'He just doesn't seem like the type to go off half-cocked,' Dr Brown was saying. 'I wonder if he heard or saw something.'

'Maybe he had a headache or couldn't sleep for some other reason,' Francesca offered. 'Reggie Wilson used to prowl around at night when his head was bothering him.'

David Brown leaned forward. 'By the way,' he said to Nicole, 'Francesca tells me that you think Wilson's instability might have been exacerbated by the headache pills he was using. You certainly seem to know your drugs. I was extremely impressed by how quickly you idenitified the particular sleeping pill I had taken.'

'Speaking of drugs,' Francesca added after a short pause, 'Janos Tabori mentioned something about a discussion he had with you concerning Borzov's death. I may not have understood him correctly, but I thought he said that you believe a drug reaction may have been involved.'

They were driving steadily across the ice. The conversation had been even in tone, apparently casual. There was no obvious reason to be suspicious.

Nevertheless, Nicole said to herself as she framed a response to Francesca's remarks, *those last two comments seemed too smooth. Almost practised.* She turned to look at David Brown. She suspected that Francesca could dissemble without effort, but Nicole was certain she would be able to tell from Dr Brown's facial expression whether or not their questions were rehearsed. He squirmed slightly under her unblinking gaze.

'Cosmonaut Tabori and I were having a conversation about General Borzov and we started speculating about what might have caused his pain,' Nicole said blandly. 'After all, his appendix was perfectly healthy, so something else must have been responsible for his acute discomfort. In the course of our conversation, I mentioned to Janos that an adverse drug reaction should be considered as one possible cause. It was not a very strong statement.'

Dr Brown seemed relieved and immediately changed the subject. However, Nicole's statement had not satisfied Francesca. *Unless I am mistaken our lady journalist has more questions*, Nicole mused. *But she isn't going to ask them right now.* She watched Francesca and could tell that the Italian woman was not paying attention to Dr Brown's monologue in the back seat. While he was discussing the reaction on Earth to Wilson's death, Francesca was deep in thought.

There was a momentary quiet after Brown finished his commentary. Nicole glanced around her at the miles of ice, the imposing cliffs on the sides of the Cylindrical Sea, and the skyscrapers of New York in front of her. Rama was a glorious world. She had a momentary pang of guilt about her distrust of Francesca and Dr Brown. *It's a shame that we humans are never able to pull in the same direction*, Nicole said to herself. *Not even when confronted by infinity.*

'I can't imagine how you have managed it.' Francesca suddenly broke the silence. She had turned to address Nicole. 'Even after all this time, not even the tabloid videos have a legitimate lead. And it doesn't take a genius to figure out when it must have occurred.'

Dr Brown was completely lost. 'What in the world are you talking about?' he asked.

'Our famous life science officer,' Francesca replied. 'Don't you find it fascinating that after all this time, the identity of her daughter's father is still unknown to the public?'

'Signora Sabatini,' Nicole said immediately in Italian, 'as I told you once before, this subject is none of your business. I will not tolerate this kind of intrusion into my private affairs –'

'I just wanted to remind you, Nicole,' Francesca interrupted quickly, also in Italian, 'that you have secrets you might not want exposed.'

David Brown stared blankly at the two women. He had not understood a word in the last exchange and was confused by the obvious tension. 'So, David,' Francesca said in a patronising tone, 'you were telling us about the mood on Earth. Do you think we're going to be ordered home? Or are we merely going to abort this particular sortie?'

'The COG Executive Council has been called into special session for later this week,' he answered after a puzzled hesitation. 'Dr Maxwell's current guess is that we will be told to abandon the project.'

'That would be a typical overreaction from a group of government officials whose primary objective has always been to minimise the downside risk.' Francesca commented. 'For the first time in history, adequately prepared human beings are exploring the interior of a vehicle built by another intelligence. Yet on Earth, the politicians continue to act as if nothing unusual has happened. They are incapable of vision. It's amazing.'

Nicole des Jardins did not listen to the rest of Francesca's conversation with Dr Brown. Her mind was still focused on their earlier exchange. *She must think I have proof about the drugs in Borzov, Nicole said to herself. There's no other possible explanation for the threat.*

When they reached the edge of the ice, Francesca spent ten minutes setting up the robot camera and sound equipment for a sequence showing the three of them preparing to 'search the alien city' for their missing colleague. Nicole's complaints to Dr Brown about the waste of time went unheeeded. She did, however, make the fact that she was annoyed obvious by refusing to participate in the video sequence. While Francesca was completing her preparations, Nicole climbed the nearby stairway and studied the city of skyscrapers. Behind and below her, Nicole could hear Francesca invoking the drama of the moment for the millions of viewers back on Earth.

'Here I stand on the outskirts of the mysterious island city of New York. It was near this very spot that Dr Takagishi, Cosmonaut Wakefield and I heard some strange sounds earlier this week. We have reason to suspect that New York may have been the professor's destination when he took off from Beta campsite last night to do some solitary and unauthorised exploration ...

'What has happened to the professor? Why does he not respond when called on the commpak? Yesterday we witnessed a terrible tragedy when journalist Reggie Wilson, risking his own life to save this reporter, was trapped inside the rover and was unable to escape the powerful claws of the crab biots. Has a similar fate befallen our Rama expert? Did the extraterrestrials who built this amazing vehicle eons ago perhaps create a sophisticated trap designed to subdue and ultimately destroy any unsuspecting visitors? We don't know for certain. But we ...'

From her vantage point on top of the wall, Nicole tried to ignore Francesca and imagine in what direction Dr Takagishi might have gone. She consulted the maps stored in her pocket computer. *He would have gone toward the exact geometrical centre of the city*, she concluded. *He was certain there was meaning in the geometry.*

35

Into the Pit

They had walked the bewildering maze of streets for only twenty minutes, but they would already have been hopelessly lost without their personal navigators. They had no thorough plan for the search. They simply wandered up and down streets in a quasi-random pattern. Every three or four minutes there would be another transmission from Admiral Heilmann to Dr Brown and the search party would have to look for a location where the signal strength was satisfactory.

'At this rate,' Nicole remarked as once again they faintly heard Otto Heilmann's voice on the communicator, 'our search is going to take forever. Dr Brown, why don't you just stay in one spot? Then Francesca and I –'

'Break. Break.' They heard Otto more clearly as David Brown moved into a space between two tall buildings. 'Did you copy that last transmission?'

'Afraid not, Otto,' Dr Brown replied. 'Would you please repeat it.'

'Yamanaka, Wakefield, and Turgenyev have covered the bottom third of the Northern Hemicylinder. No sign of Takagishi. It's unlikely that he could have gone farther north, unless he went to one of the cities. In that case we should have seen his footprints somewhere. So you're probably on the right track.

'Meanwhile we have big news here. Our captured crab biot started to move about two minutes ago. It is trying to escape, but so far its tools have barely dented the cage. Tabori is working feverishly to build a larger, stronger cage that will go around the entire apparatus. I'm bringing Yamanaka's copter back to Beta so he can give Tabori a hand. He should be here in a minute ... Wait ... There's an urgent coming through from Wakefield ... I'll put him on.'

Richard Wakefield's British accent was unmistakable although he could barely be heard by the trio in New York. 'Spiders,' he shouted in response to a question from Admiral Heilmann. 'You remember the spider biot dissected by Laura Ernst? Well, we can see six of them just beyond the southern cliff. They're all over that temporary hut we built. And something has apparently repaired those two dead crab biots, for our prisoner's brothers are trundling toward the south pole....'

'Pictures!' Francesca Sabatini screamed into the radio. 'Are you taking pictures?'

'What's that? Sorry, I did not copy.'

'Francesca wants to know if you're taking pictures,' Admiral Heilmann clarified.

'Of course, love,' Richard Wakefield said. 'Both the automatic imaging system in the helicopter and the hand camera you gave me this morning have been running without interruption. The spider biots are amazing. I've never seen anything move so fast ... By the way, any sign of our Japanese professor?'

'Not yet,' David Brown shouted from New York. 'It's slow going in this maze. I feel as if I'm looking for a needle in a haystack.'

Admiral Heilmann repeated the status of the missing person search for Wakefield and Turgenyev in the helicopter. Richard then said that they were coming back to Beta to refuel. 'What about you, David?' Heilmann asked. 'In view of everything, including the need to keep those bastards on Earth informed, don't you think you should return to Beta yourself? Cosmonauts Sabatini and des Jardins can continue the search for Dr Takagishi. If necessary we can send someone to replace you when the helicopter picks you up.'

'I don't know, Otto, I haven't –' Francesca turned off the transmit switch on David Brown's radio in the middle of his reply. He shot her an angry glance that quickly softened.

'We need to talk about this,' she said firmly. 'Tell him you'll call him back in a couple of minutes.'

Nicole was flabbergasted by the conversation that ensued between Francesca Sabatini and David Brown. Neither of them seemed to be even slightly concerned about the fate of Dr Takagishi. Francesca insisted that she had to return to Beta immediately to cover *all* the breaking stories. Dr Brown was anxious because he was away from the 'primary' action of the expedition.

Each argued that his reasons for returning were more important. What if they both left New York? No, that would leave Cosmonaut des Jardins alone. Maybe she should come with them and they could reinitiate the search for Takagishi when things calmed down in several hours ...

Nicole finally exploded. '*Never*,' she shouted suddenly at them, 'never in my life have I seen such egotistical....' She could not think of a good noun. 'One of our colleagues is missing and almost certainly needs our help. He may be injured or dying, yet all you two can do is argue about your own petty prerogatives. It's really disgusting.'

She paused a second to catch her breath. 'Let me tell you one thing,' Nicole continued, still fuming. 'I am not going back to Beta right now. I don't give a damn if you order me. I am staying here and finishing the search. At least I have my priorities straight. I know a man's life is more important than image or status or even a stupid media project.'

David Brown blinked twice, as if he had been slapped in the face. Francesca smiled. 'Well, well,' she said, 'so our reclusive life science officer knows more than we have given her credit for.' She looked over at David and then back at Nicole. 'Will you excuse us for a moment, dear? We have a few matters to discuss in private.'

Francesca and Dr Brown moved over beside the base of a skyscraper about twenty metres away and began an animated conversation. Nicole turned the other way. She was angry with herself for losing her temper. She was especially irritated that she had revealed her knowledge of their contract with Schmidt and Hagenest. *They will assume Janos told me*, she thought. *After all, we have been close friends.*

Francesca walked back to join Nicole while Dr Brown radioed Admiral Heilmann. 'David is calling for the helicopter to meet him next to the icemobile. He assures me that he can find his way out. I will stay here with you and search for Takagishi. At least that way I can photograph New York.'

There was no emotion in Francesca's pronouncement. Nicole was unable to read her mood. 'One other thing,' Francesca added. 'I promised David we would conclude our search and be ready to return to camp in four hours or less.'

The two women hardly talked during the first hour of their search. Francesca was content to let Nicole choose the path. Every fifteen minutes they stopped to radio the Beta camp and obtain an updated fix on their position. 'You're now about two kilometres south and four kilometres east of the icemobile,' Richard Wakefield told them when they stopped for lunch. He had been delegated the job of keeping track of their progress. 'You're just east of the central plaza.'

They had gone to the central plaza first, for Nicole had thought that Takagishi would have headed there. They had found an open circular plaza with many low structures, but no sign of their colleague. Since then, Francesca and Nicole had visited the two other plazas and carefully combed the length of two of the central pie portions. They had found nothing. Nicole admitted she was running out of ideas.

'This is quite an astonishing place,' Francesca responded as she began to eat her lunch. They were sitting on a square metal box about a metre high. 'My photographs can barely begin to capture it. Everything is so quiet, so tall, so ... alien.'

'Some of these buildings could not be described

without your pictures. The polyhedrons, for example. There's one in each slice, with the biggest one always just around the plaza. I wonder what they signify, if anything? And why are they located where they are?'

The emotional tension just below the surface in the two women remained suppressed. They chatted a little about what they had seen in their trek across New York. Francesca had been especially fascinated by a large trellis arrangement that they had found connecting two tall skyscrapers in the central unit. 'What do you suppose that lattice or net thing was all about?' she asked idly. 'It must have had twenty thousand loops and must have been fifty metres tall.'

'I guess it's ridiculous for us to try to understand any of this,' Nicole said with a wave of her hand. She finished her lunch and glanced at her companion. 'Ready to continue?'

'Not quite,' Francesca said purposefully. She cleaned up the remains of her lunch and put them in the garbage pouch of her flight suit. 'You and I still have some unfinished business.'

Nicole looked at her quizzically. 'I think it's time we took off the masks and faced each other honestly,' Francesca said in what was a deceptively friendly manner. 'If you suspect that I gave Valeriy Borzov some medication on the day that he died, why don't you ask me directly?'

Nicole stared at her adversary for several seconds. 'Did you?' she asked at length.

'Do you think I did?' Francesca replied coyly. 'And if so, why did I do it?'

'You're just playing the same game at another level,' Nicole said after a pause. 'You're not willing to admit anything. You just want to find out how much I know. But I don't need a confession from you. Science and technology are supporting me. Eventually the truth will be obvious.'

'I doubt it,' Francesca said casually. She jumped down from the box. 'The truth always eludes those who search for it.' She smiled. 'Now let's go find the professor.'

On the western side of the central plaza the two women

encountered another unique structure. From a distance it resembled a huge barn. The peak of its black roof was easily forty metres above the ground and it was more than a hundred metres long. There were two especially fascinating features about the barn. First, the two ends of the building were open. Secondly, although one could not see into it from the outside, all the walls and the roof were transparent from the *inside*. Francesca and Nicole took turns proving that it was not an optical illusion. Someone inside the barn could indeed see in all directions except down. In fact, the adjacent reflective skyscrapers had been precisely aligned so that all the nearby streets were visible from the inside of the barn.

'Fantastic,' said Francesca as she photographed Nicole standing on the other side of the wall.

'Dr Takagishi told me,' Nicole said as she came around the corner, 'that it was impossible to believe that New York was purposeless. The rest of Rama? Maybe. But nobody could have spent this much time and effort without some reason.'

'You almost sound religious,' Francesca said.

Nicole stared quietly at her Italian colleague. *She's needling me now*, Nicole said to herself. *She doesn't really care what I think. Maybe what anybody thinks.*

'Hey. Look at this,' Francesca said after a short silence. She had walked a few steps into the interior of the barn and was pointing at the ground. Nicole came up beside her. In front of Francesca a narrow rectangular pit was cut in the floor. The pit was about five metres long, a metre and a half wide, and quite deep, maybe as much as eight metres. Most of the bottom was in shadow. The walls of the pit ran straight up and down, without any sign of indentation.

'There's another one over here. And another there ...' Altogether there were nine pits, each constructed in exactly the same manner, scattered over the south half of the barn. In the north half, nine small spheres rested on the surface in a carefully measured array. Nicole found herself wishing for a legend of some kind, an instructional guide that would explain the meaning or purpose of all these objects. She was starting to feel bewildered.

They had crossed almost the entire length of the barn when they heard a faint emergency signal on their communicators. 'They must have found Dr Takagishi,' Nicole said out loud as she rushed out one of the open ends of the barn. As soon as she was no longer underneath the roof, the volume of the emergency signal nearly shattered her eardrums. 'Okay. Okay,' she radioed. 'We can hear you. What's up?'

'We've been trying to call you for over two minutes,' she heard Richard Wakefield say. 'Where in the hell have you been? I only used the emergency signal because of its higher gain.'

'We were inside this amazing barn,' Francesca replied from behind Nicole. 'It's like a surrealistic world, with one way mirrors and weird reflections –'

'That's great,' Richard interrupted, 'but we don't have time to chat. You ladies are to march forthwith to the closest spot on the Cylindrical Sea. A helicopter will pick you up in ten minutes. We'd come into New York itself if there was a place for us to land.'

'Why?' Nicole asked. 'What's the hurry all of a sudden?'

'Can you see the South Pole from where you are?'

'No. We have too many tall buildings in the way.'

'Something strange is happening around the little horns. Huge arcs of lightning are bouncing from spire to spire. It's an impressive display. We all feel something unusual is about to happen.' Richard hesitated a second. 'You should leave New York immediately.'

'Okay,' Nicole answered. 'We're on our way.'

She switched off the transmitter and turned to Francesca. 'Did you hear how loud the emergency signal was the moment we came out of the barn?' Nicole thought for several seconds. 'The material in the walls and roof of that building must block radio signals.' Her face now brightened. 'That explains what happened to Takagishi – he must be inside a barn, or something similar.'

Francesca was not following Nicole's line of thought. 'So what?' she said, taking one last panoramic image of the barn with her video camera. 'It's really not important now. We must hurry out to meet the helicopter.'

'Maybe he's even in one of those very pits,' Nicole continued excitedly. 'Sure. It could have happened. He was exploring in the dark. He could have fallen ... Wait here,' she said to Francesca. 'I'll only be a minute.'

Nicole dashed back inside the barn and bent down beside one of the holes. Holding the side of the pit with her hand, she shone the beam from her flashlight down into the bottom. Something was there! She waited a few seconds for her eyes to focus. It was a pile of material of some kind. She moved quickly to the next pit. 'Doctor Takagishi,' she yelled. 'Are you here, Shig?' she called in Japanese.

'Come on!' Francesca shouted at Nicole from the end of the barn. 'Let's go. Richard sounded very serious.'

At the fourth pit the shadows made it very difficult for Nicole to see the bottom even with the beam from her flashlight. She could make out some objects, but what were they? She laid down on her stomach and eased slightly into the pit at a different angle to try to confirm that the shapeless mass below her was not the body of her friend.

The lights in Rama began flashing on and off. Inside the barn, the optical effect was startling. And disorienting. Nicole glanced up to see what was happening and lost her balance. Most of her body slid into the pit. 'Francesca,' she yelled, pressing her hands against the opposite wall of the pit for support, 'Francesca, I need some help,' Nicole shouted again.

Nicole waited almost a minute before she concluded that Cosmonaut Sabatini must already have left the barn area. Her arms were tiring rapidly. Only her feet and the very bottoms of her legs were safely resting on the barn floor. Her head was next to one of the pit walls about eighty centimetres below floor level. The remainder of her body was suspended in midair, prevented from falling only by her intense arm pressure against the wall.

The lights continued to flash off and on at short intervals. Nicole lifted her head to see if she could possibly reach the top of the pit with one of her arms, while holding her position secure with the other. It was hopeless. Her head was too deep in the hole. She waited several more seconds, her desperation growing as the fatigue in her arms increased. Finally Nicole made an attempt both to throw her body upward and to grab on to the lip of the pit in one connected motion. She was almost successful. Her arms could not stop her downward momentum when she fell. Her feet followed her body into the hole and she smacked her head against the wall. She tumbled unconscious to the bottom of the pit.

36

Impact Course

Francesca had also been startled when the lights of Rama had suddenly begun to flash. Her initial impulse had been to run inside, just under the roof of the barn. Once there, she felt slightly more protected. *What's going on now?* she thought as the reflected lights from the adjacent buildings forced her to close her eyes to keep from becoming dizzy.

When she heard Nicole's cry for help, Francesca started to rush over to help her fellow cosmonaut. However, she tripped on one of the spheres and banged her knee as she fell. When she rose, Francesca could see in the strobing light that Nicole's position was very precarious. Only the backs of Nicole's shoes were visible. Francesca stood quite still and waited. Her mind had already raced ahead. She had a nearly perfect image of the pits in her memory, including a fairly accurate assessment of the depth. *If she falls she'll be injured,* she thought, *maybe even killed.* Francesca remembered the smooth walls. *She won't be able to climb out.*

The flashing lights gave an eerie overtone to the scene. As Francesca watched, she saw Nicole's body rise almost out of the pit and her hands scramble for a hold on the lip. In the next flashes of light the shoes changed angle with respect to the pit and then abruptly disappeared. Francesca heard no scream.

If she had not controlled herself, Francesca would have hurried over to the pit and looked into it. *No,* she said to herself, still standing amidst the small spheres, *I

*must not look. If by chance she is still conscious, she might see
me. Then I will have no options.*

Already Francesca was thinking about the possibilities
offered by Nicole's fall. She was certain, based on their
earlier exchange, that Nicole intended to do her utmost
to prove that Borzov had ingested a pain-inducing drug
on the last day of his life. It might even be possible for
Nicole to identify the particular compound and then
eventually, since it was not common, to trace its purchase
back to Francesca. The scenario was unlikely, even
implausible. But it could happen.

Francesca remembered using her special permits to
buy the dimethyldexil, along with a batch of other items,
at a hospital pharmacy in Copenhagen two years earlier.
At the time there had been a suggestion that the drug, in
very small doses, could produce mild feelings of
euphoria in highly-stressed individuals. A single journal
article in an obscure Swedish mental health publication
the following year had contained the information that
sizable doses of dimethyldexil would produce acute pain
that simulated appendicitis.

As Francesca walked rapidly away from the barn in a
northerly direction, her agile mind worked through all
the possibilities. She was performing her usual
risk/reward tradeoff. The primary issue she was facing,
now that she had left Nicole in the pit, was whether or
not to tell the truth about Nicole's fall. But why did you
leave her there? somebody would ask. Why didn't you
radio us that she had fallen and stand by until help could
arrive?

*Because I was confused and frightened and the lights were
flashing. And Richard had sounded so very concerned about
our leaving. I thought it would be easier for us to all talk
together at the helicopter.* Was that believable? Barely. But
it was easy to keep straight. *So I still have the partial truth
option,* Francesca thought as she passed the octahedron
near the central plaza. She realised she had walked too far
to the east, checked her personal navigator, and then
changed her direction. The lights of Rama continued to
flash.

And what are my other choices? Wakefield talked with us just outside the barn. He knows where we were. A search party would definitely find her. Unless.... Francesca thought again about the possibility that Nicole might eventually implicate her in the drugging of General Borzov. The resulting scandal would certainly result in a messy investigation and probably a criminal indictment. In any case, Francesca's reputation would be sullied and her future career as a journalist would be seriously compromised.

With Nicole out of the picture, on the other hand, there was virtually zero probability that anyone would ever learn that Francesca had drugged Borzov. The only person who knew the facts was David Brown, and he had been a co-conspirator. Besides, he had even more to lose than she did.

So the issue, Francesca thought, *is whether or not I can make up a believable story that both reduces the chance Nicole will be found and does not implicate me if she is. That's a very difficult task.*

She was nearing the Cylindrical Sea. Her personal navigator told her that she was only six hundred metres away. *Damnit*, Francesca answered herself after thinking very carefully about her situation, *I don't really have a completely safe opinion. I will have to choose one or the other. Either way there's a significant risk.*

Francesca stopped moving north and paced back and forth between two skyscrapers. As she was walking, the ground underneath her feet began to tremble. Everything was shaking. She dropped to her knees to steady herself. She heard Janos Tabori's voice very faintly on the radio. 'It's all right, everybody, don't be alarmed. It looks as if our vehicle is undergoing a manoeuvre. That must have been what the warnings were all about ... By the way, Nicole, where are you and Francesca? Hiro and Richard are about to take off in the helicopter.'

'I'm close to the sea, maybe two minutes away,' Francesca answered. 'Nicole went back to check on something.'

'Roger,' Janos replied. 'Are you there, Nicole? Do you copy, Cosmonaut des Jardins?'

There was silence on the radio.

'As you know, Janos,' Francesca interjected, 'communications are very spotty from here. Nicole knows where to meet the helicopter. She'll be along quickly, I'm certain.' She paused a moment. 'Where are the others? Is everyone all right?'

'Brown and Heilmann are on the radio with Earth. ISA management will be completely freaked out now. They were already demanding that we leave Rama before this manoeuvre began.'

'We're just boarding the helicopter,' Richard Wakefield said. 'We'll be there in a few minutes.'

It's done. I've made my choice, Francesca said to herself when Richard was finished. She was surprisingly elated. Immediately she began to rehearse her story. 'We were near the large octahedron in the central plaza when Nicole spotted an alley off to our right that we had not noticed before. The street leading to the alley was extremely narrow and she remarked that it was probably a region where communications could not penetrate. I was already tired – we had been walking so fast. She told me to go ahead to the helicopter....'

'And you never saw her again?' Richard Wakefield interrupted. Francesca shook her head. Richard was standing on the ice next to her. Beneath them the ice was vibrating as the long manoeuvre continued. The lights were on again. They had stopped their flashing when the manoeuvre began.

Pilot Yamanaka was sitting in the cockpit of his helicopter. Richard checked his watch. 'It's almost five minutes since we landed here. Something must have happened to her.' He glanced around. 'Maybe she's coming out somewhere else.'

Richard and Francesca climbed into the helicopter and Yamanaka took off. They cruised up and down the island coast, twice circling over the solitary icemobile. 'Edge into New York,' Wakefield commanded. 'Maybe we'll be able to spot her.'

From the helicopter it was virtually impossible to see the ground in the city. The copter had to fly above the tallest buildings. The streets were very narrow and the shadows played games with the eyes. Once Richard thought he saw something moving between the buildings, but it turned out to be an optical illusion.

'All right, Nicole, all right. Where the hell are you?'

'Wakefield –' Dr David Brown's sonorous voice sounded in the helicopter –' 'I want you three to come back to Beta immediately. We need to have a meeting.' Richard was surprised to hear that it was Dr Brown. Janos had been the one monitoring their communication link since they had left Beta.

'What's the hurry, boss?' Wakefield replied. 'We still haven't made our scheduled rendezvous with Nicole des Jardins. She should be coming out of New York any minute.'

'I'll give you the details when you get here. We have some difficult decisions to make. I'm certain that des Jardins will radio when she reaches the shore.'

It did not take them long to cross the frozen sea. Near the Beta campsite, Yamanaka landed the helicopter on the shaking ground and the three cosmonauts descended. The remaining four members of the crew were waiting for them.

'This is one incredibly long manoeuvre,' Richard said with a smile as he approached the others. 'I hope the Ramans know what they're doing.'

'They probably do,' Dr Brown said sombrely. 'At least the Earth thinks that they do.' He looked carefully at his watch. 'According to the navigation section in mission control, we should expect this manoeuvre to last another nineteen minutes, give or take a few seconds.'

'How do they know?' enquired Wakefield. 'Have the Ramans landed on Earth and handed out a flight plan while we've been up here exploring?'

Nobody laughed. 'If the vehicle stays at this attitude and acceleration rate,' Janos said with uncharacteristic seriousness, 'then in nineteen more minutes it will be on an impact course.'

'Impact with what?' Francesca asked.

Richard Wakefield did some quick mental computations. 'With the Earth?' he guessed. Janos nodded.

'Jesus!' Francesca exclaimed.

'Exactly,' David Brown said. 'This mission has become an Earth security concern. The COG Executive Council is meeting at this very moment to consider all contingencies. We have been told in the strongest possible language that we must leave Rama as soon as the manoeuvre is completed. We are to take nothing except the crab biot and our personal belongings. We are –'

'What about Takagishi? And des Jardins? Wakefield asked.

'We will leave the icemobile where it is, along with a rover here at Beta. They are both easy to operate. We will still be in radio contact from the Newton.' Dr Brown stared directly at Richard. 'If this spacecraft is really on an Earth impact course,' he said dramatically, 'our individual lives are no longer very important. The entire course of history is about to be changed.'

'But what if the navigation engineers are wrong? What if Rama has just happened to make a manoeuvre that momentarily intersects an Earth impact trajectory? It could be –'

'Extremely unlikely. You remember that group of short burst manoeuvres at the time of Borzov's death? They changed the orientation of Rama's orbit so that an Earth impact could be achieved with one long manoeuvre at exactly the right time. The engineers on Earth figured it out thirty-six hours ago. They radioed O'Toole before dawn this morning to expect the manoeuvre. I didn't want to say anything while everyone was out looking for Takagishi.'

'That explains why everyone is so anxious for us to clear out of here,' Janos noted.

'Only partially,' Dr Brown continued. 'There is clearly a different feeling about Rama and the Ramans down on Earth. ISA management and the world leaders on the COG Executive Council are apparently convinced that Rama is implacably hostile.'

He stopped for several seconds. as if he were reassessing his own attitude. 'I think they are reacting emotionally myself, but I cannot persuade them differently. I personally see no evidence of hostility, only a disinterest in and disregard for a wildly inferior being. But the televised account of Wilson's death has done its damage. The world's populace cannot be here beside us, cannot grasp the majesty of this place. They can only react viscerally to the horror –'

'If you don't think the Ramans have hostile intentions,' Francesca interrupted, 'then how do you explain this manoeuvre? It can't be coincidence. They or it has decided for some reason to head for the Earth. No wonder the people down there are traumatised. Remember, the first Rama never acknowledged its visitors in any way. This is a dramatically different response. The Ramans are telling us they know –'

'Hold it. Hold it,' Richard said. 'I think we're jumping to conclusions a little too fast. We have twelve more minutes before we should start pushing the panic buttons.'

'All right, Cosmonaut Wakefield,' Francesca said, now remembering that she was a reporter and activating her video camera, 'for the record, what do you think it will mean if this manoeuvre does culminate in a trajectory that impacts the Earth?'

When Richard finally spoke he was very serious. 'People of the Earth,' he said dramatically, 'if Rama has indeed changed its course to visit our planet, it is not necessarily a hostile act. There is nothing, I repeat nothing, that any of us have seen that indicates the species that created this space vehicle wishes us any harm. Certainly Cosmonaut Wilson's death was disturbing, but it was probably an isolated response from a specific set of robots rather than a part of a sinister plan.

'I see this magnificent spacecraft as a single machine, almost organic in its complexity. It is extraordinarily intelligent and programmed for long-term survival. It is neither hostile nor friendly. It could easily have been designed to track any incoming satellites and compute where the visiting spacecraft must have originated. Rama's orbit change to fly in the vicinity of the Earth might therefore be nothing more than its standard response to an encounter initiated by another spacefaring species. It may simply be coming to find out more about us.'

'Very good,' Janos Tabori said with a grin. 'That was borderline philosophical.'

Wakefield laughed nervously.

'Cosmonaut Turgenyev,' Francesca said as she changed the direction of the camera, 'do you agree with your colleague? Just after General Borzov died, you openly expressed some concern that perhaps some 'higher force', meaning the Ramans, might have had a hand in his death. What are your feelings now?'

The normally taciturn Soviet pilot stared directly into the camera with her sad eyes. 'Da,' she said, 'I think Cosmonaut Wakefield is a very brilliant engineer. But he has not answered the difficult questions. Why did Rama manoeuvre during General Borzov's operation? Why did the biots cut Wilson to pieces? Where is Professor Takagishi?'

Irina Turgenyev paused a moment to control her emotions. 'We will not find Nicole des Jardins. Rama may be only a machine, but we cosmonauts have already seen how dangerous it can be. If it is heading for the Earth, I fear for my family, my friends, for all humanity. There is no way to predict what it might do. And we would be powerless to stop it.'

Several minutes later Francesca Sabatini carried her automatic video equipment out beside the frozen sea for one final sequence. She carefully checked the time before switching on the camera precisely fifteen seconds before the manoeuvre was expected to end. 'The picture you are seeing is jumping up and down,' she said in her best journalistic voice, 'because the ground underneath us here on Rama has been shaking continuously since this manoeuvre started forty-seven minutes ago. According to the navigation engineers, the manoeuvre will stop in the next few seconds if Rama has changed course to impact the Earth. Their calculations are, of course, based on assumptions about Rama's intentions –'

Francesca stopped in mid-sentence and took a deep breath. 'The ground is no longer shaking. The manoeuvre is over. Rama is now on an Earth impact trajectory.'

37

Marooned

When Nicole awakened for the first time she was groggy and had great difficulty holding any idea fixed in her mind. Her head hurt and she could feel sharp pains in her back and legs. She did not know what had happened to her. She was barely able to find her water flask and take a drink. *I must have concussion*, Nicole thought as she fell back asleep.

It was dark when Nicole woke up again. But her mind was no longer in a fog. She knew where she was. She remembered looking for Takagishi and sliding into the pit. Nicole also remembered calling for Francesca and the painful, terrible fall. She immediately took her communicator from the belt of her flight suit.

'Hello there, Newton team,' she said as she stood up slowly. 'This is Cosmonaut des Jardins checking in. I've been, well, indisposed might be a good word. I fell down into a hole and knocked myself out. Sabatini knows where I am....'

Nicole broke off her monologue and waited. There was no response from her receiver. She turned up the gain but only succeeded in picking up some strange static. *It's dark already*, she thought, *and it had only been light for two hours at most* ... Nicole knew that the periods of light inside Rama had been lasting about thirty hours. Had she been unconscious that long? Or had Rama done the unexpected again? She looked at her wristwatch, which showed time elapsed since the start of the second sortie, and did a quick calculation. *I've been down here for thirty-two hours. Why has nobody come?*

Nicole thought back to the last minutes before she fell. They had talked to Wakefield, and then she had dashed in to check the pits. Richard always did a navigation fix when they were in two-way lock and Francesca knew exactly....

Could something have happened to the entire crew? But if not, why had nobody discovered her? Nicole smiled to herself as she fought the onset of panic. *Of course*, she reasoned, *they found me, but I was unconscious, so they decided, ...* Another voice in her head told her that her thought pattern didn't make sense. Under any circumstances, she would have been retrieved from the pit if they had found her.

She shuddered involuntarily as she feared, for a brief moment, that perhaps she would *never* be found. Nicole forced her mind to change subjects and began an assessment of the physical damage she had suffered during the fall. She ran her fingers carefully across all portions of her skull. There were several bumps, including a large one on the very back of her head. *That must have been responsible for the concussion*, she surmised. But there were no skull fractures and what little bleeding there had been had stopped hours ago.

She checked her arms and legs, then her back. There were bruises everywhere, but miraculously no bones were broken. The occasional sharp pain just below her neck suggested that she had either crushed part of a vertebra or pinched some nerves. Other than that, she would heal. The discovery that her body had survived more or less intact temporarily buoyed her spirits.

Nicole next surveyed her new domain. She had fallen in the middle of a deep but narrow rectangular pit. It was six paces from end to end and one-and-a-half paces across. Using her flashlight and outstretched arm, she estimated the depth of the hole at eight-and-a-half metres.

The pit was empty except for a jumbled collection of small metallic pieces, ranging in length from five to fifteen centimetres, that were stacked over at one end of the hole. Nicole examined them carefully under the beam from her flashlight. There were over a hundred altogether and maybe a dozen different individual types. Some were long and straight, others curved, a few jointed – they reminded Nicole of industrial trash from a modern steel mill.

The walls of the pit were absolutely straight. The wall material felt like a metal/rock hybrid to Nicole. It was cold, very cold. There were no anomalies, no wrinkles that might have been used as footholds, nothing that would encourage her to believe she could climb out. She tried to chip or scrape the wall surface using her portable medical tools. She was unable to make any mark.

Discouraged by the perfect construction of the pit walls, Nicole walked back to the metal pile to see if there was any way she could put together a ladder or scaffold, some kind of support that would elevate her to the point where she could climb out using her own strength. It was not encouraging. The metal pieces were small and thin. A quick mental calculation told her there was not enough mass to support her weight.

Nicole became even more discouraged when she ate a small snack. She realised that she had brought very little food and water with her because she had wanted to carry extra medical supplies for Takagishi. Even if she rationed it carefully, her water would only last a day and her food no more than thirty-six hours.

She shone her flashlight directly upward. The beam bounced off the roof of the barn. Thinking about the barn reminded her again of the events preceding her fall. Nicole remembered the increased amplitude of the emergency signal once she exited the building. *Great*, she thought despondently, *the interior of this barn is probably a radio blackout zone. No wonder nobody heard me.*

She slept because there was nothing else to do. Eight hours later Nicole woke up with a start from a frightening dream. She had been sitting with her father and daughter in a lovely provincial restaurant in France. It was a magnificent spring day; Nicole could see flowers

in the garden adjoining the restaurant. When the waiter
had come, he had placed a plate of escargots smothered
in herbs and butter in front of Genevieve. Pierre received
a mountainous serving of chicken cooked in a mushroom
and wine sauce. The waiter had smiled and left. Slowly it
had dawned on Nicole that there was nothing for *her*....

She had never dealt with real hunger before. Even
during the Poro, after the lion cubs took her food, Nicole
had not been seriously hungry. She had told herself
before she slept that she would carefully ration her
remaining food, but that was before the hunger pangs
had become overpowering. Now Nicole tore into her
food packets with trembling hands and only barely
stopped herself from eating all the food that was left. She
wrapped the paltry remainder, put it back into one of her
pockets, and buried her face in her hands. Nicole allowed
herself to cry for the first time since she had fallen.

She also allowed herself to acknowledge that starving
to death would be a terrible way to die. Nicole tried to
imagine what it would feel like to weaken from hunger
and then ultimately to perish. Would it be a gradual
process, each successive stage more horrible than the one
before? *Then let it come soon*, Nicole said out loud,
momentarily abandoning all hope. Her digital watch was
glowing in the dark, counting off the last precious
minutes of her life.

Several hours passed. Nicole grew weaker and more
despondent. She sat with her head bowed in the cold
corner of the pit. Just as she was about to give up
completely and accept the certainty of her death,
however, there came from inside her a different voice, an
assertive, optimistic voice that refused to let her give up.
It told her that *any* time of being alive was precious and
wonderful, that simply being conscious at all, *ever*, was
an overwhelming miracle of nature. Nicole took a slow,
deep breath and opened her eyes. *If I'm to die here*, she
said to herself, *then at least let me do it with élan*. She
resolved that she would spend whatever time remained
concentrating on the outstanding moments of her
thirty-six years.

Nicole still retained a tiny hope of being rescued. But she had always been a practical woman, and logic told her that what was left of her life was probably measured in hours. During her unhurried trip into her treasured memories, Nicole wept several times, without inhibition; tears of joy at the past recaptured; bittersweet tears because she knew, as she relived each episode, that it was probably her last visit to that particular portion of her memory bank.

There was no pattern to her wanderings through the life that she had lived. She did not categorise, measure, or compare her experience. Nicole simply lived them again as they came to her, each old event transformed and enriched by her heightened awareness.

Her mother occupied a special place in her memory. Because she had died when Nicole was only ten, her mother had retained all the attributes of a queen or goddess. Anawi Tiasso had indeed been beautiful and regal, a jet-black African woman of uncommon stature. All Nicole's images of her were bathed in soft, glowing light.

She remembered her mother in the living room of their home in Chilly-Mazarin, gesturing to Nicole to come and sit upon her lap. Anawi read a book to her daughter every night before bedtime. Most of the stories were fairy tales about princes and castles and beautiful, happy people who overcame every obstacle. Her mother's voice was soft and mellow. She would sing lullabies to Nicole as the little girl's eyes grew heavier and heavier.

The Sundays of her childhood were special days. In the spring they would go to the park and play on the wide fields of grass. Her mother would teach Nicole how to run. The little girl had never seen anything as beautiful as her mother, who had been an international-class sprinter as a young woman, racing gracefully across the meadow.

Of course Nicole remembered vividly all the details of her trip with Anawi to the Ivory Coast for the Poro. It was her mother who had held her during the nights in Nidougou before the ceremony. During those long, frightening nights, the little girl Nicole had struggled with all her fears. And each day, calmly and patiently, her mother had answered all her questions and had reminded her that many, many other girls had passed through the transitional rite without undue difficulty.

Nicole's fondest memory from that trip was of the hotel room in Abidjan, the night before she and Anawi returned to Paris. She and her mother had discussed the Poro only in passing during the thirty hours since Nicole and the other girls had finished the ceremonies. Anawi had not yet offered any praise. To be certain, Omeh and the village elders had told Nicole that she had been exceptional, but to a seven-year-old girl no appraisal is as important as the one from her mother. Nicole had summoned her courage just before dinner.

'Did I do all right, Maman?' the little girl had said tentatively. 'At the Poro, I mean.'

Anawi had burst into tears. 'Did you do all right? Did you do all right?' She had wrapped her long sinuous arms around her daughter and picked her up off the floor. 'Oh, darling,' her mother had said as she had held Nicole high above her head, 'I'm so proud of you that I could split.' Nicole had jumped into her mother's arms and they had hugged and laughed and cried for fifteen minutes.

Nicole lay on her back in the bottom of the pit, the tears from her memories rolling sideways across her face and down into her ears. For almost an hour she had been thinking about her daughter, starting with her birth and then going through each of the major events of Genevieve's life. Nicole was recalling the vacation trip to America that they had taken together, three years earlier when Genevieve had been eleven. How very close they had been on that trip, especially on the day they had hiked down the South Kaibab trail into the Grand Canyon.

Nicole and Genevieve had stopped at each of the markers along the trail, studying the imprint of two billion years of time on the surface of the planet Earth. They had lunched on a promontary overlooking the desert desiccation of the Tonto plateau. That night, mother and daughter had spread their sleeping mats, side by side, right next to the mighty Colorado River. They had talked and shared dreams and held hands throughout the night.

I would not have taken that trip, Nicole mused, beginning to think about her father, *if it hadn't been for you. You were the one who knew it was the right time to go.* Nicole's father was the conerstone of her life. Pierre des Jardins was her friend, confessor, intellectual companion, and most ardent supporter. He had been there when she was born and at every significant moment of her life. It was he whom she missed the most as she lay at the bottom of the pit inside Rama. It was he with whom she would have chosen to have had her final conversation.

There was no single memory of her father that jumped out at her, that demanded renewal above all the rest. Nicole's mental montage of Pierre framed all the events of her own life. Not all of them were happy. She remembered clearly, for example, the two of them in the savanna not far from Nidougou, silently holding hands as they both wept quietly while the funeral pyre of Anawi burned into the African night. She could also still feel his arms around her as she sobbed incessantly following her failure, at the age of fifteen, to win the nationwide Joan of Arc competition.

They had lived together at Beauvois, an unlikely pair, from a year after the death of her mother until Nicole had finished her third year of studies at the University of Tours. It had been an idyllic existence. Nicole roamed through the woods around their villa after she cycled home from school. Pierre wrote his novels in the study. In the evening Marguerite rang the bell and called them both to dinner before she climbed on her own bicycle, her day's work complete, and returned to her husband and children in Luynes.

During the summers Nicole travelled with her father throughout Europe, visiting the medieval towns and castles that were the primary venues of his historical novels. Nicole knew more about Eleanor of Aquitaine and her husband Henry Plantagenet than she knew about the active political leaders of France and Western Europe. When Pierre won the Mary Renault prize for historical fiction in 2182, she went with him to Paris to receive the award. Nicole sat in the first row in the large auditorium, dressed in the tailored white skirt and blouse that Pierre had helped her choose, and listened to the speaker extol her father's virtues.

Nicole could still recite parts of her father's acceptance speech from memory. 'I have often been asked,' her father had said near the end of his delivery, 'if I have accumulated any wisdom that I would like to share with future generations.' He had then looked directly at her in the audience. 'To my precious daughter Nicole, and all the young people of the world, I offer one simple insight. In my life I have found two things of priceless worth – learning and loving. Nothing else, not fame, not power, not achievement for its own sake, can possibly have the same lasting value. For when your life is over, if you can say "I have learned" and "I have loved", you will also be able to say "I have been happy".'

I have been happy, Nicole said as more tears ran down the side of her face, *and mostly because of you. You never disappointed me. Not even in my most difficult moment.* Her memory turned, as she knew it would, to the summer of 2184, when her life had accelerated at such a fantastic pace that she had lost control of its direction. In one six-week period Nicole won an Olympic gold medal, conducted a short but torrid affair with the Prince of Wales, and returned to France to tell her father that she was pregnant.

Nicole could remember the key events from that period as if they had happened only yesterday. No emotion in her life had ever quite matched the joy and exhilaration that she had felt when she was standing on the victory stand in Los Angeles, the gold medal around her neck and the cheers of a hundred thousand people echoing in her ears. It was her moment. For almost a week she was the darling of the world media. She was on the front page of every newspaper, highlighted in every major broadcast on sports.

After her final interview in the television studio adjoining the Olympic stadium, a young Englishman with an engaging smile had introduced himself as Darren Higgins and handed her a card. Inside was a handwritten invitation to dinner from none other than the Prince of Wales, the man who would become Henry XI of Great Britain.

The dinner was magical, Nicole recalled, her desperate situation in Rama temporarily forgotten. *He was charming. The next two days were absolutely wonderful.* But thirty-nine hours later, when she awakened in Henry's bedroom suite in Westwood, her fairy tale was suddenly over. Her prince, who had been so attentive and affectionate, was now frowning and fretful. As the inexperienced Nicole tried unsuccessfully to understand what had gone wrong, it slowly dawned on her that her flight of fantasy was over. *I was just a conquest*, she remembered, *the celebrity of the moment. I was unsuitable for any permanent relationship*.

Nicole would never forget the last words the prince had said to her in Los Angeles. He had been circling her while she was hurriedly packing. He could not understand why she was so distraught. Nicole had not replied to any of his questions and had resisted his attempts to embrace her. 'What did you expect?' he had asked finally, his frustration obvious. 'That we would ride off into the sunset and live happily ever after? Come on, Nicole, this is the real world. You must know that the British people would never accept a half-black woman as their queen.'

Nicole had escaped before Henry saw her tears. *And so, my darling Genevieve*, Nicole said to herself in the bottom of the pit in Rama, *I left Los Angeles with two new treasures. I had a gold medal and a wonderful baby girl within my body.* Her thoughts quickly skipped across the following weeks of anxiety to the desperate, lonely moment when she finally summoned her courage to talk to her father.

'I ... I don't know what to do,' Nicole had said
tentatively to Pierre on that September morning in the
living room of their villa at Beauvois. 'I know that I have
disappointed you terribly – I have disappointed myself –
but I want to ask you if it's all right. I mean, if I want to,
Papa, can I stay here and try –'

'Of course, Nicole,' her father had interrupted her. He
was softly crying. It was the only time that Nicole had
seen him cry since the death of her mother. 'We'll do
whatever's right,' he had said as he pulled her into his
embrace.

I was so lucky, Nicole thought. *He was so accepting. He
never faulted me. He never asked anything. When I told him
that Henry was the father and that I never wanted anyone
else to know, least of all Henry or the child, he promised we
would keep my secret. And he has.*

The lights came on suddenly and Nicole stood up to
survey her prison under the new conditions. Only the
centre of the pit was full lighted; both the ends were in
shadow. Considering her situation, she was feeling
amazingly cheerful and upbeat.

She looked up to the roof of the barn and through it to
the nondescript sky of Rama. Nicole thought about her
last few hours and had a sudden impulse. She had not
said a prayer in over twenty years but she dropped down
on her knees in the full light in the middle of the pit.
Dear God, she said, *I know it's a little late, but thank you
for my father, my mother, and my daughter. And all the
wonders of life*. Nicole glanced up at the ceiling. She was
smiling and had a twinkle in her eye. *And right now, dear
God, I could use a little help.*

38
Visitors

The tiny robot strode out into the light and unsheathed his sword. The English army had arrived at Harfleur.

'Once more unto the breach, dear friends,
once more,
Or close the wall up with our English dead.
In peace there's nothing so becomes a man
As modest stillness and humility:
But when the blast of war blows in our ears,
Then imitate the action of the tiger....'

Henry V, new king of England, continued to exhort his imaginary soldiers. Nicole smiled as she listened. She had spent the better part of an hour following Wakefield's Prince Hal from the debauchery of his youth, on to the battlefields fighting against Hotspur and the other rebels, and thence to the throne of England. Nicole had only once read the three Henry plays, and that had been years before, but she was well aware of the historical period because of her lifelong fascination with Joan of Arc.

'Shakespeare made you into something you never were,' she said out loud to the little robot as she bent beside it to insert Richard's baton in the 'Off' slot. 'You were a warrior, to be sure, nobody would argue with that. But you were also a cold and heartless conqueror. You made Normandy bleed under your powerful yoke. You almost crushed the life out of France.'

Nicole laughed nervously at herself. *Here I am*, she thought, *talking to a senseless ceramic prince twenty centimetres high.* She remembered her feelings of hopelessness an hour earlier after she had tried once more to work out a way to escape. The fact that her time was running out had been reinforced when she had drunk the next-to-last swig of water. *Oh well*, she mused, turning back to Prince Hal, *at least this is better than feeling sorry for myself.*

'And what else can you do, my little prince?' Nicole said. 'What happens if I insert this pin in the slot marked C?'

The robot activated, walked a few steps, and finally approached her left foot. After a long silence Prince Hal spoke, not in the rich actor's voice he had used during his earlier recitals, but instead in Wakefield's British tones. 'C stands for converse, my friend, and I have a considerable repertoire. But I don't speak until you say something first.'

Nicole laughed. 'All right, Prince Hal,' she said after a moment's thought, 'tell me about Joan of Arc.'

The robot hesitated and then frowned. 'She was a witch, dear lady, burned at the stake in Rouen a decade after my death. During my reign the north of France had been subjugated by my armies. The French witch, claiming she was sent by God....'

Nicole stopped listening and jerked her head up as a shadow crossed over them. She thought she saw something flying above the roof of the barn. Her heart pounded furiously. 'Here. I'm here,' she shouted at the top of her voice. Prince Hal droned on in the background about how Joan of Arc's success had sadly resulted in the return of his conquests to the realm of France. 'So English. So typically English,' Nicole said as she once again inserted the baton in Prince Hal's off button.

Moments later the shadow was large and completely darkened the bottom of the pit. Nicole looked up and her heart caught in her throat. Hovering over the pit, its wings spread and flapping, was a gigantic birdlike creature. Nicole shrank back and screamed involuntarily. The creature stuck its neck into the pit and uttered a set of

noises. The sounds were harsh yet slightly musical.
Nicole was paralysed. The thing repeated almost the
same set of noises and then tried – without success
because its wings were too large – to lower itself slowly
into the narrow pit.

During this brief period Nicole, her traumatic terror
giving way to normal fear, studied the great flying alien.
Its face, apart from two soft eyes that were a deep blue
surrounded by a brown ring, reminded her of the
pterodactyls that she had seen in the French museum of
natural history. The beak was quite long and hooked.
The mouth was toothless and the two talons, bilaterally
symmetrical about the main body, each had four sharp
digits.

Nicole would have guessed the avian's mass at about a
hundred kilograms. Its body, except for the face and
beak, the ends of the wings, and the talons, was covered
by a thick black material that resembled velvet. When it
was clear to the avian that it would not be able to fly
down to the bottom of the pit, it sounded two sharp
notes, pulled itself up, and disappeared.

Nicole did not move at all during the first minute after
the creature departed. Then she sat down and tried to
collect her thoughts. The adrenaline from her fright was
still coursing through her body. She tried to think
rationally about what she had seen. Her first idea was
that the thing was a biot, like all the rest of the mobile
creatures which had previously been seen in Rama. *If
that's a biot*, she said to herself, *then it's extremely
advanced*. She pictured the other biots she had seen, both
the crabs from the Southern Hemisphere and the wide
variety of weird creations filmed by the first Raman
expedition. Nicole could not convince herself that the
avian was a biot. There was something about the eyes....

She heard wings flapping in the distance and her body
tensed. Nicole cowered in the shadowy corner just as the
light in the pit was again obscured by a huge hovering
body. No, there were two bodies. The first avian had
returned with a companion, the second one considerably
the larger. The new bird stuck its neck around to look at

its companion. While the two avians jabbered back and forth, Nicole noticed that this one was covered with a polished surface, like linoleum, but in all other respects except size was identical to her first visitor. At length the new bird ascended and the strange pair landed on the side of the pit, still jabbering. They observed Nicole quietly for a minute or two. Then, after a brief conversation, they were gone.

Nicole was exhausted after her bout with fear. Within minutes after her flying visitors departed, she was curled up and asleep in the corner of the pit. She slept soundly for several hours. She was awakened by a loud noise, a crack that resounded through the barn like the report of a gun. She woke up quickly, but heard no more unexplained sounds. Her body reminded her that she was hungry and thirsty. She pulled out what was left of her food. *Should I make two tiny meals out of this*? she asked herself wearily, *or should I eat it all now and accept whatever comes*?

With a deep sigh, Nicole decided to finish off her food and water with one last meal. She was thinking that the two combined might give her enough sustenance that she could temporarily forget about food. She was wrong. While Nicole was drinking the last sip of water from her water flask, her mind was bombarded with images of the bottled spring water that she and her family always had on the table at Beauvois.

There was another loud crack in the distance after Nicole had finished her meal. She stopped to listen, but again there was silence. Her thoughts were dominated by escape ideas, all of them using the avians in some way to help her out of the pit. She was angry with herself for not having tried to communicate with them while she had the chance. Nicole laughed to herself, *Of course, they might have decided to eat me. But who's to say starving to death is preferable to being eaten.*

Nicole was sure that the avians would come back. Perhaps her certainty was reinforced by the hopelessness of her situation, but nevertheless she started making

plans for what she would do when they did return. *Hello*,
she imagined herself saying. She would stand up with an
outstretched palm and walk forcefully to the centre of the
pit, right under the hovering creature. Nicole would then
use a special set of gestures to communicate her plight –
pointing repeatedly first at herself and then the pit would
indicate that she couldn't escape; waving at both the
avians and the barn roof would ask them for their help.

Two loud sharp noises brought Nicole back to reality.
After a brief pause she heard another crack. Nicole
searched through the 'Environments' chapter in her
computerised *Atlas of Rama* and then laughed at herself
for not having recognised immediately what was
occurring. The loud reports were the sound of the ice
breaking up as the Cylindrical Sea melted from the
bottom. Rama was still inside the orbit of Venus
(although, unknown to Nicole, the last midcourse
manoeuvre had placed it on to a trajectory whose distance
from the sun was now increasing again), and the solar
input had finally brought the temperature inside Rama to
above the freezing point of water.

The *Atlas* warned of fierce windstorms, hurricanes that
would be created by the atmospheric thermal instabilities
following the melting of the sea. Nicole walked to the
centre of the pit. 'Come on, you birds, or whatever you
are,' she yelled. 'Come and get me now and let me have a
chance to escape.'

But the avians did not come back. Nicole sat awake in
the corner for ten hours, slowly growing weaker as the
frequency of the loud reports reached a peak and then
gradually diminished. The wind began to blow. At first it
was just a breeze, but it became a gale by the time the
cracks from the ice breaking up had stopped. Nicole was
completely discouraged. When she fell asleep again she
told herself that she would probably not be awake more
than once or twice more.

The winds pummelled New York as the hurricane raged
for hours. Nicole huddled lifelessly in a corner. She
listened to the howling wind and remembered sitting in a

ski chalet during a blizzard in Colorado. She tried to remember the pleasures of skiing but she could not. Her hunger and fatigue had weakened her imagination as well. Nicole sat very still, her mind devoid of thoughts except for wondering occasionally what it would feel like to die.

She couldn't remember falling asleep, but then she couldn't remember waking up either. She was very weak. Her mind was telling her that something had blown into her hole. It was dark again. Nicole crawled from her end of the pit toward the end with the jumbled metal. She did not switch on her flashlight. She bumped into something and started, then she felt it with her hands. The object was big, larger than a basketball. It had a smooth exterior and was oval in shape.

Nicole became more alert. She found her flashlight in her flight suit and illuminated the object. It was off-white and shaped like an egg. She examined it thoroughly. When she pressed on it hard, it gave slightly under the pressure. *Can I eat it?* her mind asked, her hunger so severe that she had no worries about what it might do to her.

Nicole pulled out her knife and was able to cut it with difficulty. She feverishly chopped off a chunk and forced it into her mouth. It was tasteless. Nicole spat it out and started to cry. She kicked the object angrily and it rolled over. She thought she heard something. Nicole reached out and pushed it hard, rolling it over again. *Yes*, she said to herself, *yes. That was a sloshing sound.*

It was slow work cutting through the outside with her knife. After several minutes Nicole retrieved her medical equipment and started working on the object with her power scalpel. Whatever it was, the object was made of three separate and distinct layers. The covering was tough, like the skin of a football, and relatively difficult to manipulate. The second layer was a soft, moist, royal blue compound the consistency of a melon. Inside, in the centre, were several quarts of a greenish liquid. Trembling with anticipation, Nicole stuck a cupped hand into the incision and pulled the liquid to her lips. It had an odd, medicinal taste, but it was refreshing. She drank, two hurried swallows, and then her years of medical training interceded.

Fighting against her desire to drink more, Nicole inserted the probe from her mass spectrometer into the liquid to analyse its chemical constituents. She was in such a hurry that she made a mistake with the first specimen and had to repeat the process. When the results of the analysis were displayed on the tiny modular monitor that could be affixed to any of her instruments, Nicole began to weep with joy. The liquid would not poison her. On the contrary, it was rich in proteins and minerals in the kinds of chemical combinations that the body could process.

'All right, all right!' Nicole shouted out loud. She stood up quickly and nearly fainted. More cautious now, she sat back down on her knees and began the feast of her life. She drank the liquid and ate the moist meat until she was absolutely gorged. Then she fell into a deep, satisfied sleep.

Nicole's primary concern when she awakened was to determine the quantity of 'manna melon', as she called it, that was available to her. She had been a glutton, and knew it, but that was in the past. What she needed to do now was to husband the manna melon until she could somehow enlist the aid of the avians.

Nicole measured the melon carefully. Its gross weight had originally been almost ten kilograms, but only a little over eight remained. Her assessment indicated that the inedible outer portion compromised approximately two kilograms, leaving her six kilograms of nourishment split roughly evenly between the liquid and the royal blue meat. *Let's see*, she was thinking, *three liquid kilograms makes –*

Nicole's thought processes were interrupted as the lights came on again. *Yes*, she said to herself, checking her wristwatch, *right on time, with the same secular drift*. She looked up from her watch and saw the egg-shaped object for the first time in the full light. Her recognition was immediate. *Oh my God*, Nicole thought as she walked over and traced with her fingers the brown lines wriggling on the creamy-white surface. *I had almost forgotten.* She reached into her flight suit and pulled out the polished stone that Omeh had given her on New Year's Eve in Rome. She stared at it and then glanced over at the oval object in the pit. *Oh my God*, Nicole repeated.

She replaced the stone in her pocket and removed the small green vial. 'Ronata will know the time to drink,' she heard her great-grandfather say again. Nicole sat down in the corner and emptied the vial in one gulp.

39
Waters of Wisdom

Immediately Nicole's vision began to blur. She closed her eyes for a second. When she opened them again she was blinded by a riot of bright colours, streaming by her in geometrical patterns as if she were moving very fast. In the centre of her sight, way off in the distance, a black dot emerged from the background amidst a brilliant set of alternating red and yellow forms. Nicole concentrated on the dot as it continued to grow. It rushed toward her and expanded to fill her vision. She saw a man, an old black man, running across the African savanna on a perfect starry night. Nicole clearly saw his face as he turned to climb a mountain of rocks. The man looked like Omeh but also, somewhat strangely, like her mother.

He raced up the rock mountain with amazing agility. At the top he stood in silhouette, his arms outspread, and stared into the sky at the crescent moon on the horizon. Nicole heard the sound of a firing rocket engine and turned to her left. She watched a small spacecraft descend to the surface of the moon. Two men in space suits started down a ladder. She heard Neil Armstrong say, 'That's one small step for a man, one giant leap for mankind.'

Buzz Aldrin joined Armstrong on the lunar surface and they both pointed off to their right. They were staring at the old black man standing on a nearby lunar scarp. He smiled. His teeth were very white.

His face loomed ever larger in Nicole's vision as the

lunar landscape behind him began to fade. He started to chant slowly, in Senoufo, but at first Nicole could not comprehend what he was saying. All of a sudden she realised that he was talking to *her* and that she could understand every word. 'I am one of your ancestors from long ago,' he said. 'As a boy I went out to meditate the night that people landed on the moon. Because I was thirsty, I drank deeply the waters from the Lake of Wisdom. I flew first to the moon, where I talked with the astronauts, and then to other worlds. I met the Great Ones. They told me you would come to bring the story of Minowe to the stars.'

As Nicole watched the old man's head began to grow. His teeth became vicious, long, his eyes yellow. He transformed into a tiger and leaped for her throat. Nicole screamed as she felt the teeth upon her neck. She prepared to die. But the tiger became limp; an arrow was buried deep in its side. Nicole heard a noise and looked up. Her mother, wearing a magnificent flowing red robe and carrying a golden bow, was running gracefully toward a gilded chariot parked in the middle of the air. 'Mother ... wait,' Nicole shouted.

The figure turned. 'You were seduced,' her mother said. 'You must be more careful. Only three times can I save you. Beware of what you cannot see but know is there.' Anawi climbed into the chariot and took the reins. 'You must not die. I love you, Nicole.' The winged red horses arched higher and higher until Nicole could no longer see them.

The colour pattern returned to her vision. Nicole heard music now, first far off in the distance, then much closer. It was synthetic, like the sound of crystal bells. Beautiful, haunting, ethereal. There was loud applause. Nicole was sitting in the front row at a concert with her father. On the stage an Oriental man with hair down to the floor, his eyes fixed in a gaze of rapture, stood next to three odd-shaped instruments. The sound was all around her. It made her want to cry.

'Come on,' her father said. 'We must go.' As Nicole was watching her father turned into a sparrow. He smiled at her. She flapped her own sparrow-wings and they were airborne together, leaving the concert behind. The music faded. The air rushed by them. Nicole could see the lovely Loire valley and a glimpse of their villa at Beauvois. She was content to be going home. But her sparrow-father descended instead at Chinon, farther down the Loire. The two sparrows landed in a tree on the castle grounds.

Beneath them, standing in the crisp December air, Henry Plantagenet and Eleanor of Aquitaine were arguing about the succession to the throne of England. Eleanor walked over under the tree and noticed the sparrows. 'Why hello, Nicole,' she said, 'I didn't know you were there.' Queen Eleanor reached up and stroked the sparrow's underbelly. Nicole thrilled to the softness of her touch. 'Remember, Nicole,' she said, 'destiny is more important than love of any kind. You can endure anything if you are certain of your destiny.'

Nicole smelled fire and sensed they were needed somewhere else. She and her father ascended, turning north toward Normandy. The fire smell grew stronger. They heard a cry for help and urgently flapped their wings.

In Rouen a plain girl with lights in her eyes looked up at them as they approached. The fire below had reached her feet; the first smell of burning flesh was in the air. The girl lowered her eyes in prayer as a makeshift cross was held above her head by a priest. 'Blessed Jesus,' she said, tears running down her cheeks.

'We'll save you, Joan,' Nicole shouted as she and her father dropped into the crowded square. Joan embraced them as they untied her from the stake. The fire exploded around them and everything went black. In the next instant Nicole was flying again, but this time as a great white heron. She was alone, inside Rama, flying high over the city of New York. She banked to avoid one of the avians, who regarded her with shock.

Nicole could see everything in New York in incredible detail. It was as if she had multispectral eyes with a wide range of lenses. She could spot movement in four different places. Close to the barn, a centipede biot was trudging slowly toward the south end of the building. From the vicinity of each of the three central plazas, heat was emanating from underground sources, causing coloured patterns in her infrared vision. Nicole circled down toward the barn and landed safely in her pit.

40

Alien Invitation

I must be prepared for rescue, Nicole said to herself. She had finished filling her flask with the greenish liquid from the centre of the manna melon. After carefully sectioning the moist melon flesh and putting the pieces in her old food container packets, Nicole sat back down in her usual corner.

Whew! she thought, returning to the wild mental excursion she had taken after drinking the contents of the vial. *What in the world was that all about?* Nicole recalled her vision during the Poro, when she was still a child, and the brief conversation about it that she had had with Omeh three years later when Nicole had returned to Nidougou for the funeral of her mother.

'Where did Ronata go?' Omeh had asked one evening when the old man and the girl had been alone together.

She had known immediately what he was asking. 'I became a big white bird,' she had answered. 'I flew beyond the moon and sun to the great void.'

'Ah,' he had said, 'Omeh thought so.'

And why didn't you ask him then what had happened to you? the scientist in the adult Nicole asked her former ten-year-old self. *Then maybe some of this would make sense*. But somehow Nicole knew that the vision was beyond analysis, that it existed in a realm as yet unfathomed by the deductive processes that made science so powerful. She thought instead about her mother, about how beautiful she had been in her long flowing red robes. Anawi had saved her from the tiger.

Thank you, mother, Nicole thought. She wished that she had talked longer with her.

It was a weird sound, like dozens of unshod baby feet on a linoleum floor, and it was definitely coming in her direction. Nicole didn't have much time to wonder. Seconds later the head and antennae of a centipede biot appeared at the edge of her pit and, without slowing down in any way, proceeded directly down the wall at the opposite end.

Altogether the biot was four metres long. It clambered down the wall without difficulty, placing each of its sixty legs directly against the smooth surface and holding on by some kind of suction. Nicole put on her backpack and watched for her opportunity. She was not *that* surprised by the appearance of the biot. After what she had seen in her vision, she was certain that she was going to be rescued by some means.

The centipede biot consisted of fifteen attached, jointed segments, each with four legs, and an insectlike head with a bizarre array of sensors, two of which were long and thin and resembled antennae. The jumbled pile of metal at the other end of the pit was apparently its spare parts. While Nicole was watching, the biot replaced three of its legs, the carapace for one of its segments, and two knobbly protuberances on the side of its head. The entire process took no more than five minutes. When it was finished, the biot started again up the wall.

Nicole jumped on the centipede biot's back when three-quarters of its body was heading upward. The sudden extra weight was too much. The biot lost its grasp and fell, along with Nicole, back into the pit. Moments later it tried again to scale the wall. This time Nicole waited until the entire length of the centipede was heading up the wall, hoping that the strength of the extra segments would make the difference. It was to no avail. The biot and Nicole collapsed into a heap.

One of its front legs had been severely injured during the second fall, so the biot made the necessary repairs before trying to ascend the wall a third time. Nicole, meanwhile, pulled all her strongest suture material out of her medical pack and tied one end of a long octuple thickness around the three back sections of the biot. In the other end of the suture thread she made a loop. After she had put on gloves to protect her hands and then fashioned a waistband to keep the thread from cutting, Nicole tied the loop around her waist.

This could be a disaster, Nicole realised as she imagined all the possible outcomes of her scheme. *If the thread does not hold, I could fall. The second time I might not be so lucky.*

The centipede inched its way up the wall as before. Several small steps after it was completely elongated, the biot felt Nicole's weight from below. This time, however, it did not fall. The struggling biot managed to continue slowly on its upward path. Nicole kept her body perpendicular to the surface, as if she were rock climbing, and held on to the suture thread with both her hands.

Nicole was about forty centimetres behind the last segment of the biot as they scaled the wall. When the head of the centipede reached the top of the pit, Nicole was almost halfway out. Her slow and steady climb continued as, segment after segment, a portion of the biot left the pit above her. A few minutes later, however, her progress slowed markedly, stopping altogether when the number of centipede segments remaining on the wall dropped to four. Nicole could almost touch the rear segment of the centipede if she stretched her arms above her. Only about one metre's length of the biot was still on the wall, but nevertheless it was apparently stuck. Nicole was putting too much strain on the joints attaching the rear segments.

Grim scenarios ran through Nicole's mind as she dangled more than six metres above the floor of the pit. *This is great*, she thought sarcastically, as she pulled tightly on the suture line and placed her feet firmly against the wall. *There are three possible outcomes, none of them good. The thread could break. The biot could collapse. Or I might remain suspended here forever.*

Nicole considered her alternatives. The only plan she could conceive with even a reasonable probability of success – and it was still very risky – was for her to climb up the suture thread to the last segment and then, somehow, using the body or legs of the centipede as handholds, to muscle her way to the top of the pit.

Nicole glanced down and remembered her first fall. I think I'll wait a while first and see if this machine gets moving again. A minute passed. Then another. Nicole took a deep breath. She reached up high on the suture line and pulled herself up the wall. She repeated the process with the other hand. She was now right behind the last segment. Nicole reached out and grabbed one of the legs, but as soon as she tried to put any weight on it, it pulled free from the wall.

So much for that plan, she thought after a moment's fright. She had restabilised herself just behind the biot. Nicole studied the centipede again very carefully. The carapace of each segment was made of overlapping pieces. *It might be possible to grab one of those flaps ...* Nicole reconstructed her first two attempts to ride on the back of the biot. *It was the suction force of the feet that gave out,* she thought. *Now most of the biot is on the level ground above. It should be able to hold me.*

Nicole realised that once she was on the back of the biot, she no longer had any protection against falling. To test the concept, she pulled herself to the top of the suture line and grabbed the carapace flap. She was able to get a firm grip. The only question was whether the flap could support her weight. Nicole tried to assess its strength while holding on to the sutures with her other hand for safety. So far, so good.

Nicole grasped the flap on the rear biot segment and cautiously pulled herself up, then released her grip on the suture thread. She wrapped her legs around the side of the centipede's body and pulled herself along until she could reach the next flap. The legs of the rear segment popped off the wall, but the centipede did not move otherwise.

She repeated the process twice more, moving from

segment to segment. Nicole was almost at the top. While she was on her final climb, she received a brief scare when the biot slipped a few centimetres back into the pit. Holding on breathlessly, she waited until the biot was stable and then crawled forward to the first segment that was on level ground. As she was crawling, the biot began walking again, but Nicole just rolled off sideways and landed on her back on the ground. 'Hallelujah,' she shouted.

As she stood on the wall around New York and stared out at the rolling waters of the Cylindrical Sea, Nicole wondered why there had been no answer to her call for help. The self-test status flag on her radio indicated that it was working properly, yet she had tried three separate times without success to establish contact with the rest of the crew. Nicole was well aware of the commlinks available to the cosmonauts. Failure to receive a reply meant both that no crew members were within six to eight kilometres of her at present *and* that the Beta relay station was not operational. *If Beta were working*, Nicole thought, *then they would be able to talk to me from anywhere, even the Newton.*

Nicole told herself that the crew were doubtless on board their own spacecraft, preparing for another sortie, and that the Beta communications station had probably been disabled by the hurricane. What bothered her, though, was that it had already been forty-five hours since the onset of the melting and more than ninety hours since she had fallen into the pit. Why was nobody looking for her?

Nicole's eyes scanned the sky for some sign of a helicopter. The atmosphere now contained clouds, as predicted. The melting of the Cylindrical Sea had substantially altered the weather patterns on Rama. The temperature had warmed up considerably. Nicole glanced at her thermometer and confirmed her estimate, that it was now four degrees above freezing.

The most likely situation, Nicole reasoned, returning to the question of the whereabouts of her colleagues, *is that they will return soon. I need to stay close to this wall so that I can easily be seen.* Nicole did not waste much time thinking about other, less likely scenarios. She considered only briefly the possibility that the crew had had a major disaster and nobody had yet been available to look for her. *But even in that case*, she said to herself, *I should follow the same approach. They would come sooner or later.*

To pass the time, Nicole took a sample of the sea and tested it. It had very few of the organic poisons found by the first Raman expedition. *Maybe they flourished and died while I was still in the pit*, she thought. *Anyway, they're virtually all gone now*. Nicole noted to herself that in an emergency a strong swimmer might be able to make it across without a boat. However, she recalled the pictures of the shark biots and other denizens of the sea reported by Norton and his crew and slightly modified her assessment.

Nicole walked along the ramparts for several hours. While she was sitting down quietly eating her manna melon lunch (and thinking about methods she could employ to retrieve the rest of the melon, in the event that she still wasn't rescued in another seventy-two hours), she heard what she thought was a cry coming from New York. She thought immediately of Dr Takagishi.

She tried her radio one more time. Nothing. Again Nicole checked the sky for some sign of a helicopter. She was still debating whether or not to forsake her lookout on the wall when she heard a second cry. This time she had a better fix on its location. She located the nearest stairway and walked south into the centre of New York.

Nicole had not yet updated the map of New York stored in her computer. After she crossed the annular streets near the central plaza, she stopped near the octahedron and entered all her new discoveries, including the barn with the pits and anything else she could remember. A moment later, while Nicole was admiring the beauty of the bizarre, eight-sided building, she heard a third cry. Only this time it was more like a shriek. If it was Takagishi, he was certainly making a peculiar noise.

She jogged across the open plaza, trying to close in on the sound while it was still fresh in her mind. As Nicole approached the buildings on the opposite side, the shriek sounded again. This time she also heard an answer. She recognised the voices. They sounded like the avian pair that had visited her while she was in the pit. Nicole became more cautious. She walked in the direction of the sound. It seemed to be coming from the area around the lattice nets that Francesca Sabatini had found so fascinating.

In less than two minutes, Nicole was standing between two tall skyscrapers which were connected at the ground by a thick mesh lattice that rose fifty metres into the air. About twenty metres above the ground, the velvet-bodied avian struggled against its trap. The avian's talons and wings were ensnared in the cords of the stringy lattice. It screamed again when it saw Nicole. Its larger companion, presently circling near the top of the buildings, dived down in her direction.

Nicole cowered against the facade of one of the buildings as the avian drew near. It jabbered at Nicole, as if it were scolding her, but it did not touch her. The velvet avian then said something and, after a short exchange, the huge linoleum bird withdrew to a nearby ledge about twenty metres away.

After she had calmed herself (and keeping one eye on the large avian on its perch), Nicole walked over to the lattice and inspected it. She and Francesca had not had any time to spare when they had been searching for Takagishi, so this was Nicole's first chance for a detailed examination. The lattice was made of a ropelike material, about four centimetres thick, which had some elasticity. There were thousands of intersections in the lattice, and at each one of them there was a small knot, or node. The nodes were a little sticky, but not enough to make Nicole think that the whole lattice was some kind of spider's web for catching flying creatures.

While she was studying the bottom of the lattice, the free avian flew over Nicole's head and landed close to its trapped friend. Being very careful to avoid becoming snared itself, it played with the individual strands with its talons. It also stretched and twisted the cords, with some difficulty. Next the linoleum bird gingerly stepped over to where its companion was trapped and made an awkward attempt either to break or untie the lattice links holding the other avian. When it was finished, the huge bird stepped back and stared at Nicole.

What is it doing? Nicole said to herself. *I'm certain that it's trying to tell me something....* When Nicole did not move, the avian laboriously repeated the entire demonstration. This time Nicole thought she understood that the alien creature was trying to tell her that it couldn't free its friend. Nicole smiled and waved. Then, still staying at the bottom of the lattice, she tied a few of the adjacent cords together. When she subsequently untied them, the two avians shrieked their approval. She repeated the process twice and then pointed, first at herself and then at the velvet creature trapped above her.

There was a flurry of talk in their loud, sometimes musical tongue and the larger of the pair returned to his ledge. Nicole stared up at the velvet creature. It was caught in three different places; in each case its struggle had resulted in its being wedged more tightly in the elastic cord. Nicole surmised that the avian must have been caught in the violent hurricane winds and had been blown into the lattice during the preceding night. The cords had probably deformed under the momentum of the contact, and when they had snapped back to their normal size, the great bird was trapped in the mesh.

It was not a difficult climb. The lattice was carefully anchored to the two buildings and the rope itself was heavy enough that Nicole did not sway very much. But twenty metres off the ground is a considerable height, taller than a normal six-storey building, so Nicole was having some second thoughts when she finally reached the altitude where the avian was trapped.

She was panting from the effort of her climb. She eased gingerly over to the avian to ensure that she had not misunderstood anything in their strange communication. The alien bird followed her fixedly with its huge blue eyes.

One of the wings was snared very close to the avian's

head. Nicole began trying to free the wing, first wrapping strands of the lattice around her own ankles to make certain that she would not fall. It was slow work. At one point Nicole caught a whiff of the creature's powerful breath. *I know that smell,* Nicole said to herself. It only took an instant for Nicole to connect the odour with the manna melon that she had been eating earlier. *So you eat the same thing?* Nicole thought. *But where does it come from?* Nicole wished that she could talk to these strange and wonderful creatures.

She struggled with the first knot. It was very tight. She was afraid she might injure the creature's wing if she pulled with more force. Nicole reached into her pack and retrieved her power scalpel.

Instantly the other avian was upon her, jabbering and shrieking and scaring Nicole half to death. It would not go away and permit her to proceed until Nicole moved away from the trapped bird and showed its companion how the scalpel could cut through the lattice cord.

Using the scalpel the freeing operation was completed quickly. The velvet avian soared into the air, its musical cries of happiness resounding throughout the area. Its companion joined in the celebration with shrieks of its own as the two played, almost like lovebirds, in the air above the lattice. They disappeared a moment later and Nicole climbed slowly down to the ground.

Nicole was pleased with herself. She was ready now to return to the wall and wait for the rescue that she was certain was imminent. She walked toward the north, singing a folk song of the Loire that she remembered from her adolescence.

After several minutes Nicole had company again. More accurately, she had a guide. Whenever she made a wrong turn, the velvet avian, flying overhead, would make an incredible racket. The noise would only cease when Nicole moved in the proper direction. *I wonder where we're going?* Nicole asked herself.

In the plaza area, not more than forty metres from the octahedron, the avian swooped down on an utterly unobtrusive portion of the metallic ground. It tapped its talons several times and then hovered over the spot. A covering of some kind slid away and the creature disappeared under the plaza. Twice it flew out, said something in Nicole's direction, and then descended.

Nicole understood the message. *I think I'm being invited home to meet the family*, she said to herself. *Let's just hope that I'm not the dinner.*

41

A Friend Indeed

Nicole had no idea what to expect. She was not fearful as she walked over and gazed at the hole in the ground. Curiosity was her dominant feeling. She worried momentarily that her rescue team might arrive while she was under the ground, but Nicole convinced herself that they would return later.

The rectangular cover was large, about ten metres long and six metres wide. When the avian saw that Nicole was following, it flew into the hole and waited on the third ledge. Nicole squatted beside the opening and stared into the depths. She could see some lights close by and more were flickering in the distance below her. She could not estimate accurately to what depth the corridor descended, but it was obviously more than twenty or thirty metres.

The downward climb was not easy for a non-flying species. The vertical corridor was essentially a large hole with a series of broad ledges along its sides. Each of the ledges was exactly the same size, about five metres long and one metre wide, and they were separated one from another by about two metres in depth. Nicole had to be very careful.

What light there was in the vertical corridor came from the opening to the plaza and some lanterns hanging on the walls every four ledges along the descent. The lanterns were enclosed in transparent wrappings that were very flimsy and paperlike. Each lantern contained a small, burning fire, together with some liquid substance that Nicole assumed was the fuel.

Nicole's velvet-bodied friend watched her patiently throughout the descent, always staying three ledges below her. Nicole had the feeling that if she were to slip, the avian would catch her in mid-air, but she didn't want to test her hypothesis. Her mind was running at a rapid pace. Nicole had already decided that the creatures were definitely not biots. That meant they were an alien species of some kind. *But they couldn't possibly be the Ramans*, Nicole reasoned. *Their level of technological development is totally inconsistent with this spacecraft.*

Nicole remembered from her history courses the poor and backward Mayans found in Mexico by the conquistadors. The Spanish had deemed it impossible that the ancestors of those ignorant and impoverished people could possibly have built such impressive ceremonial centres. *Could that have happened here?* Nicole wondered. *Might these strange avians be all that is left of the master species that constructed this vehicle?*

About twenty metres below the surface Nicole heard what sounded like running water. The noise increased as she dropped on to a ledge that was actually an extension of a horizontal tunnel heading off behind her. Across the vertical corridor Nicole could see a similar dark hallway going in the opposite direction, also parallel to the surface.

Her avian guide was, as usual, three ledges below. Nicole pointed down the tunnel at her rear. The creature flew up close to her and systematically hovered over each of the two ledges immediately below Nicole, making it perfectly clear that Nicole was expected to descend.

Nicole was not willing to give up so easily. She took out her flask and made a drinking motion. Then she pointed behind her at the dark tunnel. The avian fluttered about, apparently weighing the decision, and then flew over Nicole's head into the blackness. Forty seconds later Nicole saw a light in the distance that continued to grow as it approached her. The avian returned, carrying a large torch in one of its talons.

Nicole followed the avian for about fifteen metres.

They came to a room, off to the left of the tunnel, which contained a large cistern full of water. Fresh water fell into the cistern from a pipe embedded in the wall. Nicole pulled out her mass spectrometer and tested the liquid. It was virtually pure H_2O; no other chemicals were present above one part in a million. Careful to remember her manners, Nicole cupped her hands and drank from the waterfall. It was unbelievably delicious.

After she had finished drinking, Nicole continued to walk down the tunnel in the same direction. The avian went into a frenzy, flying up and down and jabbering incessantly, until Nicole reversed her descent, she noticed that the ambient light level had dropped considerably. Nicole glanced .bove her. The opening to the plaza in New York was now closed. *I hope that doesn't mean I'm here for good*, she thought.

Twenty metres further below the surface, another pair of dark horizontal tunnels ran perpendicular to the main corridor. At this second level the velvet avian, still carrying the torch, led Nicole down one of the horizontal tunnels for about two hundred metres. She followed the bird into a large, circular room with a high ceiling. The avian used its torch to light several wall lanterns around the room. Then it disappeared. It was gone for almost an hour. Nicole sat as patiently as she could, at first staring around the black room, which reminded her of a cave or grotto. There were no decorations. At length Nicole began to concentrate on how she would inform the avians that she was ready to leave.

When her velvet friend eventually returned, it brought four associates. Nicole heard them flapping their wings in the hallway and jabbering intermittently. Her avian's companion (who Nicole assumed was a mate of some kind) and two additional linoleum-surfaced creatures flew in first. They landed and then awkwardly walked up very close to Nicole to conduct a visual examination. After they had sat down on the opposite side of the room, another velvet-bodied creature, this one brown instead of black, flew in last. It was carrying a small manna melon in its talons.

The melon was placed in front of Nicole. All the avians watched expectantly. Nicole neatly cut a one-eighth section out of the melon with her scalpel, picked it up to drink a small draught from the greenish liquid in the middle, and then carried the remaining melon over to her hosts. They shrieked appreciatively, admiring the precision of the cut as they passed the melon among themselves.

Nicole watched the avians eat. They shared the melon, one with another, and at no time were any portions meted out. The two velvet avians were surprisingly deft and dainty with their talons, making as little mess as possible and leaving no waste whatsoever. The larger avians were much clumsier; their eating reminded Nicole of animals on Earth. Like Nicole, none of the avians ate the tough outer covering of the manna melon.

When the meal was over the avians, who had not talked at all while they were eating, huddled in a circle for several seconds. The huddle broke up after the brown velvet one jabbered something that sounded to Nicole like a song. One at a time, they then flew over for another closeup look at her and disappeared out the door.

Nicole sat quietly and wondered what would happen next. The avians had left the lights on in the dining room (or banquet hall, or whatever it was), but it was pitch black in the corridor outside. They clearly intended for her to stay where she was, at least for the time being. It had been a long time since Nicole had had any sleep and she was pleasantly full from the meal. *Oh well*, she said to herself, curling up on the floor after a short internal debate, *maybe a short nap will refresh me.*

In her dream she heard someone calling her name, but it was very far away. She had to strain to hear the voice. Nicole woke with a start and tried to remember where she was. She listened carefully but didn't hear anything. When she checked her watch, she learned that she had been asleep for four hours. *I'd better get out of here*, Nicole thought. *It will be dark soon and I don't want to miss my chance to be rescued.*

She moved out into the hallway and switched on her small flashlight. Nicole reached the vertical corridor in less than a minute. Immediately she began scrambling up the ledges. Just below where she had stopped during her descent for a drink of water, Nicole heard a strange noise above her. She stopped to catch her breath. She leaned slightly into the gaping hole and shone her light above, in the direction of the sound. Something large was moving back and forth on the portion of the first level that jutted out into the vertical corridor.

Nicole cautiously climbed up to the ledge directly underneath the new phenomenon and crouched beneath it. Whatever it was, it was covering each square centimetre of the ledge in front of the tunnel entrance once every five seconds. There was no way Nicole could avoid it. She couldn't possibly pull herself up and then climb to the next ledge above in less than five seconds.

She moved down to one end of her ledge and listened intently to the sound above her. When the thing turned and went in the opposite direction. Nicole pulled her head over the edge of the next level. The object was moving rapidly on treads and looked altogether like an armoured tank from the rear. She had only a brief glimpse, for the top half of the tank spun around quickly at the other end as it prepared to reverse its field.

One thing is certain, Nicole said to herself as she stood on the ledge below. *That tank is some kind of sentinel.* Nicole wondered whether or not it had any sensors – certainly it had given no indication that it had heard her – but decided that she couldn't afford to find out. *It wouldn't be much of a guard if it couldn't at least see an intruder.*

Nicole climbed slowly down the ledges to the dining room level. She was sorely disappointed and now angry with herself for having come into the avian lair in the first place. It still did not make sense to her that the avians might be holding her as a captive. After all, hadn't the creature invited her to visit after Nicole had saved his life?

Nicole was also puzzled by the tank sentinel. Its

existence was baffling, and completely inconsistent with the level of technical developement of everything else in the lair. What was its purpose. Where did it come from? *Curiouser and curiouser*, Nicole thought.

When she was back on the second underground level, Nicole looked around to see if there was any other way she could get out of the lair. There was an identical set of ledges on the opposite side of the vertical corridor. If she could jump across, then maybe....

Before seriously considering such a plan, Nicole had to determine whether or not a tank, or equivalent sentinel, was guarding the opposite horizontal tunnel on the first level. She couldn't tell from where she was standing, so, muttering to herself about her stupidity, Nicole climbed back up the ledges on her side to obtain a good view across the corridor. She was in luck. The ledge in front of the opposite tunnel was empty.

By the time she returned to the second underground level again, Nicole was fatigued from all the climbing. She stared across the corridor and at the lights in the abyss below her. She would almost certainly die if she fell. Nicole was a very good judge of distance and reckoned that it was about four metres from the edge of the ledge extension in front of her tunnel to the edge on the opposite side. *Four metres*, she mused, *four-and-a-half at the most. Allowing for some room at both ends, I need a five metre jump to clear it. In flight suit* mit *backpack*.

Nicole remembered a Sunday afternoon at Beauvois four years earlier, when Genevieve was ten and both mother and daughter were watching the 2196 Olympics on television. 'Can you still jump a long way, Maman?' the little girl had asked, having a hard time picturing her mother as an Olympic champion.

Pierre had cajoled her into taking Genevieve to the athletics field adjacent to the secondary school at Luynes. Her timing had been way off in the triple jump, but after thirty minutes of warmup and practice Nicole had managed to long jump six-and-a-half metres. Genevieve had not been that impressed. 'Mama,' her daughter had said while they were bicycling home through the green countryside, 'Danielle's big sister can jump almost that far, and she's only a university student.'

The memory of Genevieve stirred a profound sadness in Nicole. She longed to hear her daughter's voice, help her with her hair, or go boating with her on their small, private pond beside the Bresme. *We never value enough the time we have*, she thought, *until they're no longer around*.

Nicole started back down the tunnel to where the avians had left her. She wouldn't try the jump. It was too dangerous. If she slipped....

'Nicole des Jardins, where the hell are you?' Nicole froze the moment she heard the call, very faint, off in the distance. Had she imagined it? 'Nicole,' she heard again. It was definitely Richard Wakefield's voice. She ran back to the vertical corridor and started to shout. *No*, she thought rapidly, *that will wake them. It won't take me more than five minutes. I can jump....*

Nicole's adrenaline was pumping at an incredible rate. She marked off her steps and soared across the chasm with plenty of room to spare. She climbed up the ledges at breakneck speed. Toward the top she heard Wakefield calling her again.

'I'm here, Richard. Below you,' she shouted. 'Underneath the plaza.'

Nicole reached the top ledge and started pushing on the covering. It wouldn't budge. 'Shit,' she shouted as the puzzled Richard paced around in the vicinity. 'Richard come over here. Where you hear my voice. Beat on the ground.'

Richard began to knock hard on the covering. They were shouting at each other. The noise was deafening. From far below Nicole heard the flapping of wings. As the avians rose in the corridor, they began to shriek and jabber.

'Help me,' Nicole yelled at them as they drew close. She pointed up at the cover. 'My friend is out there.'

Richard continued to pound. Only the two avians who had originally found Nicole in the pit came up to where she was. They hovered around her, flapping their wings and jabbering back at the five others who were one level below. The creatures were apparently having an argument, for the black velvet avian twice extended its neck down toward its associates and uttered a fearsome screech.

The covering suddenly opened. Richard had to scramble to keep from falling in. When he looked down into the hole he saw Nicole and two gigantic bird creatures, one of which flew right by him as Nicole crawled out of the opening. 'Bloody hell!' he exclaimed, his eyes following the flight of the avian.

Nicole was overcome with joy. She ran into Wakefield's arms. 'Richard, oh Richard,' she said, 'I'm so glad to see you.'

He grinned at her and returned the hug. 'If I had known you felt like this,' he said, 'I would have come earlier.'

42

Two Explorers

'Let me get this straight. You're telling me that you're *alone*? And we have no way to cross the Cylindrical Sea?'

Richard nodded. It was too much for Nicole. Five minutes earlier she had been exultant. Her ordeal was finally over. She had imagined returning to the Earth and seeing her father and daughter again. Now he was telling her....

She walked away quickly and leaned her head against one of the buildings surrounding the plaza. Tears rolled down her cheeks as she gave vent to her disappointment. Richard followed her at a distance.

'I'm sorry,' Richard said.

'It's not your fault,' Nicole replied after she had regained her composure. 'It just never occurred to me that I might see one of the crew again and *still* not be rescued....' She stopped herself. It was not fair for her to make Richard suffer. She walked over to him and forced a smile.

'I'm not usually this emotional,' Nicole said. 'And I interrupted your story right in the middle.' She paused a second to wipe her eyes. 'You were telling me about the shark biots chasing the motor boat. You saw them first when you were about halfway across the sea?'

'More or less,' Richard replied. Her disappointment had subdued him. He tried a nervous laugh. 'Do you remember, after one of the simulations, when the review board criticised us for not having sent a pilotless version of our motor boat into the water first, just to make sure that there wasn't something peculiar to the new design that would disturb the "ecological equilibrium" in some way? Well, I thought at the time their suggestion was ridiculous. Now I'm not so certain. Those shark biots hardly bothered the Newton vessels, but they were definitely angry about my high-speed motor boat.'

Richard and Nicole had sat down together on one of the grey metal boxes that dotted the plaza area. 'I managed to dodge them once,' Richard continued, 'but I was extremely lucky. When I had no other choice I simply jumped out and swam. Fortunately for me, they were mostly after the boat. I didn't see one again while I was swimming until I was only a hundred metres from shore.'

'How long have you been inside Rama altogether now.' Nicole asked.

'About seventeen hours. I left the Newton two hours after dawn. I spent too much damn time trying to repair the communications station at Beta. But it was impossible.'

Nicole felt his flight suit. 'Except for you hair, I can't even tell you've been wet.'

Richard laughed. 'Oh, the miracles of fabric engineering. Would you believe that this suit was almost dry by the time I changed my thermals? By then I was having a hard time convincing even myself that I had spent that twenty minutes swimming in the cold water.' He looked at his companion. She was relaxing very slowly. 'But I'm surprised at you, Cosmonaut des Jardins, you haven't even asked me the most important question. How did I know where you were?'

Nicole had pulled out her scanner and was reading Richard's biometry. Everything was within tolerances, despite his recent harrowing swim. She was a little slow to understand his question. 'You *knew* where I was?' she said finally, knitting her brow. 'I thought you were just wandering around....'

'Come on, lady. New York is small, but not *that* small. There's twenty-five square kilometres of territory inside these walls. And radio around here is completely unreliable.' He grinned. 'Let's see, if I stood and called your name in each square metre, I would have to call you twenty-five million times. At one call every ten seconds – allowing myself time to listen for a response and move to the next square metre – that would be six calls a minute. So it would take four million minutes, which is slightly more than sixty thousand hours, or twenty-five hundred Earth days –'

'Okay, okay,' Nicole interrupted. She was finally laughing. 'Tell me how you knew where I was.'

Richard stood up. 'May I?' he said dramatically, extending his fingers toward the breast pocket of Nicole's flight suit.

'I suppose so,' she answered. 'Although I can't imagine what....'

Richard reached into her pocket and pulled out Prince Hal. 'He led me to you,' Wakefield said. 'You're a good man, my prince, but for a while I thought you'd failed me.'

Nicole had no idea what Richard was talking about. 'Prince Hal and Falstaff have matching navigation beacons,' he explained. 'They put out fifteen strong pulses a second. With Falstaff fixed in my hut at Beta and with an equivalent transceiver over at Alpha campsite, I could follow you by triangulation. So I knew exactly where you were – at least in terms of x-y coordinates. My simple tracking algorithm wasn't designed for excursions in z.'

'That's what an engineer would call my visit to the avian lair?' Nicole said with another smile. 'An excursion in z?'

'That's one way of describing it.'

Nicole shook her head. 'I don't know about you, Wakefield. If you really knew where I was all this time, why the hell did you wait so long....'

'Because we lost you, or thought we had, before we found you ... after I came back to retrieve Falstaff.'

'Have I become a dullard in the last week, or is this roundabout explanation incredibly confusing?'

It was Richard's turn to laugh. 'Maybe I should try to

make my presentation more orderly.' He paused to arrange his mental notes. 'I was really irritated,' he began, 'back in June when the Engineering Steering Group decided not to use navigation beacons as backup personnel locators. I had argued, unsuccessfully, that there might be emergency situations, or unforeseen circumstances, in which the signal to noise ratio on the regular voice link would be below threshold. So I equipped three of my own robots just in case....'

Nicole studied Richard Wakefield while he talked. She had forgotten that he was both amazing and amusing. She was certain that if she asked the right questions, he could talk on this subject alone for a full hour.

'...Then Falstaff lost the signal,' he was saying. 'I wasn't present myself at the time, for I was preparing to come with Hiro Yamanaka to pick you and Francesca up in the helicopter. But Falstaff has a small recorder and timetags all the data. After you didn't show up, I replayed the data from the recorder and found that the signal had abruptly disappeared.

'It came back on only briefly, while we were talking on the radio a few minutes later, but several seconds after our last conversation the signal was gone for good. The signature suggested a hardware failure to me. I thought Prince Hal had malfunctioned. When Francesca said that you had been with her up until the plaza, then I was virtually certain that Prince Hal –'

Nicole had only been listening with one ear but she bolted to attention when Richard mentioned Francesca. 'Stop,' Nicole interrupted, holding up her hand. 'What did you say she told you?'

'That you and she had left the barn together and that you had walked away from her several minutes later to look for Takagishi....'

'That's complete bullshit,' Nicole said.

'What do you mean?' Richard asked.

'It's a lie. An absolute and total untruth. I fell into that pit I told you about while Francesca was there, or at least no more than a minute after she left. She never saw me again.'

Richard thought for a moment. 'That explains why Falstaff lost you. You were in the barn all that time and the signal was blocked.' Now it was his turn to be puzzled. 'But why would Francesca make up such a story?'

That's what I'd like to know, Nicole said to herself. *She must have poisoned Borzov on purpose. Otherwise why would she deliberately....*

'Was there something between the two of you?' Richard was saying. 'I always thought I detected –'

'Probably some jealousy,' Nicole interrupted, 'going both ways. Francesca and I are light years apart.'

'You can say that again,' Richard chuckled. 'I've spent the better part of a year giving off signals that I find you intelligent and interesting and attractive. Yet I've never received anything but a restrained and courteous professional response. Francesca, on the other hand, notices if you happen to look at her with your head tilted sideways.'

'There are other, more substantive differences,' Nicole replied, not altogether displeased that Richard had finally verbalised his interest in her as a woman.

There was a momentary pause in the conversation. Nicole glanced at her watch. 'But I don't want to spend any more time talking about Francesca Sabatini,' she said. 'It's going to be dark again in an hour and we have an escape from this island to plan. We also have certain, uh, logistical issues to address, such as food, water, and other unmentionable items that made confinement in a small pit reasonably disgusting.'

'I brought a portable hut – if we need one.'

'That's great,' Nicole replied, 'I'll remember that when it rains.' She reached automatically into her backpack for some manna melon but did not pull out the food packet. 'By the way,' she said to Richard, 'did you bring any *human* food?'

The hut came in handy when they were ready for sleep. They decided to pitch it just to the side of the central plaza. Nicole felt safer being close to the avians. In some sense they were her friends and they might help if an emergency arose. They were also the only known source of food. Between them, Richard and Nicole had barely enough food and water to last for another two Raman days.

Nicole had not objected to Richard's suggestion that they share the hut. He had gallantly offered to sleep outside, 'if that would make you more comfortable,' but the huts were easily large enough for two sleeping mats as long as there were no other furnishings. Lying about half a metre apart made their conversation very easy. Nicole gave a detailed rendition of her hours alone, omitting only the part about the vial and the vision. That was too personal for her to share. Richard was fascinated by her entire story and absolutely intrigued by the avians.

'I mean, look,' he said, propping his head up on his elbow, 'try to work out how the hell they got here. From what you've said, except for that tank sentinel – and I completely agree with you that it's an anomaly – they're no more advanced than prehistoric man. What a boggle it would be to learn their secret.

'You can't rule out completely that they're biots,' he continued, barely able to contain his enthusiasm. 'They might not be impressive as biology, but Jesus, as artificial intelligence they would be state of the art.' He sat up on his mat. 'Just think about what it would mean either way. We must find out all these answers. You're a linguist, maybe you could learn to talk to them.'

Nicole was amused. 'Has it occurred to you, Richard,' she asked, 'that all of his discussion will be academic if nobody ever rescues us?'

'A couple of times.' Richard laughed. He was lying down again. 'That damn Heilmann took me aside, right before I came back inside Rama, and told me that I was acting "in violation of all procedures" by returning here. He promised me that they would not come after me under *any* circumstances.'

'So why did you come back?'

'I'm not completely certain,' he said slowly. 'I know I wanted to pick up Falstaff and see if, by some wild

happenstance, he had ever received any more signals
from your beacon. But I think there were other reasons.
The mission was becoming more politics than science. It
was obvious to me that the bureaucrats on Earth were
going to abort the mission, 'for security reasons', and the
crew was not going to return to Rama. I knew the
political discussions would continue for another day or
two.' He paused a second. 'And I wanted one last look at
the most incredible sight of my life.'

Nicole was quiet for a moment. 'You obviously
weren't afraid,' she said softly, 'because you show no sign
of fear even now. Doesn't the thought of being left to die
on board Rama bother you at all?'

'A little,' Richard answered. 'But dying in an exciting
situation is much better than living in a boring one.'
Again he propped himself up on his elbow. 'I have been
looking forward to this mission for three years. I thought
from the beginning that I had a good chance of being
selected. Except for my robots and Shakespeare, there is
nothing in my life but my work. I have no family or
friends to think of....'

His voice trailed off. 'And I'm as much afraid of going
back as I am of dying. At least Richard Wakefield,
Newton cosmonaut, has a clearly-defined purpose.' He
started to say something else but stopped himself.
Richard lay back down and closed his eyes.

43

Exobiological Psychology

'There's another reason not to give up hope,' Richard said cheerfully as soon as he saw Nicole open her eyes, 'and I forgot to mention it last night.'

Nicole had always awakened very slowly. Even as a child. She liked to savour the last part of her dream state before confronting harsh reality. At home Genevieve and Pierre both knew not to talk to her about anything important until after she had had her morning coffee. She blinked at Richard, who was shining his small flashlight in the gap between them.

'This space vehicle is now headed for the Earth,' he said. 'Even if the Newton leaves, there might be another human spacecraft here sooner or later.'

'What's that?' Nicole said, sitting up and rubbing her eyes.

'In all the excitement last night,' Richard replied, 'I left out one of the most important points. The manoeuvre – I guess you missed it because you were unconscious at the bottom of that pit – put Rama on an Earth impact course. That made our evacuation imperative.'

Richard noticed that Nicole was staring at him as if he had lost his mind. 'The spaceship is still on a hyperbola with respect to the Sun,' he clarified, 'but it's blasting full speed toward the Earth. We will impact in twenty-three days.'

'Richard,' Nicole said, longing intensely for that fresh cup of coffee, 'I do not like jokes early in the morning. If you have spent your energy making up –'

'No, no,' he interrupted her. 'I'm serious. It's true. Believe me.'

Nicole pulled out her pocket thermometer and checked it. 'Then tell me, my engineering genius, why is the temperature in here still increasing? If we are now going away from the Sun, shouldn't it be dropping?'

'You're smarter than that, Nicole.' Richard shook his head. 'The thermal input from the Sun on the exterior of Rama diffuses very slowly through the outer shell and then into the interior. The thermal conductivity is obviously very low. I wouldn't expect the temperatures to reach a peak for another two weeks at least.'

Nicole remembered enough of her basic thermodynamics to realise he was making sense. It was too early in the morning for thermal diffusion. Nicole struggled with the idea that Rama was now bound for the Earth. She asked Richard for a drink of water. *What is going on here?* she thought. *Why is Rama now headed for our planet?*

Richard must have been reading her mind. 'You should have heard the silly discussions about why Rama had changed its trajectory and what it was likely to do. There was a seven-hour conference call on the subject.'

He laughed out loud. 'The ISA has an employee, a Canadian I think, whose speciality is exobiological psychology. Can you believe it? This idiot actually participated in the conference call and offered insights into the motives behind the Raman manoeuvre.' Richard shook his head vigorously. 'All bureaucracies are the same. They drain the life out of the truly creative people and develop mindless paper-pushers as their critical mass.'

'What was the final result of the call?' Nicole asked after a short silence.

'Most of the same people guessed that Rama would go into orbit around the Earth and conduct passive remote observations. But they were in the minority. Sanity and logic took a holiday, in my opinion. Even David Brown – who acted very strangely, it seemed to me, after we returned to the Newton – acknowledged that there was a high probability that Rama would do something hostile. He clarified his position by stating that it would *not*, in reality, be a hostile act; however, its attempt to learn more about the Earth might result in actions that would be *perceived* by us as hostile.'

The agitated Richard was now standing up. 'Have you ever heard such gobbledygook in your life? And Dr Brown was one of the more coherent speakers. The entire ISA Advisory Board was polled as to which of the projected scenarios each of them favoured. Do you think that bunch of plenipotentiaries could respond simply with "I believe in Option A, direct impact with resultant destruction and climate alteration", or "I favour Option C, Earth orbit with bellicose intentions"? Hell no! Each one of them had to deliver a lecture of some kind. That weird Dr Alexander, the one who asked you all the questions after your open biometry meeting in November, even spent fifteen minutes explaining how Rama's existence had exposed a flaw in the ISA charter. As if anybody gave a shit!' Richard sat down again and put his hands on his cheeks. 'The whole thing was unbelievable.'

Nicole was now fully awake. 'I assume,' she said, sitting up on her mat, 'judging from your obvious irritation, that you disagreed with the consensus.'

Richard nodded. 'Almost three-quarters of the large group participating in the call – which included all the Newton cosmonauts as well as most of the senior scientists and executives in the ISA – were convinced that the Raman manoeuvre was likely to be harmful to the Earth in some significant way. Almost all of them focused on the same issue. Since the first Rama apparently ignored our existence altogether, they argued, the fact that Rama II altered its trajectory to achieve a rendezvous with the Earth shows that this spacecraft is operating under different principles. I certainly agree with that conclusion. But what I cannot understand is why everyone necessarily assumes that the Raman action is hostile. It seems just as likely to me that the aliens could be motivated by curiosity, or even a desire to be our benefactors in some way.'

The British engineer paused for a moment to reflect.

'Francesca says that the polls on Earth are indicating that a huge majority of ordinary people, almost ninety percent according to her, are terrified by Rama's approach. They are clamouring for the politicians to do something.'

Richard opened the hut and walked out into the dark plaza. He idly shone his flashlight on the octahedron. 'At a second meeting eighteen hours later it was decreed that the Newton team would not go inside Rama again. Technically, I am not in violation of that order, because I left the Newton before the official proclamation. But it was obvious that the order was coming.'

While the leaders of the planet Earth are discussing what to do with a spacecraft the size of an asteroid that is aimed directly at them,' Nicole said as she walked out into the plaza behind him, 'you and I have a more tractable problem. We must cross the Cylindrical Sea.' She managed a wan smile. 'Shall we do a little exploring while we talk?'

Richard directed his flashlight beam into the bottom of the pit. The manna melon was clearly identifiable but the individual pieces in the pile of jumbled metal were very hard to resolve. 'So those are spare parts from a centipede biot?'

Nicole nodded. They were kneeling side by side on the lip. 'Even in the daylight the ends of the pit are in shadows. I needed to be certain that I wasn't looking at Takagishi's body.'

'I would love to see a centipede biot repair itself.' Richard stood up and walked over to the wall of the barn. He knocked. 'And the material scientists would love this stuff. Normal radio waves are blocked both ways and you can't see in from the outside. Yet the wall is somehow tranpsarent if you're inside the barn looking out.' He turned to Nicole. 'Bring your scalpel over here. Let's see if we can cut off a piece.'

Nicole was trying to decide if one of them should drop down into the pit and retrieve the melon. It wouldn't be too difficult, assuming the suture line would hold. At length she pulled out her scalpel and walked over beside Richard.

'I'm not certain we should do this,' she said. She hesitated before applying the scalpel to the barn wall. 'In the first place, the scalpel could be damaged. We might need it later. Secondly, uh, it might be considered vandalism.'

'Vandalism?' he said rhetorically. Richard regarded Nicole with a peculiar look. 'What a curiously homocentric concept.' He shrugged his shoulders and headed toward one end of the barn. 'Never mind,' he said, 'you're probably right about the scalpel.'

Richard had entered some data into his pocket computer and was studying the small monitor when Nicole came over beside him. 'You and Francesca were standing right about here, correct?' Nicole gave him an affimative reply. 'Then you went back into the barn to look into one of the pits?'

'We've been over this before,' Nicole replied, 'why are you asking again?'

'I think Francesca saw you fall into one of the pits and intentionally misled us with that story about you wandering off to search for our Japanese professor. She didn't want anybody to find you.'

Nicole stared at Richard in the dark. 'I agree,' she responded slowly. 'But why do *you* think so?'

'It's the only explanation that makes any sense. I had a bizarre encounter with her just before I came back inside. She came into my room under the pretence of wanting an interview, supposedly to find out why I was returning to Rama. When I mentioned Falstaff and your navigation beacon, she switched off her camera. Then she became quite animated and asked me many detailed technical questions. Before she left, she told me she was convinced that none of us should ever have entered Rama in the first place. I thought she was going to beg me not to go back.

'I can understand her not wanting me to find out that she had tried to maroon you in the pit,' Richard continued after a brief pause. 'What I can't fathom is why she left you there in the first place.'

'You remember the night you explained to me why

RoSur's fault protection had failed?' Nicole said after a moment's reflection. 'That same night I also asked you and Janos if either of you had seen General Borzov....'

As they walked back in the direction of the central plaza and their hut, Nicole spent fifteen minutes explaining to Richard her entire hypothesis about the conspiracy. She told him about the media contract, the drugs Francesca had given to both David Brown and Reggie Wilson, and Nicole's personal interactions with all the principals. She did not tell him about the data cube. Richard agreed that the evidence was very compelling.

'So you think she left you there in the pit to avoid being unmasked as a conspirator?'

Nicole nodded.

Richard whistled. 'Then everything fits. It was apparent to me that Francesca was running the show when we returned to the Newton. Both Brown and Heilmann were taking orders from her.' He put his arm around Nicole. 'I wouldn't want that woman as my enemy. She clearly has no scruples whatsoever.'

44
Another Lair

Richard and Nicole had bigger concerns than Francesca.
When they returned to the central plaza, they found their
hut had disappeared. Repeated knocks on the avian cover
produced no response. The precariousness of their
situation became clearer to both of them.

Richard grew moody and uncommunicative. He
apologised to Nicole, saying that it was a characteristic of
his personality for him to withdraw from people when he
felt insecure. He played with his computer for several
hours, only stopping occasionally to ask Nicole questions
about the geography of New York.

Nicole lay down on her sleeping mat and thought
about swimming across the Cylindrical Sea. She was not
an exceptionally good swimmer. During training it had
taken her about fifteen minutes to swim one kilometre.
That had been in a placid swimming pool. To cross the
sea she would be forced to swim five kilometres through
cold, choppy water. And she might be accompanied by
lovely creatures like the shark biots.

A jolly fat man twenty centimetres high interrupted
her contemplation. 'Would you like a drink, fair lass?'
Falstaff asked her. Nicole rolled over and studied the
robot from close up. He hoisted a large mug of fluid and
drank it, spilling some on his beard. He wiped it off with
his sleeve and then he burped. 'And if you want nothing
tc drink,' he said in a heavy British accent, thrusting his
hand down into his codpiece, 'then perhaps Sir John
could teach you a thing or two between the sheets.' The

tiny face was definitely leering. It was crude, but very funny.

Nicole laughed. So did Falstaff. 'I am not only witty in myself,' the robot said, 'but the cause that wit is in other men.'

'You know,' Nicole said to Richard, who was watching from several metres away, 'if you ever become tired of being an astronaut, you could make millions in children's toys.'

Richard came over and picked up Falstaff. He thanked Nicole for her compliment. 'As I see it, we have three options,' he then said very seriously. 'We can swim the sea, we can explore New York to see if we can forage enough material to construct some kind of boat, or we can wait here until someone comes. I'm not optimistic about our chances in any of the cases.'

'So what do you suggest?'

'I propose a compromise. When it's light, let's carefully search the key areas of the city, particularly around the three plazas, and see if we can find anything that could be used to build a boat. We'll allot one Raman day, maybe two, to the exploration. If nothing turns up, we'll swim for it. I have no faith we'll ever see a rescue team.'

'Sounds all right to me. But I would like to do one thing first. We don't have a lot of food, to make a rather obvious understatement. I'd feel better if we pulled up the manna melon first, before we did any more exploring. That way we could be protected against any surprises.'

Richard agreed that establishing the food supply would probably be a prudent initial action. But he didn't like the idea of using the suture thread again. 'You were lucky in many ways,' he told Nicole. 'Not only did the line not break, it didn't even slip off that waistband you made. However, it did cut completely through your gloves in two places and almost through the waistband.'

'You have another idea?' Nicole asked.

'The lattice material is the obvious choice,' Richard replied. 'It should be perfect, provided that we don't have any trouble obtaining it. Then I can go down in the pit and spare you the trouble —'

'Wrong,' Nicole interrupted. She smiled. 'With all due respect, Richard, now is not the time for any macho derring-do. Using the lattice is a great idea. But you're too heavy. If something happened. I would never be able to pull you out.' She patted him on the shoulder. 'And I hope it doesn't hurt your feelings, but I'm probably the more athletic of the two of us.'

Richard feigned hurt pride. 'But whatever happened to tradition? The man always performs the feats of physical strength and agility. Don't you remember your childhood cartoons?'

Nicole laughed heartily. 'Yes, my dear,' she said lightly. 'But you aren't Popeye. And I'm not Olive Oyl.'

'I'm not certain I can deal with this,' he said, shaking his head vigorously. 'To discover at the age of thirty-four that I'm not Popeye ... What a blow to my self-image.' He cuddled Nicole gently. 'What do you say?' he continued. 'Should we try to sleep some more before it's light?'

Neither of them was able to sleep. They lay side by side on their mats in the open plaza, each occupied with their own thoughts. Nicole heard Richard's body move. 'You're awake too?' she said in a whisper.

'Yeah,' he answered. 'I've even resorted to counting Shakespearean characters with no success. I was up to more than a hundred.'

Nicole propped herself up on an elbow and faced her companion. 'Tell me, Richard,' she said, 'where did this preoccupation of yours with Shakespeare come from? I know you grew up in Stratford, but it's hard for me to imagine how an engineer like you, in love with computers and calculations and gadgets, could become so fascinated with a playwright.'

'My therapist told me it was an "escapist compulsion",' Richard replied a few second later. 'Since I didn't like the real world or the people in it, he said, I made up another one. Except that I didn't create it from scratch. I just extended a wonderful universe already fabricated by a genius.

'Shakespeare was my God,' Richard continued after a
moment. 'When I was nine or ten, I would stop in that
park along the Avon – the one beside all the theatres,
with the statues of Hamlet, Falstaff, Lady Macbeth, and
Prince Hal – and spend the afternoon hours making up
additional stories about my favourite characters. That
way I put off going home until the last possible moment.
I dreaded being around my father ... I never knew what
he would do –

'But you don't want to hear this –' Richard interrupted
himself suddenly – 'everyone has memories of childhood
pain. We should talk about something else.'

'We should talk about whatever we're feeling,' Nicole
responded, surprising even herself. 'Which is something
I hardly ever do,' she added softly.

Richard turned and looked in her direction. He
extended his hand slowly. She gently wrapped her fingers
around his. 'My father worked for British Rail,' he said.
'He was a very clever man, but socially clumsy, and he
had difficulty finding a job that fitted him after he
finished university at Sussex. Times were still tough. The
economy had just started to recover from the Great
Chaos....

'When my mother told him that she was pregnant, he
was overwhelmed by the responsibility of it all. He
looked for a safe, secure position. He had always scored
well on tests and the government had forced all the
national transportation monopolies, including the rail
system, to staff positions based on objective test results.
So my father became the manager of operations at
Stratford.

'He hated the job. It was boring and repetitive, no
challenge at all for a man who had an honours degree.
Mother told me that when I was very small he applied for
other positions, but he always seemed to botch the
interviews. Later on, when I was older, he never even
tried. He sat at home and complained. And drank. And
then made everyone around him miserable.'

There was a long silence. Richard was having a
difficult time struggling with the demons of his

childhood. Nicole squeezed his hand. 'I'm sorry,' she said.

'So was I,' Richard replied with a slight break in his voice. 'I was just a small child with an incredible sense of wonder and love of life. I would come home enthusiastic about something new I had learned or something that had happened at school, and my Dad would just growl.

'Once, when I was only eight, I came home from school in the early afternoon and I got into an argument with him. It was his day off and he had been drinking, as usual. Mother was out at the shops. I don't remember what it was about now, but I do recall telling him that he was wrong about some trivial fact. When I continued to argue with him, he suddenly hit me in the nose with all his might. I fell against the wall with my broken nose gushing blood. From that time on, until I was fourteen and felt I could protect myself, I never walked in that house when he was there unless I was certain that my mother was home.'

Nicole tried to imagine an adult man slugging an eight-year-old child. *What kind of human being could break his own son's nose?* she wondered.

'I had always been very shy,' Richard was saying, 'and had convinced myself that I had inherited my father's social clumsiness, so I didn't have many friends my own age. But I still yearned for human interaction.' He looked over at Nicole and paused, remembering. 'I made Shakespeare's characters my friends. I read his plays every afternoon in the park and immersed myself in his imaginative world. I even memorised entire scenes. Then I talked to Romeo or Ariel or Jaques while I was walking home.'

It was not difficult for Nicole to visualise the rest of Richard's story. *I can picture you as an adolescent*, she thought. *Solitary, awkward, emotionally repressed. Your obsession with Shakespeare gave you an escape from your pain. All the theatres were near your home. You saw your friends become alive on the stage.*

On impulse Nicole leaned over and kissed Richard lightly on the cheek. 'Thanks for telling me,' she said.

As soon as it was daylight they walked over to the lattice.

Nicole was surprised to find that the incisions she had made when she had freed the avian had all been repaired. The lattice was like new. 'Obviously a repair biot has already been here,' Richard commented, no longer particularly impressed after all the wonders he had already witnessed.

They cut off several long strands of the lattice and headed for the barn. On the way Richard tested the elasticity of the material. He found that it stretched about fifteen percent and always restored itself, albeit very slowly at times, to its original length. The restoration time varied significantly, depending on how long the piece had been fully stretched. Richard had already begun his examination of the inside structure of the cord when they arrived at the barn.

Nicole did not waste any time. She tied one end of the lattice material around a stumpy object just outside the barn and lowered herself down the wall. Richard's function was to make certain that nothing untoward occurred and to be available if there was some kind of an emergency. Down in the bottom of the pit Nicole shuddered once as she remembered how helpless she had felt there just a few days earlier. But she quickly turned her attention to her task, inserting a makeshift handle made from her medical probes deep into the manna melon and then securing the other end of the handle to her backpack. Her ascent was vigorous and uneventful.

'Well.' She smiled at Richard, as she handed him the melon to carry. 'Should we now continue with Plan A?'

'Roger,' he replied. 'Now we know where our next ten meals are coming from.'

'Nine,' Nicole corrected him with a laugh. 'I've made a slight adjustment in the estimate now that I've watched you eat a couple of times.'

Richard and Nicole marched quickly from the barn to the western plaza. They crisscrossed the open area and combed the narrow alleys nearby, but they did not find anything that would help them build a boat. Richard did have an encounter with a centipede biot, however; in the middle of their search one had entered the plaza and then moved diagonally across it. Richard had done everything possible, including lying in front of it and beating it over the head with his backpack, to try to induce the biot to stop. He had not been successful. Nicole was laughing at him when Richard returned, a little frustrated, to her side.

'That centipede is absolutely useless,' he complained. 'What the hell is it for? It's not carrying anything. It has no sensors that I can see. It just travels merrily along.'

'The technology of an advanced extraterrestrial species –' she reminded Richard of one of his favourite quotes –' will be indistinguishable from magic.'

'But that damn centipede's not magic,' he replied, a little annoyed at Nicole's laughter, 'it's goddamn stupid!'

'And what would you have done if it had stopped?' Nicole enquired.

'Why, I would have examined it, of course. What did you think?'

'I think we'd be better off concentrating our energy in other areas,' she replied. 'I don't imagine a centipede biot is going to help us get off this island.'

'Well,' Richard said a little brusquely, 'it's obvious to me already we're going about this process all wrong. We're not going to find anything on the surface. The biots probably clean it up regularly. We should be looking for another hole in the ground, like the avian's lair. We can use the multispectral radar to identify any places where the ground is not solid.'

It took them a long time to find the second hole, even though it was not more than two hundred metres from the centre of the western plaza. At first Richard and Nicole were much too restrictive in their search. After an hour, though, they finally convinced themselves that the ground underneath the plaza area was solid everywhere. They expanded their search to include the small streets and lanes nearby, off the concentric avenues. On a dead-end alley with tall buildings on three sides, they found another covering in the centre of the road. It was not camouflaged in any way. This second cover was the same size as the one at the avian lair, a rectangle ten metres long and six metres wide.

45
Nikki

'Do you think the avian cover opens in the same way?'
Nicole asked, after Richard had very carefully searched
the environs and found a flat plate on one of the buildings
that looked decidedly out of place. Pressing hard against
the plate had caused the cover to open.

'Probably,' he answered. 'We'll have to go back and
check.'

'Then these places are not very secure,' Nicole said.
The two of them walked back on to the street and knelt
down to look in the hole. A broad, steep ramp descended
from beside them and disappeared into the darkness
below. They could only see about ten metres into the
hole.

'It looks like one of those ancient car parks,' Richard
remarked. 'Back when everybody had automobiles.' He
stepped on the ramp. 'It even feels like concrete.'

Nicole watched as her companion moved slowly down
the ramp. When Richard's head was below the ground
level, he turned and spoke to her. 'Aren't you coming?'
he asked. He had switched on his flashlight beam and
had illuminated a small landing another few metres
below.

'Richard,' Nicole said from above, 'I think we should
discuss this. I don't want to be stuck....'

'Ah ha!' Richard exclaimed. As soon as his foot hit the
first landing, some lights around him automatically lit the
next phase of the descent. 'The ramp doubles back,' he
shouted, 'and continues down. Looks just the same.' He

turned and disappeared from Nicole's field of view.

'Richard,' Nicole now yelled, a little exasperated, 'will you please stop for a minute? We must talk about what we're doing.'

A few seconds later Richard's smiling face reappeared. The two cosmonauts discussed their options. Nicole insisted that she was going to stay outside, in New York, even if Richard was going to continue with his exploration. At least that way, she argued, she could guarantee that they would not be stranded in the hole.

While she was talking, Richard was standing on the first landing and surveying the area around him. The walls were made of the same material Nicole had found in the avian lair. Small strip lights, looking not unlike normal fluorescent lights on Earth, ran along the wall to illuminate the path.

'Move away just a second, will you?' Richard shouted in the middle of their conversation.

At first puzzled, Nicole backed away from the entrance to the rectangular hole. 'Farther,' she heard Richard yell. Nicole walked over and stood against one of the surrounding buildings.

'Is this far enough?' she had just finished shouting when the covering on the hole began to close. Nicole ran forward and tried to stop the motion of the cover, but it was much too heavy. 'Richard,' she cried as the hole disappeared beneath her.

Nicole pounded on the cover and remembered her own feelings of frustration when she had been locked in the avian lair. She quickly ran back over to the building and pressed the embedded flat panel. Nothing happened. Almost a minute passed. Nicole became anxious. She ran back into the street and called for her colleague.

'I'm all right here, under the cover,' he answered, bringing Nicole considerable relief. 'I found another plate near the first landing and pressed it. I think it toggles the cover closed or open, but it may have a timing delay constraint. Give me a few minutes. Don't you try to open the cover. And don't stand too near it.'

Nicole backed away and waited. Richard was correct.

Several minutes later the cover opened and he emerged from the hole with a big grin on his face. 'See,' he said, 'I told you not to worry ... Now what's for lunch?'

As they descended the ramp, Nicole heard the familiar sound of running water. In a little room about twenty metres behind the landing, they found piping and a cistern identical to those in the avian lair. Richard and Nicole both filled their flasks with the fresh, delicious water.

Outside the room, there were no horizontal tunnels leading off in both directions, only another descending ramp dropping five more metres beneath the floor. Richard's flashlight beam crawled slowly across the dark walls near the water room. 'Look here, Nicole,' he said, pointing at what was a very subtle variation in building material. 'See, it arches around to the other side.'

She followed his beam as it inscribed a long circular arc on the wall. 'It looks as if there were at least two phases of construction.'

'Exactly,' he replied. 'Maybe there were horizontal tunnels here as well, at least in the beginning, and they were sealed off later.' Neither of them said anything else as they continued their descent. Back and forth went the identical ramps. Whenever Richard and Nicole touched a new landing, the next descending ramp was illuminated.

They were fifty metres underneath the surface when the ceilings above them opened up and the ramps terminated in a large cavern. The circular floor of the cave was about twenty-five metres in diameter. There were four dark tunnels, five metres in height and equally spaced at ninety degrees around the circle, leading off from the cavern.

'Eeny, Meeny, Miny, Mo,' Richard said.

'I'll take Mo,' Nicole said. She headed toward one of the tunnels. When she was within a few metres of the entrance, the lights in the near portion of the tunnel switched on.

This time it was Richard's turn to be hesitant. He stared cautiously into the tunnel and made some quick entries into his computer. 'Does it look to you as if this tunnel curves slightly to the right? See, there at the end of the lights?'

Nicole nodded. She looked over Richard's shoulder to see what he was doing. 'I'm making a map,' he said in response to her question. 'Theseus had string and Hansel and Gretel had bread. We have them both beat. Aren't computers wonderful?'

She smiled. 'So what's your guess?' Nicole said while they were walking along in the near part of the tunnel. 'Will it be a Minotaur or a gingerbread house with a wicked witch?'

We should be so lucky, Nicole thought. Her fear was increasing as they penetrated deeper and deeper into the tunnel. She recalled that awful moment of terror in the pit when she had first seen the avian hovering over her with its beak and talons extending in her direction. An icy chill ran down her spine. *There it is again*, she said to herself, *that feeling that something terrible is going to happen*.

She stopped. 'Richard,' she said, 'I don't like this. We should turn back....'

They both heard the noise at the same time. It was definitely *behind* them, back in the vicinity of the circular cavern they had just left. It sounded like hard brushes dragging against metal.

Richard and Nicole huddled together. 'That's the same sound,' he whispered, 'that I heard the first night in Rama, when we were at the walls of New York.'

The tunnel behind them curved slightly to the left. When they looked back in that direction, the lights were off at the limit of their vision. The second time they heard the sound, however, some lights came on in the far distance almost simultaneously, indicating something was near the entrance to their tunnel.

Nicole bolted. She must have covered the next two hundred metres in thirty seconds, despite her flight suit and backpack. She stopped and waited for Richard. Neither of them heard the sound again and no new lights were illuminated in the distant reaches of the tunnel.

'I'm sorry,' Nicole said when Richard finally arrived. 'I panicked. I think I've been in this alien wonderland too long.'

'Jesus,' Richard responded with a frown. 'I've never seen anybody run that fast.' His frown changed into a smile. 'Don't feel bad, Nikki,' he said. 'I was scared shitless too. But I was frozen in place.'

Nicole continued taking deep breaths and stared at Richard. 'What did you call me?' she asked, somewhat belligerently.

'Nikki,' he replied. 'I thought it was time for me to have my own special name for you. Don't you like it?'

Nicole was speechless for ten full seconds. Her mind was millions of kilometres and fifteen years away, in a hotel suite in Los Angeles, her body experiencing wave after wave of pleasure. 'That was remarkable, Nikki, truly wonderful,' the prince had said several minutes later. She had told Henry on that night fifteen years before not to call her Nikki, that it sounded like a name for a buxom showgirl or a tart.

Richard was snapping his fingers in front of her face. 'Hello, hello. Anybody home?'

Nicole smiled. 'Sure, Richard,' she replied. 'Nikki's just fine – as long as you don't use it all the time.'

They continued to walk slowly along the tunnel. 'So where did you go back there?' Richard asked.

Somewhere I can never tell you about, Nicole mused. *Because each of us is the sum of all we have ever experienced. Only the very young have a clean slate. The rest of us must live forever with everything we have ever been.* She slid her arm through Richard's. *And have the good sense to know when to keep it private.*

The tunnel seemed endless. Richard and Nicole had almost decided to turn around when they came to a dark passage off to their right. Without hesitation they both walked inside. The lights came on immediately. Inside the room, on the big wall to the left of them, were twenty-five flat rectangular objects, arranged in five orderly rows with five columns each. The opposite wall was empty. Within seconds after their entrance, the two cosmonauts heard a high frequency, squeaky sound coming from the ceiling. They tensed briefly, but relaxed as the squeaking continued and there were no new surprises.

They held hands and walked to one end of the long narrow room. The objects on the wall were photographs, most of them recognisable as having been taken somewhere inside Rama. The great octahedron near the central plaza was featured in several of the photos. The remaining pictures were a balance between scenes of the buildings of New York and wide-angle shots of panoramas around the interior of Rama.

Three of the photographs were particularly fascinating to Richard. They depicted sleek, aerodynamically curved boats plying the Cylindrical Sea; in one of the photographs a great wave was about to crash over the top of a large boat. 'Now there's what we need,' Richard said to Nicole excitedly. 'If we could find one of them, our troubles would be over.'

The squeaking above them continued with very little modulation. A spotlight moved from picture to picture at moments when there was a pause in the squeak. Nicole and Richard easily concluded that they were in a museum on some kind of tour, but there was nothing else they could know for certain. Nicole sat down against a side wall. 'I'm having a lot of trouble with all this,' she said. 'I feel totally out of control.'

Richard sat down beside her. 'Me too,' he nodded. 'And I just arrived in New York. So I can imagine what all this is doing to you.'

They were silent for a moment. 'You know what bothers me the most?' Nicole said, trying to give some expression to the helplessness she was feeling. 'It's how very little I understood and appreciated my own ignorance. Before I came on this voyage, I thought I knew the general dimensions of the relationship between my own knowledge and the knowledge of mankind. But what is staggering about this mission is how very small the *entire range* of human knowledge might be compared to what *could* be known. Just think, the sum of everything all human beings know or have ever known might be nothing more than an infinitesimal fraction of the Encyclopedia Galactica –'

'It *is* really frightening.' Richard interrupted her enthusiastically. 'And thrilling at the same time ... Sometimes when I'm in a bookshop or a library, I am overwhelmed by all the things I don't know. Then I'm seized by a powerful desire to read all the books, one by one. Imagine what it would be like to be in the *true* library, one that combined the knowledge of all the species in the universe ... The very thought makes me woozy.'

Nicole turned to him and slapped his leg. 'All right, Richard,' she said jokingly, changing the mood, 'now that we have reaffirmed how incredibly stupid we are, what's our plan? I reckon we have already covered about a kilometre in this tunnel. Where do we go from here?'

'I propose we walk another fifteen minutes in the same direction. In my experience tunnels always lead somewhere. If we don't find anything, we'll turn around.'

He helped Nicole up and gave her a small hug. 'All right, Nikki,' he said with a wink. 'Half a league onward.'

Nicole frowned and shook her head. 'Twice is enough for one day,' she said, extending her hand toward Richard.

46

The Better Part of Valour

The huge circular hole below them extended into the darkness. Only the top five metres of the shaft were lit. Metal spikes, about a metre long, protruded from the walls, each separated from its neighbours by the same distance.

'This is definitely the destination of the tunnels,' Richard muttered to himself. He was having some difficulty integrating this huge, cylindrical hole with its walls of spikes into his overall conception of Rama. He and Nicole had walked around the perimeter twice. They had even backtracked several hundred metres down the other, adjacent tunnel, concluding from its slight curvature to the right that it probably originated from the same cavern as the tunnel they had followed earlier.

'Well,' Richard said at length, shrugging his shoulders, 'here we go.' He put his right foot on one of the spikes to test its ability to hold his weight. It was firm. He moved his left leg down to another of the spikes and descended one more level with his right leg. 'The spacing is nearly perfect,' he said, glancing back at Nicole, 'it shouldn't be a difficult climb.'

'Richard Wakefield,' Nicole said from the rim of the hole, 'are you trying to tell me that you intend to climb down into that abyss? And that you expect me to follow?'

'I don't expect anything of you,' he replied. 'But I can't see the point of turning back now. What's our alternative? Should we go back down the tunnel to the ramps and exit? For what? To see if anyone has found us yet? You saw the photographs of the boats. Maybe they're right here at the bottom. Maybe there's even a secret river that runs underground into the Cylindrical Sea.'

'Maybe,' Nicole said, starting to descend slowly now that Richard's progress had triggered another bank of lights below them,' one of those things that made the bizarre noise is waiting for us down at the bottom.'

'I'll find out,' Richard said. 'Hallooo, down there. We two human-type beings are coming down.' He waved and momentarily lost his balance.

'Don't be a showoff,' Nicole said, coming down beside him. She paused to catch her breath and look around her. Her two feet were resting on spikes and she was holding tightly to two others with her hands. *I must be insane*, she said to herself. *Just look at this place. It's easy to imagine a hundred gruesome deaths*. Richard had dropped down another pair of spikes. *And look at him. Is he totally immune to fear? Or just reckless? He actually seems to be enjoying all this*.

The third bank of lights illuminated a lattice on the opposite wall below them. It was hanging among all the spikes and, from a distance in the dim light, looked startlingly like a smaller version of the object that had been attached to the two skyscrapers in New York. Richard hurried around the cylinder to examine the lattice. 'Come over here,' he shouted at Nicole. 'I think it's the same damn material.'

The lattice was anchored to the wall by small bolts. At Richard's insistence, Nicole cut off a piece and handed it to him. He stretched it and watched it regain its shape. He studied its internal structure. 'It *is* the same stuff,' he said. His brow knitted into furrows. 'But what the hell does it mean?'

Nicole stood beside him and idly shone her flashlight into the depths below them. She was about to suggest that they climb out and head for more familiar terrain when she thought she saw a reflection from a floor about twenty metres below. 'I'm going to make you a proposition,' Nicole said to Richard. 'While you're studying that lattice cord, I'll drop down another several metres. We may be near the bottom of this bizarre well of spikes, or whatever it is. If not, then we'll abandon this place.'

'All right,' Richard said absentmindedly. He was already involved in his examination of the lattice cord, using the microscope he had taken from his backpack.

Nicole nimbly descended to the floor. 'I guess you'd better come down,' she shouted to Richard. 'There are two more tunnels, one large and one small. Plus another hole in the centre....' He was beside her immediately. He had climbed down as soon as he had seen the lower platform illuminated by lights.

Richard and Nicole were now standing on a ledge three metres wide at the bottom of the spiked cylinder. The ledge formed a ring around another smaller descending hole that also had spikes growing out of its walls. To their left and right, dark arched tunnels were cut into the rock or metal that was the base construction material for the extensive underground world. The tunnel on their left was five to six metres high; the tiny tunnel on the opposite side, one hundred and eighty degrees around the ring, was only half a metre tall.

Running out of each of the two tunnels, and penetrating half a ledge-width into the ring, were two small parallel strips of unknown material which were fastened to the floor. The strips were very close together in the smaller tunnel and more widely spaced in the other. Richard was sitting on his knees examining the strips in front of the large tunnel when he heard a distant rumble. 'Listen,' he said to Nicole, as the two of them instinctively backed away.

The rumbling increased and changed into a whining sound, as if something were moving swiftly through the air. Far off in the tunnel, which ran straight as an arrow, Richard and Nicole could see some lights switch on. They tensed. They didn't need to wait long for an explanation. A vehicle that resembled a hovering subway car burst into view and sped toward them, stopping suddenly with its front edge just over the farthest extension of the strips on the floor.

Richard and Nicole had recoiled as the vehicle had hurtled toward them. Both were dangerously close to the edge of the ring. For several seconds they stood in silence, each staring at the aerodynamic shape hovering in front of them. Then they looked at each other and laughed simultaneously. 'Okay,' Nicole said nervously, 'I get it. We've crossed into some new dimension. In this one it's just a little difficult to find the subway station … This is so totally absurd. We climb down a spiked barrel and end up in a Metro station … I don't know about you, Richard, but I've had enough. I'll take a few *normal* avians and manna melons any day of the week....'

Richard had walked over beside the vehicle. A door in the side had opened and they could both see the lit interior. There were no seats, only thin cylindrical poles, spaced in no obvious pattern, that ran the three metres from the ceiling to the floor. 'It can't go far,' Richard said, sticking his head inside the door but leaving his feet on the ledge outside. 'There isn't anywhere to sit down.'

Nicole came over to inspect for herself. 'Maybe they have no old or crippled people – and the shops are all close to home.' She laughed again as Richard leaned farther into the car so he could see the ceiling and walls more clearly. 'Don't get any crazy ideas,' she said. 'It would be certifiably insane for us to climb aboard that car. Unless we were out of food and it was our last hope.'

'I guess you're right,' Richard replied. He was definitely disappointed as he withdrew from the subway car. 'But what an amazing....' He stopped himself in mid-sentence. He was staring across the platform at the opposite side of the ledge. There, in the middle of the now-illuminated entrance to the tiny tunnel, an identical vehicle, one-tenth the size of the one next to them, was hovering off the floor. Nicole followed Richard's gaze.

'That must be the road to Lilliput over there,' Nicole said. 'Giants descend another floor and normal-sized creatures take this subway. It's all very simple.'

Richard walked swiftly around the ring. 'That's perfect,' he said out loud, taking off his backpack and setting it on the ledge beside him. He began to rummage in one of the large pockets.

'What are you doing?' Nicole asked curiously.

Richard pulled two tiny figures out of the pack and showed them to her. 'It's perfect,' he repeated, his excitement unmistakable. 'We can send Prince Hal and Falstaff. I'll only need a few minutes to adjust their software.'

Already Richard had spread his pocket computer out on the ledge beside the robots and was busily working away. Nicole sat down with her back against the wall between two spikes. She glanced over at Richard. *He is truly a rare species*, she thought with admiration, thinking back over their hours together. *A genius, that's obvious. Almost without guile or meanness. And somehow he has retained the curiosity of the child.*

Nicole suddenly felt very tired. She smiled to herself as she was watching Richard. He was absorbed in his work. Nicole closed her eyes for a moment.

'I'm sorry I took so long,' Richard was saying. 'I kept thinking of new things to add and I needed to rearrange the linkage....'

Nicole woke up from her nap very slowly. 'How long have we been here?' she said as she yawned.

'A little over an hour,' Richard answered sheepishly. 'But everything is all set. I'm ready to put the boys in the subway.'

Nicole glanced around her. 'Both the cars are still here,' she commented.

'I think they work like all the lights. I bet they will stay in the station as long as we're on the platform.'

Nicole stood up and stretched. 'So here's the plan,' Richard said. 'I have the controlling transceiver in my hand. Hal and Sir John each have audio, video, and IR sensors that will acquire data continuously. We can choose which channel to monitor on our computers and send new commands as necessary.'

'But will the signals penetrate the walls?' Nicole asked, remembering her experience inside the barn.

'As long as they don't have to travel through too much material. The system is way overdesigned in terms of signal-to-noise to accommodate some attenuation ... Besides, the large subway came at us along a straight line. I'm hoping this one will be similar.'

Richard gingerly set the two robots down on the ledge and commanded them to walk toward the subway. Doors opened on both sides as they drew near. 'Remember me to Mistress Quickly,' Falstaff said as he climbed aboard. 'She was a stupid lass, but with a good heart.'

Nicole gave Richard a puzzled glance. 'I didn't overwrite all their earlier programming,' he laughed. 'From time to time they will probably make some absurd random comments.'

The two robots stood on the subway for a minute or two. Richard hastily checked their sensors and made one more set of calibrations on the monitor. At length the doors of the subway closed, the vehicle waited for another ten seconds, and then it rushed away into the tunnel.

Richard commanded Falstaff to face the front, but there was not much to be seen out the window. It was a surprisingly long ride at a very high speed. Richard estimated that the little subway had travelled several kilometres before it finally slowed to a stop.

Richard waited before commanding the two robots to leave the subway. He wanted to make certain that they did not get off at an intermediate stop. However, there was no need to worry; the first full set of imaging data from Prince Hal and Falstaff showed that the subway had indeed reached the end of the line.

The two robots walked around the flat platform beside the vehicle and photographed more of their surroundings. The subway station had arches and columns, but it was basically one long, connected room. Richard estimated from the images that the ceiling height was about two metres. He commanded Hal and Falstaff to follow a long hallway that moved off to the left, perpendicular to the subway track.

The hallway terminated in front of another tunnel, this

one barely five centimetres high. As the robots examined
the floor, finding two tiny strips extending almost to their
feet, a subway of minuscule proportions arrived to the
station. With its door open and its interior lit, Richard
and Nicole could see that the new subway car was
identical, except for its size, to the two they had seen
before.

The cosmonauts were sitting together with their knees
on the ledge, both avidly watching the small computer
monitor. Richard commanded Falstaff to take a picture
of Prince Hal standing next to the tiny subway. 'The car
itself,' Richard said to Nicole after studying the image,
'is less than two centimetres tall. What's going to ride in
it? Ants?'

Nicole shook her head and said nothing. She was
feeling bewildered again. At that moment she was also
thinking about her initial reaction to Rama, after she had
ridden the ferry from the seal to the communication
station at the top of the Alpha stairway. *Never in my
wildest imaginings*, she thought, recalling her awe at that
first panoramic sight, *did I foresee that there would be so
many new mysteries. The first explorers hardly scratched the
surface....*

'Richard,' Nicole said, interrupting her own thoughts.

He commanded the robots to walk back down the
hallway and then glanced up from the monitor. 'Yes?' he
said.

'How thick is the outer shell of Rama?'

'About four hundred metres altogether, I think,' he
said with a slightly puzzled expression. 'But that's at one
of the ends. We have no definite way of knowing how
thick the shell is anywhere else. Norton and crew
reported that the depth of the Cylindrical Sea was highly
variable – as little as forty metres in some places and as
much as a hundred and fifty elsewhere. That would
suggest to me a shell thickness of several hundred metres
at least.'

Richard checked the monitor quickly. Prince Hal and
Falstaff were almost back at the station where they had
climbed off the subway. He transmitted a stop command

and turned to Nicole. 'Why are you asking? It's not like you to ask idle questions.'

'There's obviously an entire, unexplored world down here,' Nicole replied. 'It would take a lifetime –'

'We don't have that long,' Richard broke in with a laugh. 'At least not a normal lifetime ... But back to your thickness question, remember the entire Southern Hemicylinder has a floor level four hundred and fifty metres above the north. So unless there are some major structural irregularities – and we certainly haven't seen any from the outside – the thickness should be substantially greater in the south.'

Richard waited for Nicole to say something additional. When she remained silent for several seconds, he turned back to the monitor and continued his surrogate exploration with the robots.

There had been a good reason for Nicole's question about the thickness of the shell. She had a picture in her mind that she could not shake. Nicole was imagining coming to the end of one of these long underground tunnels, opening a door, and then being blinded by the light of the Sun. *Wouldn't it be incredible*, she was thinking, *to be an intelligent creature living in this maze of dim light and tunnels and then, by chance, to stumble on to something that would irrevocably change your entire concept of the universe? How could you return....*

'Now what in the world is that?' Richard was asking. Nicole stopped her mental drifting and focused on the monitor. Prince Hal and Falstaff had entered a large room at the opposite end of the subway station and were standing in front of a conglomeration of loose, spongelike webbing. The infrared image of the scene showed a nested sphere, inside the web, that was radiating heat. At Nicole's suggestion, Richard commanded the robots to walk around the object and survey the rest of his new domain.

The room was immense. It extended into the distance farther than the resolution of the video devices carried by the robots. The ceiling was about twenty metres high and the two side walls were separated by more than fifty metres. Several other similar spherical objects encased in spongy masses could be seen scattered about the room in the distance. A lattice, stretching almost all the way across the room but stopping five metres above the floor, dangled from the high ceiling in the foreground. Another lattice could barely be discerned a hundred metres or so behind the first one.

Richard and Nicole discussed what the robots should do next. There were no other exits from either the subway station or the large room. A panoramic image around the room revealed nothing nearby of interest except the sphere embedded in its spongy exterior. Nicole wanted to bring the robots back and leave the lair altogether. Richard's curiosity demanded at least a cursory investigation of one of the spherical objects.

The two robots were able, with some difficulty, to climb around and through the webbed material to reach the sphere in the centre. The ambient temperature increased as they neared the sphere. One of the purposes of the external material was clearly to absorb heat. When the robots reached the nested sphere, their internal monitors flashed a warning that the outside temperatures exceeded their safe operating limits.

Richard moved quickly. Directing the robots on a nearly continuous basis, he determined that the sphere was virtually impenetrable and was probably made of a thick metal alloy with a very hard surface. Falstaff banged on the sphere several times with his arm; the resulting sound damped quickly, indicating the sphere was full, possibly with a liquid. The two robots were weaving their way out of the sponge webbing when their audio systems picked up the sound of brushes dragging against metal.

Richard tried to speed up their escape. Hal was able to increase his pace but Falstaff, whose subsystem temperatures had risen too high during his proximity to the sphere, was prevented by his own internal processor logic from accelerating his actions. The brush sound continued to grow louder.

The computer monitor on the ledge between the two

cosmonauts was changed to split screen. Prince Hal reached the edge of the sponge, hit the floor, and headed for the subway without waiting for his companion. Falstaff continued to climb slowly through the webbing. 'Tis too much work for a drinking man,' he mumbled, as he crawled over another barrier.

The dragging metal sound abruptly stopped and Falstaff's camera recorded an image of a long, skinny object with black and gold stripes. Moments later the camera frame went to all black and the little robot's 'Terminal Fault Imminent' alarm began to sound. Richard and Nicole had one more fleeting glimpse of a picture from Falstaff; it showed what might have been a giant eye, from up close, a black gelatinous mixture tinged with blue. Then all transmissions from the robot, including emergency telemetry, abruptly ceased.

Meanwhile Hal had entered the waiting subway. During the several seconds before the subway left the station, the ominous dragging sound was heard again. But the subway departed anyway, with the robot inside, and started speeding through the tunnel toward the two cosmonauts. Richard and Nicole breathed a sigh of relief.

No more than a second later a loud sound like breaking glass was picked up by Prince Hal's audio system. Richard commanded the robot to turn in the direction of the sound and Hal's camera photographed a solitary black and gold tentacle in midair. The tentacle had broken the window and was moving inexorably toward the robot. Both Richard and Nicole realised what was happening at the same moment. The thing was on top of the subway! And it was coming toward them!

Nicole was climbing the spikes in a flash. Richard wasted several valuable seconds picking up his computer monitor and putting all his equipment in the backpack. He heard Prince Hal's 'Terminal Fault Imminent' alarm when he was halfway up the spikes. Richard turned around to look just as the subway pulled into the tunnel below him.

What he saw made his blood run cold. On top of the subway was a large dark creature whose central body, if

that was indeed what it was, was flattened against the
roof. Striped tentacles extended in all directions. Four of
them had pierced the windows of the train and grabbed
the robot. The thing quickly climbed off the subway and
wrapped one of its eight tentacles around the lowest
spikes. Richard didn't watch any more. He clambered up
the rest of the cylinder and started racing through the
tunnel at the top, following the steps of Nicole far ahead
of him in the distance.

As he ran, Richard noticed that the tunnel was curving
slightly to the right. He reminded himself that even
though this was not the same tunnel they had used
before, it should still lead them to the ramps. After
several hundred metres Richard stopped to listen for the
sound of his pursuer. He heard nothing. Richard had just
taken two deep breaths and started to run again when his
ears were assaulted by a terrible wail in front of him. It
was Nicole. *Oh shit*, he thought, as he rushed forward to
find her.

47

Progressive Matrices

'Never, never in my entire life,' Nicole said to Richard, 'have I ever seen anything that terrified me like that.' The two cosmonauts were sitting with their backs against the bottom of one of the skyscrapers surrounding the western plaza. They were both still breathing heavily, exhausted from their frantic escape. Nicole took a long drink of water.

'I had just started to relax,' she continued. 'I could hear you behind me – and nothing else. I decided I would stop in the museum and wait for you to catch up. It hadn't yet occurred to me that we were in the 'other' tunnel.

'It should have been obvious, of course, because the opening was on the wrong side. But I wasn't thinking logically at that moment ... Anyway, I stepped inside the room, the lights came on, and there he was, not more than three metres in front of me. I thought my heart had stopped altogether....'

Richard remembered Nicole running into his arms in the tunnel and sobbing for several seconds. 'It's Takagishi ... stuffed like a deer or a tiger ... in the opening to the right,' she had said in fits and starts. After she had regained her composure, the two of them had walked back down the tunnel together. Inside the opening, standing upright just opposite the entrance, Richard had been shocked to see Newton cosmonaut Shigeru Takagishi. He was dressed in his flight suit and looked exactly as he had the last time they had seen him at the Beta campsite. His face was fixed in a pleasant smile and his arms were at his side.

'What the hell?' Richard had said, blinking twice, his curiosity only slightly stronger than his terror. Nicole had averted her eyes. Even though she had seen the sight before, the stuffed Takagishi was much too lifelike for her.

They had only stayed in the large room for a minute. Alien taxidermy had also performed wonders on an avian with a broken wing that was hanging from the ceiling next to Takagishi. Against the wall behind the Japanese scientist was Richard and Nicole's hut, which had disappeared the day before. The hexagonal electronics board from the Newton portable science station was on the floor next to Takagishi's feet, not far from a full-scale model of a bulldozer biot. Other biot replicas were scattered around the room.

Richard had started to study the varied collection of biots in the room when they had faintly heard the familar dragging noise coming from behind them in the tunnel. They had not wasted any more time. Their flight down the tunnel and up the ramps had been broken only by a brief stop at the cistern to replenish their supply of fresh water.

'Dr Takagishi was a gentle, sensitive man,' Nicole was saying to Richard, 'with passionate feelings about his work. Just before launch I visited him in Japan and he told me that his lifelong ambition had been to explore a second Rama spacecraft.'

'It's a shame he had to die such an unpleasant death,' Richard grimly replied. 'I guess that octospider, or one of its friends, must have dragged him down here for a visit to the taxidermist almost immediately. They certainly wasted no time putting him on display.'

'You know, I don't think they killed him,' Nicole said. 'Maybe I'm hopelessly naive, but I didn't see any evidence of foul play in his ... his statue.'

'You think they just scared him to death?' Richard retorted sarcastically.

'Yes,' said Nicole firmly. 'At least it's possible.' She

spent the next five minutes explaining Takagishi's heart situation to Richard.

'I'm surprised at you, Nicole,' Richard replied after listening carefully to her disclosure. 'I had you figured all wrong. I thought you were Miss Prim and Proper, play it by the rules all the way. I never gave you credit for having a mind of your own. Not to mention a strong streak of compassion.'

'In this instance it's not clear that either was an asset. If I had faithfully enforced the rules, Takagishi would be alive and living with his family in Kyoto.'

'And he would have missed the singular experience of his life ... which brings me to an interesting question, my dear doctor. Surely you are aware, as we sit here, that the odds do not favour our escape. We are both likely to die without ever seeing another human face. How do you feel about that? Where does your death, or any death for that matter, fit into your overall scheme of things?'

Nicole looked at Richard. She was surprised by the tenor of his question. She tried without success to read the expression on his face. 'I'm not afraid, if that's what you mean,' she answered carefully. 'As a doctor I've thought often about death. And of course since my mother died when I was very young, even as a child I was forced to have some perspective on the subject.'

She paused for a moment. 'For myself, I know that I would like to stay alive until Genevieve is grown – so that I can be a grandmother to her children. But just being alive is not the most important thing. Life must have quality to be worthwhile. And to have quality we must be willing to take a few risks ... I'm not being very focused, am I?'

Richard smiled. 'No,' he said, 'but I like your general drift. You have mentioned the key word. Quality ... Have you ever considered suicide?' he asked suddenly.

'No,' Nicole replied, shaking her head. 'Never. There's always been too much to live for.' *There must be some reason for his question*, she was thinking. 'What about you?' she said after a short silence. 'Did you think about suicide during any of that pain with your father?'

'No, strangely enough,' he answered. 'My father's beatings never made me lose my zest for life. There was too much to learn. And I knew that I would outgrow him and be on my own eventually.' There was a long pause before he continued. 'But there was one period in my life when I did seriously consider suicide,' Richard said. 'My pain and anger were so great that I did not think I could endure them.'

He became silent, locked in his thoughts. Nicole waited patiently. Eventually she slipped her arm through his. 'Well, my friend,' she said lightly, 'you can tell me about it someday. Neither of us is accustomed to sharing our deepest secrets. Maybe in time we can learn. I'm going to start by telling you why I believe we are not going to die and why I think we should go over to search the area around the eastern plaza next.'

Nicole had never told anyone, not even her father, about her 'trip' during the Poro. Before she finished telling her story to Richard, not only had Nicole covered what had happened to her as a seven-year-old at the Poro, but also she had recounted the story of Omeh's visit to Rome, the Senoufo prophecies about the 'woman without companion' who scatters her progeny 'among the stars', and the details of her vision after drinking the vial at the bottom of the pit.

Richard was speechless. The entire set of stories was so foreign to his mathematical mind that he did not know how to react. He stared at Nicole with awe and amazement. At length, embarrassed by his silence, he started to speak. 'I don't know what to say....'

Nicole put her fingers to his lips. 'You don't need to say anything,' she said. 'I can read your reaction in your face. We can talk about it tomorrow, after you've had some time to think about what I told you.'

Nicole yawned and looked at her watch. She pulled her sleeping mat out of her backpack and unrolled it on the ground. 'I'm exhausted,' she said to Richard. 'Nothing like a little terror to produce instant fatigue. I'll see you in four hours.'

'We've been searching now for an hour and a half,' Richard said impatiently. 'Look at this map. There's nowhere within five hundred metres of the plaza centre that we haven't been to at least twice.'

'Then we're doing something wrong,' Nicole replied. 'There were *three* heat sources in my vision.' Richard frowned. 'Or be logical, if you prefer. Why would there be three plazas and only two underground lairs? You said yourself that the Ramans always follow a reasonable plan.'

They were standing in front of a dodecahedron that faced the eastern plaza. 'And another thing,' Richard growled to himself, 'what's the purpose of all these damn polyhedrons? There's one in every sector and the three biggest are the plazas … Wait a minute,' he said, as his eyes went from one of the twelve faces of the dodecahedron to an opposite skyscraper. His head then turned quickly around the plaza. 'Could it be?' he said. 'No,' he answered, 'that would be impossible.'

Richard saw that Nicole was staring at him. 'I have an idea,' he said excitedly. 'It may be completely farfetched … Do you remember Dr Bardolini and his progressive matrices? With the dolphins? … What if the Ramans also left a pattern here in New York of subtle differences that change from plaza to plaza and section to section? … Look, it's no crazier than your visions.'

Already Richard was on his knees on the ground, working with his maps of New York. 'Can I use your computer too?' he said to Nicole a few minutes later. 'That will speed up the process.'

For hours Richard Wakefield sat beside the two computers, mumbling to himself and trying to solve the puzzle of New York. He explained to Nicole, when he took a break for dinner at her insistence, that the location of the third underground hole could only be determined if he thoroughly understood the geometric relationships between the polyhedrons, the three plazas, and all the skyscrapers immediately opposite the principal faces of the polyhedrons in each of the nine sectors. Two hours before dark Richard dashed off hurriedly to an adjacent section to obtain extra data that had not yet been recorded on their computer maps.

Even after dark he did not rest. Nicole slept the first part of the fifteen-hour night. When she awoke after five hours, Richard was still working feverishly on his project. He didn't even hear Nicole clear her throat. She arose quietly and put her hands on his shoulders. 'You must get some sleep, Richard,' she said quietly.

'I'm almost there,' he said. She saw the bags under his eyes when he turned around. 'No more than another hour.'

Nicole returned to her mat. When Richard woke her later, he was full of enthusiasm. 'Wouldn't you know it?' he said with a grin. 'There are three possible solutions, each of which is consistent with all the patterns.' He paced for almost a minute. 'Could we go look now?' he then said pleadingly. 'I don't think I can sleep until I find out.'

None of Richard's three solutions for the location of the third lair was close to the plaza. The first one was over a kilometre away, at the edge of New York opposite the Northern Hemicylinder. He and Nicole found nothing there. They then marched another fifteen minutes in the dark to the second possible location, a spot very near the southeast corner of the city. Richard and Nicole walked down the indicated street and found the covering in the exact spot that Richard had predicted. 'Hallelujah,' he shouted, spreading out his sleeping mat beside the cover. 'Hooray for mathematics.'

Hooray for Omeh, Nicole thought. She was no longer sleepy but she wasn't anxious to explore any new territory in the dark by herself. *What comes first*, she asked herself as she was lying awake on her mat, *Intuition or mathematics? Do we use models to help us find the truth? Or do we know the truth first, and then develop the mathematics to explain it?*

They were both up at daylight. 'The days are still growing slightly shorter,' Richard mentioned to Nicole. 'But the sum of daytime and nighttime is remaining constant at forty-six hours, four minutes, and fourteen seconds.'

'How long before we reach the Earth?' Nicole enquired as she was stuffing her sleeping mat in its protective package.

'Twenty days and three hours,' he replied after consulting his computer. 'Are you ready for another adventure?'

She nodded. 'I presume you also know where to find the panel that opens this cover?'

'No,' he said confidently, 'but I bet it's not hard to find. And after we find this one, the avian lair opening will be a piece of cake because we'll have the whole pattern.'

Ten minutes later Richard pushed on a metal plate and the third covering swung open. The descent into this third hole was down a wide staircase broken by occasional landings. Richard took Nicole's hand as they walked down the stairs. They used their flashlights to find their way, as no lights illuminated their descent.

The water room was in the same place as in the other underground lairs. There were no sounds in the horizontal tunnels that led off from the central stairway at either of the two main levels. 'I don't think anyone lives here,' Richard said.

'At least not yet,' Nicole answered.

48

Welcome Earthlings

Richard was puzzled. In the first room off one of the top horizontal tunnels he had found an array of strange gadgets which he had decoded in less than an hour. He now knew how to regulate the lights and temperature throughout each particular portion of the underground lair. But if it were that easy, and all the lairs were similarly constructed, why did the avians not use the lights that had been provided? While they were eating breakfast Richard quizzed Nicole about the details of the avian lair.

'You're overlooking more fundamental issues,' Nicole said, as she took a bite of manna melon. 'The avians aren't that important by themselves. The real question is, where are the Ramans? And why did they put these holes under New York in the first place?'

'Maybe they're all Ramans,' Richard replied. 'The biots, the avians, the octospiders – maybe they all came originally from the same planet. At the beginning they were all one happy family. But as the years and generations passed, different species evolved in separate ways. Individual lairs were constructed and the –'

'There are too many problems with that scenario,' Nicole interrupted. 'First, the biots are definitely machines. The avians may or may not be. The octospiders almost certainly aren't, although a techno-logical level that could create this spaceship in the first place might have progressed further in artificial intelligence than we can possibly imagine. My intuitive sense, however, says that those things are organic.'

'We humans would never be able to distinguish between a living creature and a versatile machine created by a truly advanced species.'

'I agree with that. But we can't possibly resolve this argument by ourselves. Besides, there is another question that I want to discuss with you.'

'What's that?' Richard asked.

'Did the avians and the octospiders and these underground regions exist also on Rama I? If so, how did the Norton crew miss them altogether? If not, why are they on this spacecraft and not the first one?'

Richard was quiet for several seconds. 'I see where you're heading,' he said finally. 'The fundamental premise has always been that the Rama spacecraft were created millions of years ago, by unknown beings from another region of the galaxy, and that they were totally uninvolved with and uninterested in whatever they encountered during their trek. If they were created that long ago, why would two vehicles that were presumably built at virtually the same time have such striking differences?'

'I'm starting to believe that our colleague from Kyoto was right,' Nicole answered. 'Maybe there *is* a meaningful pattern to all this. I'm fairly confident that the Norton crew was thorough and accurate in its survey and that all the distinctions between Rama I and Rama II are indeed real. As soon as we acknowledge that the two spacecraft are different, we face a more difficult issue. *Why* are they different?'

Richard had finished eating and was now pacing in the dimly-lit tunnel. 'There was a discussion just like this, before it was decided to abort the mission. At the teleconference the main question was, why did the Ramans change course to encounter the Earth? Since the first spacecraft had not done so, it was considered hard evidence that Rama II was different. And the people participating in that meeting knew nothing of the avians or octospiders.'

'General Borzov would have loved the avians,' Nicole

commented after a short silence. 'He thought that flying was the greatest pleasure in the world.' She laughed. 'He once told me that his secret hope in life was that reincarnation was on the level and that he would come back as a bird.'

'He was a fine man,' Richard said, stopping his pacing momentarily. 'I don't think we ever properly appreciated all his talents.'

As Nicole replaced part of the manna melon in her backpack and prepared to continue the exporation, she smiled at her peripatetic friend. 'One more question, Richard?'

He nodded.

'Do you think we've met any Ramans yet? By that I mean the creatures who made this vehicle. Or any of their descendants.'

Richard shook his head vigorously. 'Absolutely not,' he said. 'Maybe we've met some of their creations. Or even other species from the same planet. But we haven't seen the main characters yet.'

They found the White Room off to the left of a horizontal tunnel at the second level below the surface. Until then the exploration had been almost boring. Richard and Nicole had walked down many tunnels and had peered into one empty room after another. Four times they had found a set of gadgets for regulating the lights and temperature. Until they reached the White Room, they had seen nothing else of interest.

Both Richard and Nicole were astonished when they entered a room whose walls were painted a crisp white. In addition to the paint, the room was fascinating because one corner was cluttered with objects that turned out, on closer inspection, to be quite familiar. There was a comb and a brush, an empty lipstick container, several coins, a collection of keys, and even something that looked like an old walkie-talkie. In another pile there was a ring and a wristwatch, a tube of toothpaste, a nail file, and a small keyboard with Latin letters. Richard and Nicole were stunned. 'Okay, genius,' she said with a wave of her hand.

'Explain all this, if you can.'

He picked up the tube of toothpaste, opened the cap, and squeezed. A white material came out. Richard put his finger in it and then placed the finger in his mouth. 'Yeuch,' he said, spitting out the paste. 'Bring your mass spectrometer over here.'

While Nicole was examining the toothpaste with her sophisticated medical instruments, Richard picked up each of the other objects. The watch in particular fascinated him. It was indeed keeping proper time, second by second, although its reference point was completely unknown. 'Did you ever go to the space museum in Florida?' he asked Nicole.

'No,' she answered distractedly.

'They had a display of the common objects taken by the crew on the first Rama mission. This watch looks exactly like the one in the display – I remember it well because I bought a similar one in the museum shop.'

Nicole walked over with a puzzled look on her face. 'This stuff isn't toothpaste, Richard. I don't know what it is. The spectra are astonishing, with an abundance of super-heavy molecules.'

For several minutes the two cosmonauts rummaged in the odd collection of items, trying to make some sense out of their latest discovery. 'One thing is certain,' Richard said, as he was trying unsuccessfully to open up the walkie-talkie, 'these objects are definitely associated with human beings. There's simply too many of them for some kind of strange interspecies coincidence.'

'But how did they get here?' Nicole asked. She was trying to use the brush but its bristles were far too soft for her hair. She examined it in more detail. 'This is not really a brush,' she announced. 'It *looks* like a brush, and *feels* like a brush, but it's useless in the hair.'

She bent down and picked up the nail file. 'And this can't be used to file any human's fingernails.' Richard came over to see what she was talking about. He was still struggling with the walkie-talkie. He dropped it in disgust and took the nail file that Nicole had extended toward him.

'So these things look human, but aren't?' he said, pulling the file against the end of his longest fingernail. The nail was unchanged. Richard gave the file back to Nicole. 'What's going on here?' he said in a frustrated tone.

'I remember reading a science fiction novel while I was at university,' Nicole said a few seconds later, 'in which an extraterrestrial species learned about human beings solely from our earliest television programmes. When they finally met us, they offered cereal boxes and soaps and other objects the aliens had seen on our television commercials. The packages were all properly designed, but the contents were either non-existent or absolutely wrong.'

Richard had not been listening carefully to Nicole. He had been fiddling with the keys and surveying the collection of objects in the room. 'Now what do all these things have in common?' he said, mostly to himself.

They both arrived at the same answer several seconds later. 'They were all carried by the Norton crew,' Richard and Nicole said in unison.

'So the two Rama space vehicles must have some kind of communication linkup,' Richard said.

'And these objects have been planted here on purpose, to show us that the visit to Rama I was observed and recorded.'

'The spider biots that inspected the Norton campsites and the equipment must have contained imaging sensors.'

'And all of these things were fabricated from pictures transmitted from Rama I to Rama II.'

After Nicole's last comment both of them were silent, each following their own thought pattern. 'But why do they want us to know all this? What is it we're supposed to do now?' Richard stood up and began to pace around the room. Suddenly he started laughing. 'Wouldn't it be amazing,' he said, 'if David Brown was right after all, if the Ramans really were completely uninterested in anything they found, but programmed their space vehicles to *act* interested in any visitors? They could

flatter whatever species they encountered by making midcourse corrections and by fashioning simple objects. What
an incredible irony. Since all immature species are probably hopelessly self-centred, the visitors to the Raman
craft would be totally occupied trying to understand an
assumed message –'

'I think you're getting carried away,' Nicole interrupted. 'All we know at this point is that this spacecraft
apparently received pictures from Rama I, and that repro-
ductions of small, everyday objects that were carried by
the Newton crew have been placed here in this room for us
to find.'

'I wonder if the keyboard is as useless as everything
else,' Richard said as he picked it up. He spelled the word
'Rama' with the keys. Nothing happened. He tried
'Nicole'. Still nothing.

'Don't you remember how the old models worked?'
Nicole said with a grin. She took the keyboard. 'They all
had a separate power key.' She pressed the unnamed
button in the upper right hand corner of the keyboard. A
portion of the opposite wall slid away, revealing a large
black square area about one metre on a side.

The small keyboard was based upon the ones that had
been attached to the portable computers on the first Rama
mission. It had four rows of twelve characters, with an
extra power button in the upper right hand corner. The
twenty-six Latin letters, ten Arabic numerals, and four
mathematical operands were marked on forty of the individual keys. The other eight keys contained either dots or
geometrical figures on their surfaces and, in addition,
could be set in either an 'up' or 'down' position. Richard
and Nicole quickly learned that these special keys were the
true controls of the Raman system. By trial and error they
also discovered that the result from striking any individual
action key was a function of the positioning of the *other*
seven keys. Thus pressing any specific command key
could produce as many as 128 different results. Altogether
then, the system provided for 1024 separate actions that
could be initiated from the keyboard.

Making a command dictionary was a laborious process. Richard volunteered for the duty. Using their own computers to keep notes, he began the process of developing the rudiments of a language to translate the special keyboard commands. The initial goal was simple – to be able to use the Raman computer like one of their own. Once the translation was developed, any given input into the Newton portable computers would contain, as part of its output, what set of key impressions on the Raman board would produce a similar response on the black screen.

Even with Richard's intelligence and computer expertise, the task was a formidable one. It was also not something that could easily be shared. At Richard's suggestion, Nicole climbed out of the lair twice during the first Raman day they were in the White Room. Both times she took long walks around New York, casting her eyes to the sky from time to time to look for a helicopter. On the second excursion Nicole went back to the barn where she had fallen in the pit. Already so much had happened that her frightening experience at the bottom seemed like ancient history.

She thought often about Borzov, Wilson, and Takagishi. All the cosmonauts had known when they left the Earth that there were uncertainties in the mission. They had trained often to handle vehicle emergencies, problems with their own spacecraft that might prove to be life threatening. But none of them had actually believed that there would be any fatalities on the mission. *If Richard and I perish here in New York*, Nicole remarked to herself, *then almost half the crew will have died. That will be the worst disaster since we started flying piloted missions again.*

She was standing outside the barn, in almost the exact spot where she and Francesca had talked to Richard on the communicator the last time. *So why did you lie, Francesca?* Nicole said to herself. *Did you think somehow my disappearance would silence all suspicion?*

On the final morning at the Beta campsite, before she and the others had set out to look for Takagishi, Nicole had transmitted all the notes in her own portable computer in Rama through the networking system to the desktop in her room on the Newton. At the time Nicole had made the data transfer to give herself extra memory, if she should need it, in her travelling computer. *But it's all there*, she recalled, *if some diligent detective ever looks for it. The drugs, David's blood pressure, even a cryptic reference to the abortion. And of course Richard's solution to the RoSur malfunction.*

On her two walks Nicole saw several centipede biots, and even a bulldozer once, at the far limit of her vision. She didn't see any avians and neither heard nor saw an octospider. *Maybe they only come out at night*, she mused as she returned to have dinner with Richard.

49

Interaction

'We're almost out of food,' Nicole said. They packed up what remained of the manna melon and stuffed it in Richard's backpack.

'I know,' he replied. 'I have a plan for you to obtain some more.'

'*Me?*' asked Nicole. 'Why is it my job?'

'Well, first of all, it only requires one person. Working with graphics on the Raman computer gave me the idea. Second, I can't spare the time. I think I'm on the verge of breaking into the operating system. There are about two hundred commands that I can't explain unless they allow entry into another level, some kind of higher-order space in the hierarchy.'

Richard had explained to Nicole during dinner that he had now figured out how to use the Raman computer like one on the Earth. He could store and retrieve data, perform mathematical computations, design graphics, even create new languages. 'But I haven't begun to tap its potential,' he had said. 'Tonight and tomorrow I must discover more of its secrets. We're running out of time.'

His plan for obtaining food was, indeed, deceptively simple. After the long Raman night (during which Richard could not have slept more than three hours), Nicole walked over to the central plaza to implement the plan. Based on his progressive matrix analysis, Richard gave her three possible locations for the panel to open the covering above the avian lair. He was so confident of his analysis that he wouldn't even discuss what she should do if she didn't find the plate. Richard was correct. Nicole found the panel easily. Then she opened the cover and shouted down the vertical corridor. There was no response.

She shone her flashlight into the darkness below her. The tank sentinel was on duty, going to and fro in front of the horizontal tunnel that led past the water room. Nicole shouted again. If she could avoid it, she did not want to descend even to the first ledge. Even though Richard had assured her he would come to her rescue if she were overdue, Nicole did not relish the prospect of being hemmed in with the avians again.

Was that a distant jabbering she heard? Nicole thought so. She took one of the coins that she had found in the White Room and dropped it into the vertical corridor. It sailed far down, hitting a ledge somewhere near the second main level. This time there was loud jabbering. One of the avians flew up into her flashlight beam and over the tank sentinel's head. Moments later the cover began to close and Nicole had to move away.

She had discussed this contingency with Richard. Nicole waited several minutes and then pushed the panel again. When she yelled into the depths of the avian lair the second time, there was an immediate response. This time her friend, the black velvet avian, flew up to within five metres of the surface and jabbered at her. It was clear to Nicole that she was being told to go away. Before the avian turned around, however, Nicole pulled out her computer monitor and activated a stored program. Two manna melons appeared on the screen in graphic depiction. As the avian watched, the melons became coloured and then a neat incision displayed the texture and colour inside one of them.

The black velvet avian had flown up closer to the opening for a better look. Now it turned and screeched back into the dark below. Within seconds a second familiar bird, the likely mate for the black velvet one, flew up and landed on the first ledge below the ground. Nicole repeated the display. The two birds talked and then flew deeper into the lair.

Minutes went by. Nicole could hear occasional jabbering from the depths of the corridor. At length her two friends returned, each carrying a small manna melon in its talons. They landed in the plaza near the opening. Nicole walked over toward the melons, but the avians continued to clutch them. What followed was (Nicole assumed) a long lecture. The two birds jabbered both individually and together, always looking at her and often tapping on the melons. Fifteen minutes later, apparently satisfied that they had communicated their message, the avians took flight, swooped around the plaza, and vanished into their lair.

I think they were telling me that melons are in short supply, Nicole thought as she walked back toward the Eastern plaza. The melons were heavy. She had one in each of the two backpacks that she had emptied that morning before she left the White Room. *Or maybe that I should not disturb them in the future. Whatever it was, we will not be welcome any more.*

She thought that Richard would be ecstatic when she returned to the White Room. He was, but not because of Nicole and the manna melons. He had a grin on his face from one ear to the other and was holding one hand behind his back. 'Wait until I show you what I have,' he said as Nicole unloaded the backpacks. Richard brought his hand around in front of him and opened it. The hand contained a solitary black ball about ten centimetres in diameter.

'I'm nowhere near figuring out all the logic, or how much information can go in the request,' Richard said. 'But I have established a fundamental principle. We can ask for and receive 'things' using the computer.'

'What do you mean?' Nicole asked, still not certain why Richard was so excited about a small black ball.

'They made this for me,' he said, handing her the ball again. 'Don't you understand? Somewhere here they have a factory and can make things for us.'

'Then maybe "they", whoever they are, can start making us some food,' said Nicole. She was a little annoyed that Richard had neither congratulated her nor thanked her for the melons. 'The avians are not likely to give us any more.'

'It will be no problem,' Richard said. 'Eventually, once we learn the full range of the request process, we may be able to order fish and chips, steak and potatoes, anything, as long as we can state what we want in unambiguous scientific terms.'

Nicole stared at her friend. With his unkempt hair, his unshaven face, the bags under his eyes, and his wild grin, he looked at the moment like a fugitive from a lunatic asylum. 'Richard,' she asked, 'will you slow down a little? If you've found the Holy Grail, can you at least spend a second explaining it to me?'

'Look at the screen,' he said. Using the keyboard he drew a circle, then scratched it out and made a square. In less than a minute Richard had carefully drawn a cube in three dimensions. When he was finished with the graphics, he put the eight action keys into a predetermined configuration and then pressed the key with the small rectangle designator. A set of strange symbols appeared on the black monitor. 'Don't worry,' Richard said, 'we don't need to understand the details. They are just asking for the dimensional specifications of the cube.'

Richard next made a string of entries from the normal alphanumeric keys. 'Now,' he said, turning back to face Nicole, 'if I have done it correctly, we will have a cube, made from the same material as that ball, in about ten minutes.'

They ate some of the new melon while they waited. It tasted the same as the others. *Steak and potatoes would be unbelievably good*, Nicole was thinking, when suddenly the end wall lifted up half a metre above the floor and a black cube appeared in the gap.

'Wait a minute, don't touch it yet,' Richard said as Nicole went over to investigate. 'Look here!' He shone his flashlight into the darkness behind the cube. 'There are vast tunnels beyond these walls,' he said, 'and they must lead to factories so advanced we couldn't even recognise them. Imagine! They can even make objects on request.'

Nicole was beginning to understand why Richard was so ecstatic. 'We now have the capability to control our own destiny in some small way,' he continued. 'If I can break the code fast enough, we should be able to request food, maybe even what we need to build a boat.'

'Without loud motors, I hope,' quipped Nicole.

'No motors,' agreed Richard. He finished his melon and turned back to the keyboard.

Nicole was becoming worried. Richard had succeeded in making only one new breakthrough in a full Raman day. All he had to show for thirty-eight hours of work (he had only slept eight hours during the entire period) was one new material. He could make 'light' black objects like the first ball, whose specific gravity was close to balsa wood, or he could make 'heavy' black objects of density similar to oak or pine. He was wearing himself out with his work. And he could not, or would not, share any of the load with Nicole.

What if his first discovery was just blind luck? Nicole said to herself as she climbed the stairs for her dawn walk. *Or what if the system cannot make anything but two kinds of black objects?* She could not help worrying about wasted time. It was only sixteen more days until Rama would encounter the Earth. There was no sign of a rescue team. At the back of her mind was the thought that perhaps she and Richard had been abandoned altogether.

She had tried to talk to Richard about their plans the previous evening, but he had been exhausted. Richard hadn't responded in any way when Nicole had mentioned to him that she was very concerned. Later, after she had carefully outlined all their options and asked his opinion about what they should do, she noticed that he had fallen asleep. When Nicole awakened after a brief nap herself, Richard was already working again at the keyboard and refused to be distracted by either breakfast or conversation. Nicole had stumbled over the growing array of black objects on the floor as she had departed the White Room for her early morning exercise.

Nicole was feeling very lonely. The last fifty hours, which she had spent mostly by herself, had passed very slowly. Her only escape had been the pleasure of reading. She had the text of five books stored in her computer. One was her medical encyclopedia, but the other four were all for recreation. *I bet all of Richard's discretionary memory is filled with Shakespeare*, she thought as she sat on the wall surrounding New York. She stared out at the Cylindrical Sea. In the far distance, barely visible in her binoculars through the mist and clouds, she could see the northern bowl where they had entered Rama the first time.

She had two of her father's novels stored in the computer. Nicole's personal favourite was *Queen For All Ages*, the story of Eleanor of Acquitaine's younger years, beginning with her adolescence at the ducal court in Poitiers. The story line followed Eleaner through her marriage to Louis Capet of France, their crusade to the Holy Land, and her extraordinary personal appeal for an annulment from Pope Eugenius. The novel culminated with Eleanor's divorce from Louis and betrothal to the young and exciting Henry Plantagenet.

The other Pierre des Jardins novel in her computer's memory was his universally-acclaimed chef d'oeuvre, *I, Richard Coeur De Lion*, a mixture of first person diary and interior monologue, set during two winter weeks at the end of the twelfth century. In the novel Richard and his soldiers, embarked on another crusade, were quartered near Messina under the protection of the Norman king of Sicily. While there the famous warrior-king and homosexual son of Eleanor of Acquitaine and Henry Plantagenet, in a burst of self-examination, relived the major personal and historical events of his life.

Nicole remembered a long discussion with Genevieve after her daughter had read *I, Richard* the previous summer. The younger teenager had been fascinated by the story, and had surprised her mother by asking extremely intelligent questions. Thoughts of Genevieve made Nicole wonder what her daughter might be doing at Beauvois at that very moment. *They have told you that I have disappeared*, Nicole surmised. *What does the military call it? Missing in action?*

In her mind's eye Nicole could see her daughter riding home from school each day on her bicycle. 'Any news?' Genevieve would probably say to her grandfather as she crossed the portal of the villa. Pierre would just shake his head sorrowfully.

It had been two weeks now since anyone has officially seen me. Do you still have hope, my darling daughter? The bereft Nicole was struck by an overwhelming desire to talk to Genevieve. For a moment, suspending reality, Nicole could not accept the fact that she was separated from her daughter by millions of kilometres and had no way to communicate with her. She rose to return to the White Room, thinking in her temporary confusion that she could phone Genevieve from there.

When her sanity returned several seconds later, Nicole was astonished at how easily her mind had tricked itself. She shook her head and sat down on the wall overlooking the Cylindrical Sea. She remained on the wall for almost two hours, her thoughts roaming freely over a variety of subjects. Toward the end of the time, when she was preparing to return to the White Room, her mind focused on Richard Wakefield. *I have tried, my British friend*, Nicole said to herself. I have been more open with you than with anyone since Henry. But it would be just my luck to be here with someone even less trusting than myself.

Nicole was feeling an undefined sadness as she trekked down the stairs to the second level and turned right at the horizontal tunnel. Her sadness changed to surprise when she entered the White Room. Richard jumped up from his small black chair and greeted her with a hug. He had shaved and brushed his hair. He had even cleaned his fingernails. Laid out on the black table in the middle of the room was a neatly sectioned manna melon. One piece sat on each of the two black plates in front of the chairs.

Richard pulled out her chair and indicated for Nicole to sit down. He went around the table and sat in his own seat. He reached across the table and took both of Nicole's hands. 'I want to apologise,' he said with great intensity, 'for being such a boor. I have behaved very badly these last few days.

'I have thought of thousands of things to tell you during these hours I've been waiting,' he continued hesitantly, a strained smile playing across his lips, 'but I can't remember most of them ... I know I wanted to explain to you how very important Prince Hal and Falstaff were to me. They were my closest friends ... It has not been easy for me to deal with their deaths. My grief is still very intense....'

Richard took a drink of water and swallowed. 'But most of all,' he said, 'I'm sorry that I have not told you what a spectacular person you are. You are intelligent, attractive, witty, sensitive – everything I ever dreamed of finding in a woman. Despite our situation, I've been afraid to tell you how I felt. I guess my fear of rejection runs very deep.'

Tears welled out of the corner of Richard's eyes and ran down his cheeks. He was trembling slightly. Nicole could tell what an incredible effort it had been for him. She brought his hands up against her cheeks. 'I think you're very special too,' she said.

50
Hope Springs Eternal

Richard continued to work with the Rama computer, but he limited himself to short sessions and involved Nicole whenever he could. They took walks together and chatted like old friends. Richard entertained Nicole by acting out entire scenes from Shakespeare. The man had a prodigious memory, and tried to play both sides in the love scenes from *Romeo and Juliet*, but every time he broke into his falsetto, Nicole would erupt with laughter.

One night they talked for over an hour about Omeh, the Senoufo tribe, and Nicole's visions. 'You understand that it's difficult for me to accept the physical reality of some of these stories,' Richard said, attempting to qualify his curiosity. 'Nevertheless, I admit that I find them absolutely fascinating.' Later he showed keen interest in analysing all the symbolism in her visions. It was obvious that he acknowledged Nicole's mystical attributes as just another component in her rich personality.

They slept nuzzling together before they made love. When they did finally have intercourse, it was gentle and unhurried, surprising both of them with its ease and satisfaction. A few nights later, Nicole was lying with her head on Richard's chest, quietly drifting in and out of sleep. He was in deep thought. 'Several days ago,' he said, nudging her awake, 'back before we became so intimate, I told you that I considered committing suicide once. At the time I was afraid to tell you the story. Would you like to hear it now?'

Nicole opened her eyes. She rolled over and put her chin on his stomach. 'Uh huh,' she said. She reached up and kissed him on the eyes before he began his tale.

'I guess you know I was married to Sarah Tydings when both of us were very young,' he started. 'It was also before she was famous. She was in her first year with the Royal Shakespeare Company and they were performing *Romeo and Juliet, As You Like It*, and *Cymbeline* in repertory at Stratford. Sarah was Rosalind and Juliet and fantastic at both.

'She was eighteen at the time, just out of school. I fell in love with her the first night I saw her as Juliet. I sent her roses in the dressing room every evening and used most of my savings to see all the performances. We had two long dinners together and then I proposed. She accepted more from astonishment than love.

'I went to do research at Cambridge after the summer was over. We lived in a modest flat and she commuted to the theatre in London. I would go with her whenever I could, but after several months my studies demanded more of my time.'

Richard stopped his narrative and glanced down at Nicole. She had not moved. She was lying partially across him, a smile of love on her face. 'Go on,' she said softly.

'Sarah was an adrenaline junkie. She craved excitement and variety. The mundane and tedious angered her. Grocery shopping, for example, was a colossal bore. It was just too much trouble for her to turn on the set and decide what to order. She also found any kind of schedule incredibly constraining.

'Lovemaking had to be performed in a different position or be accompanied by some different music every time; otherwise it was old hat. For a while I was creative enough to satisfy her. I also took care of all the routine tasks to free her from the drudgery of housework. But there were only so many hours in the day. Ultimately, despite my considerable abilities, my studies began to suffer because I was spending all my energy making life interesting for her.

'After we had been married for a year, Sarah wanted to rent a flat in London, so that she didn't need to make the long commute every night after a performance. Actually she had already been spending a couple of nights a week in London, ostensibly with one of her actress friends. But her career was soaring and we had plenty of money, so why should I say no?

'It was not long before rumours about her behaviour became quite widespread. I chose to ignore them, fearing, I guess, that she wouldn't deny them if I asked her. Then one night late, while I was studying for an examination, I received a phone call from a woman. She was very polite, although obviously distraught. She told me that she was the wife of the actor Hugh Sinclair, and that Mr Sinclair – who at that time was starring with Sarah in the American drama *In Any Weather* – was having an affair with my wife. 'In fact,' she told me, 'he is over at your wife's flat at this very moment.' Mrs Sinclair started crying and then hung up.'

Nicole reached up and softly caressed Richard's cheek with her hand. 'I felt as if my chest had exploded,' he said, remembering the pain. 'I was angry, terrified, frantic. I went to the station and took the late train to London. When the taxi dropped me at Sarah's place, I ran to the door.

'I did not knock. I bolted up the stairs and found the two of them sleeping naked in the bed. I picked Sarah up and flung her against the wall – I can still remember the sound of her head smashing into the mirror. Then I fell on him in a rage, punching his face over and over, until it was nothing but a mass of blood. It was awful....'

Richard stopped himself and began to cry noiselessly. Nicole put her arms around his heaving chest. 'Darling, darling,' she said.

'I was an animal,' he cried. 'I was worse than any father ever was. I would have killed them both if the people in the next flat hadn't restrained me.'

Neither of them said anything for several minutes. When Richard spoke again his voice was subdued, almost remote. 'The next day, after the police station and the tabloid reporters and all the recriminations with Sarah, I wanted to kill myself. I would have done it, too, if I had owned a gun. I was considering the gruesome alternatives – pills, slitting my wrists with a razor blade, jumping off a bridge – when another student called to ask me a detailed question on relativity. There was no way, after fifteen minutes of thinking about Mr Einstein, that suicide was still a viable option. Divorce, certainly. Celibacy, highly likely. But death was out of the question. I could never have prematurely terminated my love affair with physics.' His voice tailed off.

Nicole wiped her eyes and placed her hands in his. She leaned her naked body across Richard's and kissed him. 'I love you,' she said.

Nicole's sounding alarm indicated that it was daylight again in Rama. *Ten more days*, she noted after a quick mental calculation. *We'd better have a serious talk now*.

The alarm had awakened Richard as well. He turned and smiled at his sleeping partner. 'Darling,' Nicole said, 'the time has come –'

'The walrus said, to speak of many things.'

'Come on now, be serious. We have to decide what we're going to do. It's fairly obvious that we're not going to be rescued.'

'I agree,' said Richard. He sat up and reached across Nicole's mat for his shirt. 'I have been dreading this moment for days. But I guess we have finally reached the point where we should consider swimming across.'

'You don't think there's any chance of making a boat out of our black stuff?'

'No,' he answered. 'One material is too light and the other too heavy. We could probably build a hybrid that would be seaworthy, *if* we had some nails, but without any sails we would still have to row across ... our best bet is to swim.'

Richard stood up and walked over to the black square on the wall. 'My fancy plans didn't pan out, did they?' He thumped lightly on the square. 'And I was going to produce steak and potatoes as well as a boat.'

'The best laid plans of mice and men gang aft agley.'

'What a weird poet old Robbie was. I never could understand what people saw in him.'

Nicole finished dressing and started doing some stretching exercises. 'Whew,' she said. 'I'm out of shape. I haven't had any heavy physical activity in days.' She smiled at Richard, who was looking at her coyly. 'That doesn't count, you idiot.'

'It does for me,' he said with a grin. 'It's about the only exercise I've ever liked. I used to hate it at the Academy when we had those special 'physical training' weekends.'

Richard had laid out small portions of manna melon on the black table. 'Three more meals after this one,' he said without emotion. 'I guess we swim before it's dark again.'

'You don't want to go this morning?' Nicole asked.

'No,' he replied. 'Why don't you go and survey the coast and pick a spot. I found something last night on the computer that has me baffled. It won't give us food or sailboats, but it looks as if I may have finally broken through into another kind of structure.'

After breakfast, Nicole kissed Richard goodbye and wandered up to the surface. It did not take her long to reconnoitre the coast. There really were no reasons to pick one embarkation point over another. The grim reality of the coming swim oppressed Nicole. *The odds are good*, she told herself, *that neither Richard nor I will be alive when it is dark again in Rama.*

She tried to imagine what it would be like to be eaten by a shark biot. Would it be a quick death? Or would you drown aware that your legs had just been amputated? Nicole shuddered at the idea. *Maybe we should try to obtain another melon....* She knew that was useless. Sooner or later, they had to swim.

Nicole turned her back on the sea. *At least these last few days have been good*, she said to herself, not wanting to think anymore about their predicament. *He has been an excellent companion. In every way.* She allowed herself the momentary luxury of recalling their shared pleasure, then smiled and started walking back toward the lair.

★

'But what am I looking at?' Nicole asked as another image flashed up on the black square.

'I'm not completely certain,' Richard replied. 'All I know is that I have tapped into a long list of some kind. You remember that one particular command configuration that produces the lines of symbols that look like Sanskrit? Well, I was scrolling through the gibberish and eventually I noticed a pattern. I stopped at the beginning of the pattern, changed the position of the last three keys, and then hit the double dot again. Suddenly an image was on the screen. And every time I hit an alphanumeric, the picture changed.'

'But how do you know you're looking at sensor output?'

Richard entered a command and there was a change in the image. 'Occasionally I see something I recognise,' he said. 'Look at that one, for example. Couldn't that be the Beta stairway viewed from the camera in the middle of the Central Point?'

Nicole studied the picture. 'Possibly,' she said, 'but I don't see how you could ever tell for certain.'

Richard commanded the screen to change again. The next three pictures were unintelligible. The fourth one showed a feature tapering to a point at the top of the frame. 'And that one,' he said, 'couldn't it be one of the little horns, as seen from a sensor near the top of the Big Horn?'

No matter how hard she tried, Nicole could not visualise what the view would be like from the top of the giant spire in the centre of the Southern bowl. Richard continued to flip through the pictures. Only about one in five was even partially clear. 'Somewhere in this system there must be some enhancement algorithms,' he said to himself. 'Then I can sharpen up all the images.'

Nicole could tell that Richard was about to begin another long work session. She walked over to him and put her arms around his neck. 'Could I talk you into a little distraction first?' she said, reaching up and kissing him on the mouth.

'I guess so,' he replied, dropping the keyboard on the floor. 'It will probably be good for me to clear my mind.'

★

Nicole was in the middle of a beautiful dream. She was home again at her villa in Beauvois. Richard was sitting beside her on the couch in the living room and was holding her hand. Her father and daughter were opposite them in the soft chairs.

Her dream was broken by Richard's insistent voice. When Nicole opened her eyes her lover was standing over her, his voice crackling with excitement. 'Wait until you see this, darling,' he said, extending a hand to pull her up. 'It's fantastic! Somebody is still here.'

Nicole shook the dream from her mind and looked at the black square where Richard was pointing. 'Can you believe it?' he said, jumping up and down. 'There's no doubt about it. The military ship is still docked.'

Only then did Nicole realise that she was looking at a picture of the outside of Rama. She blinked her eyes and listened to Richard's rambling explanation. 'Once I figured out the code for the enhancement parameters, almost every frame became clear. That set of pictures I showed you earlier must be the realtime output from hundreds of Rama's imaging sensors. And I think I have figured out how to access the other sensor data bases as well.'

Richard was exultant. He threw his arms around Nicole and lifted her off the ground. He hugged and kissed her and bounced around the room like a lunatic.

When he finally calmed down a little, Nicole spent almost a full minute studying the image that was projected on the black square. It was definitely the Newton military ship; she could read the markings. 'So the science spacecraft has gone home,' she commented to Richard.

'Yes,' he answered, 'as I expected. I was afraid they would *both* be gone and that after we swam across the sea, we would find ourselves still trapped, this time in a larger prison.'

The same concern had bothered Nicole. She smiled at Richard. 'It's relatively straightforward then, isn't it? We swim across the Cylindrical Sea and walk over to the chairlift. Someone will be waiting for us at the top.'

Nicole started packing her belongings. Richard, meanwhile, continued to flash new images on the screen. 'What are you doing now, darling?' Nicole asked gently. 'I thought we were going to make our swim.'

'I haven't made a full pass through the sensor list since I located the enhancement parameteres,' Richard replied. 'I just want to make certain we're not missing anything critical. It will only take another hour or so.'

Nicole stopped packing and sat down in front of the screen beside Richard. The pictures were indeed interesting. Some were exterior shots, but most were images of different regions inside Rama, including the underground lairs. One magnificent photo was taken from the top of the large room where the hot spheres in their sponge webbing rested on the floor beneath the hanging lattices. Richard and Nicole watched the picture for a moment, hoping to see a black and gold octospider, but they detected no movement.

They were near the end of the list when an image of the bottom third of the Alpha stairway stunned them both. There, climbing down the stairs, were four human figures in spacesuits. Richard and Nicole watched the figures descend for five seconds and then exploded with joy. 'They're coming?' Richard said, throwing his arms into the air. 'We're going to be rescued!'

51

Escape Harness

Richard was becoming impatient. He and Nicole had been standing on the walls of New York for over an hour, scanning the skies for some sign of a helicopter. 'Where the hell are they?' he grumbled. 'It only takes fifteen minutes by rover from the bottom of Alpha stairway to the Beta campsite.'

'Maybe they're looking somewhere else,' Nicole said encouragingly.

'That's ridiculous,' Richard said. 'Surely they would go to Beta first – and even if they couldn't repair the comm system, at least they'd find my last message. I said I was taking one of the motor boats to New York.'

'They probably know that there's no place for a helicopter to land in the city. They may be coming across in a boat themselves.'

'Without first seeing if they could spot us from the helicopter? That's unlikely.' Richard turned his eyes to the sea and searched for a sail. 'A boat. A boat. My kingdom for a boat.'

Nicole laughed but Richard barely managed a little smile. 'Two men could assemble the sailboat in the supply hut at Beta in less than thirty minutes,' he fretted. 'Damnit, what's holding them up?'

In his frustration Richard switched on the transmitter in his communicator. 'Now hear this, you guys. If you're anywhere near the Cylindrical Sea, identify yourselves. And then hurry yourselves over here. We're standing on the wall and we're tired of waiting.'

There was no response. Nicole sat down on the wall. 'What are you doing?' Richard asked.

'I think you're worrying enough for both of us,' she responded. 'And I'm tired of standing up and waving my arms.' She stared across the Cylindrical Sea. 'It would be so much easier,' Nicole said wistfully, 'if we could just fly across ourselves.'

Richard cocked his head to one side and looked at her. 'What a great idea,' he said several seconds later. 'Why didn't we think of it before?' He immediately sat down and started doing some calculations on his computer. 'Cowards die many times before their deaths,' he mumbled to himself, 'the valiant never taste of death but once.'

Nicole watched her friend furiously pounding his keyboard. 'What are you doing, dear?' she enquired, glancing over his shoulder at the computer monitor.

'Three!' he shouted, after finishing a computation. 'Three should be enough.' Richard looked up at the puzzled Nicole. 'Do you want to hear the most outrageous plan in interplanetary history?' he asked her.

'Why not?' she said with a doubtful smile.

'We are going to build ourselves harnesses out of the lattice material and the avians are going to fly us across the Cylindrical Sea.'

Nicole stared at Richard for several seconds. 'Assuming we can make the harnesses,' she said sceptically, 'how do we talk the avians into doing their part?'

'We convince them it's in their own best interest,' Richard replied. 'Or alternatively we threaten them in some way ... I don't know, you can work on that issue.'

Nicole was incredulous. 'Anyway,' Richard continued, grabbing her hand and walking down the wall, 'it beats standing around here waiting for the helicopter or the boat.'

Five hours later there was still no sign of the rescue team. When they had finished making the harnesses, Richard had left Nicole at the wall and gone back to the White

Room to check through the sensor set again. He returned
with the news that he thought he had seen the human
figures in the vicinity of the Beta campsite, but that the
resolution on that particular frame had been very poor.
As they had agreed, Nicole had been calling every
half-hour on the communicator. There had been no
response.

'Richard,' she said, while he was programming some
graphics on his computer, 'why do you think the rescue
team was using the stairway?'

'Who knows?' he replied. 'Maybe the chairlift
malfunctioned and there were no engineers left.'

'It seems strange to me,' Nicole mused. *Something
about this is bothering me*, she thought, *but I don't dare
share it with Richard until I can explain it. He doesn't
believe in intuition.* Nicole glanced at her watch. *It's a
good thing we rationed the melon. If the rescue team doesn't
show up and this wild scheme doesn't work, we won't be
swimming until next daylight.*

'Preliminary design complete,' Richard stated emphatically. He waved to Nicole to join him. 'If you approve
the line drawing,' he said, pointing at the monitor in his
hand, 'then I will proceed with the detailed graphics.'

In the picture three large avians, each with one line
wrapped around its body, were flying in formation across
a sea. Dangling underneath them, and attached by three
lines, was a stick figure human being sitting in a flimsy
harness. 'Looks good to me,' said Nicole, never thinking
for a minute that such an event would actually happen.

'I can't believe we're doing this,' Nicole remarked,
pushing the plate to open the avian lair for the second
time.

Their first attempt to renew contact had resulted in the
expected cold shoulder. This second time it was Richard
who shouted into the avian lair. 'Listen to me, you
avians,' he growled in his fiercest voice, 'I need to talk to
you. Right *now*. Get up here on the double.' Nicole had
to restrain a laugh.

Richard began dropping black objects into the lair.

'See,' he grinned, 'I knew these damn things would be good for something.' Eventually they could hear some activity at the bottom of the vertical corridor. The same pair of avians they had seen many times before flew up to the top of the lair and started screeching at Richard and Nicole. They did not even look at the monitor when Richard held it out for them. When they were finished screeching, the pair flew over the top of the tank sentinel and the cover closed again.

'It's no use, Richard,' Nicole said when he asked her to open the cover a third time. 'Even our friends are against us.' She paused before pressing the plate. 'What are we going to do if they attack us?'

'They won't attack,' Richard said, indicating for Nicole to open the cover. 'But just in case, I want you to stay over there. I will deal with your feathered friends.'

There was jabbering from the lair as soon as the cover opened for the third time. Richard immediately started shouting back and pitching black objects down the corridor. One of them hit the tank sentinel and prompted a small explosion, like a gunshot.

The two usual avians flew up to the opening and screamed at Richard. Three or four of their comrades were just behind. The noise was unbelievable. Richard did not back down. He kept yelling and pointing at the computer monitor. Finally he was able to get their attention.

The group of avians watched the graphic depiction of the flight across the sea. Richard then held up one of the harnesses in his left hand and started running the demonstration on his monitor again. Frantic conversation among the avians ensued. At the end, however, Richard sensed that he had lost. As a pair of the other avians flew over the top of the tank sentinel, Richard climbed down into the lair, on to the first ledge. 'Hold it,' he shouted at the top of his lungs.

The mate of the black velvet avian lunged forward, its threatening beak no more than a metre from Richard's face. The noise from all the screeching and jabbering was deafening. Richard was undaunted. Despite the avian protests, he descended to the second ledge. Now he would not be able to escape if the cover started to close.

Again he held up the harness and pointed at the monitor. A chorus of screeches told him the response. Then, above the avian howl, he heard another sound, like a klaxon alarm announcing a fire drill at a school or hospital. All the avians immediately calmed down. They settled quietly on the ledges and stared down at the tank sentinel.

The lair was strangely silent. After a few seconds Richard heard the beating of wings and moments later a new avian flew into the vertical corridor. It rose slowly up to his level and hovered just opposite him. It had a grey velvet body and sharp grey eyes. Two thick rings of bright cherry red were wrapped around its neck.

The creature studied Richard and landed on the ledge opposite him, across the corridor. The avian which had been in that spot scurried out of the way. When the grey velvet bird spoke, it was soft and very clear. After the speech was finished, the black velvet avian flew up beside the new arrival and apparently explained the furore. Several times the two avians stared across at Richard. The last time, thinking that perhaps their nodding heads were a cue, Richard displayed the graphic flight one more time and held up the harnesses. The bird with the cherry rings flew over beside him for a closer look.

The creature made a sudden movement, frightening Richard, and he nearly fell off the ledge. What may have been avian laughter was silenced by a few words from the grey velvet leader, which then sat quite still, as if it were thinking, for over a minute. At length the avian leader gestured toward Richard with one talon, opened its huge wings, and soared out through the opening into daylight.

For several seconds Richard did not move. The great creature rose up, up into the sky above the lair and was soon followed by the two more familiar avians. Moments later Nicole's head appeared in the opening. 'Are you coming?' she asked. 'I don't know how you did it, but it looks as if our friends are ready.'

52
Flight 302

Richard pulled the harness tight around Nicole's waist and buttocks. 'Your feet will dangle,' he said, 'and at first, when the lattice cord is stretching, you will have the feeling that you're falling.'

'What if I hit the water?' Nicole asked.

'You have to trust the avians to fly high enough that you won't,' Richard replied. 'I think they're quite intelligent, especially the one with the red rings.'

'Do you think it's the king?' Nicole asked, adjusting her harness for comfort.

'Probably their equivalent,' Richard answered. 'He has made it clear from the beginning that he intends to fly in the middle of the formation.'

Richard walked up the steep incline to the wall, carrying all three harness lines in his hands. The avians were sitting quietly together, staring out at the sea. They acquiesced as he tied the harness around their midsections, just behind the backs of the wings. Then they watched his computer monitor as he again showed them the graphics of the takeoff. The avians were to lift off together, slowly, pull the harness lines taut directly over Nicole's head, and then lift her straight up before flying north across the sea.

He checked that the knots were secure and then returned to Nicole's side at the bottom of the incline. She was only about five metres from the water. 'If, by some chance, the avians do not return for me,' Richard told her, 'don't wait forever. Once you find the rescue team, assemble the sailboat and come across. I will be down in the White Room.' He took a deep breath. 'Be safe, my darling,' Richard added. 'Remember that I love you.'

Nicole could tell from the pounding of her heart that the moment of takeoff had finally arrived. She kissed Richard slowly on the lips. 'And I love you,' she murmured.

When they broke their embrace, Richard waved at the avians on the wall. The grey velvet avian cautiously rose in the air, followed immediately by its two companions. They hovered in formation directly over Nicole. She felt the three lines pull tight and was momentarily lifted into the air.

Seconds later, as the elastic cord began to stretch, Nicole was falling toward the ground again. The avians flew higher, heading out over the water, and Nicole felt as if she were a yo-yo, bouncing up and down as the cord stretched and then contracted with a jerk when the avians rose swiftly to a higher altitude.

It was an exciting flight. She touched the water once, just barely, while she was still close to shore. She was briefly frightened, but the avians lifted her quickly before anything more than her feet got wet. Once the lattice cord was at its full extension, the ride was fairly smooth. Nicole sat in her harness, her hands holding on to two of the three lines, her feet dangling below her about eight metres from the tops of the waves.

The middle of the sea was quite calm. About halfway across Nicole saw two great, dark figures swimming along beneath her, parallel to her course. She was certain they were shark biots. She also detected two or three other species in the water, including one, long and skinny like an eel, that reared itself out of the sea and watched her fly by. *Whew*, Nicole thought as she surveyed the water, *I'm certainly glad that I didn't swim.*

The landing was easy. Nicole had been concerned that the avians might not realise there was a fifty-metre cliff on the opposite side of the sea. She need not have worried. As they approached landfall in the Northern Hemicylinder, the avians gently increased their altitude.

Nicole was set down gingerly about ten metres from the edge.

The huge birds landed close by. Nicole climbed out of her harness and walked over to the avians. She thanked them profusely and tried to pat them on the backs of their heads, but they jerked away from her touch. The creatures rested for several minutes and then, at a signal from their leader, they flew off across the sea toward New York.

Nicole was surprised at the intensity of her emotions. She knelt down and kissed the ground. It was only then that she realised she had never really expected to escape safely from New York. For a moment, before she started searching for the rescue team with her binoculars, she reviewed everything that had happened to her since that fateful crossing in her icemobile. *Before New York is a lifetime ago*, she said to herself. *Now everything has changed.*

Richard untied the harness from the avian leader and dropped it on the ground. All the birds were now free. The creature with the grey velvet body craned its neck around to see if Richard was finished. The rich cherry red of its rings was even clearer in the full daylight. Richard wondered about the rings and what they signified, knowing there was a high likelihood he would never see these magnificent aliens again.

Nicole came over beside Richard. When he had landed she had embraced him passionately. The avians had boldly stared, signalling their curiousity. *They too*, Nicole thought, *must be wondering about us*. The linguist in her imagined what it would be like actually to talk to an extraterrestrial species, to begin to understand how an altogether different intelligence might operate....

'I wonder how we say goodbye and thank you,' Richard was saying.

'I don't know,' Nicole replied, 'but it would be nice....'

She stopped to watch the avian leader. It had called the other two creatures to come beside it and the three birds were standing facing Richard and Nicole. On a signal

they all spread their wings, to their full extent, and
formed into a circle. They turned around one full
revolution and then fell back into a straight line facing
the humans.

'Come on,' Nicole said. 'We can do that.'

Nicole and Richard stood side by side, their arms
outstretched, and faced their avian friends. Nicole then
put her arms on Richard's shoulders and led him through
a circular turn. Richard, who was sometimes not very
graceful, stumbled once but managed to complete the
movement. Nicole imagined that the avian leader was
smiling when she and Richard straightened out after the
revolution.

The three avians took off seconds later. Higher and
higher in the sky they rose, until they were at the limit of
Nicole's vision. Then they flew south, across the sea
toward home.

'Good luck,' Nicole whispered as they departed.

The rescue team was not in the vicinity of the Beta
campsite. In fact, Richard and Nicole had not seen any
sign of them during a thirty-minute drive in the rover
along the coast of the Cylindrical Sea. 'These guys must
really be stupid,' Richard groused. 'My message was in
plain view there at Beta. Could it be that they haven't
even come down this far yet?'

'It's less than three hours until dark,' Nicole replied.
'They may have returned to the Newton already.'

'All right, then, to hell with them,' Richard said.
'Let's have a bite to eat and then head for the chairlift.'

'Do you think we should save any of the melon?'
Nicole asked a few minutes later, while they were eating.
Richard gave her a puzzled glance. 'Just in case,' she
added.

'Just in case what?' Richard rejoined. 'Even if we don't
find that idiotic rescue bunch and must climb all the
stairs ourselves, we'll still be out of here right after dark.
Remember, we become weightless again at the top of the
stairway.'

Nicole smiled. 'I guess I'm naturally more cautious,'

she said. She put several bites of melon back into her pack.

They had driven three-quarters of the way toward the chairlift and the Alpha stairway when they spotted the four human figures in spacesuits. It looked as if they were leaving the conglomeration of buildings that had been designated as the Raman Paris. The figures were walking in the opposite direction from the rover.

'I told you the guys were idiots,' Richard exclaimed. 'They don't even have the sense to take off their spacesuits. It must be a special team, sent up in the spare Newton vehicle just to find us and bring us back.'

He steered the rover across the Central Plain in the direction of the humans. Richard and Nicole both started shouting when they were within a hundred metres, but the men in the spacesuits continued their slow procession toward the west. 'They probably can't hear us,' Nicole offered. 'They still have on their helmets and communication gear.'

A frustrated Richard drove up to within five metres of the single file line, stopped the rover, and jumped out in a hurry. He ran quickly around to the leader, shouting all the way. 'Hey, guys,' he yelled. 'We're here, behind you. All you have to do is turn around....'

Richard stopped cold as he stared at the blank expression of the man in the lead. He recognised the face. Jesus, it was Norton! He shuddered involuntarily as a tingle ran down his spine. Richard barely jumped out of the way as the four man procession walked slowly past him. Numb from the shock, he quietly studied the other three faces, none of which changed expression as they marched past. They were three other cosmonauts from the Rama I crew.

Nicole was at his side only seconds after the final figure passed him. 'What's the matter?' she said. 'Why didn't they stop?' The blood had all drained out of Richard's face. 'Darling, are you all right?'

'They're biots,' Richard mumbled. 'Goddamn human biots.'

'*Whaaat?*' Nicole replied, a streak of terror in her

voice. She ran quickly to the head of the line and stared at the face behind the helmet glass. It was definitely Norton. Every feature of the face, even the colour of the eyes and the slight moustache, was absolutely perfect. But the eyes didn't say anything.

The motion of the body, too, now that she noticed it, seemed artificial. Each pair of steps was a repeated pattern. There were only slight variations from figure to figure. *Richard is right*, Nicole thought. *These are human biots. They must have been made from the images, just like the toothpaste and the brush.* A momentary panic swelled in her chest. But we don't need a rescue team, she told herself, calming her anxiety, *the military ship is still docked at the top of the bowl.*

Richard was stunned by the discovery of the human biots. He sat in the rover for several minutes, unwilling to drive, asking questions of Nicole and himself that he could not possibly have answered. 'So what's going on here?' he said over and over again. 'Are all these biots based on real species, found somewhere in the universe? And why are they being fabricated in the first place?'

Before they drove over to the chairlift, Richard insisted that they both take many metres of video footage of the human biots. 'The avians and octospiders are fascinating,' he said as he took a special closeup of 'Norton's' leg motion, 'but this tape will blow everyone away.'

Nicole reminded him that it was less than two hours until dark and that it still might be necessary for them to climb the Stairway of the Gods. Satisfied that he had recorded the bizarre procession for posterity, Richard slid into the driver's seat of the rover and headed toward the Alpha stairway.

There was no need to perform any tests to see if the chairlift was working properly; it was running when they drove up beside it. Richard jumped out of the rover and ran into the control room.

'Someone's coming down,' he said, pointing up the lift.

'Or something,' Nicole said grimly.

The five-minute wait seemed like an eternity. At first neither Richard nor Nicole said anything. Later, however, Richard suggested that perhaps they should sit in the rover in case they needed to make a quick escape.

Each trained his binoculars on the long cable stretching upward to the heavens. 'It's a man!' cried Nicole.

'It's General O'Toole!' said Richard a few moments later.

Indeed it was. General Michael Ryan O'Toole, American air force officer, was descending in the chairlift. He was still several hundred metres above Richard and Nicole, and had not yet seen them. He was busy studying with his binoculars the beauty of the alien landscape around him.

General O'Toole had been preparing to leave Rama for the final time when, as he rode up in the chairlift, he had spotted what looked like three birds flying far to the south in the Rama sky. The general had decided to return to see if he could find those birds again. He was unprepared for the joyous greeting that awaited him when he reached the bottom of his ride.

53
Trinity

When Richard Wakefield had left the Newton to go back inside Rama, General O'Toole had been the last crew member to say goodbye. The general had waited patiently while the other cosmonauts had finished their conversations with Richard. 'You're really certain you want to do this?' Janos Tabori had said to his British friend. 'You know the full committee is going to declare Rama off limits within hours.'

'By then,' Richard had grinned at Janos, 'I will be on my way to Beta. Technically I will not have violated their order.'

'That's bullshit,' Admiral Heilmann had interjected tersely. 'Dr Brown and I are in charge of this mission. We have both told you to stay on board the Newton.'

'And I've told you several times,' Richard said firmly, 'that I left some personal items inside Rama that are very important to me. Besides, you know as well as I do that there's nothing for any of us here to do over the next couple of days. Once the abort decision is definitely made, all the major scheduling acitivities will be on the ground. We will be told when to undock and head for Earth.'

'I will remind you, one more time,' Otto Heilmann had replied, 'that I consider what you are doing an act of insubordination. When we return to Earth I intend to prosecute to the fullest –'

'Save it, will you, Otto,' Richard interrupted. There was no rancour in his tone. He adjusted his spacesuit and started to put on his helmet. As always Francesca was recording the scene on her video camera. She had been strangely silent since her private conversation with Richard an hour earlier. She seemed detached, as if her mind were somewhere else.

General O'Toole walked up to Richard and extended his hand. 'We haven't spent much time together, Wakefield,' he said, 'but I've admired your work. Good luck in there. Don't take any unnecessary chances.'

Richard had been surprised by the general's warm smile. He had expected the American military officer to try to talk him out of leaving. 'It's magnificent in Rama, General,' Richard had said. 'Like a combination of the Grand Canyon, the Alps, and the Pyramids all at once.'

'We've lost four crew members already,' O'Toole replied. 'I want to see you back here safe and sound. God bless you.'

Richard finished shaking the general's hand, put on his helmet, and stepped across into the airlock. Moments later, when Wakefield was gone, Admiral Heilmann was critical of General O'Toole's behaviour. 'I'm disappointed in you, Michael,' he said. 'From that warm sendoff the young man might have concluded that you actually approved of his action.'

O'Toole faced the German admiral. 'Wakefield has courage, Otto,' he said. 'And conviction as well. He is not afraid of either the Ramans or the ISA disciplinary process. I admire that kind of self-confidence.'

'Nonsense,' Heilmann rejoined. 'Wakefield is a brash, arrogant schoolboy. You know what he left inside? A couple of those stupid Shakespearean robots. He just doesn't like taking orders. He wants to do what's uppermost on his own personal agenda.'

'That makes him a lot like the rest of us,' Francesca remarked. The room was quiet for a moment. 'Richard is very smart,' she said in a subdued tone. 'He probably has reasons for going back into Rama that none of us understand.'

'I just hope he comes back before dark, as he promised,' Janos said. 'I'm not certain I could stand to lose another friend.'

The cosmonauts filed out of the atrium into the hallway. 'Where's Dr Brown?' Janos asked Francesca as he walked along beside her.

'He's with Yamanaka and Turgenyev. They're reviewing possible crew assignments for the trip home. As shorthanded as we are, a lot of crosstraining will be necessary before we leave.' Francesca laughed. 'He even asked me if I could be a backup navigation engineer. Can you imagine that?'

'Easily,' Janos replied. 'You could probably learn any of the engineering assignments at this point.'

Behind them Heilmann and O'Toole shuffled down the corridor. When they reached the hall leading to the private crew quarters, General O'Toole started to leave. 'Just a minute,' Otto Heilmann said. 'I need to talk to you about something else. This damn Wakefield thing almost made it slip my mind. Can you come to my office for an hour or so?'

'Essentially,' Otto Heilmann said, pointing at the unscrambled cryptogram on the monitor, 'this is a major change to the Trinity procedure. It's not surprising. Now that we know much more about Rama, you would expect the deployment to be somewhat different.'

'But we never anticipated using all five weapons,' O'Toole responded. 'The extra pair were only loaded on board in case of failures. That much megatonnage could vapourise Rama.'

'That's the intent,' Heilmann said. He sat back in his chair and smiled. 'Just between us chickens,' he said, 'I think there's a lot of pressure on the general staff down there. The feeling is that Rama's capabilities were vastly underrated initially.'

'But why do they want to put the two largest weapons in the ferry passageway? Surely a single megaton bomb would accomplish the desired result.'

'What if it didn't explode for some reason? There has to be a backup.' Heilmann leaned forward eagerly on his desk. 'I think this change to the procedure clearly defines the strategy. The two at the end will ensure that the structural integrity of the vehicle will be absolutely destroyed – that's essential to guarantee that it is impossible for Rama to manoeuvre again after the blast. The other three bombs are scattered around the interior to make certain that no part of Rama is safe. It's equally important that the explosions should result in enough velocity change that all the remaining pieces miss the Earth.'

General O'Toole constructed a mental image of the giant spacecraft being annihilated by five nuclear bombs. It was not a pleasant picture. Once, fifteen years before, he and twenty other members of the COG general staff had flown into the South Pacific to watch a hundred-kiloton weapon explode. The COG system engineering personnel had convinced the political leaders, and the world press, that one nuclear test was necessary 'every twenty years or so' to ensure that all the old weapons would indeed fire in an emergency. O'Toole and his team had observed the demonstration, ostensibly to learn as much as possible about the effects of nuclear weapons.

General O'Toole was deep in his memory, recalling the spine-tingling horror of that fireball rising in the peaceful South Pacific sky. He was not aware that Admiral Heilmann had asked him a question. 'I'm sorry, Otto,' he said. 'I was thinking about something else.'

'I had asked you how long you thought it might take to get approval for Trinity.'

'You mean in our case?' O'Toole said with disbelief.

'Of course,' Heilmann responded.

'I can't imagine it,' O'Toole said quickly. 'The weapons were included in the mission manifest solely to guard against openly hostile actions by the Ramans. I even remember the baseline scenario – an unprovoked attack against the Earth by the alien spacecraft, using high technology weapons beyond the capabilities of our defences. The current situation is altogether different.'

The German admiral studied his American colleague. 'No one ever envisioned the Rama spacecraft on a collision course with the Earth,' Heilmann said. 'If it does not alter its trajectory, it will gouge an enormous hole in the surface and kick up such dust that the temperatures will drop all over the world for several years … At least, that's what the scientists say.'

'But that's preposterous,' O'Toole argued. 'You heard all the discussion during the conference call. No rational person really believes that Rama will actually hit the Earth.'

'Impact is only one of several disaster scenarios. What would you do if you were chief of staff? Destroying Rama now is a safe solution. Nobody loses.'

Visibly shaken by the conversation, Michael O'Toole excused himself from the meeting with Admiral Heilmann and headed for his room. For the first time in his entire association with the Newton mission, O'Toole thought that he might actually be ordered to use his RQ code to activate the weapons. Never before, never for a moment, had he considered that the bombs in the metal containers at the back of the military ship were anything more than a palliative for the fears of the civilian politicians.

Sitting at the computer terminal in his room, the concerned O'Toole recalled the words of Armando Urbina, the Mexican peace activist who had advocated a total dismantling of the COG nuclear arsenal. 'As we have seen both at Rome and Damascus,' Señor Urbina had said, 'if the weapons exist, they can be used. Only if there are no weapons at all can we guarantee that human beings will never again suffer the horror of nuclear devastation.'

Richard Wakefield did not return before Raman nightfall. Since the communication station at Beta had been knocked out of commission by the hurricane (the Newton had monitored the breakup of the Cylindrical Sea and the onset of the windstorm through telemetry relayed by Beta before it was silenced), Richard had moved out of communications range when he was halfway across the Central Plain. His last transmission to Janos Tabori, who had volunteered to man the commlink, had been typically Wakefield. As the signal from inside Rama was fading, Janos, in a lighthearted tone, had asked Richard how he wanted to be remembered 'to his fans' in case he was 'swallowed by the Great Galactic Ghoul'.

'Tell them that I loved Rama not wisely, but too well,' Richard had shouted into his communicator.

'What's that?' Otto Heilmann had puzzled. The admiral had come looking for Janos to discuss a Newton engineering problem.

'He killed her,' Janos had said, trying without success to lock up the signal again.

'Who killed ... what are you talking about?'

'It's not important,' Janos had answered, spinning around in his chair and floating into the air. 'Now, what can I do for you, Herr Admiral?'

Richard's failure to return was not considered serious until several hours after the following Raman dawn. The cosmonauts remaining on the Newton had convinced themselves the night before that Wakefield had become absorbed in some task ('probably fixing the Beta comm station,' Janos had offered), had lost track of the time, and had decided not to take a solitary ride out in the dark. But when he didn't return in the morning, a feeling of gloom began to pervade the conversation of the crew.

'I don't know why we won't admit it,' Irina Turgenyev said suddenly during a period of quiet at dinnertime. 'Wakefield is not coming back either. Whatever got Takagishi and des Jardins got him as well.'

'That's ridiculous, Irina,' Janos replied heatedly.

'Da,' she remarked. 'That's what you've always said. Ever since the beginning, when General Borzov was cut to pieces. Then it was an accident that the crab biot attacked Wilson. Cosmonaut des Jardins disappears down an alley....'

'Coincidence,' Janos shouted, 'all coincidence!'

'You're stupid, Janos,' Irina shouted back. 'You trust everybody and everything. We should blow the damn thing to pieces before it does any more –'

'Stop, stop, you two,' David Brown said loudly as the

two East European colleagues continued to argue.

'All right now,' added General O'Toole. 'We're all a little tense. There's no need for us to quarrel.'

'Will anyone be going in to look for Richard?' the emotional Janos asked no one in particular.

'Who would be crazy enough –' Irina began to respond.

'No,' interrupted Admiral Heilmann firmly. 'I told him that his visit was unauthorised and that we would not come after him in any circumstances. Besides, Dr Brown and the two pilots tell me that we can barely fly the two Newton ships home with the manpower remaining – and their analysis assumed Wakefield was with us. We cannot take any more risks.'

There was a long and sombre silence at the dinner table. 'I had planned to tell everyone when the meal was over,' David Brown then said, standing up beside his chair, 'but it looks to me as if this group could use some good news now. An hour ago we received our orders. We're to depart for Earth at 1-14 days, a little over a week from now. Between now and then we will cross-train the personnel, rest for the voyage home, and make certain that all the Newton engineering systems are working properly.'

Cosmonauts Turgenyev, Yamanaka, and Sabatini all shouted their approval. 'If we're going to leave without returning to Rama,' Janos enquired, 'why are we waiting so long? Surely we can be well enough prepared in three or four days.'

'As I understand it,' Dr Brown replied, 'our two military colleagues have a special task that will occupy most of their time – and some of ours – for much of the next three days.' He glanced over at Otto Heilmann. 'Do you want to tell them?'

Admiral Heilmann stood up at his place. 'I need to discuss the details first with General O'Toole,' he said in a ringing voice. 'We'll explain it to everyone else in the morning.'

O'Toole didn't need Otto Heilmann to show him the message that had been received only twenty minutes before. He knew what it said. In compliance with the procedure, there were only three words:

Proceed with Trinity.

54

Once A Hero

Michael O'Toole could not sleep. He tossed and turned, switched on his favourite music, and repeated both the 'Hail Mary' and 'Our Father' liturgies over and over. Nothing worked. He longed for a distraction, something that would make him forget his responsibilities and allow his soul some repose.

PROCEED WITH TRINITY, he said to himself at last, focusing on the true cause of his disquiet. What exactly did that mean? Use the teleoperator fork lifts, open up the containers, pick up the weapons (they were about the size of refrigerators), check out the subsystems, put the bombs in a pod, carry them over to the Rama seal, ferry them to the heavy load elevator....

And what else? he thought. One more thing. It wouldn't take much more than a minute at each weapon, but it was by far the most important. Each bomb had a redundant pair of tiny numerical keyboards on its side. He and Admiral Heilmann each had to use the keyboards to input a special sequence of digits, an RQ code it was called, before the weapons could be activated. Without those codes the bombs would remain absolutely dormant, forever.

The original debates over whether or not to include nuclear weapons in the limited Newton supply manifest had echoed through the corridors of COG military headquarters in Amsterdam for several weeks. The ensuing vote had been close. It was decided that the Newton would carry the nuclear weapons, but to allay widespread concern, it was also decided to implement rigorous safety measures that would guard against their unwarranted use.

During these same meetings, the COG military leadership avoided public outcry by placing a top secret classification on the fact that the Newton was transporting nuclear bombs to its rendezvous with Rama. Not even the civilian members of the Newton crew had been told about the existence of the weapons.

The secret working group on Trinity Safety Procedures had met seven times at four different locations around the world prior to the Newton launch. To make the deployment process immune to untoward electronic inputs, manual action had been chosen as the method of activation for the nuclear weapons. Thus neither a lunatic on the Earth nor a frightened cosmonaut on the Newton could trigger the process with a simple electronic command. The current COG chief of staff, a brilliant but passionate disciplinarian named Kazuo Norimoto, had expressed concern that without electronic command capability the military was unduly dependent upon the humans selected for the mission. He had been persuaded, however, that it was far better to depend on the Newton military officers than to worry about a terrorist or fanatic somehow gaining possession of the activation code.

But what if one of the Newton military officers were seized by panic? How could the system be protected against a unilateral act of nuclear warfare by a crew member? When all the discussions were completed, the resultant safety system was relatively simple. There would be three military officers in the crew. Each of them would have an RQ code known only to himself. Manual input of any two of the long numerical sequences would arm the nuclear devices. The system was thus protected against either a recalcitrant officer or a frightened one. It sounded like a foolproof system.

But our current situation was never considered in the contingency analyses, O'Toole thought as he lay in his bed. *In the event of any dangerous action, either military or civilian, each of us was supposed to designate an alternate to learn our code. But who would have thought that an appendectomy was dangerous? Valeriy's RQ died with him. Which means the system now requires two for two.*

O'Toole rolled over on his stomach and pressed his face against the pillow. He now understood clearly why he was still awake. *If I don't input my code those bombs cannot be used.* He remembered a luncheon on the military ship with Valeriy Borzov and Otto Heilmann during the leisurely cruise toward Rama. 'It's a perfect set of checks and balances,' the Soviet general had joked, 'and probably played a role in our individual selections. Otto would pull the trigger at the slightest provocation and you, Michael, would agonise over its morality even if your life were threatened. I'm the tie-breaker.'

But you are dead, General O'Toole said to himself, *and we have been ordered to activate the bombs.* He rose from the bed and walked over to his desk. As he had done all his life when facing a tough decision, O'Toole pulled a small electronic notebook from his pocket and made two short lists, one summarising the reasons for following his orders to destroy Rama and the other presenting arguments against it. He had no strictly logical reasons to oppose the destruction command – the giant vehicle was probably a lifeless machine, his three colleagues were almost certainly dead, and there was a non-trivial implied threat to the Earth. But still O'Toole hesitated. There was something about committing such a flagrantly hostile act that offended his sensibilities.

He returned to his bed and rolled over on his back. *Dear God*, he prayed, staring at the ceiling, *how can I possibly know what is right in this situation? Please show me the way.*

Only thirty seconds after his morning alarm. Otto Heilmann heard a soft knock on his door. General O'Toole walked in moments later. The American was already dressed for the day. 'You're up early, Michael,' Admiral Heilmann said, fumbling for his morning coffee, which had been heating automatically for five minutes already.

'I wanted to talk to you,' O'Toole said pleasantly. He

courteously waited for Heilmann to pick up his coffee packet.

'What is it?' the admiral asked.

'I want you to call off the meeting this morning.'

'Why?' Heilmann replied. 'We need some assistance from the rest of the crew, as you and I discussed last night. The longer we wait to get started, the more chance we will delay our departure.'

'I'm not ready just yet,' O'Toole said.

Admiral Heilmann's brow furrowed. He took a long sip from his coffee and studied his companion. 'I see,' he said quietly. 'And what else is needed before you will be ready?'

'I want to talk to someone, General Norimoto perhaps, to understand why we are destroying Rama. I know you and I talked about it yesterday, but I want to hear the reasons from the person giving the order.'

'It is a military officer's duty to follow orders. Asking questions could be viewed as a disciplinary breach –'

'I understand all that, Otto,' O'Toole interrupted, 'but this is not a battlefield situation. I am not refusing to comply with the order. I just want to be certain....' His voice trailed off and O'Toole stared off in the distance.

'Certain of what?' Heilmann asked.

O'Toole took a deep breath. 'Certain that I'm doing the right thing.'

A video conference with Norimoto was arranged and the Newton crew meeting was delayed. Since it was the middle of the night in Amsterdam, it was some time before the encoded transmission could be translated and presented to the COG chief of staff. In his typical manner, General Norimoto then requested several more hours to prepare his response, so that he could obtain 'staff consensus' on what he was going to say to O'Toole.

The general and Admiral Heilmann were sitting together in the Newton military control centre when the transmission from Norimoto arrived. General Norimoto was dressed in his full military uniform. He did not smile when he greeted the Newton officers. He put on his glasses and read from a prepared text.

'General O'Toole, we have carefully reviewed the questions contained in your last transmission. All your concerns were included on the issues list that was discussed here on Earth before we reached the decision to proceed with Trinity. Under the unique provisions contained in the ISA-COG operating protocols, you and the other Newton military personnel are temporarily part of my special staff; therefore, I am your commanding officer. The message that was transmitted to you should be treated as an order.'

General Norimoto managed just a glimmer of a smile. 'Nevertheless,' he continued reading, 'because of the significance of the action contained in your order and your obvious concern about its repercussions, we have prepared three summary statements that should help you to understand our decision:

'One. We do not know if Rama is hostile or friendly. We have no way of obtaining additional data to resolve the issue.

'Two. Rama is hurtling toward Earth. It might impact with our home planet, take hostile action once it's in our neighbourhood, or perform benign activities that we can't define.

'Three. By implementing Trinity when Rama is still ten or more days away, we can guarantee the safety of the planet, regardless of Rama's intentions or future actions.'

The general paused for the briefest of moments. 'That is all,' he then concluded. 'Proceed with Trinity.'

The screen went blank. 'Are you satisfied?' Admiral Heilmann asked.

'I guess so,' O'Toole sighed. 'I didn't hear anything new, but I shouldn't have expected anything else.'

Admiral Heilmann looked at his watch. 'We've wasted almost an entire day,' he said. 'Should we have the crew meeting after dinner?'

'I'd rather not,' O'Toole replied. 'This episode has exhausted me and I hardly slept at all last night. I'd prefer to wait until the morning.'

'All right,' Heilmann said after a pause. He stood up

and put his arm on O'Toole's shoulder. 'We'll get started first thing after breakfast.'

In the morning General O'Toole did not attend the scheduled crew meeting. He phoned Heilmann and asked the admiral to proceed with the discussion without him. O'Toole's excuse was that he had a 'vicious stomach upset'. He doubted if Admiral Heilmann believed his explanation, but it didn't really matter.

O'Toole watched and listened to the meeting on the television in his room, never interrupting or adding to the proceedings. None of the other cosmonauts seemed particularly surprised that the Newton was carrying a nuclear arsenal. Heilmann did a thorough job of explaining what was to be done. He enlisted the help of Yamanaka and Tabori, as he and O'Toole had discussed, and outlined a sequence of events that would conclude with the weapons deployed inside Rama in seventy-two hours. That would leave the crew another three days to prepare for departure.

'When will the bombs detonate?' Janos Tabori asked nervously after Admiral Heilmann was finished.

'They will be set to explode sixty hours after our scheduled departure. According to the analytical models, we should be out of the debris field in twelve hours, but for safety we have specified, in our procedure, that the weapons will not be exploded unless we are at least twenty-four hours away ... If our departure is delayed because of some crisis, we can always overwrite the detonation time by electronic command.'

'That's reassuring,' Janos remarked.

'Any more questions?' Heilmann asked.

'Just one,' Janos said. 'As long as we're inside Rama putting these things in their proper locations, I assume that it's all right if we look around for our lost friends. In case they may be wandering....'

'The timeline is very tight, Cosmonaut Tabori,' the admiral replied, 'and the deployment itself, inside the structure, only takes a few hours. Unfortunately, due to delays in our starting the procedure, we will place the

weapons in their designated positions during the time that
Rama is dark.'

Great, O'Toole thought in his room. *That's something
else that can be blamed on me*. All in all, though, he felt that
Admiral Heilmann had handled the meeting very well. *It
was nice of Otto not to say anything about the code*, O'Toole
told himself. *He probably figures I'll come around. And he's
probably right.*

When O'Toole woke up from a short nap it was past lunch
time and he had a ravenous hunger. There was nobody in
the dining room except Francesca Sabatini; she was
finishing her coffee and studying some kind of engineering
data on her computer monitor.

'Feeling better, Michael?' she said when she saw him.

He nodded. 'What are you reading?' O'Toole asked.

'This is the executive software manual,' Francesca
replied. 'David is very concerned that without Wakefield
we won't even know if the Newton software is working
properly or not. I'm learning how to read the self-test
diagnostic output.'

'Whew,' O'Toole whistled. 'That's pretty heavy for a
journalist.'

'It's really not that complicated.' Francesca laughed.
'And it's extremely logical. Maybe in my next career I'll be
an engineer.'

O'Toole made himself a sandwich, picked up a package
of milk, and joined Francesca at the table. She put a hand
on his forearm. 'Speaking of next careers, Michael, have
you given any thought to yours?'

He looked at her quizzically. 'What are you talking
about?'

'I'm trapped in the usual professional dilemma, my dear
friend. My duties as a journalist are in direct conflict with
my feelings.'

O'Toole stopped chewing. 'Heilmann told you?'

She nodded. 'I'm not stupid, Michael. I would have
found out sooner or later. And this is a big, big story.
Maybe one of the biggest of the mission. Can't you see the
trailer on the nightly news: 'American general refuses to

follow order to destroy Rama. Tune in at five?'

The general became defensive. 'I haven't refused. The Trinity procedure does not call for me to input my code until after the weapons are out of the containers....'

'...and ready for placement in the pods.' Francesca completed the sentence. 'Which is about eighteen hours from now. Tomorrow morning as near as I can figure ... I plan to be on hand to record the historic event.' She rose from the table. 'And Michael, in case you're wondering, I haven't mentioned your call to Norimoto in any of my reports. I may refer to your conversation with him in my memoirs, but I won't publish them for at least five years.'

Francesca turned around and looked directly in O'Toole's eyes. 'You're about to go from being an international hero to a bum overnight, my friend. I hope you've carefully considered all the ramifications of your decision.'

55

The Voice of Michael

General O'Toole spent the afternoon in his room, watching on television as Tabori and Yamanaka checked out the nuclear weapons. He was excused, on the basis of his presumed stomach upset, from his assigned task of checking the weapon systems. The procedure was surprisingly straightforward and matter-of-fact; no-one would have suspected that it was designed to destroy the most impressive work of engineering ever seen by mankind.

Before dinner O'Toole placed a call to his wife. The Newton was rapidly approaching Earth now, and the delay time between transmission and reception was under three minutes. Old-fashioned two-way conversations were again possible. His talk with Kathleen was cordial and mundane. General O'Toole thought briefly about sharing his moral dilemma with his wife, but he realised that the videophone was not secure and decided against it. They both expressed excitement about being reunited in the very near future.

The general ate dinner with the crew. Janos was in one of his boisterous moods, entertaining the others with stories about his afternoon with 'the bullets', as he insisted on calling the nuclear bombs. 'At one point,' Janos said to Francesca, who had been laughing nonstop since his narrative began, 'we had all the bullets lightly anchored to the floor and lined up in a row, like dominoes. I scared the shit out of Yamanaka. I pushed the front one over and they all fell, clang, bang, in every direction. Hiro was certain they were going to explode.'

'Weren't you worried that you might injure some critical components?' David Brown asked.

'Nope,' Janos replied. 'The manuals that Otto gave me said that you couldn't hurt those things if you dropped them from the top of the Trump Tower. Besides,' he added, 'they aren't even armed yet. Right, Herr Admiral?'

Heilmann nodded and Janos launched into another story. General O'Toole drifted away, into his own mind, struggling impossibly with the relationship between those metal objects in the military ship and the mushroom-shaped cloud in the Pacific....

Francesca interrupted his reverie. 'You have an urgent call on your private line, Michael,' she said. 'President Bothwell will be on in five minutes.'

The conversation at the table stopped. 'Well,' said Janos with a grin, 'you must be some special person. It's not just everybody who receives a call from Slugger Bothwell.'

General O'Toole excused himself politely from the table and went to his room. *He must know*, he was thinking as he waited impatiently for the call to connect. *But of course. He's the President of the United States.*

O'Toole had always been a baseball fan and his favourite team was the Boston Red Sox. Baseball had gone into receivership at the height of the Great Chaos, in 2141, but a new group of owners had put the leagues back in business four years later. When Michael was six, in 2148, his father had taken him to Fenway Dome to watch a game between the Red Sox and the Havana Hurricanes. It was the beginning of a lifelong love affair for O'Toole.

Sherman Bothwell had been a left-handed, power-hitting first baseman for the Red Sox between 2172 and 2187. He had been immensely popular. A Missouri boy by birth, his genuine modest and old-fashioned dedication to hard work were as exceptional as the 527 home runs he had hit during his sixteen years in the major leagues. During the last year of his baseball career,

Bothwell's wife had died in a terrible boating accident. Sherman's uncomplaining dedication to the responsibility of raising his children as a single parent was widely applauded.

Three years later, when he married Linda Black, the darling daughter of the governor of Texas, it was obvious to many people that Sherman had a political career in mind. He advanced through the ranks with great speed. First lieutenant governor, then governor and presidential hopeful. He was elected to the White House by a landslide in 2196; it was anticipated that he would soundly defeat the Christian Conservative candidate in the forthcoming general election of 2200.

'Hello, General O'Toole,' the man in the blue suit said, with a friendly smile, when the screen was no longer blank. 'This is Sherman Bothwell, your president.'

The president was using no notes. He was leaning forward in a simple chair, his elbows resting on his thighs and his hands folded in front of him. He was talking as if he were sitting beside General O'Toole in someone's living room.

'I have been following your Newton mission with great interest – as has everybody in my family, including Linda and the four kids – ever since you launched. But I have been *especially* attentive these last several weeks, as the tragedies have rained down upon you and your courageous colleagues. My, my. Who would have ever thought that such a thing as that Rama ship could exist. It is truly staggering....

'Anyway, I understand from our COG representative that the order has been given to destroy Rama. Now I know that decisions like that are not made lightly, and that it places quite a large responsibility on folks like yourself. Nevertheless, I'm certain it's the right action.

'Yessirree, I know it's correct. Why, you know my daughter Courtney – that's the eight-year-old – she wakes up with nightmares almost every night. We were watching when you all were trying to capture that *bi-ot*, the one that looked like a crab, and my, it was positively awful. Now Courtney knows – it's been all over the television – that Rama is heading *di-rectly* for the Earth and she is really scared. Terrified. She thinks the whole country will be overrun by those crab things and that she and all her friends will be chopped up just like journalist Wilson.

'I'm telling you all this, General, because I know you're facing a big decision. And I've heard on the grapevine that you may be hesitant to destroy that humungous spacecraft and all its wonders. But General, I've told Courtney about you. I've told her that you and your crew are going to blow Rama to smithereens long before it reaches the Earth.

'That's why I called. To tell you that I'm counting on you. And so is Courtney.'

General O'Toole had thought, before listening to the President, that he might take advantage of the call and lay his dilemma in front of the leader of the American people. He had imagined that he might even question Slugger Bothwell about the nature of a species that destroys to protect against an unlikely risk. But after the practically perfect short speech from the ex-first-baseman, O'Toole had nothing to say. How could he refuse to respond to such a plea? All the Courtney Bothwells on the entire planet were counting on him.

After sleeping for five hours O'Toole awakened at three o'clock. He was aware that the most important action of his life was facing him. It seemed to him that everything he had done, his career, his religious studies, even his family activities, had been preparing him for this moment. God had trusted him with a monumental decision. But what did God want him to do? His forehead broke out in a sweat as O'Toole knelt before the image of Jesus on the cross that was behind his desk.

Dear Lord, he said, clasping his hands earnestly, *my hour approaches and I still do not see Thy will clearly. It would be so easy for me just to follow my orders and do what everyone wants. Is that Thy desire? How can I know for certain?*

Michael O'Toole closed his eyes and prayed for

guidance with a fervour surpassing any he had ever felt previously. As he prayed, he recalled another time, years before, when he had been a young pilot working as part of a temporary peacekeeping force in Guatemala. O'Toole and his men had awakened one morning to find their small air base in the jungle completely surrounded by the right-wing terrorists who were trying to bring the fledgling democratic government to its knees. The subversives wanted the planes. In exchange they would guarantee safe passage to O'Toole and his men.

Major O'Toole had taken fifteen minutes to deliberate and pray before deciding to fight it out. In the ensuing battle the planes were destroyed and almost half his men were killed, but his symbolic stand against terrorism emboldened the young government and many others throughout Central America at a time when the poor countries were struggling desperately to overcome the ravages of two decades of depression. O'Toole had been awarded the Order of Merit, the highest COG military accolade, for his exploits in Guatemala.

On board the Newton years later, General O'Toole's decision process was much less straightforward. In Guatemala the young major had not had any questions about the morality of his actions. His order to destroy Rama, however, was altogether different. In O'Toole's opinion, the alien ship had not taken any overtly bellicose actions. In addition, he knew that the order was based primarily on two factors: fear of what Rama *might* do and the uproar of xenophobic public opinion. Historically, both fear and public opinion were notoriously unconcerned about morality. If somehow he could learn what Rama's true purpose was, then he could....

Below the painting of Jesus on the desk in his room was a small statue of a young man with curly hair and wide eyes. This figure of St Michael of Siena had accompanied O'Toole on every journey he had made since his marriage to Kathleen. Seeing the statue gave him an idea. General O'Toole reached into one of the desk drawers and pulled out an electronic template. He switched on the power, checked the template menu, and accessed a concordance indexing the sermons of St Michael.

Under the word 'Rama', the general found a host of different references in the concordance. The one that he was looking for was the only one marked in a bold font. That specific reference was the saint's famous 'Rama sermon', delivered in camp to a group of five thousand of Michael's neophytes three weeks before the holocaust in Rome. O'Toole began to read.

'As the topic for my talk to you today, I am going to address an issue raised by Sister Judy in our council, namely, what is the basis for my statement that the extraterrestrial spacecraft called Rama might well have been the first announcement of the second coming of Christ. Understand that at this point I have had no clear revelation one way or the other; God has, however, suggested to me that the heralds of Christ's next coming will have to be extraordinary or the people on Earth will not notice. A simple angel or two blowing trumpets in the heavens won't suffice. The heralds must do things that are truly spectacular to engage attention.

'There is a precedent, established in the old testament prophecies foretelling the coming of Jesus, of prophetic announcements originating in the heavens. Elijah's chariot was the Rama of its time. It was, technologically speaking, as much beyond the understanding of its observers as Rama is today. In that sense there is a certain conforming pattern, a symmetry that is not inconsistent with God's order.

'But what I think is most hopeful about the arrival of the first Rama spacecraft eight years ago – and I say 'first' because I am certain there will be others – is that it forces humanity to think of itself in an extraterrestrial perspective. Too often we limit our concept of God and, by implication, our own spirituality. We belong to the universe. We are its children. It's just pure chance that our atoms have risen to consciousness here on this particular planet.

'Rama forces us to think of ourselves, and God, as beings of the universe. It is a tribute to His intelligence that He has sent such a herald at this moment. For as I have told you many times, we are overdue for our final evolution, our recognition that the entire human race is but a single organism. The appearance of Rama is another signal that it is time for us to change our ways and begin that final evolution.'

General O'Toole put down the template and rubbed his eyes. He had read the sermon before, just before his meeting with the pope in Rome in fact, but somehow it had not seemed as significant then as it did now. *So which are you, Rama?* he thought. *A threat to Courtney Bothwell or a herald of Christ's second coming?*

During the hour before breakfast General O'Toole was still vacillating. He genuinely did not know what his decision would be. Weighing heavily upon him was the fact that he had been given an explicit order by his commanding officer. O'Toole was well aware that he had sworn, when he had received his commission, not only to follow orders, but also to protect the Courtney Bothwells of the planet. Did he have any evidence that this particular order was so immoral that he should violate his oath?

As long as he thought of Rama only as a machine, it was not too difficult for General O'Toole to countenance its destruction. His action would not, after all, kill any Ramans. But what was it that Wakefield had said? That the Raman spaceship was probably more intelligent than any living creature on Earth, including human beings? And shouldn't superior machine intelligence have a special place among God's creations, perhaps even above lower life forms?

Eventually General O'Toole succumbed to fatigue. He simply had no energy left to deal with the unending stream of questions without answers. He reluctantly decided to cease his internal debate and prepared to implement his orders.

His first action was again to memorise his RQ code, a specific string of 50 integers between 0 and 9 that was known only by him and the processors inside the nuclear weapons. O'Toole had personally entered his code and checked that it had been properly stored in each of the weapons before the Newton mission had been launched from Earth. The string of digits was long to minimise the probability of its being duplicated by a repetitive, electronic search routine. Each of the Newton military officers had been counselled to derive a sequence that met two criteria: the code should be almost impossible to forget and should not be something straightforward, like all the phone numbers in the family, that an outside party might work out easily from the personnel files.

For sentimental reasons, O'Toole had wanted nine of the numbers in his code to be his birthdate, 3-29-42, and the birthdate of his wife, 2-7-46. He knew that any decryption specialist would immediately look for such obvious selections, so the general resolved to hide the birthdates in the fifty digits. But what about the other forty-one? That particular number, forty-one, had intrigued O'Toole ever since a beer and pizza party during his sophomore year at MIT. One of his associates then, a brilliant young number theorist whose name he had long since forgotten, had told O'Toole in the middle of a drunken discussion that 41 was a 'very special number, the initial integer in the longest continuous string of quadratic primes'.

O'Toole never fully comprehended what exactly was meant by the expression 'quadratic prime'. However, he did understand, and was fascinated by, the fact that the string 41, 43, 47, 53, 61, 71, 83, 97, where each successive number was computed by increasing the difference from the previous number by two, resulted in exactly forty consecutive prime numbers. The sequence of primes ended only when the forty-first number in the string turned out to be a non-prime, namely 41 x 41 + 1681. O'Toole had shared this little-known piece of information only once in his life, with his wife Kathleen on her forty-first birthday, and he had received such a lacklustre response that he had never told anybody about it again.

But it was perfect for his secret code, particularly if he

disguised it properly. To build his fifty-digit number, General O'Toole first constructed a sequence of forty-one digits, each coming from the sum of the first two digits in the corresponding term in the special quadratic prime sequence beginning with 41. Thus '5' was the initial digit, representing 41, followed by '7' for 43, '1' for 47 (4 + 7 + 11 and then truncate), '8' for 53, etc. O'Toole next scattered the numbers of the two birthdates using an inverse Fibonacci sequence (34, 21, 13, 8, 5, 3, 2, 1, 1) to define the locations of the nine birthday integers in the original forty-one digit string.

It was not easy to commit the sequence to memory, but the general did not want to write it down and carry it with him to the activation process. If his code was written down, then anyone could use it, with or without his permission, and his option to change his mind again would be precluded. Once he had memorised the sequence, O'Toole destroyed all his computations and went to the dining room to have breakfast with the rest of the cosmonauts.

'Here's a copy of my code for you, Francesca, and one for you, Irina, and the final one goes to Hiro Yamanaka. Sorry, Janos,' Admiral Heilmann said with a big smile, 'but I'm all out of bullets. Maybe General O'Toole will let you enter his code into one of the bombs.'

'It's all right, Herr Admiral,' Janos said wryly. 'Some privileges in life I can do without.'

Heilmann was making a big production out of activating the nuclear weapons. He had had many copies of his fifty-digit number printed out and had enjoyed explaining to the other cosmonauts how clever he had been in the conception of his code. Now, with uncharacteristic flair, he was allowing the rest of the crew to participate in the process.

Francesca loved it. It was definitely good television. It occurred to O'Toole that Francesca had probably suggested such a staging to Heilmann, but the general didn't spend much time thinking about it. O'Toole was too busy being astonished by how calm he himself had become. After his long and agonising soul-searching, he was apparently going to perform his duty without qualms.

Admiral Heilmann became confused during the entering of his code (he admitted that he was nervous) and temporarily lost track of where he was in his sequence. The system designers had foreseen this possibility and had installed two lights, one green and one red, immediately above the numerical keyboards on the side of the bomb. After every tenth digit one of the two lights would illuminate, indicating whether or not the previous decade of code was a successful match. The safety committee had expressed concern that this 'extra' feature compromised the system (it would be easier to decrypt five ten-digit strings than one fifty-digit string), but repeated human engineering tests prior to launch had shown that the lights were necessary.

At the end of his second decade of digits, Heilmann was greeted by the flashing red light. 'I've done something wrong,' he said, his embarrassment obvious.

'Louder,' shouted Francesca from where she was filming. She had neatly framed the ceremony so that both the weapons and the pods appeared in the picture.

'I've made a mistake,' Admiral Heilmann proclaimed. 'All this noise has distracted me. I must wait thirty seconds before I can start again.'

After Heilmann had successfully completed his code, Dr Brown entered the activation code on the second weapon. He seemed almost bored; certainly he didn't push the keyboard with anything approaching enthusiasm. Irina Turgenyev activated the third bomb. She made a short but passionate comment underscoring her belief that the destruction of Rama was absolutely essential.

Neither Hiro Yamanaka nor Francesca said anything at all. Francesca, however, did impress the rest of the crew by doing her first thirty digits from memory. Considering that she had supposedly never seen Heilmann's code until an hour earlier, and had not been alone for more than two minutes since then, her feat was quite remarkable.

Next it was General O'Toole's turn. Smiling comfortably, he walked easily up to the first weapon. The other cosmonauts applauded, both showing their respect for the general and acknowledging his struggle. He asked everyone please to be quiet, explaining that he had committed his whole sequence to memory. Then O'Toole entered the first decade of digits.

He stopped for a second as the green light flashed. In that instant an image flashed into his mind of one of the frescoes on the second floor of the shrine of St Michael in Rome. A young man in a blue robe, his eyes uplifted to the heavens, was standing on the steps of the Victor Emmanuel Monument, preaching to an appreciative multitude. General O'Toole heard a voice, loudly and distinctly. The voice said 'No.'

The general spun round quickly. 'Did anybody say anything?' he said, staring at the other cosmonauts. They shook their heads. Befuddled, O'Toole turned back to the bomb. He tried to remember the second decade of digits. But it was no good. His heart was racing at breakneck speed. His mind kept saying, over and over again, *What was that voice?* His resolve to perform his duty had vanished.

Michael O'Toole took a deep breath, turned around again, and walked across the huge bay. When he passed his stunned colleagues he heard Admiral Heilmann yell, 'What are you doing?'

'I'm going to my room,' O'Toole said without breaking stride.

'Aren't you going to activate the bombs?' Dr Brown said behind him.

'No,' replied General O'Toole. 'At least, not yet.'

56

An Answered Prayer

General O'Toole stayed in his room for the rest of the day. Admiral Heilmann dropped by about an hour after O'Toole's failure to enter his code. After some meaningless small talk (Heilmann was terrible at that sort of thing), the admiral asked the all-important question.

'Are you ready to proceed with the activation?'

O'Toole shook his head. 'I thought I was this morning, Otto, but....' There was no need for him to say anything more.

Heilmann rose from his chair. 'I've given orders for Yamanaka to take the first two bullets to the passageway inside Rama. They'll be there by dinner if you change your mind. The other three will be left in the bay for the time being.' He stared at his colleague for several seconds. 'I hope you come to your senses before too much longer, Michael. We're already in deep trouble at headquarters.'

When Francesca came in with her camera two hours later, it was clear from her choice of words that the attitude toward the general, at least among the remaining cosmonauts, was that O'Toole was suffering from acute nervous tensions. He wasn't being defiant. He wasn't making a statement. None of the rest of the crew could have tolerated those alternatives, because they would all look bad by association. No, it was obvious that there was something wrong with his nerves.

'I've told everyone not to bother you with calls,' Francesca said compassionately as she glanced around the room, her television mind already framing the images of the coming interview. 'The phones have been ringing like crazy, especially since I sent down the tape from this morning.' She walked over to his desk, checking the objects on its top. 'Is this Michael of Siena?' Francesca asked, picking up the small statue.

O'Toole managed a wan smile. 'Yes,' he said. 'And I think you know the man on the cross in the picture.'

'Very well,' Francesca replied. 'Very well indeed.... Look, Michael, you know what's coming. I would like this interview to paint you in the best possible light. Not that I'm going to treat you with kid gloves, you understand, but I want to make certain that those wolves down there hear your side of the story –'

'They're already screaming for my hide?' O'Toole interrupted.

'Oh, yes,' she answered. 'And it will get much worse. The longer you delay activating the bombs, the more wrath will be aimed at you.'

'But why?' O'Toole protested. 'I haven't committed a crime. I've simply delayed activating a weapon whose destructive power exceeds –'

'That's irrelevant,' Francesca retorted. 'In *their* eyes, you haven't done your job, namely to protect the people on the planet Earth. They're frightened. They don't understand all this extraterrestrial crap. They've been told that Rama will be destroyed and now you've refused to remove their nightmares.'

'Nightmares,' mumbled O'Toole, 'that's what Bothwell....'

'What about President Bothwell?' enquired Francesca.

'Oh, nothing,' he said. He looked away from her probing eyes. 'What else?' O'Toole asked impatiently.

'As I was saying, I want you to look as good as possible. Comb your hair again and put on a fresh uniform, not a flight suit. I'll daub a little make-up on your face so you don't look washed out.' She returned to the desk. 'We'll place your family photos in full view next to Jesus and Michael. Think carefully about what you're going to say. Of course, I'll ask why you failed to activate the weapons this morning.'

Francesca walked over and put her hand on O'Toole's shoulder. 'In my introduction I will have suggested that you've been under a strain. I don't want to put words in your mouth, but admitting a little weakness will probably play well. Particularly in your country.'

General O'Toole squirmed while Francesca finished the preparations for the interview. 'Do I have to do this?' he asked, becoming more and more uncomfortable as the journalist rearranged his room.

'Only if you want anybody to think you're not Benedict Arnold,' was her curt reply.

Janos came in to visit just before dinner. 'Your interview with Francesca was very good,' he lied. 'At least you raised some moral issues that all of us should consider.'

'It was dumb of me to bring up all that philosophical crap,' O'Toole fretted. 'I should have followed Francesca's advice and blamed everything on my fatigue.'

'Well, Michael,' said Janos, 'what's done is done. I didn't come in here to review the events of the day. I'm certain you've done that plenty of times already. I came in here to see if I could be any help.'

'I don't think so, Janos,' he replied. 'But I do appreciate the thought.'

There was a long hiatus in the conversation. At length Janos stood up and shuffled toward the door. 'What do you do now?' he asked quietly.

'I wish I knew,' O'Toole answered. 'I don't seem to be able to come up with a plan.'

The combined Rama-Newton spacecraft continued to hurtle toward the Earth. With each passing day the Rama threat loomed greater, a huge cylinder moving at hyperbolic speed toward what would be a calamitous impact if no new midcourse corrections were made. The estimated crash point was in the state of Tamil Nadu, in south India, not far from the city of Madurai. Physicists were on the network news every night, explaining what could be expected. Shock waves and ejecta became terms bandied about at dinner parties.

Michael O'Toole was vilified by the global press. Francesca had been right. The American general became the focus of a world's fury. There were even suggestions that he should be court-martialled and executed, on board the Newton, for his failure to follow orders. A lifetime of important accomplishments and selfless contributions was forgotten. Kathleen O'Toole was forced to leave the family apartment in Boston and take refuge with a friend in Maine.

The general was tortured by his indecision. He knew that he was doing irreparable damage to his family and his career by his failure to activate the weapons. But each time he convinced himself he was ready to execute the order, that loud and resounding 'No' echoed again in his ears.

O'Toole was only marginally coherent in his final interview with Francesca, the day before the scientific ship left to return to the Earth. She asked some very tough questions. When Francesca asked him why, if Rama were going to orbit the Earth, it had not yet made a deflection manoeuvre, the general perked up momentarily and reminded her that aerobraking – dissipating energy in the atmosphere as heat – was the most efficient method of achieving orbit around a planetary body with an atmosphere. But when she gave him a chance to amplify his statement, to discuss how Rama might reconfigure itself to have aerodynamic surfaces, O'Toole did not answer. He just stared at her distractedly.

O'Toole came out of his room for the final dinner the night before Brown, Sabatini, Tabori and Turgenyev departed for home. His presence spoiled the last supper. Irina was extremely unpleasant to him, upbraiding the general venomously, and refusing to sit at the same table. David Brown ignored him altogether, choosing instead to discuss in excruciating detail the laboratory being designed in Texas to accommodate the captured crab biot. Only Francesca and Janos were friendly, so General O'Toole returned to his room straight after dinner without formally saying goodbye to anyone.

The next morning, less than an hour after the scientific ship had left, O'Toole buzzed Admiral Heilmann and asked for a meeting. 'So you have finally changed your mind?' the German said excitedly when the general entered his office. 'Good. It's not too late yet. It's only 1-12 days. If we hurry we can still detonate the bombs at 1-9.'

'I'm getting closer, Otto,' O'Toole replied, 'but I'm not there yet. I've been thinking about all this very carefully. There are two things I would still like to do. I'd like to talk to Pope John-Paul and I want to go inside to see Rama for myself.'

O'Toole's response left Heilmann deflated. 'Shit,' he said. 'Here we go again. We'll probably....'

'You don't understand, Otto,' the American said. He stared fixedly at his colleague. 'This is good news. Unless something totally unexpected occurs, either during my call to the pope or while I'm exploring Rama, I'll be ready to enter my code the minute I come out.'

'Are you certain?' Heilmann asked.

'I give you my word,' O'Toole replied.

General O'Toole held nothing back in his long, emotional transmission to the pope. He was aware that his call was being monitored, but it no longer mattered. A single thing was uppermost in his mind: making the decision to activate the nuclear weapons with a clear conscience.

He waited impatiently for the reply. When Pope John-Paul V finally appeared on the screen, he was sitting in the same room in the Vatican where O'Toole had had his audience just after Christmas. The pope was holding a small electronic pad in his right hand and occasionally glanced down as he spoke.

'I have prayed with you, my son,' the pontiff began in his precise English, 'particularly during this last week of your personal turmoil. I cannot tell you what to do. I do

not have the answers any more than you do. We can only
hope together that God, in His wisdom, will provide
unambiguous answers to your prayers.

'In response to some of your religious enquiries,
however, I can make a few comments. I offer them to you
in the hope that they will be helpful ... I cannot say
whether or not the voice you heard was that of St
Michael, or if you had what is known as a religious
experience. I can affirm that there is a category of human
experience, usually called religious for lack of a better
term, that exists and cannot be explained in purely
rational or scientific terms. Saul or Tarsus was definitely
blinded by a light from the heavens as part of his
conversion to Christianity, before he became the apostle
Paul. Your voice may have been St Michael. Only you
can decide.

'As we discussed three months ago, God certainly
created the Ramans, whoever they were. But he also
created the viruses and bacteria that cause human death
and suffering. We cannot glorify God, either individually
or as a species, if we do not survive. It seems unlikely to
me that God would expect us to take no action if our very
survival were threatened.

'The possible role of Rama as a herald for the second
coming of Christ is a difficult issue. There are some
priests inside the church who agree with St Michael,
although they are a distinct minority. Most of us feel that
the Rama craft are too spiritually sterile to be heralds.
They are incredible engineering marvels, to be sure, but
there is nothing about them that suggests any warmth or
compassion or any other redeeming characteristic that is
associated with Christ. It therefore seems very unlikely
that Rama has any strictly religious significance.

'In the end it is a decision you must make yourself.
You must continue your prayers, as I'm certain you
realise, but perhaps you should expect a little less fanfare
in God's response. He does not speak to everyone in the
same way; nor will each of His messages to you come in
the same form. Please remember one more thing. As you
explore Rama in search of God's will, the prayers of

many on Earth will go with you. You can be certain that God will give you an answer; your challenge is to identify and interpret it.'

John-Paul ended his transmission with a blessing and a recitation of the Lord's prayer. General O'Toole knelt automatically and spoke the words along with his spiritual leader. When the screen was blank, he reviewed what the pontiff had said and felt reassured. *I must be on the right track*, O'Toole said to himself. *But I should not expect a heavenly proclamation with accompanying trumpets.*

O'Toole was not prepared for his powerful emotional response to Rama. Perhaps it was the sheer scale of the spacecraft, so much larger than anything ever built by human beings. Perhaps also his long confinement on the Newton and heightened emotional state contributed to the intensity of his feelings. Whatever the reasons, Michael O'Toole was totally overwhelmed by the spectacle as he made his solitary way into the giant spacecraft.

There was no specific feature that dominated the rest in O'Toole's mind. His throat caught and his eyes brimmed with tears of wonder on several different occasions: riding down the chairlift on his initial descent and looking out across the Central Plain, with its long illuminated strips which were Rama's light; standing beside the rover on the shores of the Cylindrical Sea and staring through his binoculars at the mysterious skyscrapers of New York; and gawking many times, like all the cosmonauts before him, at the gigantic horns and buttresses that adorned the southern bowl. O'Toole's dominant feelings were awe and reverence, much as he had felt the first time he had entered one of the old European cathedrals.

He spent the Raman night at Beta, using one of the extra huts left by the cosmonauts on the second sortie. He found Wakefield's message dated two weeks earlier, and had a momentary desire to assemble the sailboat and cross over to New York. But O'Toole restrained himself and focused on the true purpose of his visit.

He admitted to himself that although Rama was a spectaculiar achievement, its magnificence should not be a relevant factor in his evaluation process. Was there anything he had seen that would cause him to alter his tentative conclusion? *No*, he grudgingly answered his own question. When the lights came on again inside the giant cylinder, O'Toole was confident that before the next Raman nightfall he would activate the weapons.

Still he procrastinated. He drove the entire width of the coastline, examining New York and the other vistas from different vantage points and observing the five-hundred-metre cliff on the opposite side of the sea. On one last pass through the Beta campsite, O'Toole decided to pick up some odds and ends, including a few personal mementoes left behind by the other crew members in their hasty retreat from Rama. Not many items had escaped the hurricane, but he found some souvenirs that had been trapped in corners against the supply crates.

General O'Toole took a long nap before he guided the rover back to the bottom of the chairlift. Realising what he was going to do when he reached the Newton, O'Toole knelt down and prayed one last time before ascending. Shortly into his ride, when he was still less than half a kilometre above the Central Plain, he turned his chair and looked back across the Raman panorama. *Soon this will all be gone*, O'Toole thought, *enveloped in a solar furnace unleashed by man*. His eyes lifted from the plain and focused on New York. He thought he saw a moving black speck in the Raman sky.

With trembling hands he lifted his binoculars to his eyes. In a few seconds O'Toole located the enlarged speck. He quickly changed the binocular resolution and the speck split into three parts, each a bird soaring in formation far off in the distance. O'Toole blinked but the image did not change. There were indeed three birds flying in the Raman sky!

Joy filled General O'Toole. He yelled with delight as he followed the birds with his binoculars until he could no longer see them. The remaining thirty minutes of the ride to the top of the Alpha stairway seemed like a lifetime.

The American officer immediately climbed into another chair and descended again into Rama. He wanted desperately to see those birds one more time. *If I could somehow photograph them*, he thought, planning to drive back to the Cylindrical Sea if necessary, *then I could prove to everyone that there are also living creatures in this amazing world*.

From two kilometres above the floor, O'Toole searched in vain for the birds as he descended. Only slightly disheartened by his failure to find them, he was subsequently dumbfounded by what he saw when he dropped his binoculars from his eyes and prepared to disembark from the chair. Richard Wakefield and Nicole des Jardins were standing side by side at the bottom of the lift.

General O'Toole embraced them each with a vigorous hug and then, with tears of happiness running down his cheeks, he knelt on the soil of Rama. 'Dear God,' he said as he offered his silent prayer of thanks. 'Dear God,' he repeated.

57

Three's Company

The three cosmonauts talked avidly for over an hour.
There was so much to tell. When Nicole told of her fright
upon encountering the dead Takagishi in the octospider
lair, O'Toole was momentarily silent and then shook his
head. 'There are so many unanswered questions here,' he
said, staring up at the high ceiling. 'Are you really
malevolent after all?' he asked rhetorically.

Richard and Nicole both praised the general's courage
in not entering his code to activate the weapons. They
were also both horrified that the COG had ordered the
destruction of Rama. 'It is absolutely unforgivable for us
to use nuclear weapons against this spaceship,' Nicole
said. 'I am convinced that it is not fundamentally hostile.
And I believe that Rama manoeuvred to intercept the
Earth because it has a specific message for us.

Richard lightly chided Nicole for developing her opinion more on the basis of emotions than facts. 'Perhaps,' she
rejoined, 'but there is a serious logical flaw as well in this
decision to destroy. We now have hard evidence that this
vehicle communicated with its predecessor. There is good
reason to suspect that a Rama III is out there somewhere,
probably coming in this direction. If the Rama fleet *is*
potentially hostile, there is no way the Earth will be able to
escape. We may succeed in destroying this second craft –
but in so doing we will almost certainly alert their next
ship. Since their technology is so much more advanced
than ours, we would have no possibility of surviving their
concerted attack.'

General O'Toole looked at Nicole with admiration. 'That's an excellent point,' he said. 'It's a shame you weren't available for the ISA discussions. We never considered –'

'Why don't we postpone the rest of this conversation until we're back on the Newton?' Richard said suddenly. 'According to my watch, it will be dark again in another thirty minutes, before any of us have reached the top of the lift. I don't want to ride in the dark any longer than is necessary.'

Each of the three cosmonauts believed that they were leaving Rama for the last time. As the remaining minutes of light dwindled, each gazed intently at the magnificent alien landscape stretching out into the distance. For Nicole, the dominant feeling was one of elation. Cautious by nature with her expectations, until this moment in the chairlift she had not allowed herself the intense pleasure of believing that she would ever again hold her beloved Genevieve in her arms. Her mind was now flooded by the bucolic beauty of Beauvois and she imagined in detail the joy of her reunion scene with her father and daughter. *It could be as little as a week or ten days*, Nicole said to herself expectantly. By the time she reached the top she was having difficulty containing her jubilation.

During his ride Michael O'Toole reviewed, one more time, his activation decision. When dark came to Rama, suddenly and at the predicted moment, he had finished developing his plan for communicating his conclusion to the Earth. They would phone ISA management immediately. Nicole and Richard would summarise their stories and Nicole would present her reasons for thinking that the destruction of Rama would be 'unforgivable'. O'Toole was convinced that his order to activate the weapons would then be rescinded.

The general switched on his flashlight just before his chair reached the top of the stairway. He stepped off in the weightless environment and stood beside Nicole. They waited for Richard Wakefield before proceeding together around the ramp to the ferry passageway, only a hundred metres away. After the trio had boarded the ferry and were ready to move through the Rama shell toward the Newton, Richard's flashlight beam fell on a large metal object on the side of the passage. 'Is that one of the bombs?' he asked.

The nuclear weapon system did indeed resemble an oversized bullet. *How curious*, Nicole thought, recoiling as an instant shudder ran through her system. *It could be any shape of course, I wonder what subconscious aberration made the designers choose that particular form....*

'But what's that weird contraption at the top?' Richard was asking O'Toole.

The general's brow furrowed as he stared at an unfamiliar object illuminated by the centre of the beam of light. 'I don't know,' he confessed. 'I've never seen it before.' He disembarked from the ferry. Richard and Nicole followed him.

General O'Toole shuffled over to the weapon and studied the strange attachment fixed above the numerical keyboard. It was a flat plate, slightly larger than the keyboard itself, that was anchored by angular joints to the sides of the weapon. On the underside of the plate, momentarily retracted, were ten tiny punches – at least, that's how they appeared to O'Toole. His observation was confirmed seconds later when one of the punches extended and hit the number '5' on the keyboard several centimetres below. The '5' was followed by a '7', and then by eight more numbers before a green light flashed the successful completion of the first decade.

Within seconds the apparatus entered ten more digits and another green light flashed. O'Toole froze in terror. *My God*, he thought, *that's my code! Somehow they've broken....* His panic subsided an instant later when, after the third decade of digits, the red light announced that an error had been made.

'Apparently,' General O'Toole said a short time later in response to an enquiry from Richard, 'they have jerry-rigged this scheme to try to enter the code in my absence. They only have the first two decades correct. For a moment I was afraid....' O'Toole paused, aware of strong emotions stirring within him.

'They must have assumed you weren't coming back,' Nicole said in a matter-of-fact tone.

'If Heilmann and Yamanaka did it,' O'Toole replied. 'Of course we can't rule out completely the possibility that the contraption might have been placed there by the aliens ... or even the biots.'

'Extremely unlikely,' Richard commented. 'The engineering is much too crude.'

'At any rate,' O'Toole said, opening his backpack for some tools to disconnect the apparatus, 'I'm not taking any chances.'

At the Newton end of the passageway, O'Toole, Wakefield, and des Jardins found the second bomb fitted with the same apparatus. The trio watched it punch out one code attempt – with the same result, a failure somewhere in the third decade – and then they disabled it as well. Afterwards they opened up the seal and departed from Rama.

Nobody greeted them when they stepped inside the Newton military ship. General O'Toole assumed that both Admiral Heilmann and Yamanaka were asleep and went immediately to the bedrooms. He wanted to talk to Heilmann in private anyway. But the two men were not in their rooms. It did not take long to confirm, in fact, that the other two cosmonauts were nowhere in the comparatively small living and working area of the military ship.

A search of the supply area in the back of the ship was also futile. However, the threesome did discover that one of the EVA pods was missing. This discovery raised another perplexing set of questions. Where could Heilmann and Yamanaka have gone in the pod? And why had they violated the top-priority project policy that at least one crew member should always stay on board the Newton?

The three cosmonauts were puzzled as they returned to the control centre to discuss their possible courses of action. O'Toole was the first to raise the spectre of foul play. 'Do you think those octospiders, or even some of the biots, might have come on board? After all, it's not difficult to enter the Newton unless it's in Self-Protection Mode.'

Nobody wanted to say what all three of them were thinking. If someone or something had captured or killed their two colleagues on the ship, then it might still be around and *they* might be in danger themselves....

'Why don't we call the Earth and announce that we're alive?' Richard said, breaking the silence.

General O'Toole smiled. 'Great idea.' He moved over to the control centre console and activated the panel. A standard system status display appeared on the large screen. 'That's strange,' the general commented. 'According to this, we have no video link with the Earth presently. Only low rate telemetry. Now why would the data system configuration have been changed?'

He keyed in a simple set of commands to establish the normal multichannel high-rate link with the Earth. A swarm of error messages appeared on the monitor. 'What the hell?' Richard exclaimed. 'It looks as if the video system has died.' He turned to O'Toole. 'This is your speciality, General. What do you make of all this?'

General O'Toole was very serious. 'I don't like it, Richard. I've only seen this many error messages one time before – during one of our early simulations when some nincompoop forgot to load the communications software. We must have a major software problem. The probability of that many hardware failures in such a short time span is essentially zero.'

Richard suggested that O'Toole subject the video communications software to its standard self-test. During the test, the diagnostic printout reported that the error buffers in the self-test algorithm had overflowed when the procedure was less than one percent complete. 'So the vidcomm software is definitely the culprit,' Richard said, analysing the data in the diagnostic. He entered some commands. 'It's going to take a while to straighten it out.'

'Just a minute,' Nicole interrupted. 'Shouldn't we

spend our time trying to make some sense out of all this new information before we start on any specific tasks?' The two men stopped their activity and waited for her to continue. 'Heilmann, Yamanaka, and one pod are missing from the ship,' Nicole said, walking slowly around the control centre, 'and someone was trying to automatically activate the two nuclear bombs in the passageway. Meanwhile the vidcomm software, after functioning properly for hundreds of days – counting all the preflight simulations – has suddenly gone haywire. Do either of you have a coherent explanation for all this?'

There was a long silence, 'General O'Toole's suggestion of a hostile invasion of the Newton might work,' Richard offered. 'Heilmann and Yamanaka might have fled to save themselves and the aliens could have deliberately screwed up the software.'

Nicole was not convinced. 'Nothing I have seen suggests that any aliens, or even any biots for that matter, have been inside the Newton. Unless we see some evidence....'

'Maybe Heilmann and Yamanaka were trying to break the general's code,' Wakefield invented, 'and they were afraid –'

'Stop, Stop,' Nicole shouted suddenly. 'Something's happening to the screen.' The two men turned around just in time to see Admiral Otto Heilmann's face materialise on the monitor.

'Hello, General O'Toole,' Heilmann said with a smile from the huge screen. 'This videotape was triggered by your entering the Newton airlock. Cosmonaut Yamanaka and I prepared it just before we departed in one of the pods three hours before 1-9 days. We were ordered to evacuate less than an hour after you went inside to explore Rama. We delayed as long as we could but eventually had to follow our instructions.

'Your personal orders are simple and straightforward. You are to enter your activation code into the two weapons in the ferry passageway and the three remaining in the bay. You should depart in the final pod no more than eight hours thereafter. Don't be concerned about the electronic devices in operation on the two bombs in the Raman shell. COG military headquarters ordered them put in place to test some new top secret decryption techniques. You will discover they can easily be disabled with pliers and/or wirecutters.

'An extra, emergency propulsion system has been added to the pod and its software has been programmed to guide you to a safe location, where you will rendezvous with an ISA tug. All you need to do is code in the exact time of your departure. However, I must stress that the new pod-navigation algorithms are valid *only* if you leave the Newton *before* 1-6 days. After that time, I am told the guidance parameters become increasingly invalid and it will be almost impossible to rescue you.'

There was a short pause in Heilmann's delivery and his voice took on an increased sense of urgency. 'Don't waste any more time, Michael. Activate the weapons and go directly to the pod. We have already supplied it with the food and other essentials that you will need … Good luck on your voyage home. We'll see you back on Earth.'

58
Hobson's Choice

'I'm certain that Heilmann and Yamanaka were being extremely cautious,' Richard Wakefield explained. 'They probably left early so they could take extra supplies. And with these lightweight pods, each extra kilogram can be critical.'

'*How critical?*' asked Nicole.

'Well – it could make all the difference between getting into a safe orbit round Earth – or shooting past it so quickly that we couldn't be rescued.'

'Does that mean,' O'Toole enquired sombrely, 'that only one of us might be able to use the pod?'

Richard paused before answering. 'I'm afraid that's possible; it's a function of the time of departure. We'll have to do some quick calculations to determine exactly. But personally I see no reason why we shouldn't consider flying this entire spacecraft. I was trained as a backup pilot after all ... We have only limited control authority, since the ship is so large, but if we jettison everything we don't absolutely need, we may be able to do it ... Again, we'll need to do the computations.'

Nicole's assignments from General O'Toole and Richard were to check the supplies which had been placed in the pod, determine their adequacy, and then approximate both the mass and packaging volume required to support either two or three travellers. In additon Richard, still favouring flying back to Earth in the military ship, asked Nicole to go through the Newton supply manifest and estimate how much mass could be thrown overboard.

While O'Toole and Wakefield used the computers in the control centre, Nicole worked alone in the huge bay. First she examined the remaining pod very carefully.

Although the pods were normally used by a single person for local extravehicular activity, they had also been designed as emergency escape vehicles. Two people could sit behind the tough, transparent front window with a week's supplies on the shelves at the rear of the small cabin. *But three people?* Nicole wondered. *Impossible. Someone would have to squeeze into the shelf space. And then there would not be adequate room for the supplies.* Nicole thought momentarily about being confined to the tiny shelves for seven or eight days. *It would be even worse than the pit in New York.*

She looked through the supplies that had been hastily thrown into the pod by Heilmann and Yamanaka. The food allocation was more or less correct, both in quantity and variety, for a one-week voyage; the medical kit, however, was woefully inadequate. Nicole made a few notes, constructed what she considered to be a proper supply list for a two-person crew, and estimated the mass and packaging requirements. She then started to cross the bay.

Her eyes were drawn to the bullet-shaped nuclear weapons lying placidly on their sides right beside the pod airlock. Nicole walked over and touched the bombs, her hands idly running across the polished metal surface. *So these are the first great weapons of destruction,* she thought, *the outcome of the brilliant physics of the twentieth century.*

What a sad commentary on our species, Nicole mused, as she was walking among the nuclear bombs. *A visitor comes to see us. It cannot speak our language, but it does discover where we live. When it turns the corner on to our street, while its purpose is still utterly unknown, we blast it into oblivion.*

She shuffled across the bay toward the living quarters, aware of a profound feeling of sadness deep within her. *Your problem,* Nicole said to herself, *is that you always expect too much. From yourself. From those you love. Even from the human race. We are as yet too immature a species.*

A momentary wave of nausea forced Nicole to stop for a moment. *What's this?* she thought. *Are these bombs making me ill?* In the back of her mind Nicole recalled a similar feeling of nausea fifteen years before, two hours into her flight from Los Angeles to Paris. *It can't be,* she told herself. *But I'll check just to be certain....*

'That's the second reason why the three of us cannot fit in a single pod. Don't feel bad, Nicole. Even if the physical space could accommodate our bodies and the requisite supplies, the velocity-change capability of the pod with all that mass is barely enough to close the orbit around the Sun. Our chances of being rescued would be virtually nil.'

'Well,' Nicole replied to Richard, trying to be cheerful, 'at least we still have the other option. We can go home in this big vehicle. According to my estimates, we can dump in excess of ten thousand kilograms –'

'I'm afraid it doesn't matter,' General O'Toole interrupted.

Nicole looked at Richard. 'What's he talking about?'

Richard Wakefield stood up and walked over to Nicole. He took her hands in his. 'They screwed up the navigation system too,' Richard said. 'Their automatic search algorithms, the big number-crunchers being used to try to decrypt O'Toole's code, were overlaid into the general purpose computers on top of the vidcomm and navigation subroutines. This ship is useless as a transportation module.'

General O'Toole's voice was distant and lacked its usual upbeat timbre. 'They must have started only minutes after I left. Richard read the command buffers and found out that the decryption software was uplinked less than two hours after my departure.'

'But why would they incapacitate the Newton?' Nicole asked.

'Don't you understand?' O'Toole said with passion. 'The priorities had changed. Nothing was as important as detonating the nuclear weapons. They didn't want to waste the time from the radio signals to go back and forth to Earth. So they moved the computations up here, where each successive candidate code could be commanded from the computer without delay.'

'In fairness to mission control,' Richard interjected, now pacing around the room, 'we should acknowledge that the fully-loaded Newton military ship actually has less orbit change capability than a two-person pod with an auxiliary propulsion system. In the eyes of the ISA safety manager, there was no increased risk associated with making this craft inoperable.'

'But none of this should have happened in the first place,' the general argued. 'Damnit! Why couldn't they just have waited for my return?'

Nicole sat down abruptly in one of the available chairs. Her head was spinning and she felt momentarily dizzy. 'What's the matter?' Richard said, approaching her with alarm.

'I've been having occasional periods of nausea today,' Nicole replied. 'I think I'm pregnant. I'll know for certain in about twenty minutes.' She smiled at the dumbfounded Richard. 'It's extremely rare for a woman to become pregnant within ninety days of an injection of neutrabriolate. But it has happened before. I don't suppose –'

'Congratulations,' an enthusiastic General O'Toole suddenly interrupted. 'I had no idea that the two of you were planning to have a family.'

'Nor did I,' Richard replied, still looking shocked. He gave Nicole a vigorous hug and held her close. 'Nor did I,' he repeated.

'There will be no more discussion of this subject,' General O'Toole said emphatically to Richard. 'Even if Nicole weren't pregnant with your child, I would insist that the two of you go in the pod and leave me here. It's the only sensible decision. In the first place, we both know that mass is the most critical parameter and I am by far the heaviest of us. In addition, I am old and you two are both quite young. You know how to fly the pod; I've never even trained inside it a single time. Besides,' he added dryly, 'I will be court-martialled on Earth for refusing to follow orders.

'As for you, my good doctor,' O'Toole continued moments later, 'I don't need to tell you that you are carrying a very special baby. He or she will be the only human child which was ever conceived inside an extraterrestrial space vehicle.' He stood up and glanced around. 'Now,' he said, 'I propose we open a bottle of wine and celebrate our last evening together.'

Nicole watched General O'Toole glide over to the larder. He opened it and started rummaging around. 'I'm perfectly happy with fruit juice, Michael,' she said. 'I shouldn't drink more than a single glass of wine now anyway.'

'Of course,' he replied quickly. 'I temporarily forgot. I was hoping that we could do something special on this last night. I wanted to share one last time....' General O'Toole stopped himself and brought the wine and juice back to the table. He handed cups to both Richard and Nicole. 'I want you both to know,' he said quietly, his mood now subdued, 'that I cannot imagine a finer pair of people than the two of you. I wish you every success, especially with the baby.'

The three cosmonauts drank in silence for several seconds. 'We all know it, don't we?' General O'Toole said in a barely audible tone. 'The missiles must be on their way. How long do you figure I have, Richard?'

'Judging from what Admiral Heilmann said on the tape, I would say that the first missile will reach Rama at 1-5 days. That would be consistent both with the pod being outside the debris field and the deflection velocities that must be imparted to the surviving pieces of the spacecraft.'

'You two have lost me,' Nicole said. 'What missiles are we talking about?'

Richard leaned over toward her. 'Both Michael and I are certain,' he said gravely, 'that the COG has ordered a missile strike against Rama. They had no assurance that the general would ever return to the Newton and enter his code. And the search algorithm with the automatic punch was a long shot at best. Only a missile strike could guarantee that Rama would not have the capability of harming our planet.'

'So I have a little more than forty-eight hours to make my final peace with God,' General O'Toole said after reflecting for several seconds. 'I have lived a fabulous life. I have much to be thankful for. I will go into His arms without regret.'

59
Dream of Destiny

As Nicole stretched her arms over her head and to her sides, she brushed agianst Richard on her left and one of the water containers hanging slightly out of the shelf behind her. 'It's going to be crowded,' she observed, squirming in her seat.

'Yes, it is,' Richard replied distractedly. His attention was focused on the display in front of the pilot's seat in the pod. He entered some commands and waited for the response. When it finally came, Richard frowned.

'I guess I'll make one more attempt to repackage the supplies,' Nicole said with a sigh. She turned around in her seat and stared at the shelves. 'I could save us some room and fourteen kilograms if our rescue was guaranteed in seven days,' she said.

Richard did not respond. 'Damnit,' he muttered when a set of numbers appeared on the display.

'What's the matter?' Nicole asked.

'There's something not quite right here,' Richard said. 'The navigation code was developed for considerably less payload mass – it may not converge if we lose one of the accelerometers.' Nicole waited patiently for Richard to explain. 'So if we have any hiccoughs along the way, we will probably have to stop for several hours and reinitialise.'

'But I thought you said there was plenty of fuel for the two of us?'

'Plenty of fuel, yes. However, there are some subtleties in the reprogrammed navigation algorithms that assume the pod contains less than a hundred kilograms, basically only O'Toole and his supplies.'

Nicole could read the concern in Richard's brow. 'We're all right, I think, if there are no malfunctions,' he continued. 'but no pod has ever been operated under conditions like this.'

Through the front window they could see General O'Toole walking across the bay toward them. He was carrying a small object in his hand. It was TB, one of Richard's tiny Shakespearean robots.

'I almost forgot I had him,' O'Toole said a minute later after he had been thanked profusely by Richard. Cosmonaut Wakefield was soaring around the supply depot like a joyous child, a wide smile on his delighted face.

'I thought I'd never see any of them again,' Richard yelled from one of the side walls where his exuberant momentum had carried him.

'I was passing your room,' General O'Toole shouted back, 'just before the scientific ship departed. Cosmonaut Tabori was arranging your things. He asked me to keep that particular robot, just in case....'

'Thank you, thank you, Janos,' Richard said. He walked carefully down the wall and anchored himself to the floor. 'This is a very special one, Michael,' he said with a gleam in his eye. He switched on TB's power. 'Do you know any Shakespearean sonnets?'

'There's one that Kathleen especially likes, if I can recall it. I think the first line is, "That time of year thou mayst"....'

'That time of year thou mayst in me behold
When yellow leaves, or none, or few, do hang
Upon those boughs which shake against the cold,
Bare ruined choirs where late the sweet birds sang.
In me thou seest the twilight of such day
As after sunset fadeth in the west....'

The feminine voice coming from TB startled both Nicole and General O'Toole. The words struck a resonant chord in O'Toole; he was deeply moved and a few tears welled up in the corners of his eyes. Nicole took the general's hand and squeezed it compassionately when TB was finished with the sonnet.

'You didn't say anything to Michael about the problems you found with the pod navigation,' Nicole said. She and Richard were lying side by side in one of the small bedrooms on the military ship.

'No,' replied Richard quietly. 'I didn't want to worry him. He believes that we are going to be safe and I don't want him to think differently.'

Nicole extended her arm and touched Richard. 'We could stay here, darling – then at least Michael would survive.'

He rolled over toward her. She could tell that he was looking at her even though she couldn't see him very clearly in the dark. 'I thought about that,' Richard said. 'But he would never accept it ... I even thought about sending you by yourself. Would you want to do that?'

'No,' Nicole answered after thinking for a moment. 'I don't think so. I'd rather go with you, unless....'

'Unless what?'

'Unless there really is a big difference in the odds. If one of us can survive but two of us are almost certainly doomed, it doesn't make much sense –'

'I can't give you an accurate probabilististic assessment,' Richard interrupted. 'But I don't think there's a major difference if we go together. My knowledge of the pod and its system might almost be worth the extra mass. But either way, we're better off in the pod than if we stay here.'

'You're absolutely convinced that missiles are on the way, aren't you?'

'Yes, indeed. Nothing else makes sense. I would bet that such a contingency plan was under development as soon as Rama changed course and headed for the Earth.'

They were silent again. Nicole tried to sleep but was unsuccessful. They had both decided to rest for six hours before departing so that they could store some energy for what would doubtless be an exhausting voyage. Nicole's mind, however, would not turn off. She kept imagining General O'Toole perishing in a nuclear fireball.

'He really is a wonderful man,' Nicole said very quietly. She wasn't certain if Richard was still awake.

'Yes, he is,' Richard answered in the same tone. 'I envy his inner strength. I can't imagine giving up my own life for someone else so willingly.' He paused for a moment. 'I guess that comes from his deep religious beliefs. He doesn't see death as an end, only as a transition.'

I could do it, Nicole thought. *I could give up my life for Genevieve. Maybe even for Richard and this unborn baby. Perhaps in O'Toole's religion everyone is part of his family.*

Richard, meanwhile, was struggling with his own emotions. Was he being selfish in not insisting that Nicole go alone? Could he really justify the extra risk of his presence in terms of his extra skills? He dismissed the questions and tried to think of something else.

'You haven't said much about the baby,' Nicole said softly after another short silence.

'I haven't really had time to integrate him, or her, into what's going on,' Richard replied. 'I guess I've been insensitive ... You know I'm happy about it. I just want to wait until we're rescued before I start thinking seriously about what it will be like to be a father.' He leaned over and gave Nicole a kiss. 'Now, darling, I hope you won't think I'm being rude, but I'm going to try to sleep. It could be a long time before we have another opportunity....'

'Of course,' she said. 'I'm sorry.' Nicole's mind drifted to another picture, this one of a small baby. *I wonder if he'll be intelligent*, she thought. *And will he have Richard's blue eyes and long fingers?*

Nicole was curled up in a ball in the corner of the dimly-lit room. The taste of manna melon was still in her mouth. She was awakened by a strange tapping on her shoulder. Nicole glanced up and saw the grey velvet avian bending over her. The cherry rings around its neck glowed in the dark. 'Come,' it said pleadingly. 'You must come with us.'

She followed the avian into the hallway and turned to

the right, away from the vertical corridor. The other
avians were standing quietly against the wall. They were
all watching her carefully. The whole procession
followed the grey avian down the tunnel.

In a few moments the tunnel expanded into a large
room. There was a solitary small light, on the far wall,
but otherwise the room was dark. Others were present,
but Nicole could not see them clearly. Occasionally she
glimpsed their silhouettes as they moved across the beam
from the single light source. Nicole started to say
something but the avian leader interrupted her. 'Shh,' it
said, 'they will be here soon.'

Nicole heard a noise coming toward them from the
opposite side of the room. It sounded like a cart with
wooden wheels moving on a dirt path. As it approached,
the avians around Nicole backed up and pressed against
her. Moments later there was a fire in front of them.

A bier was resting on top of a burning cart. Nicole
gasped. Her mother's body, dressed in regal green robes,
lay on top of the bier. In the light from the fire Nicole
could see some of the others in the room. Richard was
smiling at her, holding the hand of a dark little girl about
two years old. General O'Toole was very close to the fire,
kneeling in prayer beside it. Behind him were a variety of
biots and two or three odd forms that must have been
octospiders.

The flames consumed the bier and began to burn her
mother's body. Her mother rose slowly from her supine
position. When Anawi turned in Nicole's direction, her
face changed. It was Omeh's head on top of her mother's
body.

'Ronata,' he said distinctly, 'the prophecies must be
heeded. The Senoufo blood will be spread, even unto the
stars. Minowe will be left behind. Ronata must travel
with those who come from far away. Go now, and save
the strange ones and Ronata's children.'

60

Return to Rama

I can't believe I'm doing this, Nicole said to herself as she carried her final ferry-load of supplies to the heavy elevator at the top of the Beta stairway. It was dark inside Rama. The beam from her flashlight shone into the black void.

The dream had been so incredibly vivid that Nicole had been completely disorientated for more than five minutes after she woke up. Even now, almost two hours later, when she closed her eyes Nicole could see Omeh's face perfectly and hear this magical voice intoning the words. *I hope Richard doesn't wake up before I'm gone*, Nicole thought. *There's no way he would ever understand*.

She returned to the ferry and made one last trip through the shell toward the Newton. For thirty minutes she had been drafting her goodbye remarks in her mind, but now that the moment had come, Nicole was apprehensive. 'Dear Michael and dearest Richard,' she would begin, 'last night I had the most compelling dream of my life. The old Senoufo chieftain Omeh appeared to me and told me that my destiny was with Rama.'

Nicole passed through the airlock and entered the control centre. She sat down in front of the camera and cleared her voice. *This is ridiculous*, she thought, just before she turned on the lights. *I must be insane*. But the power of Omeh's image in her mind calmed all of her last minute doubts. Moments later she continued with her final remarks to her friends.

'There is no way I can summarise in this short farewell the importance of Omeh and my African background in my life. Michael, Richard can tell you some of the Senoufo stories as the two of you fly home to Earth. Suffice it to say that I have never been misled by the old shaman. I know well that voices in a dream have no substance and are most likely creations of my own subconscious, but nevertheless I have decided to follow the directions Omeh gave me.

'I intend to do whatever I can to communicate to Rama that nuclear missiles may be on the way. I don't know exactly how I will accomplish this, but I will have some hours to plan while I am assembling the sailboat to cross the Cylindrical Sea. I do remember, Richard, our discussion about the keyboard commands that might lead into the higher hierarchy....

'It is extremely difficult for me to say goodbye like this, and I am keenly aware that it is a poor substitute for a final embrace. But if you two were awake, you would never let me go back inside Rama ... I love you, Richard, never doubt it for a moment. I know it's unlikely, but maybe somehow, someday we will be united in another place. I promise you that if I survive to give birth to our child, I will never cease telling her about the intelligence, wit, and sensitivity of her father.

'I have one last request. If it turns out that either of you reach home safely and I never return to the Earth, please explain to Genevieve what happened to me. Tell her the whole story, about the dream, the vial and the vision, and the Poro when I was a child. And tell her that I loved her with all my heart.'

Tears were flowing down Nicole's cheeks when she finished her message. She stood up and rewound the tape. She played it for a minute, to make certain that it had recorded properly, and then walked over to the airlocks. *Goodness*, she thought as she put on her helmet, *I'm really going to do it*.

During Nicole's eerie descent on the chairlift in the dark she had strong misgivings abut her decision to return. It was only her supreme self-discipline that allowed her to chase away the lingering fears. As she climbed into the rover and started to drive toward the Cylindrical Sea, Nicole thought about how she would communicate with the intelligence governing Rama. *I'll definitely use* pictures, she said to herself, *and wherever possible the precise language of science. That much I have learned from Richard.*

The thought of Richard rekindled her anxieties. *He'll think that I have abandoned him,* she worried. *And how can I really expect him to think otherwise?* Nicole recalled the depressing first days of her pregnancy with Genevieve and how very lonely she had been, having nobody with whom she could share her feelings. Again she felt a strong call to turn around and leave Rama. Her introspection was broken by the spectacular arrival of light. Dawn had come again to Rama. As before, Nicole was mesmerised by the sights around her. *There's nothing like this anywhere in the universe.*

When she reached what had been the Beta campsite, she first found and started to unpack the large sailboat. It had been packed at the bottom of a large storage container. It was in good shape. Working to assemble the sailboat kept Nicole from brooding too much about her decision to leave the Newton. Mechanical assembly was not her forte. She almost despaired once when she had to disassemble a major fitting that had taken her ten minutes to put together in the first place. The entire exercise reminded her of several frustrating Christmas Eves at Beauvois when she and Pierre had worked almost all night to put Genevieve's new toys together. *There ought to be a law that stores can only sell assembled toys,* Nicole laughingly muttered as she struggled with the direction for the sailboat.

Nicole carried the hull of the boat down the steps and placed it next to the water. Each of the major substructures she assembled on the cliff above, where the light was brighter. She was so engrossed in her work that she did not hear the footsteps until they were only two or three metres away. When Nicole, who was working on her knees, turned to her right and saw something approaching her from very close, she was frightened almost out of her wits.

Moments later she and Richard were kissing and hugging. 'O'Toole's coming too,' he said, sitting down next to Nicole and immediately beginning to work on the sailboat. 'At first, when I explained that I wasn't leaving without you, that whatever life I could have on Earth wouldn't mean anything if you weren't with me, he told me that you and I were both crazy. But after we talked, and I explained to him that I thought we had a decent probability of warning the Ramans, he decided that he'd rather spend his last hours with us than take a chance on a lonely and painful death in the pod.'

'But I thought you said that it would be a safe trip for a solitary passenger?'

'It's not completely clear. The software loaded in the pod is a nightmare. You can tell from the programming that it was done hastily. And how could it have been checked properly? O'Toole by himself might have had a better chance than the two of us together ... But remember, he would face serious problems upon his arrival on Earth. That court martial comment was not idle chatter.'

'I don't think that Michael was afraid of a court martial. He might have wanted to spare his family, but –'

A shout from the distance interrupted their conversation. General O'Toole was waving at them from an approaching rover. 'But I don't understand,' Nicole said. 'How did he get here so quickly? You didn't walk, did you?'

Richard laughed. 'Of course not. I left a beacon at the bottom of the chairlift. After I arrived at Beta and saw that you had removed the sailboat and its parts, I sent the rover back on automatic.'

'That was brave of you,' Nicole said. 'What if I had set sail during the extra time that it took you to find me on foot?'

Richard peered over the cliff at the boat's hull down next to the water. 'Actually you've done better than I expected,' he said with a tease in his voice. 'You might have finished in another hour or two.'

He grabbed Nicole's hands as she tried to hit him.

General O'Toole was the only practised sailor among the three of them. Soon after they reached the midpoint of their sail, he relegated Richard to holding an oar as a possible weapon in case the pair of shark biots that were shadowing them decided to attack. 'It's not Marblehead or the Cape,' O'Toole said as he stared across at New York, 'but it's definitely an interesting sail.'

During the voyage Richard tried, without success, to convince a nervous Nicole that the shark biots were unlikely to bother them. 'After all,' he told her, 'they didn't bother the boats at all during the first Rama expedition. They must have capsized me because of something special in the design of our new motor boats.'

'How can you be so certain?' Nicole asked, staring uncomfortably at the grey shadows in the water beside them. 'And if they are not going to attack us, why have they been following us for so long?'

'We're a curiosity, that's all,' Richard replied. Nevertheless, he braced himself when one of the shadows suddenly veered toward the boat. It disappeared underneath them and joined its companion on the other side. 'See,' he said, releasing his grip on the oar, 'I told you there was nothing to worry about.'

They moored the sailboat on the New York side before climbing up the nearby stairway. Since General O'Toole had never been to New York before and was naturally very curious about what he was seeing, Richard went ahead to start working on the computer while Nicole gave the briefest of tours to O'Toole along the way.

By the time Nicole and the general reached the White Room, Richard already had some progress to report. 'My hypothesis was correct,' he said only seconds after the other two had joined him. 'I'm fairly certain that I now have accessed the entire sensor list. They must have radar or its equivalent on board. While I'm trying to locate it, why don't you two develop a flow diagram for how we will communicate our warning. Remember, keep it simple. We probably don't have more than twenty-four hours until the first missile arrives.'

Twenty-four hours, Nicole said to herself. *One more day.* She glanced over at Richard, hard at work at the keyboard, and General O'Toole, who was looking at some of the black objects still scattered in one of the corners. Nicole's momentary feelings of fondness for the two men were quickly truncated by a sharp burst of fear. The reality of their predicament overpowered her. *Will we all die tomorrow?* she wondered.

61

Endangered Spacecraft

'We really shouldn't be surprised,' Richard said without emotion. The three of them were sitting in front of the large black screen. 'All of us expected it.'

'But we hoped otherwise,' O'Toole interjected. 'Sometimes it's depressing to be proven correct.'

'Are you positive, Richard,' Nicole asked, 'that each of those blips represents an object in space?'

'I don't think there's any doubt,' Richard replied. 'We know for certain that we're looking at sensor output. And look, I'll show you how to change the fields.' Richard called to the screen a display that showed a cylinder, definitely Rama, at the centre of a set of concentric circles. Next he keyed in another pair of commands, resulting in motion on the screen. The cylinder became smaller and smaller, ultimately collapsing to a point. The size of the concentric circles around the cylinder also diminished during the motion and new circles appeared at the edge of the screen. Eventually a group of dots, sixteen in all, appeared on the right side of the display.

'But how do you know they are missiles?' Nicole queried, indicating the small points of light.

'I don't,' Richard said. 'But I do know they are flying objects nearly on a straight line between Rama and the Earth. I suppose they might be peace envoys, but I doubt it seriously.'

'How long?' O'Toole asked.

'It's hard to tell exactly,' Richard answered after a moment's pause. 'I'd estimate eighteen to twenty hours until the first one. They're spread out more than I would have expected. If we track them for an hour or so, we'll have a more precise estimate of the impact time.'

General O'Toole whistled and then reflected for several seconds before speaking. 'Before we try to tell this spacecraft that it's about to undergo a nuclear attack, will you answer one simple question for me?'

'If I can,' Richard replied.

'What makes you think that Rama can protect itself from these incoming missiles, even if we are able to communicate the warning?'

There was a protracted silence. 'Do you remember one time, Michael, almost a year ago,' Richard said, 'when we were flying together from London to Tokyo and we started talking about religion?'

'You mean when I was reading Eusebius?'

'I think so. You were telling me about the early history of Christianity ... Anyway, right in the middle of the discussion I suddenly asked you why you believed in God. Do you remember your answer?'

'Of course,' O'Toole replied. 'It's the same response I gave my oldest son when he declared himself an atheist at the age of eighteen.'

'Your answer on the plane perfectly captures my attitude in this current situation. We know that Rama is extremely advanced technologically. Certainly when it was designed there must have been some consideration of a possible hostile attack ... Who knows, maybe it even has a powerful propulsion system that we haven't yet discovered and will be able to manoeuvre out of the way. I bet –'

'Can I interrupt for a second?' Nicole said. 'I wasn't with you two on the flight to Tokyo. I'd like to know how Michael answered your question.'

The two men stared at each other for several seconds. Finally General O'Toole responded. 'Faith informed by thought and observation,' he said.

'The first part of your plan is not too difficult, and I agree with the approach, but I have no mental picture of how we will communicate the yield, or how to tie the nuclear chain reaction to the incoming missiles unambiguously.'

'Michael and I will work on those items while you develop the graphics for the first segment. He says he remembers his nuclear physics reasonably well.'

'Remember not to make too many assumptions,' Richard reminded Nicole. 'We must make certain that each part of the message is self-contained.'

General O'Toole was not with Richard and Nicole at that moment. After two hours of intense work he had walked away, out into the tunnel, about five minutes earlier. His two colleagues suddenly worried about his absence. 'He's probably going to the bathroom,' Richard said.

'He might be lost,' Nicole replied.

Richard moved over to the entrance to the White Room and called into the corridor. 'Hullo, Michael O'Toole,' he said. 'Are you all right?'

'Yes,' came the answer from the direction of the central stairway. 'Can you and Nicole come around here for a minute?'

'What's up?' Richard enquired a few moments later when he and Nicole joined the general at the foot of the stairway.

'Who built this lair?' O'Toole asked, his eyes focused on the ceiling high above him. 'And why do you think it was created in the first place?'

'We don't know,' Richard answered impatiently, 'and I don't think we'll resolve the issue in the next few minutes, or even hours. Meanwhile, we have work –'

'Indulge me for a little while,' O'Toole interrupted firmly. 'I need to have this discussion before I can proceed.' Richard and Nicole waited for him to continue. 'We are rushing pell mell toward sending a warning to whatever intelligence is in control of this vehicle. Presumably, we are doing this so that Rama will be able to take measures to protect itself. How do we know that's the right action for us? How do we know that we're not being traitors to our species?'

General O'Toole waved his arms at the large cavern

around him. 'There must be some reason, some grand plan for all this. Why were all those fake human objects left in the White Room? Why did the Ramans invite us to communicate with them? Who and what are the avians and the octospiders?' He shook his head, frustrated by all the unanswered questions. 'I was uncertain about destroying Rama; but I'm equally uncertain about sending the warning. What if Rama escapes the nuclear attack because of us and then destroys the Earth anyway?'

'That's extremely unlikely, Michael. The first Rama sailed through the solar system –'

'Just a minute, Nicole, if you don't mind,' Richard interrupted softly. 'Let me try to answer the general.'

He walked over and put his arm on General O'Toole's shoulder. 'Michael,' Richard said, 'what has impressed me the most about you since the first time we met has been your ability to understand the difference between the answers we can know, as a result of deduction or the scientific method, and those questions for which there is not even a valid logical approach. There is no way whatsoever that we can understand what Rama is all about at this juncture. We don't yet have enough data. It's like trying to solve a system of simultaneous linear equations when there are many more variables than constraints. Multiple hypersurfaces of correct solutions exist.'

O'Toole smiled and nodded his head. 'What we do know,' Richard continued, 'is that a fleet of missiles is now approaching Rama. They are probably armed with nuclear warheads. We have a choice, to warn or not to warn, and we must make it based on the information available to us at this moment.'

Richard pulled out his small computer and walked over beside O'Toole. 'You can represent this entire problem as a 3 x 2 matrix,' he said. 'Assume there are three possible descriptions of the Raman threat: never hostile, always hostile, and hostile only if attacked. Let these three situations represent the rows of matrix. Now consider the decision facing us. We can either warn them, or choose not to. Note that it is only a *successful* warning that matters. So there are two columns to the matrix, Rama warned and Rama not warned.'

O'Toole and Nicole both looked over Richard's shoulder as he constructed the matrix and displayed it on his small monitor. 'If we now look at the outcomes of the six events represented by the individual elements in this matrix, and try to assign some probabilities wherever we can, we will have all the information we need to make our decision. Do you agree?'

General O'Toole nodded, impressed by how quickly and concisely Richard had structured their dilemma. 'The outcome of the second row is always the same,' Nicole now offered, 'independent of whether or not we warn them. If Rama is truly hostile, with their more advanced technology it makes no difference whether we warn them or not. Sooner or later, with this vehicle or one that comes in the future, they will either subjugate or destroy the human race.'

Richard paused a moment to ensure that O'Toole was following the conversation. 'Similarly,' he then said slowly, 'if Rama is *never* hostile, it cannot be wrong to warn them. In neither case, warned or unwarned, is the Earth in danger. And if we are successful in telling them about the nuclear missiles, then something extraordinary will have been saved.'

The general smiled. 'So the only possible problem, O'Toole's Anxiety, if you want to call it that, comes if Rama was not originally intending to be hostile, but will change its mind and attack the Earth once it learns that nuclear missiles have been launched against it.'

'Precisely,' said Richard. 'And I would argue that our warning itself would probably be a mitigating factor in that potentially hostile case. After all —'

'All right. All right,' O'Toole replied. 'I see where you're headed. Unless a very high probability is assigned to the case I'm worried about, the overall analysis suggests a better result from warning the Ramans.' He suddenly laughed. 'It's a good thing you don't work for COG military headquarters, Richard. You might have convinced me with logic to activate the code....'

'I doubt it,' Nicole said. 'Nobody could have made a solid case for that kind of paranoia.'

'Thank you,' the general smiled, 'I'm satisfied. You were very persuasive. Let's go back to work.'

Driven by the relentless approach of the missiles, the threesome worked tirelessly for hours. Nicole and Michael O'Toole designed the warning message in two discrete segments. The first segment, much of which was background to establish the basic communication technique, presented all the trajectory mechanics, including the Rama orbit as the vehicle entered the solar system, the two Newton craft leaving the Earth and joining just before rendezvous with the alien ship, the two Raman manoeuvres changing its trajectory, and finally the sixteen missiles blasting off from the Earth toward a Rama intercept. Richard, his long hours of work at the keyboard and black screen now paying off, transformed all these orbital events into graphic line drawings while the other two cosmonauts struggled with the complexity of the remainder of the message.

The second segment was exceedingly difficult to design. In it the humans wanted to explain that the incoming missiles carried nuclear warheads, that the explosive power of the bombs was generated by a chain reaction, and that the heat, shock, and radiation resulting from the explosion were all enormously powerful. Presenting the fundamental picture was not the challenge; quantifying the destructive power in any terms that could be understood by an extraterrestrial intelligence was a formidable obstacle.

'It's impossible,' an exasperated Richard exclaimed when both O'Toole and Nicole insisted that the warning was not complete without some indication of the explosion temperature and the magnitude of the shock and radiation fields. 'Why don't we just indicate the quantity of fissionable material in the process? They must be great at physics. They can compute the yield and other parameters.'

Time was running out and all three of them were becoming exhausted. In the final hours, General O'Toole succumbed to fatigue and, at Nicole's insistence, took a substantial nap. His biometry output had indicated that his heart was in stress. Even Richard slept for ninety minutes. But Nicole never allowed herself the luxury of rest. She was determined to work out some way to depict graphically the destructive power of the weapons.

When the men awakened, Nicole convinced them to append to the second segment an additional short section demonstrating what would happen to a city or forest on Earth if a one-megaton nuclear bomb exploded in the vicinity. For these pictures to make any sense, of course, Richard had to expand his earlier glossary, in which he had defined the chemical elements and their symbols with mathematical precision, to include some more measures of size. 'If they understand this,' he grumbled as he laboriously included scale tick marks beside his line drawings of buildings and trees, 'then they're smarter than even I gave them credit for.'

Finally the message was completed and stored. They reviewed the entire warning one last time and made a few corrections. 'Of the commands that I have never been able to understand,' Richard said, 'there are five that I have reason to suspect may be links to a different level processor. Of course, I am only guessing, but I believe it's an educated guess. I will transmit our message five times, using each of these particular commands a single time, and hope that our warning somehow reaches the central computer.'

While Richard entered all the proper commands into the keyboard, Nicole and General O'Toole went for a walk. They climbed up the stairway and wandered around the skyscrapers of New York. 'You believe that we were meant to board Rama and find the White Room, don't you?'

'Yes,' Nicole answered.

'But for what purpose?' asked the general. 'If the Ramans just wanted to make contact with us, why did they go to such elaborate lengths? And why are they risking our misinterpretation of their intent?'

'I don't know,' Nicole said. 'Maybe they're testing us in some way. To find out what we're like.'

'Goodness,' O'Toole replied, 'what a terrible thought. We may be catalogued as the creatures who launch nuclear attacks against visitors.'

'Exactly,' said Nicole.

Nicole showed O'Toole the barn with the ditches, the lattice where she had rescued the avian, the stunning polyhedrons, and the entrances to the other two lairs. She was becoming very tired, but she knew that she would not sleep until everything was resolved.

'Should we head back?' O'Toole said after he and Nicole had walked down to the Cylindrical Sea and verified that the sailboat was still intact where they had left it.

'All right,' Nicole answered wearily. She checked her watch. It was exactly three hours and eighteen minutes until the first nuclear missile would arrive at Rama.

62

The Final Hour

Nobody had spoken for five minutes. Each of the three cosmonauts sat enmeshed in their own private world, aware that the first missile was now less than an hour away. Richard raced through all the sensor outputs hurriedly, searching vainly for any indication that Rama was taking some protective action. 'Shit,' he muttered, looking again at the closeup radar picture that showed the lead missile drawing closer and closer.

Richard walked over to where Nicole was sitting in the corner. 'We must have failed,' he said quietly. 'Nothing has changed.'

Nicole rubbed her eyes. 'I wish I weren't so tired,' she said. 'Then maybe we could do something interesting for our last fifty minutes.' She smiled grimly. 'Now I know what it must be like to be on Death Row.'

General O'Toole approached from the other side of the room. He was holding two of the small black balls in his left hand. 'You know,' he said, 'I have often wondered what I would do if I ever had a specified, finite time before I died. Now here I am, and my mind keeps focusing on a single thing.'

'What's that?' Nicole asked.

'Have either of you ever been baptised?' he replied tentatively.

'Whaaat?' exclaimed Richard with a laugh of surprise.

'I thought not,' said General O'Toole. 'What about you, Nicole?'

'No, Michael,' she answered. 'My father's Catholilcism was more tradition than ceremony.'

'Well,' persisted the general. 'I'm offering to baptise you both.'

'Here? Now?' enquired the astounded Wakefield. 'Are my ears deceiving me, Nikki, or did I just hear this gentleman suggest that we spend the last hour of our life being baptised?'

'It won't take –' O'Toole started to say.

'Why not, Richard?' Nicole interrupted O'Toole. She stood up with a bright smile on her face. 'What else do we have to do? And it's a hell of a lot better than morbidly sitting around here waiting for the great fireball.'

Richard almost cackled. 'This is wonderful!' he enthused. 'I, Richard Wakefield, lifelong atheist, am considering being baptised on an extraterrestrial spaceship as the final action of my life. I love it!'

'Remember what Pascal wrote,' Nicole teased.

'Ah, yes,' Richard replied. 'A simple matrix from one of the world's great thinkers. "There may or may not be a God; I may or may not believe in Him. The only way I can lose is if there is a God and I do not believe in Him. Therefore I shall believe in Him to minimise my risk."' Richard chuckled. 'But I did not agree to believe in God, only to be baptised.'

'So you'll do it,' Nicole said.

'Why not?' he replied, parroting her earlier comment. 'Maybe that way I don't have to stay in Limbo with the virtuous pagans and unbaptised children.' He grinned at O'Toole. 'All right, general, we're all yours. Do your thing.'

'Now you listen closely to this, TB,' Richard said. 'You're probably the only robot ever to be in a human's pocket during a baptism.'

Nicole nudged Richard in the ribs. The patient General O'Toole waited a few moments and then began the ceremony.

At Richard's insistence, they had left the lair and walked out into the open plaza. Richard had wanted 'the sky of Rama overhead' and neither of the other two had objected. Nicole had gone over to the Cylindrical Sea to fill the baptismal flask with water while General O'Toole completed his preparations. The American general was taking the baptism seriously but was apparently not offended by Richard's lighthearted banter.

Nicole and Richard knelt down in front of O'Toole. He sprinkled water on Richard's head. 'Richard Colin Wakefield, I baptise thee in the name of the Father, and the Son, and the Holy Spirit.'

When O'Toole had not moved. 'Richard,' he said softly, 'could I ask you to kneel again? I would like to say a short prayer.'

'What's this?' Richard asked. 'First a baptism, now a prayer?' Nicole looked up at him. Her eyes asked him to accede. 'All right,' he said. 'I guess I might as well go all the way.'

'Almighty God, please hear our prayer,' the general said in a strong voice. He also was kneeling now. His eyes were closed and his hands were clasped in front of him. 'We three have gathered here in what may be our final hour to pay homage to Thee. We beseech Thee to consider how we may serve Thee if we continue to live and, if it be Thy will, we ask Thee to spare us a painful and horrible death. If we are to die, we pray that we may be accepted into Thy heavenly kingdom. Amen.'

General O'Toole stopped for just a moment and then began to recite the Lord's prayer. After he had said, 'Our father, Who art in heaven, Hallowed be Thy name....', the lights in the great spaceship were abruptly extinguished. Another Raman day was over. Richard and Nicole waited respectfully until their friend had finished the prayer before pulling out their flashlights.

Nicole thanked the general and gave him a small hug. 'Well, here we are,' Richard said nervously. 'Twenty-seven minutes and counting. We've had a baptism and a prayer. What should we do now? Who has an idea for the last, and I mean the very last, amusement. Should we sing? Dance? Play some kind of game?'

'I would prefer to remain up here by myself,' General

O'Toole said solemnly, 'and face my death in atonement and prayer. And I imagine the two of you would like to be alone together.'

'All right, Nikki,' Richard said. 'Where shall we share our final kiss? On the shore of the Cylindrical Sea or back in the White Room?'

Nicole had been awake for thirty-two consecutive hours and was absolutely exhausted. She fell into Richard's arms and closed her eyes. At that moment scattered flashes of light intruded upon the new blackness of the Raman night.

'What's that?' General O'Toole asked anxiously.

'It must be the horns,' Richard answered excitedly. 'Come on, let's go.'

They ran to the south edge of the island and stared at the massive, enigmatic structures in the Southern bowl. Filaments of light were darting between different pairs of the six spires surrounding the great monolith in the centre. The yellow arcs seemed to sizzle in the air, undulating gently back and forth in the middle while remaining connected to one of the little horns at each end. A distant cracking sound accompanied the spectacular sight.

'Amazing,' said O'Toole, overcome with awe. 'Absolutely amazing.'

'So Rama is going to manoeuvre,' Richard said. He could hardly contain himself. He hugged Nicole, then O'Toole, and finally kissed Nicole on the lips. 'Whoopee!' he yelled as he danced along the wall.

'But Richard,' Nicole shouted after him, 'isn't it too late? How can Rama move out of the way in such a short time?'

Richard ran back to his colleagues. 'You're right,' he said breathlessly. 'And those damn missiles probably have terminal guidance anyway.' He started running again, this time heading back toward the plaza. 'I'm going to watch on the radar.'

Nicole glanced over at General O'Toole. 'I'm coming,' he said. 'But I've already run enough for one day. I want to watch this show for another few seconds. You can go on without me if you want.'

Nicole waited. As the two of them walked briskly toward the plaza, General O'Toole thanked Nicole for allowing him to baptise her. 'Don't be silly,' she replied. 'I'm the one who should thank you.' She put her hand on his shoulder. *The baptism itself wasn't that important*, she continued in her private thoughts. *It was obvious that you were concerned about our souls. We agreed primarily to show our affection for you.* Nicole smiled to herself. At least I think that was the reason....

The ground underneath them began to shake vigorously and General O'Toole stopped, momentarily frightened. 'That's apparently what happened during the last manoeuvre,' Nicole said, steadying both of them by taking the general's hand, 'although I was personally lying unconscious at the bottom of the pit and missed the entire event.'

'Then the light show was just an announcement of the manoeuvre?'

'Probably. That's why Richard was so elated.'

They had barely opened the lair covering when Richard bolted up the stairs. 'They've done it!' he exclaimed. 'They've done it!'

O'Toole and Nicole stared at him as he caught his breath. 'They've deployed some kind of mesh or net – I don't know exactly what it is – about six, maybe eight hundred metres thick – all around the spacecraft.' He turned around. 'Come on,' he said, dashing down the steps three at a time.

Despite her fatigue. Nicole responded to his excitement with a final burst of adrenaline. She bounded down the stairs after Richard and ran to the White Room. He was standing in front of the black screen, flipping back and forth from the exterior image that showed the new material around the vehicle to the radar view that depicted the incoming missiles.

'They must have understood our warning,' he said to Nicole. Richard jubilantly picked her up off the ground, gave her a kiss, and held her in the air. 'It worked, darling,' he shouted. 'Thank you, oh thank you.'

Nicole too was excited. But she was not yet convinced

that Rama's action would prevent the destruction of the vehicle. After General O'Toole came in and Richard explained to him what they were seeing on the screen, there were only nine minutes left. Nicole had butterflies the size of footballs in her stomach. The ground continued to shake as Rama extended its manoeuvre.

The nuclear missiles obviously had terminal guidance, for despite the fact that Rama was definitely changing its trajectory, the missiles continued to approach along a straight line. The closeup radar picture showed that the sixteen attackers were quite spread out. Their estimated impact times ranged over a period slightly less than an hour.

Richard's frenetic activity increased. He paced wildly around the room. At one point he pulled TB out of his pocket, put him down on the floor, and began talking rapidly to the little robot as if TB were his closest friend. What Richard said was barely coherent. One moment Richard was telling TB to prepare for the coming explosion; a second later he was explaining to him how Rama was going to miraculously evade the incoming missiles.

General O'Toole was trying to remain calm, but it was impossible with Richard flying around the room like a Tasmanian devil. He started to say something to Richard, but decided instead to step outside into the tunnel for some quiet.

During one of the rare moments that he was not moving, Nicole walked over to Richard and grabbed his hands. 'Darling,' she said, 'relax. There's nothing we can do.'

Richard looked down for a second at his friend and lover and then threw his arms around her. He kissed her wildly and then sat down on the shaking floor, pulling her down beside him. 'I'm scared Nicole,' he said, his body trembling. 'I'm really scared. I hate not being able to do anything.'

'I'm frightened too,' she replied gently, taking his hands again. 'And so is Michael.'

'But neither of you *act* scared,' Richard said. 'I feel like an idiot bouncing around here like Tigger in *Winnie-the-Pooh*.'

'Everyone confronts death in a different way,' Nicole said. 'All of us feel fear. We just deal with it in our own, individual fashion.'

Richard was calming down. He glanced over at the big monitor and then at his watch. 'Three more minutes until the first impact,' he said.

Nicole put her hands on his cheeks and kissed him softly on the lips. 'I love you, Richard Wakefield,' she said.

'And I love you,' he answered.

Richard and Nicole were sitting quietly on the floor, holding hands and watching the black screen, when the first missile reached the edge of the dense mesh that surrounded Rama. General O'Toole was standing behind them in the doorway – he had returned to the room about thirty seconds earlier. At the moment the missile made contact, the impacted part of the mesh yielded, cushioning the blow but allowing the missile to penetrate deeper into the netting. Simultaneously, other pieces of the mesh wrapped themselves rapidly about the missile, spinning a thick cocoon with amazing speed. It was all over in a fraction of a second. The missile was about two hundred metres from the outer shell of Rama, already enclosed in a thick wrapping, when its nuclear warhead detonated. The mesh on the screen flew around a little, but there was only a barely perceptible nudge inside the White Room.

'Wow!' said Richard first. 'Did you see that?'

He jumped up and approached the screen. 'It happened so fast,' Nicole commented, coming up beside him.

General O'Toole mumbled a very short prayer of thanks and joined his colleagues in front of the screen. 'How do you think it did that?' he asked Richard.

'I have no idea,' Richard replied. 'But somehow that cocoon contained the explosion. It must be a fantastic material.' He flipped back to the radar image. 'Let's watch his next one more closely. It should be here in a few –'

There was a brilliant flash of light and the screen went black. Less than a second later a sharp lateral force hit them hard, knocking them to the floor. The lights went out in the White Room and the ground stopped shaking. 'Is everyone all right?' Richard asked, groping for Nicole's hand in the dark.

'I think so,' O'Toole replied. 'I hit the wall, but only with my back and elbow.'

'I'm fine, darling,' Nicole answered. 'What happened?'

'Obviously that one exploded early, before it reached the net. We were hit by the shock wave?'

'I don't understand,' O'Toole said. 'The bomb exploded in a vacuum. How could there be a shock wave?'

'It wasn't technically just a shock wave,' Richard replied, standing up as the lights came back on and the ground began to shake again. 'Hey, how about that!' he interrupted himself, 'the famous Raman redundancy scores again. You okay?' he said to Nicole, who looked unsteady as she was standing up.

'I bruised my knee,' she answered, 'but it's not serious.'

'The bomb destroyed the rest of its own missile,' Richard said, now answering O'Toole's question as he searched through the sensor list for the redundant imaging and radar outputs, 'vaporising most of the casing and reducing the rest to fragments. The gas and debris moved outward at enormous speeds, creating the wave that hit us. The mesh attenuated the size of the shock.'

Nicole moved over against the wall and sat down. 'I want to be ready for the next one,' she said.

'I wonder how many bumps like that Rama can survive,' Richard said.

General O'Toole came over and sat down beside Nicole. 'Two down and fourteen to go,' he said. They all smiled. At least they weren't dead yet.

Richard located the redundant sensors a few minutes later. 'Uh oh,' he said as he surveyed the remaining blips on the screen. 'Unless I'm mistaken, the last bomb that

exploded was many kilometres away. We were lucky.
We'd better hope one doesn't detonate just outside the
mesh.'

The trio watched while two more missiles were
trapped and wrapped in the material surrounding Rama.
Richard stood up. 'We have a brief respite now,' he said.
'It will be three minutes or so before our next impact –
then we'll have four more missiles in a hurry.'

Nicole rose to her feet also. She saw that General
O'Toole was holding his back. 'Are you sure you're all
right, Michael?' she asked. He nodded, still watching the
screen. Richard came over beside Nicole and took her
hand. A minute later they sat down together against the
wall to wait for the next impact.

They didn't wait long. A second lateral force, much
stronger than the first one, hit them within twenty
seconds. Again the lights went out and the floor stopped
shaking. Nicole could hear O'Toole's laboured breathing
in the dark. 'Michael,' she said, 'are you hurt?'

When there was no immediate reply, Nicole started
crawling in his direction. That was a mistake. She was
not braced against anything when the powerful third
blast hit. Nicole was thrown savagely into the wall,
hitting it with the side of her head.

General O'Toole stayed beside Nicole while Richard
went up into New York to survey the city. The men
spoke quietly when Richard returned. he reported only
minor damage. Thirty minutes after the final missile had
been trapped, the lights came back on and the ground
started shaking again. 'You see,' Richard said with a
strained grin, 'I told you we'd be all right. They always
do everything important in threes.'

Nicole remained unconscious for almost another hour.
During the last few minutes she was vaguely aware of
both the vibration of the floor and the conversation on
the opposite side of the room. Nicole opened her eyes
very slowly.

'The net effect,' she heard Richard say, 'is to increase
our velocity along the hyperbola. So we will cross the

Earth's orbit much earlier than previously, long before the planet itself has arrived.'

'How close will we come to the Earth?'

'Not too close. It depends on when this manoeuvre ends. If it stopped now we would miss by a million kilometres or so, more than twice the distance to the Moon.'

Nicole sat up and smiled. 'Good morning,' she said cheerfully.

The two men came over beside her. 'Are you all right, darling?' Richard asked.

'I think so,' Nicole said, feeling the bump on the side of her head. 'I may have headaches for a while.' She looked at the two men. 'What about you, Michael? I seem to remember being worried about you just before the big blast.'

'The second one knocked the wind out of me,' O'Toole replied. 'Luckily I was better prepared for the third bomb. And my back seems fine now.'

Richard started to explain what he had learned from the output of Rama's celestial sensors. 'I heard the last part of it,' Nicole said. 'I gather we're now going to miss Earth altogether.' Richard helped her to stand up. 'But where are we headed?'

Richard shrugged his shoulders. 'No planetary or asteroidal targets are anywhere close to our present trajectory. Our hyperbolic energy is increasing. If nothing changes we will escape from the solar system altogether.'

'And become interstellar travellers,' Nicole said quietly.

'If we live that long,' added the general.

'For my part,' Richard said with a playful smile, 'I am not going to worry about what happens next. At least not yet. I plan to celebrate our escape from the nuclear phalanx. I vote we go upstairs and introduce Michael to some new friends. Should it be the avians or the octospiders?'

Nicole shook her head and smiled. 'You're hopeless, Wakefield. Let me not in any way inhibit....'

'Let me not to the marriage of true minds
Admit impediments;'

TB suddenly interrupted. All three of the cosmonauts
were startled. They stared down at the tiny robot and
then erupted with laughter.

'...love is not love
Which alters when it alteration finds
Or bends with the remover to remove.
Oh no, it is an ever-fixed mark....'

Richard picked up TB and switched him off. Nicole and
Michael were still laughing. Richard embraced each of
them individually. 'I can't think of three better travelling
companions,' he said, holding the little robot over his
head, 'wherever it is we're going.'

Afterword

by Arthur C. Clarke

Writing is a lonely profession, and after a few decades even the most devout egotist may occasionally yearn for company. But collaboration in any work of art is a risky business, and the more people involved, the smaller the chances of success. Can you imagine *Moby Dick* by Hermann Melville & Nat Hawthorne? *Or War and Peace* by Leo Tolstoy and Freddie Dostoyevsky. With Additional Dialogue by Van Turgenev?

Certainly I never imagined, until a few years ago, that I would ever collaborate with another writer on a work of fiction. *Non-fiction* was different: I've been involved in no less than 14 multi-author projects (two with the Editors of *Life*, and you don't get more multiplex than that). But fiction – no way! I was quite sure I would never let any outsider tamper with my unique brand of creativity....

Well, a funny thing happened on the way to the word-processor. Early in 1986 my agent Scott Meredith called me in his most persuasive 'Don't-say-no-until-I've-finished' mode. There was, it seemed, this young genius of a movie producer who was determined to film something – *anything* – of mine. Though I'd never heard of Peter Guber, as it happened I had seen two of his movies (*Midnight Express, The Deep*), and been quite impressed by them. I was even more impressed when Scott told me that Peter's latest, *The Color Purple*, had been nominated for half-a-dozen Oscars.

However, I groaned inwardly when Scott went on to say that Peter had a friend with a brilliant idea he'd like me to develop into a screenplay. I groaned, because there are no new ideas in sf, and if it really was brilliant I'd have thought of it already. And I *hate* screenplays; they are incredibly boring, almost unreadable, and, as far as I'm concerned, unwritable. Like a musical score, they're a necessary intermediate stage in a production. Writing them requires considerable specialised skills, but they have no literary or artistic value of their own. (A musical score is at least pretty to look at.)

Then Scott explained who the friend was, and I did a double-take. The project suddenly looked very exciting indeed, for reasons that had nothing to do with Peter Guber, but a lot to do with Stanley Kubrick.

Flashback. Twenty years earlier, in *2001: A Space Odyssey*, Stanley and I had visited the moons of Jupiter – never dreaming that these completely unknown worlds would, in fact, be reconnoitred by robots long before the date of our movie. In March and July 1979, the two Voyager probes revealed that Io, Europa, Ganymede and Callisto were stranger places than we'd dared to imagine. The stunning views of Jupiter's giant satellites made it possible – no, imperative – for me to write *2010: Odyssey Two*. This time around, the Jovian sequences could be based on reality, not imagination; and when Peter Hyams filmed the book in 1984, he was able to use actual images from the Voyager spacecraft as backgrounds for much of the action.

Spectacular though the results of 1979 missions were, it was confidently hoped that they would be quite surpassed within a decade. The Voyager spacecraft spent only a few hours in the vicinity of Jupiter, hurtling past the giant planet and its moons on the way to Saturn. But in May 1986, NASA planned to launch Galileo, an even more ambitious space probe. This would make not a brief fly-by, but a *rendezvous*; Galileo would spend two years, starting in December 1988, on a detailed survey of Jupiter and its major moons. By 1990, if all went well, there would be such a flood of new information about these exotic worlds that a third Space Odyssey would be inevitable. *That* was what I was planning to write; I'd hitched my wagon to Galileo, and could hardly care less about some amateur science-fiction author's ideas. How to turn him down politely? I was still pondering this when Scott continued:

'Peter Guber wants to fly out to Sri Lanka, just for thirty-six hours, to introduce this guy to you. His name is Gentry Lee, and let me explain who he is. He works at the Jet Propulsion Laboratory, and he's the Chief Engineer on Project Galileo. Have you heard of that?'

'Yes,' I said faintly.

'And before that, he was Director of Mission Planning for the Viking landers, that sent back those wonderful pictures from Mars. Because he felt the public didn't appreciate what was going on in space, he formed a company with your friend Carl Sagan to make *Cosmos* – he was manager of the whole TV series –'

'Enough!' I cried. 'This man I have to meet. Tell Mr Gabor to bring him here right away.'

'The name,' said Scott, 'is *Guber*. Peter Guber.'

Well, it was agreed that the two of them would fly out to Sri Lanka, and if I liked Gentry's idea (and, equally important, Gentry) I'd develop an outline – perhaps a dozen pages, which would give characters, locations, plot and all the basic elements from which any competent script-writer could generate a screenplay.

They arrived in Colombo on 12 February 1986 – just two weeks after the *Challenger* disaster. 1986 was going to be *the* Big Year for Space, but now the entire NASA programme was in total disarray. In particular, Galileo would be delayed for years. It would be 1995 before there could be any further news from the moons of Jupiter. I could forget about *Odyssey Three* – just as Gentry could forget about doing anything with Galileo except getting it back from the Cape and putting it in mothballs.

Happily, the Guber-Lee-Clarke Summit went well, and for the next few weeks I filled floppy discs with concepts, characters, backgrounds, plots – anything which seemed even remotely useful to the story we'd decided to call *Cradle*. Someone once said that writing a book of fiction consists of the elimination of alternatives.

Very true: at one time I calculated that, if I used all the elements I'd created in every possible combination, there'd be enough material for half a billion different *Cradles*.

I sent the one I finally selected, in the form of a 4,000 word outline, to Gentry. He liked it, and flew out to Sri Lanka again so that we could fill in the details. During a three-day marathon up in the mountains above the ancient capital, Kandy, despite the distraction of the most gorgeous panorama I know, we completed an 8,000 word demi-hemi-semi-final version which eventually became the basis of the novel. From then onwards, we were able to collaborate by making frequent phone calls, and flying yards of printout across the Pacific.

The writing took the best part of a year, though of course we were both involved in other projects as well. When I discovered that Gentry had a considerably better background in English *and French* literature than I did (by now I was immune to such surprises) I heroically resisted all attempts to impose my own style on him. This upset some longtime ACC readers, who when *Cradle* appeared under our joint names were put out by passages where I might have done a little more sanitising. The earthier bits of dialogue, I explained, were the result of Gentry's years with the hairy-knuckled, hard-drinking engineers and mathematicians of JPL's Astrodynamics Division, where the Pasadena cops often have to be called in to settle barefisted fights over Bessel functions and non-linear partial differential equations.

Yet so far, to the best of my knowledge, no school board has demanded that *Cradle* be removed from its shelves. I mention this because I have just discovered, to my astonished indignation, that this actually happened to *Imperial Earth* a decade ago. What's more, the board concerned then went on to ban *any* collection containing *anything* I'd ever written.

I wish I'd known about this at the time. I would have enjoyed telling these apprentice Ayatollahs that the 'Books for the Blind' version of the novel that offended them was recorded by a lady very unlikely to promote porn. She happens to be married to England's First Law Lord.

Although *Cradle* was originally conceived as a movie project, and a treatment was prepared for Warner Films, the chances of it ever reaching the screen now seem remote. By bad luck, a whole string of underwater extraterrestrial movies appeared around the time of the book's publication, and most of them sank without trace.

But Peter Guber, I'm happy to say, has gone on from strength to strength. His latest productions, *The Witches of Eastwick*, *Gorillas in the Mist* and *Rain Man* have been very well received; even this short list shows his interest in unusual and worthwhile projects. Maybe he'll make *Cradle* when the cycle comes round again, as it inevitably will. 'There is a tide in the affairs of men' – and of movies.

Though I'd greatly enjoyed working with Gentry, when we'd finished rocking *Cradle* I had no plans for further collaboration – because Halley's Comet was now dominating my life, as it had failed to dominate terrestrial skies. I realised that its next appearance, in 2061, would provide a splendid opportunity for a third Space Odyssey. (If the much-delayed Galileo does perform as hoped in 1995, and beams back megabytes of new information from the Jovian system, there may be a Final Odyssey. But I make no promises.)

By the summer of 1987, *2061: Odyssey Three* was doing very nicely in the bookshops, thank you, and I was once again beginning to feel those nagging guilt pains that assail an author when he's not Working On A Project. Suddenly, I realised that one was staring me right in the face.

Fifteen years earlier, the very last sentence of *Rendezvous With Rama* had read: 'The Ramans did everything in threes.' Now, those words were a last-minute afterthought when I was doing the final revision. I had not – cross my heart – any idea of a sequel in mind; it just seemed the correct, open-ended way of finishing the book. (In real life, of course, no story ever ends.)

Many readers – and reviewers – jumped to the conclusion that I had planned a trilogy from the beginning. Well, I hadn't – but now I realised it was a splendid idea. And Gentry was just the man for the job: he had all the background in celestial mechanics and space hardware to deal with the next appearance of the Ramans.

I quickly outlined a spectrum of possibilities, very much as I had done with *Cradle*, and in a remarkably short time *Rama II* was born. *The Garden of Rama* and *Rama Revealed* will follow during the 1989-91 period.

So once again Gentry Lee is communicating across the Pacific for brainstorming sessions in the Sri Lankan hills, and the postman is complaining about the bulky printouts he has to balance on his bicycle. This time round, however, technology has speeded up our intercontinental operations. The fax machine now allows us to exchange ideas almost in real time; it's far more convenient than the Electronic Mail Link Peter Hyams and I used when scripting *2010* (see *The Odyssey File*).

There is much to be said for this kind of long-distance collaboration; if they are too close together, co-authors may waste a lot of time on trivia. Even a solitary writer can think of endless excuses for not working; with two, the possibilities are at least squared.

However, there is no way of demonstrating that a writer is neglecting his job; even if his snores are deafening, his sub-conscious may be hard at work. And Gentry and I knew that our wildest excursions into literature, science, art or history might yield useful story elements.

For example, during the writing of *Rama II* it became obvious that Gentry was in love with Eleanor of Aquitaine (don't worry, Stacey – she's been dead for 785 years) and I had tactfully to dissuade him from devoting pages to her amazing career. (If you wonder how E of A could have the remotest connexion with interstellar adventures, you have pleasures in store.)

I certainly learned a lot of French and English history from Gentry that they never taught me at school. The occasion when Queen Eleanor berated her son, the intrepid warrior-king Richard the Lionheart *in front of his troops* for failing to produce an heir to the throne must have been one of the more piquant moments in British military history. Alas, there was no way we could work in this gallant but gay Corleone, who was often a Godfather, never a Father ... very unlike Gentry, whose fifth son arrived towards the end of *Rama II*.

But you will meet Gentry's most cherished creation, the yet-to-be-born Saint Michael of Siena. One day, I am sure, you'll encounter him again, in books that Gentry will publish under his own name, with the minimum of help or hindrance from me.

As I write these words, we're just coming up to the midway point of our four-volume partnership. And though we think we know what's going to happen next – I'm sure the Ramans have quite a few surprises in store for us....

Acknowledgements

Many different people contributed to this novel during numerous conversations over a two-year period. Those whose comments or insights were especially valuable include Bebe Barden, Paul Chodas, Clayton Frohman, Michael Glassman, Bruce Jakosky, Roland Joffe, Gerry Snyder, and Ian Stewart.

Lou Aronica, Malcolm Edwards, and Russ Galen each made significant contributions to the book. Their editing insights were essential in shaping the final structure of the novel.

Special thanks are extended to Father Martin Slaught, whose religious acumen was indispensable in creating General O'Toole, and Peter Guber, who enabled the authors to meet for the first time over three years ago.

Finally, no acknowledgement would be complete without bouquets for Mr Lee's family. His wife Stacey and five young sons, Cooper, Austin, Robert, Patrick, and Michael, generously allowed him to make the necessary trips halfway around the world to Sri Lanka and granted him the private time that was required for the integration of this novel.